Slough Library Services

Please return this book on or before the date shown on your receipt.

To renew go to:
Website: **www.slough.gov.uk/libraries**
Phone: **03031 230035**

LIB/6198

OH66

THE BUTLINS GIRLS

A comforting story set against the nation's favourite holiday camp, from bestselling author of *The Woolworths Girls*

Molly Missons hasn't had the best of times recently. Having lost her parents, now some dubious long-lost family are attempting to steal her home and livelihood... After a horrendous ordeal, Molly applies for a job as a Butlins auntie and leaves for Skegness. Molly finds true friendship in Freda, Bunty and Plum. But the biggest shock is discovering that star of the silver screen, Johnny Johnson, is working at Butlins as head of the entertainment team. Johnny takes an instant liking to Molly and she begins to shed the shackles of her recent traumas. Is he the distraction she needs – or is he too good to be true?

THE BUTLINS GIRLS

THE BUTLINS GIRLS

by

Elaine Everest

Magna Large Print Books
Long Preston, North Yorkshire,
BD23 4ND, England.

British Library Cataloguing in Publication Data.

A catalogue record of this book is
available from the British Library

ISBN   978-0-7505-4550-1

First published in Great Britain in 2017 by Pan Books
an imprint of Pan Macmillan

Published in Large Print 2018 by arrangement with
Macmillan Publishers International Ltd.

Magna Large Print is an imprint of Library Magna Books Ltd.

Printed and bound in Great Britain by
T.J. (International) Ltd., Cornwall, PL28 8RW

This book is not sanctioned or endorsed in any way by Butlin's Skyline Limited

*To my parents
for deciding that holiday camps
were perfect for our family and encouraging us
to join in – with everything!
Thank you x*

Prologue

Molly Missons gazed around in awe. So this was Butlins. Whitewashed buildings, bordered by rhododendrons, gave a cheerful feeling to a world still recovering from six years of war. The Skegness holiday camp covered a vast area, much larger than Molly had expected.

If it were not for a helpful bus conductor, she'd have alighted far too early, when first spotting row upon row of flags fluttering in the early May sunshine. As it was, the bus followed the boundaries of the camp and pulled up at the visitor entrance. The conductor helped her from the vehicle, passing her suitcase down from the steep step. With a cheery call of 'Hi-de-hi!', he waved goodbye.

Up ahead, she could see a long white building with the words 'Our true intent is all for your delight' emblazoned on the front wall for everyone to view. She thought it was a genuine welcome. Neat borders of shrubs and what looked like a children's play area were extremely inviting to this first-time visitor. What was missing were people. She couldn't see a single one. Molly knew the start of the holiday season was still days away, but surely there should be staff around the place? She pulled a letter from her coat pocket and checked the words. Yes, she had arrived on the right day, albeit several hours early. Such were the trains from Kent that if she'd caught the only other train from her connection in London to Lincolnshire, Molly would have arrived two hours late for her new job and not made a good impression.

But where was she to go? Molly chewed her lip and looked around in bewilderment, hoping someone would come to her rescue.

'You look lost, m'dear,' a gruff voice called out from behind her.

She jumped, not expecting her wishes to be answered so soon. Spinning round, Molly spotted an elderly man peering through a hatch in the window of a military-style gatehouse at the side of the road.

'Yes, I am a little,' she called back. 'I know I'm in the right place, but I have no idea where to go or what to do next.' Molly felt her chin wobble slightly. It had been a long journey into the unknown. If only she was at home once more, chatting with her mum in the kitchen while they prepared the evening meal. Sadly, that was never going to happen, however much she wished. It was a foolhardy idea to come to Butlins. It had been her best friend, Freda, who'd suggested applying for a job at the newly opened holiday camp. Despite fighting it back, a tear splashed onto her cheek.

'There, there, missy – there's no need for tears. Just you get yourself in here and I'll sort things out for you or my name's not Spud Jenkins. You can leave your suitcase out there. It won't come to any trouble.'

Molly sat on the wooden chair Spud nudged towards her. 'I'm so sorry. It's been a long journey. I'm just tired. Once I know where I have to report, I'm sure I'll feel better.'

Spud watched her thoughtfully as he struck a match over a single gas ring, which came to life with a loud pop. Shaking a battered kettle to check it contained enough water, he placed it onto the now flickering flame. 'I take it this is your first visit to Butlins?'

Molly nodded as she took a handkerchief from her handbag and wiped her eyes. 'Yes, it is. You must think I'm so silly.'

'Not for one minute. You'd be surprised how many times I've been a shoulder to cry on. Boyfriend troubles, homesickness... I've heard it all in here.'

Molly looked around Spud's domain. With windows on three sides, there wasn't much in the way of privacy, but then she supposed he needed to see who was coming and going from the camp. 'Do you work in here all the time?'

'Ever since the governor started building the camp back in 1935.' He glanced proudly at a framed photograph on his desk. 'The Royal Navy even let me stay on for the duration to do odd jobs and the like. I was no good to man or beast with this leg.' He tapped his left leg. 'Shrapnel from the First War,' he announced proudly. 'The governor put in a good word for me.'

'The governor?' Molly queried, peering more closely at the two figures in the photograph. 'Is that Billy Butlin?' She recalled seeing his face on posters when she had her interview.

'The one and only. He's a good sort is the governor. He takes care of his employees as well as the campers.'

15

Molly could see that the elderly man was proud of his boss. 'Will he visit the camp this summer, do you think?'

Spud took two chipped cups from hooks on the wall, close to where the kettle was starting to boil, and measured Camp coffee into each, followed by a generous spoonful of sugar. 'I don't see why not. He always used to pop in to see how things were going and to meet the punters. That was before we closed for the duration. He likes to meet the new staff as well. A popular man, but he doesn't suffer fools gladly. I suppose you'd say he's charismatic. Yes, that's the word, charismatic.'

'I don't know much about Mr Butlin. I've been concentrating more on the job I have to do – and working out how to get here.' She fell silent as she thought of her home and the friends she'd left behind.

Spud could see the young woman was close to tears again. 'Now, you tell me what job you've been signed up for. You've got the looks of a dancer. Am I right? Or perhaps you're the new Punch and Judy man?'

Molly giggled. 'I'm not much of a dancer, but Punch and Judy sounds fun.'

Spud grinned back. She was a pretty little thing when she wasn't looking so sad. He'd always had a soft spot for green-eyed girls with chestnut curls. 'That's the way to do it!' he said in a squeaky voice, and they both burst out laughing.

'I'm not really skilled at anything much, but I used to help my mum with the Brownies and Girl Guides until I joined the Women's Land Army. I helped her after returning home as well. When I

16

had my interview with Butlins, they thought I'd be able to assist with the children.'

'So you're Miss Molly Missons who is going to be a Butlins auntie?'

'How did you know that?' Molly gasped, but then saw Spud was looking towards a list on a clipboard hanging near the door.

Spud tapped the side of his nose and winked. 'Not much gets past me,' he said. 'I reckon you'll be run off your feet once all those nippers arrive with their parents. They'll keep you busy.'

'I'm sure I will, but I'm not convinced I'm right for the job. I've had no formal training or anything.'

Spud pointed to the photograph. 'Do you think the governor did when he opened this camp in 1936? Why, he was a showman. He'd never owned a big holiday camp like this. This was the first. He had an idea and went along with it. He learned what was wanted and came up with the goods.'

Molly frowned. 'A showman?'

'Travelling fairs, funfairs. You've seen them, haven't you?'

She nodded. 'Oh yes. I always visited the travelling fair when it came to Erith Recreation Ground, near my home. It was magical.'

Spud smiled as her face lit up. 'There you go, then. Chances are the governor knew them. He knows all the showmen. It's a close community. He had hoopla stalls before he ran his own fairgrounds. He even brought the first dodgems into the country.'

Molly did like the elderly man with the big smile. Knowing Spud would be on duty by the main

17

entrance to the camp meant she could pop in and speak to him from time to time. He seemed to sense she was afraid and alone.

'Now, you drink your coffee and I'll walk you up to the staff office. They'll soon take care of you. By tomorrow you'll have made some friends and it'll feel as though Butlins has been your home forever.'

Molly sipped the hot coffee generously enriched with evaporated milk, which Spud had poured from a tin can. She wasn't so sure she'd make friends as quickly as the man seemed to think, but she'd do her best. She wouldn't be her father's daughter if she didn't at least try. For now, she couldn't go home. It wasn't safe to do so. Instead, she'd have to make the best of things. At least it would be fun. There were worse places to run away from home to.

Spud pulled out a photograph album. The cover had seen better days, but inside was a treasure trove of his memories. 'Look at this.' He pointed to a newspaper cutting of fields that reached on forever. In the distance, there was a brief glimpse of the sea. Pointing to a corner of the picture, he declared proudly, 'This is about where we are sitting now.'

Molly was fascinated and looked closer. 'How long ago would this have been?'

Spud scratched his chin and thought for a while. 'I'd say eleven or twelve years back. Those muddy fields were used to grow turnips, among other things, before the governor started building.'

'I ploughed a few fields like that when I was in the Women's Land Army. It was hard work,'

18

Molly said with a smile.

Spud looked at her with admiration. 'Built of stern stuff, then?' he asked.

'I'm not afraid of hard work if that's what you mean,' she replied.

'Just like the governor. He didn't have much money, but he had a dream, and look what he's done here. "A week's holiday for a week's pay." No one can argue with that, now can they?'

Molly agreed. She recalled the quote from a poster she'd seen stuck to the wall of her favourite chip shop back home.

Spud flicked through the pages, stopping where he'd pasted a piece of cardboard. 'What do you think of that?'

'It looks like a piece off an old cigarette packet with a sketch and a few numbers on it.'

'That's the governor's design for a chalet. He was always jotting ideas down on scraps of paper and the back of cigarette packets. He let me have this one,' he said proudly. 'Did you know Adolf tried to wipe out the camp? He dropped over fifty bombs here during the war. That Lord Haw-Haw broadcast that the Germans had sunk the battle-ship HMS *Royal Arthur* and that all hands had gone down with the ship. That's what the navy called the camp during the war,' he added, notic-ing Molly's puzzled frown. 'The silly buggers thought Butlins was a battleship.' He roared with laughter. 'Gawd help them if they'd damaged Butlins. The governor would have been after them all and had their guts for garters,' he chuckled.

'You seem to be very fond of Mr Butlin,' Molly said.

19

'You could say that. He gave me a job when not many people would. He even gave me my name.'

'Your name?'

'You don't think I was christened "Spud", do you?' he laughed. 'Lord bless you. No, my name is Sebastian Jenkins. The governor said "Sebastian" was too much of a mouthful and decided to call me "Spud" seeing as how we were standing in a potato field at the time. I suppose I was lucky we weren't in one of the turnip fields.'

Molly laughed until her sides ached. Spud was certainly a tonic. She started to flick through the pages and had just come across a row of enamel lapel badges when the roar of an engine announced the arrival of a car outside.

'That'll most likely be one of your colleagues arriving for duty,' Spud said as he unhooked his clipboard and headed towards the door.

He'd hardly turned the handle when a shriek and a loud expletive were heard from outside. Molly stood up and peered out of the window to see a well-dressed man helping a smartly turned-out woman to her feet. Molly gasped. The woman had tripped over the suitcase Molly had left at the edge of the road by the gatehouse. This was evident by the fact the lid was lying open and a few items of Molly's best lingerie were now fluttering in the breeze. Rushing to follow Spud outside to offer her apologies to the woman, and hide her underwear, she careered straight into the man, who had been offering his assistance.

'I'm most awfully sorry. I do hope your companion isn't injured,' she blurted out, her attention taken by her best nightdress as it tried to

20

escape the suitcase.

'Well, well, if it isn't Molly Missons,' the man declared with more than a hint of irony in his voice.

Molly froze, wishing a large hole would appear in the road and swallow her up. It was Johnny Johnson, the last man on earth she wished to see here.

1

Molly Missons stepped back from arranging flowers on her parents' grave and brushed a tear from her cheek. Today, 28 February, should have been their silver wedding anniversary. Instead, it marked the sixth month of their passing and the sixth month she had been alone without a single living relative. Molly prayed fervently that her parents were now watching over her with the same love they'd shown their only child while they were alive. It was the only thought she'd clung on to during those first months of raw grief.

Molly shivered. It felt like rain. She pulled on black woollen mittens and tugged the matching knitted beret over her ears, instantly taming her mop of chestnut curls into submission. From where she stood, at the highest point of Brook Street Cemetery, she could see the town of Erith set out below and, just beyond that, the River Thames. The world was facing a new future filled with hope after many years of war, but Molly felt as though the world as she knew it had ended the day a policeman had knocked on the front door. Today, the river was as grey as the sky, completely devoid of colour, just as Molly's life had become since that fateful day in August 1945.

'I still can't believe they're no longer here,' her friend Freda said sadly, linking her arm with Molly's as they headed through the large iron gates to the bus stop. 'I fully expect to walk into the church hall and see your mum setting up the toadstool ready for the Brownies to dance round during their pack meeting.' Not as tall as her friend and with her short light brown hair tucked into a bobbled cap, she didn't look much older than the Brownies she helped out with, despite being in her mid-twenties and holding down a responsible job as a supervisor in the Woolworths across the road from Molly's parents' business.

Molly nodded, a brief smile of remembrance crossing her sad face. The Brownies and Girl Guides had played a big part in her mum's life. 'Mum loved them so much. She would have been proud to see how many turned up in uniform for the memorial service.'

'Do you think you will return to us soon? The younger Brownies keep asking when they will see Tawny Owl again. They don't really understand what's happened.'

Molly raised her hand, alerting the driver of an approaching bus as it laboured up the steep hill to the cemetery gates. 'I suppose I should. Mum wouldn't want me to mope around like I've been doing. I often have the feeling she is sitting on my shoulder telling me to get on with my life. In fact,

I'll join you this week. It's time I did my utmost to resume as normal a life as possible.'

Freda, sitting down next to her friend on the bus, reached into her handbag for her purse and handed over some coins to the conductor for their fare. 'Molly, your mum would have been so proud of you since … since the accident. Why, you've kept your dad's business running, and there's not a speck of dust in the house.' Freda didn't add that it worried her Molly had yet to pack away her parents' possessions. The large Victorian house in Avenue Road looked as though Norman and Charlotte Missons had simply left for a few hours and would return at any moment. Norman's pipe was on the occasional table by his armchair, and Charlotte's apron still hung on a hook in the kitchen, ready for her to pull on and prepare the family meal. Freda knew it gave Molly comfort to see her parents' things around the house, but it was time her friend moved on and thought of her future.

Molly smiled. 'I don't want to let standards drop. Mum would be mortified if I had a visitor and the house was less than perfect. I must say it's hard getting home from the shop each evening and having to think about preparing a meal and doing the housework.'

Freda was deep in thought as the bus continued its journey towards Erith. The last thing she wanted to do was upset her friend. She could see that Molly was exhausted, not only from the shock of losing her parents and staying on top of the house but also from keeping Norman's iron-monger's running. There was also the responsibility of having a member of staff, who required a pay packet at the end of each week. 'How are you managing at the shop now you have to be book-keeper and owner?'

Molly sighed. 'We're keeping our heads above water, as Dad used to say. If it weren't for George and his knowledge of everything to do with the ironmongery business, I'd really be floundering. Thankfully, I picked up the administration side of things from Mum in the year after I left the Land Army. As you know, I was only ever going to help out at the shop while I decided what to do with my future.' A future without my parents, she thought to herself as she gazed through the grimy window of the bus at the rows of terraced Victorian houses they passed. For a moment, she was lost in thoughts of what might have been.

'There's plenty of time. For now, you need to take care of yourself. You may well become an expert in the ironmongery business,' Freda said with a smile. 'Whatever you decide, you know I'll be here to help you.'

'I don't feel I'm an asset to the business. I'm at a loss to know the difference between a nut and a bolt, or indeed the uses for the many nails we have in stock. I'm embarrassed to say that when I covered for George on his day off last week and someone enquired about a plumb line, I advised him to visit the greengrocer's.'

Freda giggled. 'That would have made your dad laugh.'

Molly nodded. 'Yes, he'd have reminded me of that for many a day.'

Freda was pleased to see a glimpse of the old

Molly appear. It had been a while since her friend's green eyes had sparkled with fun as they'd enjoyed a joke or chatted about their favourite screen idol. 'I was wondering if you would do me a favour, Molly. It's my birthday this week. As I only have this afternoon off from Woolies, would you like to come to see a film at the Odeon? If you aren't up to it, then I'll understand.'

'You have no idea how much I would love to celebrate your birthday with you,' Molly said. 'You'd be helping me get back to normal. It's time I started to do something more than go to work. I'm sure it couldn't be wrong to visit the cinema. It will be my treat. In my muddled state, I seem to have lost track of important events like the birthdays of good friends like you. I'm sorry, Freda.'

Freda had worried about inviting Molly to the cinema, but perhaps this just might help her turn the corner after the tragic loss of her parents. 'You've nothing to be sorry for.' She checked her watch. 'We have an hour before the early show starts. Would you like to pop into the Prince of Wales for a drink, or perhaps the cafe for a bite to eat?'

Molly thought for a moment. 'Can I be an absolute bore and stop by the shop? It's almost closing time and I'd like to check that everything's as it should be.'

'You are not a bore at all. You know I love visiting your shop. I find it fascinating.'

Molly laughed. 'You are funny. You're the only woman I know who is interested in the iron-mongery trade. Even Mum left the shop side of

25

things to Dad and just helped out with the paper-work.'

'It's something I know well after serving on a counter with similar goods at Woolworths. I don't profess to be an expert, but I know the difference between a hammer and a screwdriver.'

The bus soon arrived in the town of Erith, which nestled on the south side of the River Thames a little way from London, and the two girls walked the short distance down the High Street to the double-fronted shop. There were few shoppers, as it was early closing in the town. Norman Missons had always been of the belief that his shop should stay open every day as he offered an essential service to the people of Erith, selling, as he did, everything from pounds of tintacks to galvanized watering cans. His wife, Charlotte, had put her foot down when he'd suggested opening on a Sunday. She feared the wrath of their church and also valued their afternoon trips out in the car. It had been on a trip to Canterbury that Norman had done his best to avoid a child who'd run out into the road and they'd met their untimely deaths.

As Molly and Freda approached Missons Iron-monger's, they could see faithful employee George Jones preparing to close up shop for the day. He dragged a dustbin full of mops and brooms in from the pavement at the front of the shop before returning for a sign advertising a popular brand of paraffin.

George stopped to tap his cap and nod to Molly. 'Good afternoon, Molly. Did your visit go well?'

Molly smiled at the grey-haired man. She had

26

known him as far back as she could remember. Along with his wife, Kath, he had been such a support after the accident that took his employer and good friend from him, and George had done his best to keep the business running smoothly ready for when Molly was able to pick up where her father had left off.

'The headstone is now in place, George, and the daffodils look beautiful in their marble pot. Please thank Kath for me.'

George nodded. 'We always picked the first bunch of daffs for your mum, so it's only fitting we still pick them for her now.' He glanced towards the highly polished dark wood counter as he entered the shop with a box of wooden clothes pegs in his hands.

Molly, who was following close behind with a tray of blue-and-white enamel mugs, stopped dead in her tracks. Upon the counter, in a green-tinted glass vase, stood a bunch of daffodils, bringing a shaft of sunshine to this drab February day. This was where her mum always placed George's annual gift. For just a second Molly expected to see Charlotte Missons in her white overalls polishing the wooden counter until it shone. She silently scolded herself for such a foolish notion.

Freda stepped over the threshold and closed her eyes in delight, breathing in the aroma of paraffin oil and lavender-scented floor wax. She'd often visited the shop during her lunch hour from Woolworths to chat to Molly's mum about Brownie and Girl Guide projects and would stop to lend a hand. Weighing quantities of nails on the large brass scales and tipping them into brown paper

27

bags never ceased to thrill as she lined them up ready for George to place onto shelves. If she didn't enjoy her job at Woolworths so much, she would have jumped at the chance to work alongside Molly's parents in the family business. 'Can I help you with anything, Mr Jones?'

'No, young lady. Everything's in hand. Get yourself off and enjoy what's left of your half-day, and take Molly with you. It's time she started to get out a bit more.'

'I'll do that, George. In fact, Molly's coming with me to the Odeon shortly to see *Now, Voyager*.'

'She'll enjoy that. The missus went with her sister the other day and hasn't stopped talking about that actor Paul Henreid ever since. You'd never believe she saw the film the last time it was on at the Odeon by the way she went on and on about it.' George looked at the large clock at the back of the shop. 'You'd better get a move on or the best seats will be gone.' He called out to Molly, 'You get yourself off or the B-movie will have started. I'll finish up here.'

Molly looked up from where she was sifting through a pile of envelopes. 'I'm all done, George. I'll put the post in Dad's office and be on my way.' She still could not call the back room by anything other than the name by which it had been known since she was a young child. Entering the office, she tossed the paperwork into a wooden tray, then noticed a small white envelope with her own name written on it in neat copperplate writing. It was most likely another condolence card, she thought, as she tucked it away in her handbag to read later, along with another, which she noted came from

28

her dad's solicitor, Mr A. C. Denton.

The two girls reached the cinema just as the lights went down and sat enthralled throughout the first film, in which handsome secret agent Clive Danvers saved the country from invasion by uncovering a dastardly plot. It was the main feature, though, that Molly and Freda looked forward to more, and they were not disappointed.

Freda looped her arm through Molly's as they dashed across the High Street to a fish-and-chip shop on the other side. They joined a queue of people waiting for fried fish, both breathing in the aroma of chips and vinegar in the steamy shop. 'That must be the most romantic film I've ever seen,' Freda sighed.

'I'm so pleased you asked me to come with you. It took my mind off my own life for a few hours,' Molly said. She glanced at the posters pasted to the white-tiled walls of the chip shop. A forthcoming jumble sale at Christ Church and an Easter funfair and circus at the recreation ground that backed onto her house. She was pleased that some of the Rec, as the locals called it, was back to how it used to be and no longer used to 'dig for victory'. A third poster caught her eye. 'Look, Freda – Butlins holiday camp is having a grand opening in May. Mum had wanted to holiday there before the war started, but then Dad heard the camp had been taken over by the services. Perhaps we could take a trip in the summer?'

'I'd like that,' Freda said excitedly. Since moving to Erith in 1938 she'd fallen in love with the Kentish seaside towns and visited Margate and Ramsgate whenever she could. She wrinkled her nose in thought. 'Where is Skegness?'

'It's up in Lincolnshire somewhere. A fair way to travel. We'd have to find out how to get there. I'm told we would stay in wooden huts and join the other holidaymakers for our meals. They have entertainment, and there's also a swimming pool. Everything is included for a lovely holiday.'

'It does sound wonderful. Is Butlins just in the one place?'

'From what I remember Mum telling me, they have a few different holiday camps. For some reason, she was keen on visiting the one in Skegness.'

The girls chatted excitedly as they inched their way up the queue towards the high green-and-cream shop counter.

'Been to see that *Now, Voyager*, have you?' a rosy-cheeked woman asked as she wrapped a portion of cod and chips in a copy of yesterday's *Erith Observer*.

'We have, Vi. Bette Davis is so sophisticated. The change in her appearance by the end of the film was almost a miracle,' Molly exclaimed.

'I thought the same when I see it with my old man. It'd be no use me dressing like Bette Davis working in here, though,' she guffawed, brushing strands of greying hair from her hot face. 'What can I get for you two girls this evening?'

Molly opened her purse. 'It's my treat, seeing as how it's almost your birthday, Freda. Rock and chips twice, please, Vi.'

Freda went to protest but could see that it was a losing battle. 'Thank you. Rock salmon would be nice. Can you leave them open, please, Vi?'

Vi nodded as she shook the bubbling fat from a basket of chips and tipped them into a large metal hopper at the front of the counter. 'We need more chips out here, Bill,' she bellowed towards an open door at the back of the shop. 'It's your birthday?' she said to Freda. 'Well, many happy returns, love, and plenty of them. Here's a saveloy each from me. I've been meaning to say thank you for taking our Jeanie under your wing at Woolies. She loves her job on the biscuit counter. Been the making of her, it has. She's even walking out with a nice young man from the shoe shop next door. He's no Paul Henreid, though,' she added with another belly laugh. 'But then my Jeanie's no film star, come to that.'

The girls both laughed as they watched Vi tip their fish and chips onto squares of paper and place a long saveloy sausage on top before folding newspaper around each parcel, leaving a gap from which to eat from. 'Help yourself to salt and vinegar.'

'No chance of Jeanie's fella lighting two cigarettes and handing one to her to smoke, like they did in the film?' Freda asked with a sigh. 'What was it she said to him?'

'"Don't let's ask for the moon. We have the stars,"' Molly said with a dreamy look on her face.

'Me and my Bill tried that the other night after we see the film,' Vi said with a grin.

Molly's eyes grew wide at the thought. She'd known the rotund Vi for many years, along with her pint-sized husband, Bill. 'Was it romantic, Vi?' she asked, before blowing on a hot chip and popping it into her mouth.

'Romantic? Bless my soul.' She started to laugh as tears rolled down her cheeks. 'Bill took one puff of those fags and nigh on coughed his guts up. We'll not bother with romance again.'

Still giggling, the two friends headed out into the dark evening, the fish and chips warming their hands as they headed to a bench nearby.

'I'm full up,' Molly said a short while later, as she wiped her mouth with her handkerchief. 'It was very good of Vi to throw in the saveloys, but I really can't eat mine.'

'You're right there. They won't go to waste, though – I'll take the scraps back for Nelson. He'll love them. That dog eats anything,' Freda said, folding the newspaper round the scraps. 'Do you fancy coming back for a cup of cocoa?'

'No, thanks. I'll head home. I want to have an early night to be at the shop on time for deliveries.' Molly knew that Freda's landlady kept an open house for family and friends, but at the moment she preferred not to be where people were aware of her loss. She still couldn't trust herself not to burst into tears when people showed their concern.

'Enjoy your sleep and dream of Paul Henreid,' Freda laughed.

'He's a little on the old side for me, thank you very much.'

Freda thought for a minute. 'Perhaps the dashing actor in the first film. What was his name?'

'Johnny Johnson. I've seen him in a few films. He always plays the handsome hero.'

Freda nudged Molly as she pulled on her gloves.

'So you're in love with a movie star, are you? I must admit he is extremely handsome. I've spotted him myself in a few films. He has a beautiful singing voice. It is such a shame he has only appeared in two musicals. Do you think he's English or American?'

Molly thought for a moment of the tall, dark-haired matinee idol. She wasn't going to admit to Freda that she was sweet on the actor and made sure she saw any film he appeared in. 'He's always been in English films, but who are we to know? If his acting is that good, he could be any nationality.'

'I have some old movie magazines in my room. I'll see if there's anything about him. We may as well find out about the mystery man you've fallen in love with.'

Molly pushed Freda's arm and laughed. 'Get off home, you daft thing. I'm no more in love with Johnny Johnson than you are Paul Henreid.' She hugged Freda. 'Have a lovely birthday and I'll see you in the week.'

As Molly headed away from the High Street and walked up the tree-lined avenue to her home, she thought about the handsome movie star. She was never going to admit to her friend that she dreamed about Johnny at night as well as during quiet moments at work. It was the only time she managed not to think about her parents.

2

Molly was still coming to terms with arriving home to a darkened house. The large, detached property set back from the road, close to the town of Erith, didn't seem as welcoming now she lived there alone. The houses in leafy Avenue Road had been built for the town's well-to-do in the past century and, with their bay windows and generous front gardens, still attracted the wealthier trades-people from Erith. Norman Missons had been proud to live in a street that showed how well his business was doing. With her mother no longer there to welcome her, though, the house seemed quiet and empty.

She turned her key in the lock and entered the large hallway, quickly reaching for the light switch. The homely room was flooded with light, picking out a framed photograph on the wall that had been taken on Charlotte and Norman's wedding day. Molly looked at it as she removed her coat and hat, placing them next to her parents' coats on the hall stand. They looked so young and in love. Who was to know they would be taken so soon and not live long enough to enjoy their old age together? Molly felt the anger and the unjustness she'd bottled up start to bubble to the surface. Life was so unfair – so bloody unfair.

Drawing the forest-green velvet curtains in the large bay windows of the front room, Molly lit a taper and held it to the kindling in the grate. She always made sure that before she left home each morning, there was a fire prepared and ready to light the moment she came home from work. In the kitchen, she already had the makings of a meal. The three years she'd spent working in the Land Army had taught her how to utilize her time as efficiently as possible. They had also taught her not to be afraid of hard work. After the filling fish-and-chip meal with Freda, Molly decided the shepherd's pie could be saved for tomorrow.

She poured milk into a small pan and placed it on the stove to heat for her nightly cup of cocoa. Freda had been a good friend, especially since the day Molly heard that her parents had been involved in an accident. Freda had moved in with her during those first dark weeks, forcing her to eat even when Molly had no idea whether it was night or day. When the tears finally came, it was Freda who held her while she sobbed. Freda had little family to speak of, apart from a brother in the navy, although she did have some wonderful friends and colleagues who worked alongside her at Woolworths. Once Freda had returned home, Freda's landlady had sent food and offered a bed if Molly couldn't face being alone in the large house in Avenue Road. Molly may not have any blood relatives, but she certainly had friends who cared.

Carrying a cup and saucer into the front room and settling in her dad's armchair by the fireside, Molly reached for her handbag and took out the two envelopes. The letter from Mr Denton, the family solicitor, requested she attend his office in

Pier Road at her earliest convenience to discuss her father's will. Molly was sure that everything would be straightforward, as her dad had never said otherwise. She'd visit tomorrow afternoon when it was quiet in the shop. She opened the second envelope with reluctance: people had been so kind with their condolences, but the well-meant messages of sympathy still broke her heart to read. Many an evening had been spent crying over her best vellum notepaper as she wrote to thank her parents' friends for their kind thoughts. The funeral had been well attended, the Missons family being thought of highly in the busy town. Fellow business owners and town councillors had filled the pews of Christ Church before following the cortège to the graveyard on the other side of town. An obituary in the *Erith Observer* had been glowing in its praise of the well-known couple. Freda had saved the newspapers that covered Mr and Mrs Missons's accident and the funeral for a time when Molly was ready to read them. Molly was so thankful that she had.

Carefully opening the envelope, and making a mental note to save the stamp for Freda to add to the Brownies' charity collection, she scanned the single page, covered in an untidy handwritten scrawl, and frowned. Surely this couldn't be right.

My dearest child,

I am saddened to hear of the loss of my cousin-in-law and his wife, and must apologize for my tardiness in contacting you so many months after their untimely deaths. I have only just returned from South Africa

36

*with my son, Simon, where I have property and busi-
ness interests. Be assured I will arrive shortly so we can
discuss your future and the property that is bequeathed
to me under the terms of your father's will.*
   Your devoted relative,
   Harriet

Molly read the page several times. She had never
heard her parents speak of any relatives, let alone
a Harriet and her son, Simon. Granted, her parents' past was a mystery to her, but surely if there
had been a family disagreement of some kind,
she would have been told. After all, she was an
adult and deserved to know about her family –
even more so now she was alone in the world.

'How can she be your devoted relative when
you've never met her?' Freda whispered as she
handed the sheet of paper back to Molly. 'There's
not even a proper address. It must be a forgery.'
   Not knowing what to make of the letter, Molly
had opened her shop in Pier Road, one of the
busy shopping streets of Erith, the next morning
and then crossed the road to Woolworths to show
her friend. Freda, a supervisor in the busy store,
was aware that it was against shop policy for staff
to chat to friends while on duty. However, it was
important that she spoke to her friend as soon as
possible.
   'Freda, I don't feel that someone who wasn't
related to me would go to the trouble of writing
such a letter. Do you?'
   Freda thought for a moment. 'I'm not so sure.
Stranger things have happened.'

37

Molly laughed. 'Oh, Freda, that's only in the cinema and those crime novels you like to read. This is real life. It's nice to know I have a relative, even if Mum and Dad had reasons not to tell me about her. I've never had a cousin, or a second cousin, come to that. I wonder what Simon is like.'

'I think you should show this to Mr Denton and see what he has to say about this relative. I'm surprised he hasn't told you about your dad's will yet, and why did your parents not mention the house would be left to a stranger?'

'I suppose Dad never thought that he and Mum would die so young. Even during the war we never spoke of what would happen if...' Molly bit her lip to stop the tears that threatened to fall.

'The best thing is for you to see that solicitor. He will know what's to be done.'

Molly placed the letter in her pocket. 'He has written to me a few times since the funeral, but I've not been able to face discussing my future. It makes things so final.' She felt a lump forming in her throat and couldn't speak.

Freda reached out and gripped Molly's hand. 'Come on, Molly. You've done so well up to now. I'm sure your dad will have left you well provided for. The shop is doing better than many of the businesses in town. That must count for something. Why, everyone seems to want bits and bobs from Missons to patch up their homes now that the war's over.'

As Molly crossed the road back to her shop, she thought of Freda's reassuring words. But was Missons doing well? Every week she was putting off suppliers who were asking for payments. Although the weekly takings kept them afloat, there seemed to be a backlog of debts to pay. She fell asleep each night wondering how to settle the reminders that came in the post. Molly had dipped into her post-office savings account more than once rather than have deliveries refused, but still the shop seemed to live from hand to mouth. Was she doing something wrong? She would have to bite the bullet and go through her dad's office with a fine toothcomb. She couldn't believe the shop had been running at a loss.

The office of A. C. Denton was situated above the bank chambers just up the road from her dad's shop. It had only taken a couple of minutes to cross the busy road to the office of the solicitor who had always taken care of Norman Missons's business and private affairs. Molly climbed the steep staircase and entered a chilly room where a young man was seated at a desk. She could smell paraffin from a little stove in the corner of the room. It did nothing to warm the small area. Molly recalled that Mr Denton had an account with Missons and it was some time since it had been settled. Perhaps she should write a note to remind him. However, it didn't seem the polite thing to do. Many people in the town who had paid their respects at the funeral had accounts with the shop. She couldn't insult her parents' friends by reminding them of their debts. They would be sure to bring their accounts up to date in time.

The young man glanced up with a bored expression on his face. 'Can I help you? I'm Mr Timothy Denton, junior partner.'

Molly fumbled in her handbag for the letter sent by Mr Denton. 'I received this from Mr Denton Senior requesting I call into the office at my earliest convenience. It says it concerns my dad's will.' She held it out to him as she sat down on the hard wooden seat across the desk from his own, which he'd indicated with a wave of his hand. She felt sick and dizzy, and had to fight off the thought of fleeing from the office. Did she want to hear what her dad had decided about the house and business, if indeed he had made a decision?

The young man frowned as he read the letter. 'This was written a few weeks ago. I'm afraid my uncle is now out of the office on an urgent family matter abroad.'

Molly rose to leave. 'Then I'll return another time. I have been a little tardy in reading my post recently. Please forgive me.'

He raised his hand. 'I am sure I can assist you. This should be straightforward.'

Molly sat down and watched as he rummaged through filing cabinets and cupboards before returning to his desk to sift through an untidy pile of files heaped in a wire tray. By now he was muttering to himself and there were beads of sweat on his brow. He tugged at his wing collar as if it were choking him, before giving a loud sigh. 'Ah! Here we are.' He pulled a single sheet of paper from a thin folder.

Molly could see him scanning the page before placing it on his desk. He removed his spectacles and leaned back in his chair. 'Everything seems to be in order. Your father, Norman Sydney Missons, left his house and business to your mother. You can inform her that she has nothing to worry about. As soon as my uncle returns, he will speak with your mother and give her the necessary paperwork to sign. Perhaps you could convey this to her and give her my most sincere condolences at her sad loss.' He nodded as if to dismiss her.

Molly didn't know whether to sob her heart out or laugh out loud. If only she could convey his message. If only. She pulled herself together. 'Mr Denton, I'm afraid you are under the illusion that my mum is alive. If she were, I can assure you she would be sitting here herself. She died with my dad. There's only me now. I have no siblings. I need to know about the house. It seems a distant relative is under the impression they now own my home.'

Timothy Denton had the good grace to look embarrassed and muttered his apologies. He placed the spectacles back on his nose and scrutinized the document closely. 'This is dated September 1919. There is no mention of a child,' he said pointedly.

'There wouldn't be. I wasn't born until March 1921. At that time, my parents had been married but a few months and had just settled in Erith. My dad's business was in its infancy.'

'You say a relative claims the house now belongs to her?'

Molly nodded. 'She is the widow of my dad's cousin.'

'Have you seen any documentation?'

Molly handed him the letter from Harriet. 'This letter is the first I knew of any living relative. I was under the impression I didn't have any family.'

Timothy Denton glanced at the letter and handed it back. 'There is the possibility that a later will has been made and that your relative now owns your parents' property. As there is no mention of a business, I feel that is safe. Perhaps it is time to think of moving on to pastures new? Are you planning to marry, perhaps?'

'You mean let a man take responsibility for my future, Mr Denton?' Molly rose to her feet, indignant at his words. 'I would be failing my parents if I thought my future was just to be a wife and mother. I feel I should await your uncle's return for guidance. Thank you for your time.'

Molly left the office silently fuming as she strode through the High Street and headed for home. Thank goodness George had offered to lock up the shop. She was in no mood for polite chatter with customers after such a troubling experience. Perhaps she should have thought more about her future and planned her life. It had been so easy to move back home with Mum and Dad after her Land Army days and simply help out in the shop. No doubt if her parents had not had their accident, she would have coasted through life and not had to worry about her future.

Although only late afternoon, it was already getting dark as Molly approached home. Up ahead, she could see a man helping an older woman alight from a taxicab. Could these be the relatives of whom she had only just heard? Now within a few yards of the couple, she could hear the man reprimand the driver for not carrying the suitcases to the front door. The driver simply tapped his cap in acknowledgement of the sharp words and climbed back into his vehicle.

'Hello. Are you Cousin Harriet?' Molly asked as she reached the couple's side.

The older woman turned to face Molly. 'If you are the daughter of my much-loved and dearly departed cousin-in-law Norman, then yes, I am.'

Molly frowned. How could someone miss a loved one when, as far as Molly could recall, they had never set foot over the threshold of her family home? To her knowledge, her dad had not received any correspondence from this relative, as he would often open letters over breakfast and mention any snippet of information he thought would be of interest to his wife and daughter. Perhaps they had resumed contact while Molly was working in the Land Army. Yes, that must be the answer. But she had been back in Erith since last summer. Surely one of her parents would have mentioned this cousin?

Molly felt the woman scrutinize her appearance. She tried to straighten her coat, aware her eyes would still be puffy from recent tears and her cheeks red from hurrying home. The lady in front of her reminded Molly very much of a portrait of the late Queen Victoria that had hung on the wall of her primary school, resplendent in widow's weeds with a small black bonnet pinned to her silver hair. Cousin Harriet was, however, as thin as the late queen had been portly.

She pointed a silver-handled walking stick towards Molly. 'Help my son with our cases. We have business to discuss and should not do so in the street.' She gazed up to the house and nodded approvingly. 'We shall be very comfortable here, very comfortable indeed.'

Later, as Molly climbed into her bed, she thought back to the uncomfortable evening as she had fed and cleared up after her two guests. Guests? Molly had the distinct feeling they were here to stay. Aware the elder of her relatives would want the best room in the house, she had excused herself from the dinner table after serving them shepherd's pie, which the pair had tucked into with relish, and gone to her parents' bedroom. Her heart ached as she cleared a drawer of her mum's dressing table and her dad's tallboy. She pulled clothes from one of the two wardrobes, telling herself not to stop and breathe in the scent and the memories of her parents as she carried the clothes to the box room. She would decide what to do with them later. She knew that her parents would expect her to make any guest welcome, regardless of the reason for their visit.

She checked the smaller spare bedroom. Freda stayed in the room occasionally, so it was aired and ready for occupation. Cousin Simon would have to make do with sleeping there, as the other bedroom still required decorating. It had sustained damage to the windows in the last days of the war, and although it now had replacement windows, her dad had not got round to papering and painting the room. Besides that, it contained cupboards and boxes brimming over with Brownie and Girl Guide equipment, but Molly was not prepared to move anything that meant so much to her mum. She stopped and took a deep breath. 'Pull yourself together, Molly,' she muttered to herself. Taking fresh sheets from the airing cupboard, she quickly made up the beds and threw open the large windows in her parents' room, which overlooked the front garden of the house, in order to air it. The cool evening air blew away the last of her mum's fragrance. Squaring her shoulders, Molly went downstairs to join her new family.

'So you see, my dear, it works out rather splendidly. We can all live here as one big, happy family until I decide what to do with the property. Who knows' – she gave a little giggle that seemed out of place coming from a woman of her age – 'you and Simon may just make your own union and then I could consider leaving the house to you and my grandchildren.' She smiled indulgently at her son, who, after discovering Norman's best whisky in the sideboard, had partaken until falling into a deep sleep in Norman's favourite armchair by the fireside. His collar studs now undone and a little dribble escaping his thin lips, he was oblivious to his mother's words. 'Then again, he may meet a suitable young lady, meaning you would have to find other accommodation.'

Molly tried not to look horrified. She had taken an instant dislike to Simon, who had ignored her apart from eyeing her occasionally in an uncomfortable way that made Molly's skin creep. If her dad had decided that his property should be left to a cousin and that cousin's wife was now here to claim her inheritance, then who was she to argue? Norman Missons had been a good and kind man; he would always do what was right.

45

'I wonder if I may see the will, please?' Molly asked. 'I didn't know of Dad's requests, and with the shock of the accident, it never crossed my mind until now that this would not be my home.'

Cousin Harriet waved her hand to dismiss Molly's words. 'I have the letters from my solicitor somewhere. Please don't worry yourself with such details. Everything is in order. Now, I think it's time for a little drink before I retire for the night. It has been a long and tiring day. Have you put hot-water bottles in our beds? We do feel the cold since our return from South Africa. Even though the journey took many weeks by sea and fellow travellers were able to get used to the colder climes, I'm afraid my old bones are still not used to the British weather.'

3

'You're going to what?' Freda hissed as she placed four china frogs round an ornate papier-mâché toadstool. Her words echoed around the empty hall of Northend Baptist Mission as they prepared for a special Brownie pack meeting.

Molly arranged a display of paper water lilies on the mirror next to where the toadstool sat and stepped back to admire their handiwork. 'The perfect toadstool by a lily pond.' She glanced at Freda, knowing that her friend was angered by her earlier words. 'I said I'm considering marrying Simon.'

'You've only known him a few weeks. Have you suddenly fallen head over heels in love with a cousin you never knew existed until three weeks ago?'

'Second cousin,' Molly replied, quietly aware that just outside the hall, mothers and their Brownie daughters were gathering for the special evening in which new members would be enrolled in the Brownie movement and cease being called Tweenies. She placed six brass badges on a side table and checked each one was shining brightly. They would be pinned to the girls' uniforms once they were accepted into the pack and had recited the Brownie Promise, in which they swore to do their best and be good Brownies.

'Are you doing your best?' Freda asked as she brushed down the skirt of her Brown Owl uniform. She'd been over the moon with excitement when the district commissioner had offered her the position of leader of the Brownie pack. Molly had assured her friend that she was the perfect replacement for her mum and was happy to remain as her assistant. She enjoyed being called Tawny Owl and had returned to helping out at the weekly meetings after her new-found relations had installed themselves in her parents' house. The two girls looked very smart in their official blue uniforms. Molly's hair, pinned back into a French pleat, with a navy hat on top, made her look older and more mature.

Molly frowned. 'I don't know what you mean.'

'Are you doing your best to carry on as your mum would have wanted? Would she have liked you marrying a man you hardly know just to keep

47

a roof over your head?' Freda looked concerned. She had seen how in just a few weeks her friend had been taken over by Harriet and her son, and Molly never seemed to have a second to herself unless it was to go to work.

'Things have changed since ... since Mum and Dad died. I have no choice...'

Freda laid a hand on her friend's arm. 'There is always a choice, Molly, and as long as I'm your best friend, I'll be here to ensure you make the right choice, whether you like it or not.'

'I don't feel I have much option. Not if I want to keep hold of my home. Cousin Harriet has been good to me. She could have shown me the door once she moved in. For whatever reason, Dad left the house to his cousin, and Harriet said there was no mention of me in the will. It is only her Christian duty that is keeping a roof over my head. It seems she did a lot of charity work when in South Africa.'

Freda snorted angrily. 'Christian duty? She has yet to show you this will. Do you even know it exists? Now, let's invite our guests into the room and start the proceedings, shall we? I have a few hours off tomorrow afternoon. I suggest we have afternoon tea at Hedley Mitchell's and decide what you should do next.'

Molly gave a weak smile. She had hoped her friend would be able to advise her. Harriet and Simon had swept her along on a wave of change since they stepped over the threshold at Avenue Road. She'd even had to rescue the Brownie property her mum had so lovingly cared for, after she arrived home from work one evening to discover the room clear and all equipment heaped in a pile at the end of the garden ready for a bonfire. She felt her chin start to wobble and tears prick her eyes. 'Tea and a chat would be lovely.'

The evening was a great success. The little girls were so pleased to see their Tawny Owl back with them once more, and their mothers were able to chat with Molly about their memories of her mum and dad, and understood when Molly was tearful and had to leave the room several times to compose herself. The people of Erith were such a caring community. Molly couldn't think of anywhere else in the world she would rather live.

Arriving back at the house in Avenue Road, she popped her head round the door of the front room. It felt strange to see Cousin Harriet and her son sitting in Norman and Charlotte's favourite armchairs. She tried to put it to the back of her mind and found it hard to do so. 'I'm home. It's been a long day, so I thought I'd go straight to bed and read for a while, if that's all right?'

Harriet leaned over to the wireless and turned it off. 'It's early yet, Molly. Simon was thinking of taking you out for the evening. Weren't you, Simon?'

He looked at the grandfather clock in the corner of the room and raised an eyebrow in Molly's direction. 'I thought a drink down the Prince of Wales would be in order.'

An alcoholic drink was the last thing Molly was interested in, but she feared Simon's anger. She'd witnessed how quickly his face turned red, and one morning she'd seen him clench his fists when berating the milkman for rattling milk bottles too loudly after a night spent sleeping on the sofa, his drunken state having stopped him from climbing the stairs to his bedroom. When in the presence of her relative, she often found herself treading on eggshells. She could see an empty whisky glass on a side table. No doubt he'd been partaking of her dad's best whisky yet again. It seemed to be a nightly habit.

'A drink would be nice, thank you. I'll get my coat.'

Simon gave her a glance and sneered. 'Perhaps change into something a little more becoming. I prefer not to have a Girl Guide on my arm when I enter a public house.'

Molly bit her lip rather than say what was on her mind. 'Give me five minutes.' She dashed upstairs to her bedroom and flung open the door of her wardrobe. She wasn't prepared to look 'becoming' for Simon and instead opted for a flower-patterned dress with rows of pearl buttons down the front. The green background to the pink flowers suited her complexion and complemented the auburn highlights in her hair. Dabbing a little lavender water behind her ears and checking her lipstick, she went downstairs to join her relatives.

'I thought Harriet would be coming with us,' Molly said as she looked around the empty room.

'Mother's taken your lead and is having an early night,' Simon said. 'I suggest we make a move before they start to shout last orders.'

Molly was grateful that the pub was just a short walk down the avenue, as she felt uncomfortable holding on to Simon's arm. He'd taken her hand as they'd left the house and tucked it through his

50

arm in a possessive manner. She had wanted to snatch her hand back but thought it might have caused a scene.

Entering the busy pub, Simon headed straight for the bar, indicating a free table where Molly should sit. He hadn't asked what drink she preferred, which worried her somewhat.

Returning with a tray, Molly was pleased to see what looked like a glass of lemonade beside a tankard of beer and a whisky short.

'Drink up. There's plenty more where that came from.'

Molly sipped her drink and shuddered. 'It's gin!'

'A drop of mother's ruin won't hurt you. You must have had more than that when you were in the Land Army,' he said with a knowing wink.

'I'm not sure what you mean. We had to work long hours on the farm. There wasn't much time for drinking,' Molly added, feeling hurt at his insinuation. She had enjoyed a good social life but didn't feel that it was Simon's business to know what she did during the war.

'Don't get all uppity with me. Lots of things happened during the war that women don't wish to talk about now. Drink up and I'll get another round in.'

Molly took a gulp of her drink. It was preferable to arguing with Simon. So what if some girls were over-friendly with men during wartime? It didn't mean that she had been. Molly respected herself too much to take things too far. For now, she'd try to be friendly with Simon and let him see she was a decent girl.

Molly had sipped three drinks by the time the

landlord rang the bell for last orders. Standing to pull on her coat, she felt a little light-headed. It had been a long day, what with working at the shop and then running the busy Brownie pack meeting. Simon's hands lingered a little too long on her shoulders as he stood behind, helping her on with her coat.

'Thank you, Simon. I can manage now,' Molly said, stepping away from his grasp and heading towards the door.

'Night, Doreen,' Simon called to the barmaid as he followed Molly out into the night. Molly looked back to see the barmaid who'd been serving Simon all night blow a kiss in his direction.

Simon again took her hand and tucked it through his arm, but this time Molly was grateful for something to hold on to, as the night air made her feel even more dizzy than she had inside the pub. He set out at a brisk pace that made her need to hurry to keep up with him. At this pace, she felt worse, and just a little sick. They were soon indoors. Hanging up her coat on the hall stand, Molly moved towards the kitchen. 'I'll make us a cup of tea before I retire for the night.'

A rough hand grabbed her shoulder and pulled her back. 'A cup of tea is not what I want at this moment,' Simon said as he pushed Molly roughly to the wall. Holding her by her hair, he forced his lips onto hers, probing her mouth with his tongue. 'This is more like it,' he said as he leaned away and wiped his mouth.

Molly wanted to scream, but who was there to help her? If Harriet heard a commotion, Simon would be sure to make an excuse. Besides, she didn't want the elderly woman to see she'd had a little too much to drink. Molly knew she needed to escape before it was too late. But was it already too late? She could hear his laboured breathing and tasted blood where he'd caught her lip with his rough kiss.

With his tight hold on her hair, Simon reached for the front of Molly's dress and cursed as he found it hard to undo the small pearl buttons with one hand. Swearing loudly, he tore at the fabric, the buttons bursting under the force. Both hands at once started to explore Molly's breasts, and try as she might, she could not push the heavily built man away from her. 'Please ... Simon don't hurt me.'

Simon just grunted and started to tear at the flimsy fabric beneath her dress, his mouth taking command of her now naked breast.

Molly willed herself not to panic. She thought back to what the older women in the Land Army had told her when they'd sat chatting about their amorous encounters and also the unwanted attention they sometimes encountered when walking home in the blackout with soldiers they met at dances. Taking a deep breath, she pushed Simon's shoulders. As he took a step back, she raised her knee with as much force as possible. Simon groaned in pain, stumbling backwards and knocking her parents' photograph from the hall stand as she fled towards the living room. It would have been ideal to head for the front door, but it meant passing her cousin. Dashing into the room, she reached for the brass door handle and attempted to close it on Simon, but already he was coming to his senses and heading in her direction. As the heavy door closed, he put his shoulder forward, shoving it open. Such was the force that Molly staggered against a small side table and fell onto a rug close to the fire. Whatever should I do next? she thought. If only she'd had time to reach the large bay windows, Molly could have escaped into the street and called to one of the neighbours for help. Now it was too late and Simon was towering over her, his face red with anger.

'You can't escape me, little cousin,' he growled as he knelt down, unbuttoning his trousers as he did so.

Molly looked from left to right. There was no escape. Even in his drunken state Simon was in control of the situation. It was then she noticed the brass poker lying on the hearth. If only she could reach it. But how, with Simon so close? He would be sure to notice. It took her just a second to decide.

'You've come to your senses.' Simon smiled as Molly reached for him and pulled him down. She felt bile burn her throat and resisted the urge to gag. As his attention focused on sliding his hand up her thigh, Molly reached slowly for the heavy poker. Gripping the handle, she swung it with as much strength as she could muster across Simon's back. It made contact with his right shoulder and he screamed in pain before slumping like a sack of coal on top of her.

Fearing for her life, she pushed the heavy weight from her and fled the room. All thought of leaving the house left her mind as she ran upstairs to her bedroom and locked herself in. Had she killed him?

Molly sat on her bed for a while to gather her thoughts. There was no sound in the house. Harriet must have slept through the noise. Removing her torn dress, she threw it into the corner of the room. Tomorrow, it would go in the dustbin. Even if the dress could be repaired, Molly would never be able to wear it again without thinking of what happened. She poured a little cold water into a bowl from a matching jug sat on a marble-topped washstand, then splashed her hot face with the cool water, scrubbing the taste of alcohol and Simon from her mouth before pulling on a nightdress and dressing gown, tying the belt tightly round her waist, all the time listening for any sound from downstairs.

Molly couldn't climb into bed without knowing what had happened to Simon. She might have killed him. Who would believe her side of the story if that was the case? She quietly turned the lock in her bedroom door and pulled the door open, gasping in shock as she came face to face with her second cousin.

Simon raised his hands in surrender. 'You win this time, Molly, but mark my words – be more friendly towards me in future or you will lose this house and become homeless. Mother intends that we marry, but there are more fish in the sea if you continue to be obstinate.' His eyes bore into her as he delivered his warning.

Molly gripped the front of her dressing gown tightly to her breast. She recalled the woman in the pub and how she blew a kiss to Simon. Would she be made homeless because of a barmaid?

Watching as Simon headed to his bedroom, rubbing the shoulder that had been struck with the heavy brass poker, Molly knew she had to make plans for her future or goodness knows what would happen.

The girls were seated in the genteel surroundings of Hedley Mitchell's tearooms. Even though they were just yards down the road from where they worked, the tearooms were only visited on special occasions.

Freda wiped crumbs from her mouth. 'These egg sandwiches are delicious. I know we could make them at home and chat round the kitchen table, but afternoon tea at Mitchell's is such a treat, isn't it?'

Molly sipped her tea and nodded. 'Just to be away from the house and able to talk without Cousin Harriet asking questions is a treat.'

'What has she been asking you?'

'It's rather strange. She was looking at Mum and Dad's wedding photograph the other day and wanted to know where they were married. Then she asked about Dad's parents. I reminded her that until she wrote to me, I had never known any family. I would have thought she would have known about such things, wouldn't you?'

Freda nodded. 'It does sound rather strange. Did she say how long she lived in South Africa?'

'Yes. It was just after our chat about Mum and Dad's wedding. She told me how her late husband, Bert, was a missionary and they'd not been home to England these past twenty-five years.'

'All the same, you'd have thought she'd have

kept in touch with family back home. Are you sure your parents never mentioned them?'

Molly shook her head. The curls around the small hat perched on her head bounced in the sunlight that shone through the window of the tea-room. 'No, we never spoke about family. Apart from my parents saying we were alone in the world, I have no recollection of them even discussing my grandparents. It sounds so strange now I come to think of it, but we were a happy family – life before they came to Kent and set up a home and business was never mentioned.'

Freda, too, thought it strange, but then, not everyone had a happy family life. Her own family had not been perfect, and apart from an occasional postcard, she seldom heard from her mother these days. If it weren't for her brother, Lenny, she too would be alone like Molly. Thank goodness for friends, she thought to herself. 'So what's all this about marrying Simon?'

Molly sighed. 'Cousin Harriet keeps pointing out to me that I must think of my future. She even referred to me as a "spinster", would you believe? Honestly, you'd think I'd never had the occasional boyfriend or worked away during the war.'

Freda, who was envious of her friend's time spent in the Land Army, laughed. 'From the tales you've told me, you were never short of an escort. But why marry Simon?'

'Harriet keeps talking about him settling down and having a family. It was pointedly told to me that she's left everything to Simon in her will and she's made it clear that if we marry, I'll be taken care of and can stay at my parents' house.' Her lips trembled as she thought of what happened last night. Molly had left the house early that morning, not wishing to face Harriet or Simon, and only stayed long enough to straighten the living room and pick up glass from the broken frame that held her parents' photograph. Fortunately, the photograph had not been damaged. It would be repaired and as good as new before too long. The morning had been spent shut away in her dad's office at the ironmonger's. Not that much work had been done. Molly didn't want to explain to George why she was so shaken. What had happened wasn't something she could talk about with the old man.

'Are you all right, Molly? You look awfully pale. You've hardly eaten a thing. Is that a cut on your lip?' Freda asked as she peered across the small table at the mark on Molly's bottom lip, which, despite carefully applied lipstick, could still be seen.

Molly nodded as unshed tears overflowed and cascaded down her cheeks. 'Can we go somewhere more private and talk? I'm in fear of my life,' she started to sob.

Freda quickly paid the waitress before diners and staff spotted Molly's distress. Picking up Molly's handbag, she encouraged her friend to pull on her coat and led her out of Mitchell's and down the High Street towards the River Thames.

Standing by the small pier and breathing in the cold air that blew from the river, Freda turned to her chum. 'Now, tell me everything.'

The words poured from Molly's lips. Once she started talking, she couldn't stop. She told of the many times Simon had made her feel uncomfort-

58

able, and although she could fend off Harriet's many questions, while her relative managed to ignore anything Molly asked about her dad's earlier life, she was always conscious of Simon's eyes on her.

'But why does that make you fear for your life?' Freda asked. 'Not that I'm questioning your feelings,' she added quickly.

Molly stared out over the river that she'd known all her life. As a child, she'd paddled in the water during hot summers. Trips on the paddle steamer *Kentish Queen* down to the seaside towns of Southend and Margate had been special treats. Now, there were just ships painted battleship grey anchored off the shore, alongside Thames barges and tugs going about their work. She'd never felt so close to throwing herself into the water and saying goodbye to the predicament she found herself in. She took a deep breath and told Freda what had happened after the Brownie meeting the previous night.

When she'd finished, she turned to Freda and whispered, 'Please help me. I don't know what to do.'

4

Freda looked right then left before dashing over busy Pier Road, an excited grin on her face. Erith seemed extra busy today, she thought, as she weaved her way round adults and children out doing their shopping. Nodding to a few of her customers from Woolworths and mouthing, 'Excuse me,' and, 'Thank you,' in her haste to reach Missons Ironmonger's, she was aware that she only had twenty minutes left of her lunch hour. If only she'd started to read the *Erith Observer* before eating her sandwich, she would already have reached Molly and explained her marvellous idea. Five minutes had been wasted signing out of Woolies and changing out of her maroon uniform. Staff were not allowed to wear their work overalls outside the store. Freda would have chanced just pulling on her coat but the store manager was already in a grumpy mood because a new member of staff had dropped a box of biscuits onto the freshly waxed shop floor. She wasn't about to risk the wrath of Miss Billington if she was caught breaking staff rules. Freda included Betty Billington as a friend, after sharing some special times with her and surviving the war years together at Woolies, but this was work, and friendship was for when they stepped away from the store.

Reaching the ironmonger's, she spotted Molly, feather duster in hand, tidying cans of paint that were part of an impressive display in the large shop window. Freda waved the newspaper aloft as she called out, 'Molly, I have the answer to your prayers.'

Molly waved back to Freda. 'Hello. You're a welcome sight. I could do with a break. Let's go and sit down and you can tell me why you are so excited.' Molly led Freda through the shop to her dad's office. Moving a pile of price cards from an old bentwood chair, she indicated to Freda to take a seat. Molly sat in the leather-upholstered office chair that had been her dad's for as long as she could remember. 'Shouldn't you be at work?' she asked, glancing at the clock.

'I have fifteen minutes left, but I spotted this advertisement in the *Erith Observer* and just couldn't wait until closing time to tell you about it. What do you think?' she asked, thrusting the folded newspaper across the desk.

Molly looked puzzled as she scanned the advertisements in the popular local newspaper. 'A sale of household goods at Mitchell's. A day trip to see the bluebells. How will this help my predicament, Freda?' Molly had spent a long night locked in her bedroom listening to every creak in the old house in case it was Simon seeking her out. She desperately wanted to feel safe again but was confused as to why her friend was so excited.

Freda let out an exaggerated sigh and turned the newspaper over to where an article extolled the virtues of a holiday at the soon-to-reopen Butlins holiday camp.

'As much as we both said how exciting it would be to have a holiday at Butlins, I don't think now's the time–'

Freda interrupted her friend. 'No, read the bottom of the article,' she said, pointing to the page.

A small furrow crossed Molly's brow as she concentrated on the words before putting the newspaper down on the desk. 'A job at Butlins in Skegness? Whatever could I do?'

Freda grabbed the newspaper excitedly. 'They are looking for all kinds of live-in staff from cleaners to entertainers. You are sure to be selected for something. Just think – you could have months away from Erith and be free of nasty Simon and his attentions.'

Molly nodded thoughtfully. 'It is an idea. But would this not mean Harriet and Simon would have won and I'd lose the house, let alone Dad's business? I can't understand why they've not been poking their noses in around here. After all, they know it exists.'

There was a tap and a polite cough, followed by George peering round the partially open door. 'Forgive me for interrupting your private conversation but I may be able to enlighten you with regards your relatives. I couldn't help but hear what you were talking about.'

'Come in, George.' Molly vacated her seat and offered it to the old man. 'Please, what can you tell me about Harriet and Simon?'

George looked troubled. Usually a polite, unassuming man, he seemed uncomfortable with what he was about to say. 'My Kath told me to mind my own business, but since it happened, we've both chewed the problem over and think you should know.'

'Know what?' both the girls said in unison.

'I lied to your relatives, Molly. Knowing you as I have since you was born, I thought I was doing what was best, but now I'm not so sure. Kath said I was an interfering old busybody, even though she said she'd have done the same if she'd been in my situation. The thing is, I don't like your new-found relatives and wouldn't trust them further than I could spit. There, I've said it, and that's why I lied to them.' George pulled out a large white handkerchief from the pocket of his brown overalls and wiped his sweating brow.

Molly gasped. In all the years she'd known him, she'd not seen George so passionate about something. He was usually such a quiet man, and went about his daily job without a care in the world. Even when her parents had died, he'd just calmly carried on, keeping the business running and ensuring everything was in order. 'George, please, you must tell us what happened.'

George looked towards the closed door nervously. 'It was the other day. You and Freda had not long left to see the matinee of *The Way to the Stars*. It was quiet in the shop when your dad's cousin and her son appeared. I'd seen them loitering outside while I'd been helping Den Godwin load up his van with paper and paint for that big job down West Street.'

Molly nodded. It had been a big order. She made a mental note to check if Den had paid his account up to date yet.

'Well, they followed me back into the shop and the man closed the door behind us and turned the sign to closed. I was a bit nervous, but then thought an elderly woman and a man in a collar and tie weren't likely to rob us. Besides, I had that old truncheon under the counter in case we ever had any trouble. She introduced herself as the person who had inherited from your dad and had come along to check out the shop.'

'It's strange she appeared on the day that we went to the pictures,' Freda said. 'I'm sure we invited Harriet and Simon to join us.'

'We did,' Molly agreed. It had been in the days

63

she was still getting to know the new members of her family and was doing her utmost to make them feel welcome in the town that was to be their home. 'Go on, George.'

'She made it clear that they were here to see the business and to look at the books. While she was talking to me, her son was trying the handle to the office. As you know, I keep the door of your dad's office locked when I'm alone in the shop, and proper glad I was to have done it that day, I can tell you.'

'What did they say?' Freda urged. She was aware she should by now be heading back to work but couldn't bear to miss what George had to say.

'It was more what I said.' George looked ashamed. 'I said as like I was now the rightful owner of Missons Ironmonger's as Norman and me had been equal partners: after his untimely passing, the business was all mine. I even said they was welcome to accompany me to meet Mr Denton, our solicitor, if they didn't believe me and we'd show them the agreement that had been drawn up.'

Molly beamed. 'George, well done! However did you think of that so quickly?'

'It was something that me and the missus had been chatting about, but that's for another time. Mind you, I was sweating a bit in case they called my bluff. Thankfully, I know Mr Denton is away from his office for a while so they couldn't poke their noses in there.'

Freda jumped to her feet and gave George a big kiss. 'I'd like to stay and listen to the rest of the story but I'll get the sack if I'm too late. Catch up after work and have a fish-and-chip supper?' she asked Molly.

'Why don't you both come to our house? I know Kath would love to see you. It has been a while.'

Freda and Molly quickly agreed. George and his wife were like family to Molly and always made both girls welcome in their home. 'That would be nice, George, but I insist on bringing fish and chips for everyone,' Molly said with a grin. She felt as though a big weight had lifted from her shoulders. At least for now her cousin could not get her hands on the shop, even if there was a legal document somewhere that stated her dad had left everything to his relative.

'Get that newspaper off the table, George. The girls will be here in a few minutes. They'll want to be eating their tea, not watch you checking the football results,' Kath Jones scolded her husband. She glanced towards the dresser. 'Do you think I should use my best plates?'

George stretched his arms and yawned. 'It is only young Molly and her friend coming round for a bite to eat. You've known the girl since the day she was born. Why stand on ceremony just to eat some fish and chips?'

Kath shrugged her shoulders. 'The poor girl's been through so much lately. I thought I'd make the meal a bit special, like.' She looked towards her best plates lined up on the dresser. 'Perhaps I'll just...'

He knew his wife meant well. They'd watched as Molly had mourned the deaths of Norman and Charlotte, and had been there to support her even though they were in shock themselves. George had lost a good friend in Norman, and Kath had been very close to Charlotte Missons. Not only had George worked alongside Norman in the shop, but the men had spent many a night fire-watching from the roof of the Erith shop along with other traders from the town. Both too old to be called up to do their bit, they'd turned their hands to anything to protect the people of Erith during the six years of war. 'Molly doesn't need special treatment – she wants things to be normal. We are the nearest thing she has to family, and family don't stand on ceremony, so you leave those dinner plates on the shelf. Christmas is soon enough to bring them down. Besides, they survived Hitler's bombs, so why risk me dropping one now, eh?'

Kath patted her husband's shoulder as she took the evening paper from him, then shook a clean tablecloth over the table, smoothing the starched cotton until she was happy with it. 'You're forgetting she has family now, George, strange as it is them appearing out of nowhere like that.'

George nodded. 'It is a bit queer, love. However, at the moment I'm more worried about that Simon and the way he's treating Molly.' George had been all for going to sort the man out there and then when Molly had explained. He'd only calmed down when Molly promised to keep out of Simon's way.

Kath tutted. 'I've been thinking about that since you told me. I don't want her under the same roof as that man a minute longer than she needs to be.'

George sighed. 'As much as I agree with you, love, I can't see as there's much we can do. Molly

66

is over the age of consent and can live where she wishes. Though no man should do what that bloke did. If I was ten years younger...'

'You'd need to be thirty years younger to sort him out, George. He's not like the folk from round here, who know we sort out any wrong-doers ourselves. He'd go running to the cops even though he was the one who's done wrong. No, let's try my plan first.'

George reached down to rub the ear of his old dog, Henry, as he looked sharply at his wife. 'It's time you told me what you are up to, Kath. I don't like the idea of that chap messing with you.'

'Don't talk to me as if I'm daft, George. I'm well aware I'm no match for the young bully. No, what I have in mind will be done with words not deeds. Now, get that smelly mutt from out of my kitchen while I butter some bread. Molly and Freda will be here soon with our supper and I'm not halfway near ready for them.'

George saluted his wife's back as she reached into a drawer for her bread knife, and nudged the grey-faced elderly dog under the table where he couldn't be seen but would be sure to receive a few tasty treats from his devoted owner.

'That was good,' George exclaimed as he leaned back from the table and loosened the belt on his trousers, much to Kath's annoyance. 'You can't beat a good bit of fresh fish.'

'I don't know, George – I'm a big fan of Kath's rabbit stew and dumplings,' Molly added quickly, noticing Kath's stern glance towards her husband.

Kath beamed as she stood to collect the plates.

She loved to cook. 'I'm planning on making a stew this coming Wednesday. There'll be plenty for all of you, so don't be shy about coming round here, you.'

'That would be lovely, Mrs Jones. Now, sit yourself down. Molly and me will do the clearing-up,' Freda said as she took Kath's arm and propelled her back to her seat.

Kath sat back at the table and absentmindedly stroked Henry's head. George held his breath, but Kath never commented on the dog still being in the kitchen, where he'd enjoyed discreetly fed titbits from George and the girls. 'Now, Molly, how's about you tell me what happened with that Simon? I've heard George's version, but men don't give all the details.'

George pulled himself to his feet and reached for Henry's lead, which was hanging from a brass hook at the side of the dresser. 'I'll leave you to it while I take Henry for a short walk.' He nodded to the girls and headed for the back door, followed by his faithful friend.

Molly found it easy to explain in detail what had happened with Simon as she washed the plates at the stone sink. She was in sympathetic company, and although worried about the future, she knew she had friends who would support her.

Kath gasped in horror while she listened to Molly's words but then clapped in delight as she explained how she had escaped. 'Well done, girl. I'd have done the same in your situation. It's a shame about your mum and dad's photograph, though. Are you sure it's only the glass that is damaged?'

'Yes, I'll soon get it mended.'

'I reckon that was your mum and dad looking out for you.' Kath nodded wisely.

'I like to think so, Kath,' Molly said as a lump formed in her throat. 'But what am I going to do in the future if he makes advances like that again?'

Freda nudged Molly's arm. 'Don't forget about Butlins.'

'Butlins?' Kath said. 'I thought they was still closed.'

Freda reached into her handbag and pulled out the page she'd torn from the *Erith Observer*. 'I told Molly she should apply for a job at Butlins. It would give her some breathing space away from Erith while things settle down and she decides what to do next. That's if she doesn't hear from her parents' solicitor before then.'

Kath read the newspaper article and smiled. 'It could be the answer, Molly, love. Not that we wouldn't miss you,' she added quickly, looking at the young girl's sad face.

The three women chatted about the article and the kind of jobs Molly thought she could do at the holiday camp in Skegness.

Molly picked up the newspaper and read the details again. 'But what can I do with myself until Butlins opens? It's weeks before that happens and I can't avoid Simon all that time. That's if I get a job. They may think I'm not fit for a position there.'

'Stick the kettle on, Molly. I tell you about my little idea,' Kath said. 'George and me may well spend a week at the holiday camp this summer. I quite fancy a break by the sea and not having to cook for a week.'

'What's all this about a holiday?' George asked as he came in through the back door. 'It's a bit nippy out there to be thinking of such things.'

'Sit yourself down, George, and listen to what I have to say.'

George did as he was told. He wasn't one to argue with his wife when she spoke to him like that.

Much later, George followed Molly as she let herself into the house in Avenue Road. It was only a short walk from his house in Cross Street, but so different. George and Kath's home was a cosy two-up two-down with a small bathroom on the back that George had added himself with help from Norman Missons. He was pleased he'd seen her home as Simon was in the front room and looked none too steady on his feet.

'Why, Mr Jones, to what do we owe this pleasure so late in the evening?' He looked pointedly at the grandfather clock, which would soon strike ten o'clock.

George gave Simon a nod. He was finding it hard to appear friendly to a man he disliked so intensely. 'I'm just seeing Molly safely to her bedroom door,' he replied.

The comment was wasted on Simon, who yawned loudly.

'I'll see you at work tomorrow morning, George. Thank you for walking me home,' Molly said as she headed up the stairs.

George waited in the hall until he heard Molly turn the key in the lock of her bedroom door. As he started to leave the house, he was aware of the dark, brooding glare on Simon's face.

Molly awoke with a start. A faint light through a chink in her bedroom curtain showed that dawn was fighting the night sky. She could hear footsteps rushing down the stairs, a curse as someone stumbled and muttering as the bolts on the heavy front door were slid back. Slipping her feet into her shoes, she reached for a large bag she'd carefully packed before climbing into bed the night before. Smiling to herself, she realized that today was the day she made plans for her future.

'Molly,' Simon called from downstairs, 'your friend is at the door. There seems to be some kind of problem.'

Molly leaned over the banister, trying to hold back the smile that was doing its utmost to pin itself to her face. 'My goodness, whatever is the matter?'

'It's me ... Freda. You're needed at George and Kath's house. She's had one of her turns.'

'How awful. I'll be with you in two shakes, Freda. Just let me pull on some clothes.'

Back in her room, Molly slipped off her dressing gown to reveal her outdoor clothes underneath. She had decided not to waste one tiny moment once her friend came to rescue her. Pulling a comb through her hair and checking she had her purse in her pocket, Molly grabbed the heavy bag and headed downstairs.

Simon was standing at the front door, yawning. He'd not invited Freda in and didn't seem concerned that Molly's dearest friend was quietly

71

crying into her handkerchief. Molly pushed past him and gave Freda a quick hug. 'Thank you for coming to get me. Whatever happened?'

'Oh, it was just awful, Molly. George is waiting for the doctor to arrive. Kath keeps calling for you. You know what she's like when she gets like this.'

The two girls hurried down the path. As Molly pulled the gate closed behind her, she called back to Simon, 'I don't know how long I'll be. I'll send a message once the doctor's been.'

Simon nodded and closed the door without speaking a word.

Molly and Freda walked to the end of the road before stopping to laugh together, knowing that Simon would not be able to see them from the house if he were to look from a window.

Freda wiped her eyes. 'My goodness, I did enjoy that. I didn't go overboard with the tears, did I?'

'It was perfect. Besides, I don't think Simon was awake enough to realize he was being tricked. Let's get to Kath and George's before she takes a turn for the worse.'

The two friends linked arms and walked the short distance to the older couple's house still giggling. Kath's plan had worked perfectly.

'Another slice of toast, Molly?'

Molly rubbed her stomach. 'I'm fit to bursting, Kath, thanks very much. If I eat another mouthful, I'll not get out of my chair to open the shop on time.'

'You're not going to the shop today, young miss,' George said as he wiped a piece of bread round his plate, soaking up the last of the egg yolk and bacon fat. 'Kath has plans for you.'

Molly was puzzled. Kath's idea had worked a treat, so why couldn't she go to work in the ironmonger's shop with George?

Kath smiled at her husband and the young woman she'd known since the day she was born. She knew Molly would no longer be able to live under the same roof as a man who couldn't be trusted. They needed to get her away to safety. It had to be done at a time when Harriet wasn't around to ask questions. Molly had explained how the older woman was slow to rise each morning, so Kath knew they had to strike in the early hours. It had been agreed that Freda would be the one to hammer on the door of the large house in Avenue Road and be the bearer of bad news. Kath was aware that George was likely to land a punch on Simon's nose, such was his hatred of the man who had caused such fear in a young girl. Kath felt the same way and knew they had to do the best they could to protect the daughter of the friends they so desperately missed.

She went to the dresser and opened a drawer, taking out notepaper and the advertisement from the *Erith Observer.* 'You, young lady, are going to write a letter to Butlins and enquire about a vacancy. As much as we'd love you to live here with us, we both know you are not safe from Simon. Just like Freda, we are aware that something isn't quite right about Harriet and her son coming to Erith. We intend to do our best to get to the bottom of this, but we can't do anything until Mr Denton is back in his office. In the meantime,

you are going to enjoy yourself and work somewhere we all know you will be safe. You have been
through a lot these past months, Molly, and for
now we will take care of things. Just look after
yourself and have some fun, my love.'

Molly was touched by Kath's words. 'But–'

Kath raised her hand to silence Molly. 'I won't
say we won't miss you – it'll break my heart knowing you're not working with my George every day
– but it's all for the best. Why, I'd never forgive
myself if anything happened to you. The day we
heard the terrible news of your parents' accident, I
recalled a conversation I'd once had with Charlotte. I promised that if anything should happen to
her and Norman, we would both look out for you
until the day we drew our last breath. So, no more
arguing – let's get that letter written and in the
postbox, shall we? It will be delivered tomorrow
and with luck we will hear back within a few days.
Don't forget to give our address as your home. We
don't want that unsavoury pair getting wind of our
plan.'

Molly couldn't speak. Kath and George, along
with her friend Freda, were the nearest thing to
family that she had. She couldn't think of Harriet
or Simon as relatives, however much she tried. She
was heartened that she still had people around her
who cared for her future like her parents had
done.

George got to his feet and wiped his mouth with
the back of his hand. He kissed his wife's cheek
and patted Molly's shoulder. 'Best you don't argue
with Kath when she's like this, Molly. I learned
that a long time ago.'

Kath slapped her husband playfully. 'Be off with you, old man, and open that shop.'

George winked at Molly and headed off to work.

Molly took the notepaper from Kath and sat down to write. She wasn't completely sure that Butlins was the right place for her, but as her friends had such faith in her and cared for her future, she would do the best she could not to let them down.

5

Molly tugged the front of her jacket straight, checking her reflection in a nearby shop window to make sure the seams of her stockings were straight. There were still ten minutes before her interview for a job at Butlins.

'Don't stand there dithering or all the jobs will be gone,' Freda said, giving her a shove towards the impressive entrance of the West End hotel. 'The world and his neighbour seem to be heading into the hotel. I'm surprised they need so many workers for a holiday camp.'

Molly plucked up courage and stepped into the plush foyer of the hotel. Nodding to a uniformed doorman, who pointed to a sign that showed she had to take a lift to the first floor, she gave Freda a weak grin. 'Here we go. You will come with me, won't you?'

'You bet. I wouldn't miss this for the world. I'm

rather tempted to have an interview myself. It's so exciting.'

Molly laughed at her friend. 'You know you'll never leave Woolworths. You have a good job there and know nearly all your customers by their first names.'

'So do you and you're planning on leaving the area.'

'I wish I had a choice and didn't have to leave the town I love and my home,' Molly replied as they stepped into the lift, along with four other young women.

Freda could have slapped herself. Why ever did she say that? 'Me and my big mouth. I'm sorry, Molly. I didn't mean what I said,' she whispered as the lift doors closed and they were whisked upwards.

Molly squeezed her arm. 'Don't be a chump. I know you didn't. Regardless of the reasons for attending this interview, it is rather exciting. I didn't realize this hotel would be so posh. I just hope I don't have lipstick on my teeth or a ladder in my stockings.'

'Of course you don't. You look sophisticated and refined. I must ask Maisie to make up a suit for me like that. You look so different with your hair pinned up.'

'I'm just grateful your friend Maisie was able to run it up for me. How she has time to do anything with young twins is beyond me. Do you think Mum would have approved of her fabric being made into such a modern outfit?'

'She'd have loved it. I'm so pleased I dug around a little when your cousin and that son of hers were out. I was only checking to see if there was any more Brownie equipment in the tallboy in your parents' room when I spied it in a brown paper parcel. Perhaps your mum even meant the fabric to be a gift for you. I feel it was meant to be.'

Molly nodded. It was meant to be. She looked at her reflection in the mirrored wall of the lift, hardly recognizing the elegant, self-assured woman looking back at her. The grey flannel suit, cinched in at the waist with a matching belt, suited her trim figure. She made a mental note to buy something from one of the West End stores as a little thank you to Maisie. 'I'm a very fortunate person to have such good friends,' she told Freda. 'Everyone has been so good to me since Mum and Dad died.'

'There is something else,' whispered Freda, passing her an envelope as the lift doors silently slid open onto a long hallway carpeted in deep red with plush velvet wall hangings and large oil paintings in ornate frames along the wall.

'Oh my God. Look at all this. Can it get any posher?'

'You've been in a similar place.' Freda grinned.

'I don't think so,' Molly declared, fanning herself with the envelope that Freda had just passed to her.

'Yes, you have. Doesn't it remind you of the foyer of the Erith Odeon?'

Both girls giggled, as indeed the posh St Claire Hotel was decorated in the same rich red colours as their favourite local cinema.

They shuffled forward in the queue, getting

77

closer to the open double doors at the end of the hall. Up ahead, a young woman and a few suited young men were directing applicants either left or right as they reached them.

'Open your envelope,' Freda insisted as they approached the head of the queue.

Molly didn't feel it was quite the place to do so but didn't wish to upset her friend. She pulled out a card and smiled. 'Thank you. It's lovely. But you didn't need to buy me a birthday card. Having you accompany me to London and going for tea at Lyons Corner House is enough of a treat.'

'Open the card,' Freda whispered as the girl in front of them was directed through the doors.

'Oh, I don't know what to say. Tickets to see the show *Me and My Girl*. I've always wanted to see that musical. Isn't it closing soon?'

'Tonight is the last performance. We were lucky to get them.'

Molly hugged her friend and jumped up and down in excitement. 'I can't believe it. Thank you, oh, thank you, Freda. I thought perhaps we'd have time to fit in a film, but never a live musical, and one of the best in town.'

A man appeared at the open doorway and raised his eyebrows at Molly. The two girls froze, then composed themselves.

'This way, please. Give your name at the table and collect a name badge. You will be directed to the correct interview desk.'

Freda and Molly walked towards the area he'd pointed out, now extremely subdued.

'I'm sure I've seen him somewhere before,' Freda said.

'You have,' Molly whispered back in case he heard her.

Freda looked over her shoulder. The man's eyes were on them, or rather on Molly. 'I don't... Oh my goodness. Surely it's not...'

'Yes. It's Secret Agent Clive Danvers, also known as actor Johnny Johnson,' Molly said, grinning at her friend's shocked face.

'Surely a film star doesn't work at Butlins. It must be a mistake. They do say everyone has a double somewhere,' Freda considered.

Molly looked back to where the man was standing. She'd know the actor anywhere. She saw him most nights in her dreams. The way he stood. The way his eyes twinkled in the moonlight. The arrogant line of his jaw when questioning his foe... Yes, that was most certainly Johnny Johnson. As she watched the movie star across the room, their eyes met. Molly's stomach gave a little flip. He was as attractive in real life as he was on the silver screen.

The next hour was spent filling out a long application form about her hobbies and home life as well as previous jobs. She was pleased that she was able to mention the years she spent as a land girl and how much she'd enjoyed helping her mum with the Brownies and Guides. She remembered to give George and Kath's home as her current address. That part was easy, as in the weeks since Kath's pretend illness, when Freda had called Molly from her bed to help the stricken older woman, she had not set foot inside her family home in Avenue Road. Often the urge to walk up the long footpath to the front door, place a key in the lock and step into the house overwhelmed her. To be able to go into the kitchen, touch familiar objects and imagine Charlotte Missons baking a cake or simply sitting at the table chatting about the day's events was something Molly longed to do just one more time.

George and Kath treated her like the daughter they'd never had. Their home was her home. She was given a key and told to bring her friends round whenever she wished. Molly felt truly loved. They also made sure that Molly was never alone when she left their little terraced house in Cross Street just in case she bumped into her father's cousins. Better to be safe than sorry, George often said. Indeed, it was George, accompanied by Freda, who would walk to Avenue Road to collect items of clothing that Molly required or to find Brownies equipment for the meetings. Fortunately, Freda had cupboard space in the church hall to store the pack's equipment so she wouldn't need to visit Avenue Road after Molly left Erith.

Molly did continue to work at the shop with George, but they made sure she stayed in the storeroom or in the little office as much as possible. If she didn't have to talk to Harriet or Simon, she couldn't be tripped up over the story they'd concocted and was safe from Simon's grasp. There was still no news from Mr Denton, the family solicitor, who remained out of the country, according to his nephew.

Molly met with Freda after handing in her completed form and headed to the end of the long room, where refreshments were being served. Freda had brought along her knitting but found herself chatting to family and friends of other hopeful candidates when shown to a side of the room away from where the interviews were taking place.

'I must say the Butlins uniform looks rather smart. I really like the red blazer and white pleated skirt female staff are wearing. So much better than my Woolworths uniform. The outfit alone tempts me to try for a job,' Freda said.

Molly knew her friend was joking. She was settled in Erith and her job as a supervisor at Woolworths. Freda loved living with Ruby Caselton in Alexandra Road and was a popular member of her extended family. 'I'd like you to join me at Butlins for a holiday if I secure a position, but I'd rather you stay living in Erith and keep me posted on what is happening. Who knows, once the summer season is over, I might be able to return and live in my own home. Things might go back to how they used to be when Mr Denton returns to his office and a will can be located.' A shadow fell across her face as she realized things would never be quite the same without her parents, but she dashed the thought away. Today was hopefully the beginning of her new life. It was also her twenty-fourth birthday and she had a special treat to look forward to at the theatre.

Freda smiled. She'd like nothing better than her friend to own what was rightly hers and not be fearful of the nasty Simon or his grasping mother. She knew there was something not quite right about the couple turning up out of the blue as they had done. However, until they knew what was happening, it was better Molly stayed away. Her

81

friends would do all they could to find out the truth and protect what rightfully belonged to her. She helped herself to a toasted teacake from a smiling waitress. 'What happens next?'

'We have to report to another room, where we will be given a talk about Butlins and how we are expected to behave on and off duty. Family and friends are allowed to sit in and listen, as they will no doubt be visiting the camp during the summer and will have some idea of what we have to do. After that, I find out if I've been selected and what job they have decided would best suit me.'

'Count me in. I really want to know more about Butlins. I think we ought to make a move. It looks as though people are heading towards the meeting.'

Molly placed her coffee cup on the table being used for refreshments and thanked the waitress. The waiting staff also wore Butlins uniforms and had friendly smiles on their faces. Everyone seemed so happy, whatever work they were undertaking.

The two girls followed a small crowd into a side room and were ushered to their seats. Molly was dismayed to find herself in the front row. She would have preferred to be nearer the back, but it looked as though everyone else had the same idea. In front of Molly's seat was a small raised area with a table and two chairs.

Silence descended over the room as a side door opened and a woman dressed in the red Butlins uniform appeared. She stepped onto the stage and smiled at the eager faces in front of her. 'Welcome, my friends. I am sure that before too long I will be calling many of you colleagues. My name is Connie Sinclair. I am chief staff officer at Butlins, Skegness. For those of you chosen to work in the camp, I am the person you will come to with work queries. My office processes leave applications and work rotas, as well as what most of you are interested in, pay packets.'

There was a small round of applause at this point and Connie Sinclair waited until the noise had subsided before continuing with her talk about working at Butlins. 'I'm sure there will be many questions about employment and we have five minutes to take a few questions before I introduce another new member of the team.' There followed a few questions from the floor, ranging from where staff ate to what their medical facilities were like and what time off they were entitled to. Connie looked a little stern when she replied that it was customary to start work before requesting leave.

Freda leaned towards Molly and whispered, 'She may look nice but I reckon she can be a tyrant.'

Molly giggled and was about to reply when she felt Connie Sinclair looking at her. She went quiet at once and felt her cheeks start to burn with embarrassment. She just hoped she hadn't blotted her copybook before she'd even been offered a job.

Connie looked back to her audience. 'I'd now like to introduce our entertainment adviser. Whatever your job description, and however many hours you work each day, there will be times when you will be involved in entertaining the holiday-makers. Here is the man Mr Butlin has invited to show us how to carry out our job to the best of our ability. Ladies and gentlemen, please welcome Mr Johnny Johnson.'

There were gasps around the room as many women recognized the man they'd seen on cinema screens often during the war years. Molly felt Freda's elbow in her ribs and heard a snort of laughter from her friend. 'So he was who we thought he was when we first arrived. Who'd have guessed you'd meet the man of your dreams at Butlins?'

'I believe many women have,' Molly replied as she felt her already red cheeks start to glow even more. How would she ever be able to work with a man who made her heart beat faster every time she saw him on the silver screen? In the flesh he was even more handsome. She could see glimmers of the self-assured actor as he shook hands with Connie and nodded to the audience before taking his place on the stage. Molly hoped there was a different side to him and that Johnny Johnson the actor was a different man to Johnny Johnson Butlins entertainment adviser, or there would be holidaymakers swooning wherever he went, not to mention the staff, she thought, as she looked over her shoulder to the twittering females, who would surely be putty in his hands. There would be interesting times ahead with a matinee idol at Butlins.

Johnny cleared his throat and his audience settled down to listen. He made no mention of his acting career, but it was there, like an elephant in the room.

'Thank you, ladies … and gentlemen,' he added as an afterthought, noticing a scattering of males present. 'You have already heard much of the entertainment side of Butlins from my colleagues. Perhaps some of you visited Butlins before it closed for the duration. However, my plan is to ensure that the entertainment this season is bigger and brighter than ever before. We will have entertainers visiting the camp each week. Some you will recognize from radio and stage. As well as carrying out their own duties, our staff will have the opportunity to join cabaret spots and shows. We intend Butlins to be at the forefront of holiday entertainment, ensuring our visitors return year after year to our camps. Before too long, there will be more camps spread across the country. Who knows, perhaps one day there will be holiday-makers travelling overseas to be entertained by staff just like you.'

Molly gulped. She knew staff would be expected to mix with visitors and would never really be off duty, but to get on stage and sing or dance, surely not? She didn't exactly have two left feet, and she could hold a tune, but on stage in front of people was a different matter completely. She felt the compulsion to run away back to Erith and her friends. Her thoughts drifted to the past... With a start, Molly realized that Johnny had started to talk again and tried to concentrate.

'...Even when off duty, you will be representing Butlins. How you act reflects upon your employer. Always ask yourself if you need that second drink, or whether you are being just a little too reserved. Keep a smile on your face and try to have a willing attitude.'

A hand was raised in the audience and Johnny

nodded to the young man to speak. 'Can we invite a holidaymaker out to dinner?'

Johnny smiled. 'We would not be human if we did not fall in love from time to time.' A small sigh could be heard from the audience. No doubt from a fan of Johnny's alter ego. 'As I've already mentioned, you are at Butlins to work, so whether you fall in or out of love, be circumspect at all times. Now, let us consider some situations that might arise while we are on duty.' He stepped down from the stage and walked to the edge of the front row of seats, stopping at a young man. 'Sir a young lady is overcome by the summer sun while you are leading a keep-fit class. What should you do?'

The man grinned and mentioned loosening her clothing, much to the amusement of those listening.

Johnny laughed with them. 'I do not advise it, unless you wish to be visited by the local constabulary and possibly find yourself at the Labour Exchange looking for another job.'

He pointed to an older woman sitting in the next row, who said to give the fainting holidaymaker a sip of water and ask a female member of staff to escort her to the medical block.

Moving along the front row, he stopped at a young woman and looked at her name badge. 'Deirdre, you are off duty in the ballroom and a gentleman approaches you. He is slightly the worse for drink. How do you react?'

Deirdre thought for a moment. 'Well, Johnny ... I mean Mr Johnson,' she faltered. 'I would call a male colleague and request his assistance. I would try not to create a scene. After all, the gentleman concerned is on holiday and is entitled to … relax. I would ask my colleague to assist the man outside for some fresh air. Perhaps take him to a coffee bar until he feels better.' She blushed as Johnny praised her considerate actions.

Molly did wonder how Deirdre would act if she came face to face with her inebriated second cousin Simon. At once the image of his groping hands and insistent ways came into her mind. She shuddered just as Johnny came to a standstill in front of her. He held out his hand and she took it.

'Then we have the wallflower who is lost in a world of her own. Gentlemen, there will always be a lady who is not dancing. It may be that her partner is not a dancer. She may be holidaying alone.' He looked at the name badge on Molly's lapel. 'Molly, would you care to dance?'

Molly rose to her feet and gazed into Johnny's eyes as he took her into his arms and held her close. She had often dreamed of this moment and now it was happening.

She felt the blood pounding in her head and at once became light-headed. Johnny took a few steps of what could have been a waltz, but it was all Molly could do to hang on tightly in case she fainted. A look of pain shot across his face as she stumbled and trod heavily on his foot. Johnny groaned and let go of her hand, indicating to Molly to return to her seat. The magical moment had passed.

As he limped back to the stage in an exaggerated manner, Johnny turned to his audience. 'Of course, it does help if the lady knows her left foot from her right.'

The room erupted into laughter and Molly, wishing the ground would open up and swallow her, slid further into her seat, unhappy that he had made a joke of her mishap.

'That was rather ungallant of him,' Freda said. 'He's not quite the gentleman he portrays in the movies, is he?'

Molly couldn't speak. She was disappointed in what should have been a dream come true. Looking up to where Johnny now sat on the stage, she noticed he was watching her. A soft smile flickered across his face. Was he enjoying her humiliation?

'Gosh, I never thought we'd get away. I'd have faded away to nothing if we'd not had time for a meal before heading to the theatre,' Freda said as she looked at the menu. They had chosen to eat at Lyons Corner House as it was Freda and Molly's favourite place to dine on their rare trips to London. 'What shall we have?'

Molly glanced at the menu. 'I don't feel that hungry.'

'You must eat something. Don't let that wretched man spoil your day. It wasn't your fault he caught you off guard when he asked you to dance. Anyone would have felt dizzy having to stand up in front of a crowd of strangers like that. I think I'll have Welsh rarebit.'

'It wasn't that so much as what happened afterwards,' Molly said, trying hard to suppress the feelings that surfaced every time Johnny Johnson came up in conversation. She could still feel his strong arms as he held her close and the beating of

88

his heart – and the fluttering of her own. Would she ever be able to separate the romantic movie star Johnny Johnson from the mocking entertainment adviser?

'It wasn't your fault that someone knocked your arm. Anyone would have spilt tea under those circumstances. Hmm, yes, the rarebit does look nice.'

'But it was *me* who spilt the tea, and the look he gave me...' Molly would never forget that moment. It would be frozen in time. All around them, staff arrived to mop up the mess and put things straight while Molly apologized profusely, but it was his puzzled, then cynical expression as he watched Molly's face before walking away from her that troubled her.

'Don't worry – I'm sure it's all been forgotten by now. Besides, you were offered a job and that's all that matters. Now, you'd better decide what to order as our waitress is on her way over. Why don't we both have the Welsh rarebit? We have two hours before the musical starts, and a Butlins children's auntie shouldn't be late for the show!'

Molly grinned and pushed her encounter with the man who so often frequented her dreams to the back of her mind. Her future was beginning to look rosy once more.

6

'Freda, I can't thank you enough for my lovely birthday surprise. This is a day I'll remember for a long time,' Molly said, linking her arm through her mate's as they left the Victoria Palace Theatre and stepped onto the busy London street.

'I'm sorry the seats were up in the gods, but it was good, wasn't it? We have three-quarters of an hour before our train departs. Shall we go to the stage door and watch the stars leave? We may even manage to collect a few autographs.' Both girls had purchased souvenir programmes of *Me and My Girl*, the most popular musical in London.

'That would be wonderful,' Molly said, and they headed to the side door of the theatre, both humming the title song from the show and giggling when they sang the wrong words.

It seemed that they were not the only ones in a happy mood, because as they joined the already large crowd waiting for the stars of the show to appear, many others were enjoying themselves and singing enthusiastically. A loud cheer erupted as the door opened and a group of young actors appeared. Although not yet well known, their autographs were eagerly sought by many people present. The performers stopped and signed autograph books and programmes before disappearing down the street with a parting wave to the theatregoers.

Molly shivered. It was now very cold, and there'd been a shower of rain while they'd been at the theatre, judging by the puddles in the uneven road. She tried to avoid them so as not to spoil her best shoes. Nearby, a man started to sing another tune from the show. Before long she found herself being pulled along arm in arm with others walking up and down the side road by the theatre singing 'The Lambeth Walk'. After shouting a loud 'oi!' at the end of the song, she headed back to the stage door, where she could see Freda patiently waiting. The door started to open again and there was a rush to get to the front to see the major stars of the show. People were chanting for Lupino Lane and his co-star Valerie Tandy. As the stars appeared and waved to the crowd, those at the back again started to sing and a row of people were soon strolling arm in arm and doing 'The Lambeth Walk' once more. Not wanting to appear to be a spoilsport, Molly again joined in with the rousing song. She would much rather have been closer to the stars of the show and hoped that Freda had managed to obtain at least one autograph before the stars climbed into their limousine. The car edged down the road and disappeared into the distance, and the crowd started to disperse. Molly headed back to the stage door to join Freda as the door again opened and a couple left, an elegant blonde woman, swathed in a mink stole over an ivory silk gown, accompanied by a man wearing a top hat and tails. The woman held on to his arm possessively. No doubt heading off to a late post-theatre dinner, Molly thought, a little enviously. How the other half live!

'All right for some, love, isn't it?' the man holding on to Molly's arm said. 'Me and the missus have gotta go catch the bus. No taxicab home for us.'

They both jumped onto the pavement as a shiny black taxi screeched to a halt close by. Molly leaped to one side as a wave of muddy water from a large puddle whooshed up towards her. She escaped the worst of it but shrieked as cold water seeped through one shoe to her stockinged foot. The water squelched between her toes. What a state to travel home in. Her shoe was sure to be ruined.

Molly was not the only one to shriek loudly. Looking up, she could see the beautiful young starlet shaking water from her mud-splattered ivory silk dress. Water dripped from her face. The woman glared at Molly. 'You stupid, stupid girl. Look what you've done to my gown. Johnny, do something!'

'I'm sorry but this is not my fault.' Molly started to explain.

The man in evening dress stepped forward and took the woman by the arm.

Molly couldn't believe her eyes. It was Johnny Johnson with his lady friend. They made a handsome couple, or had until a couple of moments ago.

Leading his agitated companion to the cab, he helped her inside before turning to face Molly. 'Well, well, if it isn't Molly Missons. You seem to have a way of getting into scrapes.' He gave a slight nod of his head and followed the woman into the vehicle.

Molly watched open-mouthed in astonishment as the taxi left, once more splashing her with rainwater, this time filling her other shoe.

Within days a letter confirming Molly's position as a Butlins children's auntie arrived at George and Kath's house. She would be part of a team that entertained children during the day with games and competitions, leaving their parents free to enjoy the adult events. The emphasis was on fun and making sure that every member of the family had an enjoyable time while at Butlins. Molly couldn't help but wonder if her experiences with the Brownies and Girl Guides would really equip her with the skills required to provide all-day entertainment for children. She was relieved, at least, that the toddlers and babies would be cared for elsewhere, in a special block where all eventualities would be covered. There, qualified nursery nurses would look after the little ones, even preparing bottles and food for the younger children. In the evenings, part of Molly's job would be to help out with chalet patrol and she would be provided with a bicycle in order to cover row upon row of chalets listening for crying children. Aware she had not cycled since her Land Army days, and then not that successfully, she had borrowed George's bike to brush up on her skills. It would be one less thing to worry about once in Skegness.

Molly's job started four days before the holiday camp welcomed the first of its visitors. With just under three weeks to go, she began to panic about what to take with her. She would be supplied with her Butlins uniform, along with shorts and blouses, but for off duty and evenings, she'd be able to wear her own clothes. Her other problem was that she didn't have a suitcase large enough to carry her worldly possessions via train to Skegness. She knew her parents had suitcases in the loft at Avenue Road but didn't think it would be possible to get into the house, find a stepladder and rummage around without Harriet or Simon becoming aware. Plus, what to tell her cousins? She couldn't vanish for the summer without them becoming suspicious. Although Erith was a bustling town, for her not to return to Avenue Road at some point, or to bump into her cousins, would appear extremely strange. Molly voiced her concerns one evening as she helped Kath prepare the evening meal in the cosy kitchen.

Kath stopped mashing the potatoes to think. 'You have a point there, Molly. From what I've been told, that Harriet doesn't miss a trick. You are going to have to visit her and make some excuse as to why you'll not be around for the summer.'

'I really don't want to lie to her. As much as I dislike her and Simon for how they've disrupted my life, I'm not one for telling fibs.'

Kath looked at Molly's sad face. 'It's not such a big problem. Let's get this food on the table. George will be home soon and I reckon he'll come up with an answer. In the meantime, watch those bangers and onions in the pan or they'll burn.'

Molly quickly shook the large frying pan. 'They're fine. There is something else, Kath...'

'Spit it out, girl.'

'It's Mum and Dad's grave. Would you keep an eye on it while I'm away? Do a bit of weeding every so often so it doesn't get overgrown? I reckon Freda will help out as well.'

'Bless my soul, I thought I'd already told you,' she said, piling the fluffy mashed potato into a dish and placing it in the oven to keep warm. 'I plan to go up the cemetery twice a week. I'm even planting a few extra bulbs in the garden so there's always something nice to leave in the vase up there.'

Molly left the pan she was watching and gave the older woman a hug. 'That's a big weight off my mind. Thank you, Kath.'

Kath reached into the pocket of her apron for her handkerchief and wiped her nose. 'I was very fond of your mum. She'd not say a harsh word about even the devil himself. There's much of her in you, you know. I miss her a lot. Popping up to Brook Street Cemetery with a few flowers isn't any trouble, and each time I'm there I'll tell your mum, and your dad, what you're up to. They'd be so proud of their girl and how she's coping.'

'I'm not sure they'd be impressed with me going to work at Butlins. Dad would laugh if he knew I was to be an "auntie" entertaining the children. He was always reminding me how I once lost two Brownies on a ramble along the riverbank.'

'Don't you be so sure. They were that proud when you went off to join the Land Army and there was you not knowing one end of a garden spade from the other.'

Molly snorted with laughter. 'I did find it hard to begin with, but I wasn't alone. We had no choice other than to stick it out until we won the war.'

'What's all this, then? I could hear the laughter as I came in the gate,' George said, entering through the back door. 'She hasn't burned my dinner again, has she?' he asked, nudging Kath as he hung his coat on a hook behind the door.

'Honestly, George, Molly only let the cabbage boil dry that once. You'll never let her forget that, will you?' Kath said, nodding to Molly to check the sausages again before George noticed they were turning a little black. 'We was saying as how Molly thinks she should go and tell those cousins of hers that she is going away.'

George pulled the evening paper from the pocket of his jacket and sat at the kitchen table. 'I don't see why she should,' he said, before turning to the sports page.

'George Jones, you're a fool. What if they come calling here looking for Molly? What will we say when they know she isn't living here and not likely to be back by late September?'

George sighed. He could see he wasn't going to get a moment of peace until his wife had answers to her questions. 'Tell me this, and I don't want to upset you, Molly, love. How long is it you've been living under this roof?'

Molly started to think as Kath tried to add the weeks up on her fingers.

'I'll tell you. It's been a good few weeks. They've not been near nor by, have they? Furthermore, I've seen them both walk by the shop on numerous occasions and not even look our way. That Simon has been sitting at the bar engrossed with that brassy barmaid in the Prince of Wales most days, so his attention is elsewhere for a while. What makes you think they even care where Molly is or what she's doing?'

'My God, you're right, old man. A bit of me thinks that Molly should be insulted, but then it just shows what money-grabbing people they are,' Kath said with a shocked look on her face. 'I hope this hasn't upset you, love?'

Molly grinned. 'Not one bit. It's a relief really. This whole time I've been thinking they'd be wanting to know what I'm up to when most likely they don't care about me at all. At least I can head off to Lincolnshire and not worry about the pair of them.'

'That's where you're wrong. It's half-day tomorrow, so we're going to visit that solicitor and see if there is any news. Then we will take a walk up the avenue to the house and collect a few bits for you as if nothing has changed.'

'What?' Kath and Molly said in unison.

George tapped his head with a knowing smile. 'Stands to reason that if the pair of them aren't worried about what you've been doing all this time, it won't bother them when you walk in the door. However, if they act shifty, then we know they're up to something.' He picked up his newspaper and started to read the football results as if nothing had been said.

'My, but you're a cunning bugger,' Kath said. 'I think I'll come with you to see the looks on their faces.'

'No, you don't. The pair of them have been told you're poorly. We can at least keep that side of the story running, just to be on the safe side. Now, are we going to eat those bangers before they burn any more?'

'I'll just make a drop of gravy to cover them,'

Kath said, winking at Molly.

It was a beautiful spring day as Molly and George crossed Queens Road, headed over the small railway bridge and up the tree-lined avenue towards Molly's home. Molly was due to start her job at Butlins in two days' time and all she had on her mind was her packing and the reception she would receive from Harriet and Simon. They'd not had much luck at her dad's solicitor's office. Mr Denton was still absent from his office. His nephew was no more help than he had been when Molly had visited previously. She doubted there would be a further will. After all, how many wills would a man make in his short life? There was the one at Mr Denton's office, made before her birth, when her parents had not long arrived in Erith after their marriage, and Harriet claimed she had another showing the house was hers. There was unlikely to be a third. However, she felt she owed it to George to wait until Mr Denton returned from wherever he had departed to. George had been very patient while Mr Denton's nephew turned out box after box looking for anything relating to Norman and Charlotte Missons's business.

It was apparent that Timothy Denton had not kept a tight ship while in charge of the business. The office was dustier than before, with the remains of several days' packed lunches strewn over the desk and cups collecting mould. If it hadn't been for Molly wanting to get to the bottom of her parents' wishes, she would have left the office and never returned.

As they sat watching, it became obvious to both

Molly and George that the solicitor's nephew was not going to find the paperwork they so desperately wished to see. George made a polite cough and nodded to Molly. She pulled an envelope from her handbag. 'I have to go away for a few months. In my absence, I wish Mr George Jones to act on my behalf. I also require all correspondence to be sent to his address in Cross Street, Erith. Here are my instructions.' She handed over the envelope and bid good day to the young man.

Reaching the gate of the house in Avenue Road, Molly waited for a moment to take a deep breath and gather her thoughts. George patted her hand to show his support. 'Come on, Molly – they can't hurt you. I won't let them.'

Molly smiled at George. 'Let's get it over with, shall we?'

They entered the silent house and had walked the length of the hallway before they heard Harriet's voice from the front room. 'So you've come home at last, have you?'

'Hello, Harriet. Have you met George Jones? George was a good friend of my dad's. It's his wife, Kath, who has been poorly.'

George stepped forward to shake hands with Harriet, who just nodded in his direction. 'As I told you when we met recently at Missons, Norman and I were partners in the shop. Meself and the wife have known young Molly since the day she was born. She's a good kid. I don't know what I'd have done without her while Kath's been so poorly.'

Harriet nodded, her beady eyes moving between

the elderly man and the young woman beside him. George sat down, trying to act as casual as was possible under the circumstances.

'Tell me, Mr Jones, why is your name not on the shop alongside my late cousin-in-law's? To me, that seems strange if, as you told me previously, you were business partners.'

Molly held her breath. She would have loved to have told the woman to mind her own business, but they needed to stay calm and keep their wits about them.

'The shop isn't named after Norman. The simple truth is that we decided to name it after young Molly here, but we couldn't really call an ironmonger's business "Molly's", could we?' He laughed as he said it, but his joke fell on stony ground. 'Me and the missus were never blessed with children. It just wasn't meant to be. Molly will inherit the shop from me. It's what we agreed and what is in my will.'

Harriet's jaw dropped. She stayed silent while Molly tried not to smile. George was a gem!

'Anyway, no more of this morbid talk. We just called by to let you know that Molly will be going away for a few weeks and we need to collect some of her things.'

Molly couldn't believe that George was telling Harriet that she was leaving Erith. She felt as though she was watching her life collapse as Harriet discovered her plans for the summer.

Harriet rose from her chair. 'I'm making tea. Would you both care for a cup?'

'Not for us, love. We ought to get Molly's things and make a move. I need to get up into the loft as well and find her suitcase. We don't like to leave my wife alone for too long. She's still not a hundred per cent fit.'

Harriet turned at the doorway. 'I could have sworn I spotted her in the High Street last week,' she said, a frown appearing on her forehead.

'She has good days and bad days,' George explained casually. 'In fact, that is why we need Molly's suitcase. Our doctor has advised a few weeks by the sea for the invalid, and as I can't leave the shop, it stands to reason that Molly will travel with her. We have relatives down in Cornwall they will be staying with.'

Molly sighed. Yet another of George's plans. She wished he would let her know when he was about to announce something so she could paint the right expression on her face.

'To be honest, Molly, I was hoping you would return home before too long. This is a large house and I'm not able to keep on top of the housework. Your contribution to the weekly housekeeping would be welcome as well,' Harriet said without a glimmer of sympathy for George's words.

Molly couldn't think what to say as Harriet's eyes bore into her.

Thankfully, George came to the rescue. 'Once my Kath is on her feet and completely fit, I'm sure Molly will be back with you. Could your son not help out until then?'

'My son is a businessman, not a skivvy, Mr Jones. Besides, it would not look right if his lady friend saw him doing household chores,' Harriet said with a sniff before heading to the kitchen.

'Lady friend, eh?' George said to Molly as they

101

made their way upstairs. 'It looks as though things have been progressing at a fair speed down at the Prince of Wales. I did hear that particular bar-maid's not one to let the grass grow under her feet.'

'George, shh,' Molly scolded. 'Harriet might hear you.'

'People what listen at keyholes don't ever hear good of themselves,' George pointed out. 'Now, how do I get into the loft?'

Molly pointed up the staircase to the entrance in the ceiling close to her bedroom door. 'You are going to need a stepladder. There should be one in the garden shed.'

George nodded. 'You get started finding what you need. Don't worry if it takes two trips – we can always store things in our house. I'd feel happier knowing your possessions are being looked after. I don't trust those two not to dispose of your property.'

Molly watched George head back down the stairs before going to her parents' bedroom. She noticed Harriet had made herself at home very quickly; she went through the drawers in the dressing table to check if there was anything re-maining that belonged to her mum before Harriet beat her to it. Taking a pillowcase from the airing cupboard, she carefully added a few items of make-up and several bottles of perfume. If she closed her eyes, she could almost feel her mum nearby as the light fragrances reached her nostrils. Molly gave herself a mental shake. She didn't have time to reminisce. Harriet could appear at any time.

Opening the wardrobe, she was surprised to see all her mother's clothes had been removed, apart from her favourite fur coat as well as a fur stole and deep-green crushed-velvet evening dress Charlotte had purchased but not had chance to wear before the accident. What had Harriet done with the other clothing, and why had she kept these items? Molly pulled them from the hangers, and tucking them under her arm, she went to her own room. Opening the door, she saw all her mother's clothing heaped on the bed. Harriet must have removed everything from the bedroom and just kept back a few choice items for her own use. Molly felt fury boiling up inside her. She wanted to confront the woman and ask why she'd not waited for her to return before touching her mother's possessions.

Molly froze as she heard Harriet call from the bottom of the stairs in a syrupy-sweet voice, 'Molly, dear...'

She went to the top of the stairs. Why was Harriet talking like that? 'Yes, Harriet. What can I do for you?' It took great effort for Molly not to snarl at her cousin.

'You may notice that I've moved a few of your mother's items to your bedroom. Simon's young lady is interested in taking them off your hands. She will be round later to collect them.'

Molly dared not reply. She had never felt such anger. She was sure that if she'd arrived later that day, Simon's girlfriend from the pub would have waltzed off with her mum's clothes and Molly would not have been consulted. But what was she to do with them? Whatever happened, she was the one to decide how to dispose of her mum's belongings.

She cleared a small space on the bed and sat down to think.

George appeared minutes later a little red in the face. 'I've got the stepladder. I'll pop up into the loft and find the suitcase... You're not taking all that, are you?' he said, peering at the pile of clothing.

'This is all of Mum's possessions. That awful woman is giving them to that strumpet down the pub now she's got her claws into Simon.'

George tried not to smile. He was sure Molly had never met a strumpet in her life, let alone knew what one was. However, he felt sorry for the girl. Now wasn't the time to tell her that a few clothes weren't important. She needed to learn that for herself. Her memories were in her head, not in a wardrobe. He walked to the small window and looked out for a few moments. 'I have an idea that just might work. While I climb up into the loft and find a suitcase, I want you to fold up all those clothes and anything else you want to take with you and put them on the floor.'

Molly nodded. She had no idea what George was up to, but she'd do as she was told. She had complete faith in whatever he suggested. She got straight to work as he disappeared into the loft.

While Molly folded the garments, she gazed around the room. What else should she take? Mementos of her parents were of paramount importance. She would need her summer dresses, and most definitely shoes for dancing if she were to work in the ballroom of the holiday camp. She was still contemplating what to take with her when George reappeared, huffing and puffing as he manoeuvred his way out of the loft hatch, pulling a large suitcase behind him. Molly dashed forward to help him.

'I've seen some other cases up there. This was the largest. I suggest we take most of them and pack as much as we can.'

'Won't Harriet think it strange if I take more than one?'

'If she asks, I'll say we lost ours in an air raid and haven't yet had a reason to replace them.'

'Honestly, George, I'm getting worried about all these stories you're making up. Does Kath know you do this?'

George chuckled. 'Chance would be a fine thing. Kath can read me like a book. I think she'd agree with what we are about to do,' he said as he blew dust from the case, opened the lid and lay it on the floor.

Molly was puzzled. 'I don't understand, George. Surely we are just going to pack a case or two?'

George ignored Molly's question and pulled back the heavy pink eiderdown, followed by a layer of blankets. Tugging the sheets from the bed, he threw them onto the floor, then remade the bed.

'George, I don't think Kath is short of bed sheets,' Molly said with a baffled expression. She'd seen the woman's well-stocked airing cupboard when helping out with the washing and ironing. 'Whatever are you doing?'

'Watch and see.' He smiled, his face now a deep shade of pink, perspiration appearing on his brow.

He spread one of the sheets on the bed and started to pile Charlotte Missons's neatly folded clothes in the middle, adding the clothes that Molly had taken from her chest of drawers. 'Do you happen to have a strong belt or perhaps a length of rope?'

Now even more puzzled and wondering what George was up to, she went to the chest of drawers. Pulling out a well-polished leather belt that used to be part of her Tawny Owl uniform, she handed it to George. 'I still don't understand what you are doing.'

He pulled the sides of the sheet together into a large, bulky parcel and secured it with the belt, tugging it a few times to test it wouldn't slip. Carrying the bundle to the window, he checked it wasn't too large to be passed through the gap. Nodding his head with a satisfied smile on his face, he went back to the second sheet and proceeded to do the same. 'I need another belt. Do you have one?'

Still unsure of George's motives, she took another belt from a gabardine mac hanging in her wardrobe and he secured the second bundle and again checked it wouldn't fall open when tugged. 'Now, I'm going back up in that loft to get the other cases. You start packing your bits and pieces in that case.'

'But what about my clothes? I wanted to take some of those with me,' Molly said, looking at the two large bundles in front of the bedroom window. They resembled the bundles that were collected by the bag-wash man on laundry day.

George simply winked and climbed the ladder.

Molly sighed and started to pack her possessions into the case. She wrapped the more delicate items in her underwear and covered them with a couple of thick cardigans so they wouldn't be damaged or make a noise when carried. She pulled open drawers and even checked under the bed in case she had missed something.

A cough from the doorway made her look up with a start. Simon was stood there, his tie askew, buttons undone on his shirt, and was that a lipstick mark on his cheek? Molly looked at the distance between them. Without thinking twice, she dashed forward and grabbed for the door handle, intent on slamming the door in his face. However, she was a second too slow, for Simon put his hand out and stopped the door from closing.

'What do you want, Simon?' she asked loudly, hoping that George would hear from where he was in the loft. Although she didn't want to be within arm's reach of her cousin, she also didn't want him to spot the two large bundles on the floor. He was bound to ask some uncomfortable questions. Even though she wasn't sure what George was going to do with the clothing, she knew he was thinking of her.

'I've come to see you, little cousin,' he smirked. 'You know what they say – absence makes the heart grow fonder.' He reached out and grabbed her blouse, pulling her forward so she couldn't escape.

Knowing George was nearby made Molly feel brave. She didn't dare think what would have happened if she'd been alone with the brute.

Simon's mouth sought hers. She felt her stomach lurch as a strong taste of whisky and cigarettes overcame her. Glancing up, she saw George, his face red with anger, looking down on them from the stepladder. In his hand he held a smaller version of the suitcase that Molly had just finished packing. He threw it down towards Simon, while Molly pushed with all her strength. The case hit her cousin fair and square on the head.

Simon blinked for a moment, unsure of what had happened, before swaying and stumbling on the top step of the steep staircase. Molly watched in horror as Simon's body seemed to crumple and fold as he fell down the first few steps. In his drunken state, Simon couldn't break his fall. Had they killed him? No – he lay there stunned and groaning but conscious.

'What is all the noise?' Harriet called out from the front room.

Molly looked up to where George was waving at her to go back into the bedroom and pull the door to. She did as she was told before Harriet could spot her. Composing herself, she stood behind the door until she heard George clamber down the stepladder. She then opened the bedroom door.

'Whatever is the commotion?' George asked in all innocence as he placed another case by the one that had hit Simon.

Harriet shrieked as she spotted her son. 'Help, Molly ... Mr Jones... My son has collapsed.'

George went down to where Simon was lying. 'Come on, lad. It looks as though you've had one too many. Let's get you downstairs and sobered up, shall we?' Looking down to Harriet's horrified face, he said, 'Time to put the kettle on, love.'

Molly watched as George heaved Simon into the front room and then returned to her bedroom, where she began quickly stuffing her belongings into the two new cases. George joined her as she tried to lift the largest case to carry it downstairs.

'Leave that for a moment.' He opened the bedroom window and took the first of the two bundles of clothing. He swung the bundle by the belt and let it drop to the ground below. The second bundle followed soon after. Closing the window and picking up the suitcases, he grinned at Molly. 'Got everything?'

Molly nodded. 'How are we going to carry the bundles of clothing?'

'Don't worry – they're safe for a while in the side alleyway. I'll get Ted Sayers to give me a lift to collect them when I see him at the New Light for our darts match. Let's just get you home before Kath starts to worry.'

7

'Don't look so frightened. Come in and take a seat. I'll be with you in a minute.'

Molly recognized Connie Sinclair from her interview in London. As she placed her suitcase down and sat in the proffered chair, she hoped this meeting would be more pleasant than the encounters she'd had with Johnny Johnson, the other

Butlins officer. Life was going to be a barrel of laughs if he remained as miserable and cynical as he had an hour ago, when she'd seen him at the Butlins gatehouse. After all, it wasn't her fault his girlfriend had tripped over her suitcase, or that the cabbie had splashed his other lady friend with mud outside the Victoria Palace Theatre the other day. Come to that, it hadn't been her fault that someone nudged that cup of tea from her hand that ended up drenching the wretched man. She felt a giggle coming on as she decided that perhaps she *was* responsible for trampling on his feet when he asked her to dance. The giggle vanished immediately, to be replaced by a scowl. He was such an arrogant man. Would she be able to work within a hundred yards of Johnny Johnson without something awful happening? Her days at Butlins would be numbered if that dreadful man kept coming near her.

Connie Sinclair looked up from her paperwork and frowned. 'Are you feeling unwell, Molly?'

'I'm fine, Miss Sinclair. Just a little tired after my long journey,' she replied, realizing her thoughts must have shown on her face.

Pull yourself together or they will think you're mad, she scolded herself.

Connie placed her paperwork into a file and pushed it to one side of her desk. She smiled at Molly. 'This must seem so strange after your previous job in' – Connie checked a sheet of paper in front of her – 'Erith. Why, that's in Kent and not far from my home town of Bromley.' She glanced over the sheet of paper, her expression softening. 'I see you've recently lost your parents.'

110

Molly nodded, willing herself not to cry. She had thought that now she was away from home, no one would comment on her recent loss. 'Yes, it was rather a shock, but coming to Butlins will help me to move on with my life. I promise I won't be miserable and depress the holidaymakers,' she added as an afterthought, just in case Miss Sinclair considered her a liability to the company.

'I'm sure you won't. We pride ourselves on our choice of staff. In fact, I feel that you will have great empathy with those campers who have lost family members in the war. Now,' she said, clapping her hands together, 'I have an hour to spare, so I'll give you a quick tour of the camp and take you to the stores to collect your uniform. You can leave your suitcase in reception for now.'

Molly followed Connie out into the large reception area. She tried to imagine it packed with excited holidaymakers collecting the keys to their chalets and anticipating the joys of a week of holiday fun. She noticed a small group of women and two young men standing nervously by their suitcases.

'Jolly good. It looks as though more new staff have arrived,' Connie said to Molly. 'Leave your case with theirs and I'll give you all the grand tour. Not that we can cover the entire camp. There just isn't time,' she added as they approached the group and introductions were made. 'Once you have your uniforms and have settled into your chalets, you have the rest of the day free to explore. Tomorrow, your training starts in earnest. Follow me and try to keep up,' she called out loudly so the people at the back could hear.

111

Molly stepped in line beside a pretty blonde girl. 'Hello. I'm Molly Missons.'

'Bunty Grainger.' The girl smiled back, holding her hand out for Molly to shake. 'Pleased to meet you. This is all rather exciting, isn't it?'

'To be honest, I'm finding it a bit daunting. The camp is so large. I'm sure I shall get lost.'

'If you do get lost, you can head to one of the "lost child" posts and we can collect you.'

The two girls giggled, which attracted raised eyebrows from Connie Sinclair. 'Keep up, ladies, and no gossiping in the ranks,' she added with a twinkle in her eye. 'We are passing the dining room. Over there is our swimming pool. I hope you can all swim. You will be allocated a dining time and house duties when we meet for staff training tomorrow.'

Molly and Bunty gazed through the windows to where rows of tables and chairs were being set out by staff. 'It's hard to believe so many people will be sitting down to eat in there on Saturday,' Molly said in awe.

'I've been told there is to be more than one sitting as well. That's a lot of food,' Bunty added. 'Look out – we're losing the group.'

The two girls hurried to catch up with their colleagues, marvelling at gardeners planting out flowering plants and rose bushes along the roadside in long stretches of neat beds.

'I love roses,' Bunty sighed.

'You should have been here three weeks ago. All that was growing here then were bloody big air-raid shelters,' one of the gardeners said as he stood up to stretch his back. 'The governor's had us all

112

working flat out digging out the shelters and planting the rose beds. This is just as it was before war broke out.'

Molly could see how proud he was of his work.

'Who is the governor?' Bunty asked.

'That's Billy Butlin,' Molly explained. The Butlins staff she'd met so far seemed incredibly proud of their boss. She hoped she'd get to meet him before the season ended.

'Keep up, ladies,' Connie called as she disappeared round a corner.

As they caught up with the group, who were now standing by a signpost, the girls could see rows of chalets, again bordered by grassed areas and even more bright flowers.

'It's wonderful,' Bunty sighed. 'I've never seen anything like it.'

Connie turned to check that the little group was all together before pointing out tennis courts, a gymnasium, a putting green and billiard room. 'Further over there, you will find the nursery, chapel, children's area and also our medical centre. We cover every eventuality at Butlins,' she added proudly.

'That's where I'll be based,' Bunty said, pointing towards the children's area.

'Me too. Are you going to be a Butlins auntie?' Molly asked.

'Yes. It's comforting to know someone else I'll be working with. Even if we only met a short while ago,' Bunty said with a nervous smile.

Molly felt the same. Just knowing one friendly face among thousands in this large holiday camp gave her a boost. Bunty seemed a cheerful sort.

113

She may well have fun here after all. Travelling up from London had given her time to think about the life she was leaving behind, if only for a few months. Her last day had been spent sorting a flurry of last-minute queries at the shop, despite George assuring her that he could cope. She had caught up with all business correspondence, leaving her dad's office bright and clean for George to use. Molly had placed an advertisement in the *Erith Observer* for a lad to work for them and young Jack had started work three days before Molly left Erith. He was bright and cheerful, and would be able to help out around the shop and also serve customers when George had to pop out on business.

On the afternoon before she headed to Skegness, Molly, accompanied by Kath, paid a visit to Brook Street Cemetery. It was a lovely spring day as the women pulled a few weeds from round the headstone and placed fresh flowers in the vase. Kath left Molly for a while so she could be alone with her thoughts. She felt as though she was deserting them. Goodness knows what they would have made of Harriet and Simon. But, then, the cousins would have had no need to have visited Erith if they weren't beneficiaries of her dad's will. It was a real mess and she could see no way out of it apart from going away for a while until the dust settled and she could speak to her family solicitor and ask his advice.

She knelt by the grave for a little while longer, saying a quiet prayer for Charlotte and Norman, until Kath's hand on her shoulder brought her back to the present. 'Come on, love – we'll miss that bus if we don't look sharp. I'll be up here twice a week, if not more, so you needn't worry about the grave being kept tidy. You're not the only one who misses them, you know.'

Molly got to her feet and gave the old woman a hug. She was blessed to have such good friends in Kath and George.

'Now, I suggest we stop off at Hedley Mitchell's and treat ourselves to afternoon tea. I think your mum would have approved of that, don't you?'

Molly nodded in agreement. Blowing a silent kiss to her parents, she left the cemetery, giving a final look over her shoulder as they headed to the bus stop.

By the time they arrived back at Kath's house in Cross Street, Freda had packed the largest of the suitcases that George had taken from the loft at Avenue Road. Molly had little else to do but relax with her closest friends and think of her journey to Skegness the next morning.

The chalet where Molly was to live during her time at Butlins was sparse but clean. She'd been thrilled when she'd learned that Bunty could share with her, and the two girls had excitedly collected their suitcases from reception and headed along the long rows of identical chalets until they'd reached their home from home. Opening the door, they'd both exclaimed how snug it was with three beds in such a small area. They'd been told that until more chalets had been restored, after six years of use by the navy, Butlins staff would have to share three to a chalet.

'I'm sure we'll manage,' Molly said. 'Once we

unpack and push our suitcases under our beds, there will be plenty of room. We can wash our smalls out in the hand-basin and perhaps hang a line across the veranda for them to dry.'

'As long as we don't have water dripping off our drawers while we sit out on the veranda sunbathing,' Bunty giggled.

Molly joined in. Bunty was such a laugh. They would be able to make their chalet very comfortable, somewhere to relax when they weren't on duty.

She set to unpacking her clothes, shaking out creases from the pretty summer dresses she would wear when not on duty. Carefully hanging them up on a short wooden pole that all three girls would have to share, she smiled to herself as she thought how she'd deliberated over what to bring with her to Butlins and what to leave behind at George and Kath's house. Molly had been in such a quandary that it had been a relief to find, upon returning from the cemetery, that Freda had finished the packing, thus making the task much easier. Freda had made the right choices. Molly's friend knew her so well.

Returning to the suitcase to lift out her soap bag and shoes, Molly's fingers touched a solid object. With a frown on her face, she pulled out a small, worn leather attaché case, recognizing it as belonging to her mum. Why was it in her suitcase? Flicking back two brass clasps, she raised the lid. Inside, she found faded family photographs taken before the war. Freda must have packed them thinking Molly would like mementos from home. It must have been with the suitcases George found

116

in the loft at Avenue Road. She placed it carefully back into the suitcase, thinking she'd sift through the photos when she was alone.

They'd just finished putting away their possessions when there was a loud banging on the door and a posh voice called out, 'Open up, gals. I've misplaced my blinking key.'

Molly opened the door, her chin almost hitting the ground as a tall woman wearing jodhpurs, a thick green pullover and a hacking jacket strode into the room carrying a large holdall and swinging a riding hat on her arm.

'Hey up, the cavalry's arrived.' Bunty grinned. 'Hello. You must be our fellow inmate. I'm Bunty Grainger, and this is Molly Missons.'

The woman threw her holdall to the ground and flopped onto the one unmade bed. 'Phew. What a to-do! The bloody donkeys would not get out of the lorry, no matter how many carrots we dangled in front of them. I reckon we'll have trouble there, girlies.'

Molly and Bunty looked at each other and frowned.

Seeing the looks on their faces, the woman let out a belly laugh and jumped to her feet. 'Plum Appleby, pony and donkey rides for the children, at your service. Best you stand downwind of me when I've been mucking out the stables.'

The three girls burst out laughing. Butlins was going to be an absolute hoot living with these two, Molly thought to herself.

For Molly, the next couple of days passed in a haze of meeting colleagues, learning her duties and finding her way around the vast holiday camp. She was enchanted by the Viennese dance hall and an olde worlde pub called the Pig and Whistle Inn. Even though she was busy from dawn to dusk, she felt the strain of the past months fall away and soon she was relaxed and ready to welcome the many hundreds of guests who would arrive by bus, car, train and coach the next day. She and her colleagues would first greet guests in the main reception area, helping parents to register the younger children for the nursery and then directing holidaymakers to their chalets. Every visitor would be given the name of their 'house' for the week, which would determine at what times they would eat in the large dining room she'd spotted on the day they'd arrived, and where she'd so far enjoyed delicious shepherd's pie, jam roly-poly and steak-and-kidney pudding as tasty as any her mum had made, all cooked by onsite chefs and served by the well-trained waiters and waitresses.

Molly, Bunty and Plum had decided to take a walk down to the beach next to the camp, where they could enjoy the mild, quiet evening before the invasion of visitors the following day. Kicking off their shoes, they sat on the sand looking out to sea. The tide was in and lapped quietly on the shore yards from where they sat.

'My feet are killing me,' Plum declared, kicking off her sandals. 'I may well go for a paddle in a minute.'

'I'm not surprised. You must have walked miles with those ponies and horses. I thought you were supposed to ride them,' Molly said.

With her hair loose from the tight bun she kept

it in while working, and dressed in a pretty cotton printed skirt and white blouse, Plum looked more like a woman and less like a jockey about to take part in the Grand National. She scrubs up well, as George would say, Molly thought to herself.

'I've been getting them used to their surroundings ready for when they have to give rides to the youngsters,' Plum explained.

'I feel a bit sorry for them, giving rides all day long with excitable children on their backs,' Bunty said, who lay on her side, running her fingers through the soft sand as she picked out shells and made a small pile next to her.

'Don't be,' Plum said, getting to her feet and dipping her toes in the incoming tide. 'I've split them into three teams so they don't have to work every day. Plus the stables are the best available, with stable hands at their beck and call, and the best food this side of Skegness.'

'I bet their stable mates don't snore,' Bunty said pointedly to Plum.

Plum ignored the comment as she looked along the beach to where twinkling lights from the Butlins funfair could be seen in the early evening sky. 'What fun,' she said, pointing to the fairground. 'I haven't thrown wooden balls at a coconut since I was a young gal.'

Bunty was on her feet at once and striding along the beach. The strains of music from a steam organ could be heard across the sand. 'The organ's playing "The Waltz of the Flowers". Come on, you two. It must be open.'

Molly struggled to catch up with her two new chums as they ran across the sandy beach towards the bright lights. It was May and the days were becoming warmer, but the evening was turning chilly. Molly pulled her arms through the cardigan she'd slung across her shoulders. 'Wait for me,' she shouted, but the girls were now far ahead of her and didn't hear her cries. Kicking off her white sandals in exasperation, she picked them up and managed to run much faster in the loose sand.

Entering the fairground was like stepping into another world. Even without the holidaymakers, who would arrive in their droves tomorrow, it was busy. Molly assumed that the fair also attracted locals. She made a decision to discover towns and villages in the vicinity of the holiday camp when she had time.

Plum was waving to her from where she was standing alongside Bunty in a short queue for the dodgem cars. 'I've always wanted to ride on one of these. Come and join us,' she shouted above the din of the music and men calling out to the punters to throw a hoop or take a ride on the flying boats.

Molly had never been keen on the way the cars bumped into each other. It was all rather rough. 'I'm not sure,' she faltered until she saw the disappointment on Plum's face. 'Have you never been on them?'

Plum shrugged her shoulders, trying to hide her disappointment. 'My mother thought it wasn't very ladylike,' she sighed.

'What? You work with horses. Surely that's more energetic than a fairground ride?' Molly asked.

Plum gave one of her loud laughs. 'Goodness, no! In our set, the folk are out with the hounds most days. That is considered normal,' she added, noticing Molly's perplexed expression.

'It's not normal where I come from. Are you really posh?' she asked in awe.

Molly's question caused Plum to roar with laughter once more. 'The folk aren't royalty, but they've been around since the year dot. Though there is a bit of the landed gentry about them.'

'Gosh, that must be wonderful,' Molly said, imagining hunt balls and manor houses.

For a moment, Plum's smile disappeared. She looked sad. 'It's not all it's cracked up to be. It can be a lot to live up to.' She nudged Bunty, who was in a daydream. 'Wake up, there. We are next in the queue. Who's coming on with me?'

'I'd rather just watch, if you don't mind,' Bunty said wistfully.

'Oh, I'll come with you, then,' Molly said, climbing into a dodgem car that had just been vacated. 'But you can be the driver.'

The car headed off, the girls shrieking loudly as they were bumped from behind by two young lads. Molly grabbed the sides of the little vehicle. She was convinced she would be thrown out. It was fun but just a touch scary. Plum chased the lads, trying to bump them back. Looking over at Bunty, Molly could see the girl watching across the dodgems to where a man was guiding a long length of sheet music into the organ. He raised his hand in recognition and Bunty waved back excitedly and headed off into the crowd towards him until Molly lost sight of her.

How strange, Molly thought to herself. Bunty hadn't mentioned that she knew anyone who

121

worked on the fairground, though she supposed it was none of her business. She knew so little about. Bunty and Plum, and this evening had shown there was much to learn about her new friends. She wasn't convinced either was completely happy. What a trio they made!

8

'Oh my goodness. Whatever is that noise?' Plum groaned as she buried her head beneath her pillow.

'You'd better get used to it. We'll be living with that sound from now on.' Molly laughed as she straightened her bedcovers, then picked up her towel and soap bag before pulling on a coat over her nightdress. 'It's Radio Butlins, and there will be broadcasts from dawn to dusk, waking the inmates and telling them when to eat and what events are happening. I think it's fun.'

'Fun? What's fun about some woman with a plum in her voice waking me from my slumbers?'

Bunty and Molly burst out laughing as Plum disappeared under her bedcovers.

'What's so funny?'

'We are laughing because your name is Plum and you have a posh voice,' Bunty said, trying to keep a straight face in case Plum was offended.

Plum peeped out and grinned at them. 'No one is that posh! Now, call me in half an hour. I only need a quick wash in the basin. I'll be stinking of donkeys before the hour's out.'

'You're always with those animals. That's why you missed the staff meeting when they told us about Radio Butlins.'

'So who's the daft one?' a muffled voice said from beneath the bedcovers.

'I'm off to have a bath,' Molly said. 'Don't forget we have our final staff meeting before the first holidaymakers arrive. Not that I expect to see you there,' she muttered to the now snoring Plum. Molly headed for the bathroom block, leaving Bunty and Plum snuggled in their beds.

Although still early, the sun was already peeping out from behind the clouds. It bode well for the reopening of Butlins. Molly felt a stirring of excitement at the thought of so many people arriving to enjoy a week of fun after enduring the deprivation of six years of war. She waved to the ground staff, who were out watering flowerbeds. They'd worked wonders in the weeks since the navy had returned the camp to Billy Butlin. Little remained to show that this had been an important part of the armed services' fight to win the war.

She enjoyed a leisurely soak in the hot water, knowing that come tomorrow, there would be queues for the facilities that Butlins provided for its guests. Wrapping a towel round her head turban style, Molly pulled on her clothes and headed back to the chalet. Turning the corner into the long aisle of identical chalets that led to her own home from home, she was deep in thought about the day ahead. It would be the first time she'd worn her uniform of pleated skirt, white blouse and red blazer. Flat shoes were the order of the day, as she'd be on her feet for ages welcoming the holidaymakers and showing them to their chalets. The Butlins aunties were on duty in reception, encouraging parents to allow their youngsters to join in games and fun so the older members of the party would be able to enjoy some time to themselves. In the meetings and training sessions, Molly had suggested games that she'd devised for the Brownies and Guides in the past that would be of interest to the children on holiday. A nature trail had been planned for the first full day for junior holidaymakers to enjoy. Hopefully, the day would be as bright and sunny as it was today.

'Whoa there. Didn't you hear me call your name?'

Molly stopped dead in her tracks, then turned. 'Hello, Mr Johnson. Did you wish to speak to me?' Molly had done her best to avoid Johnny Johnson since arriving at the camp. Whenever she was close to him, things seemed to happen that made her feel uncomfortable. Thankfully, Molly had yet to meet the lady who had fallen over her suitcase on the day she arrived at the camp. In fact, she felt uncomfortable now. Johnny stood in front of her, already dressed in his uniform of white trousers and open-necked shirt. His red jacket, identical to all male staff members, had several enamel badges on the lapel, including one that had the word 'Butlins' and the year, '1946'. Molly was aware her face was shiny from the recent hot bath and that her damp hair was still wrapped in a towel. 'I have to dry my hair and get ready for the meeting,' she explained, starting to walk away from him.

'Wait. I just need to ask you something.'

Molly imagined that if this were one of his films and she were his leading lady, he would pull her into his arms and kiss her tenderly. She felt her cheeks start to burn for thinking such a thing. 'Ask me something?'

'I understand you are leading the children's nature trail. I wondered if I could attend?'

Molly, still flustered from thoughts of Johnny's kisses, answered abruptly. 'Mr Johnson, you are in charge of entertainment in the camp. You do not need my permission to join in with the children's activities.'

Johnny paused for a moment, a slight frown on his brow. 'I noticed the suggestions you made to entertain our younger holidaymakers. They seem just the thing to keep the youngsters amused. I'd like to check them out. We want the children to enjoy themselves. However, I'll keep out of your way...'

That was kind, Molly thought to herself. She didn't need one of the bosses breathing down her neck while she did her work.

'I don't wish to have something tipped over me or be tripped up, so I'll follow behind,' he continued.

Molly opened her mouth to answer the infuriating man but realized she dared not say what she truly thought. Aware he was watching her closely with an unnerving twinkle in his eye, she chose her words with care. 'Thank you. You're welcome to join us. We are meeting outside reception at ten o'clock.' She turned to hurry away. What was it with that man?

The towel round her hair chose that moment to fall to the ground. With exasperation she reached down to retrieve it, spilling the contents of her wash bag. Her face burning scarlet, Molly heard a chuckle as Johnny walked away.

Molly and Bunty both agreed they'd never worked so hard. The hours sped by as they welcomed holidaymakers, gave directions, and chatted to the children for whom they would be caring over the next week. Molly made sure to tell as many parents as possible about her nature trail taking place the following morning. More than one child showed little enthusiasm until she mentioned rock pools and crabs. Parents looked relieved to be able to have a few hours to themselves to relax after travelling to Skegness.

'I do believe your nature trail is going to be a big hit,' Bunty said as she pointed out to a family where their children were to meet the next morning.

'I hope so, especially with Johnny Johnson coming along to check us out,' Molly said ruefully.

'I can't help thinking I know him from somewhere,' Bunty said thoughtfully as they both looked across to where Johnny was helping a group of elderly ladies down steep steps from a coach that had just arrived.

'You mean you don't know who he is?' Molly was amazed. 'Do you not go to the cinema?'

'No. I've not been for a few years. There wasn't a cinema near where I lived.'

'Surely you've read a movie magazine. He's

been in plenty. I have a collection of them at home...' Molly's words faltered as she realized Bunty could make fun of her knowing so much about their new boss. However, Bunty looked sad and had little to say.

'No, I haven't seen many magazines either,' she said, turning to welcome a family and point them towards reception, where tea and orange squash were being served to weary travellers. 'I take it Mr Johnson has worked in the movies.'

Molly just nodded. Her new friend's whole demeanour had changed. Was Bunty hiding something? 'Yes, he is ... was ... a matinee idol.'

The girls continued welcoming guests until they were relieved by other Butlins redcoats so they could take a tea break. Molly had been thrilled when she'd been put into Kent House. Not only would she be part of the campers' fierce competition to be 'house of the week' but she would also be reminded of the county she loved so much.

Both girls kicked off their shoes and relaxed while they sipped their hot tea after tucking into a sticky bun. 'I think I'm going to enjoy working here, as long as my feet don't complain too much,' Molly said, flicking stray crumbs from the lapels of her new red blazer.

'I think it's wonderful. I could work here forever,' Bunty said with a contented look on her face.

'What work did you do before coming here?' Molly asked. Bunty was a happy person to be around, but Molly knew little about her life before Butlins.

Bunty shrugged her shoulders. 'This and that. Nothing important. I thought Plum would have joined us, but she seems to have disappeared,' Bunty said, confirming Molly's idea that her new friend did not wish to talk about her life before she came to Butlins.

'The last time I saw her, she was walking down the drive towards the gatehouse. Perhaps she had to see Spud about something. No doubt we will see her before too long. We have donkey rides for the younger children at three o'clock and pony rides for the older ones. She'll turn up by then.'

Molly was still wondering about Bunty's silence and Plum's disappearance when she noticed Johnny Johnson approaching their table. She smiled a welcome through gritted teeth, carefully slipping her feet back into her shoes in case she was reprimanded for sloppiness while on duty. Standing as close as he was, Molly had to crane her neck to look up at the man and try to control her breathing as her heart beat a little faster. She could smell his spicy cologne and fought hard to remind herself that this man had ridiculed her on more than one occasion.

He acknowledged Bunty with a nod of his head and turned to Molly. 'I was leaving my correspondence at the post desk when I spotted this with your name on it. I thought it may be important.' He held out a postcard with the image of Erith on one side.

'Thank you,' Molly murmured. She knew it would be from Freda, as she'd seen the same postcards on sale in Woolworths and had wondered who would think to send a postcard from her home town. Now she knew.

A smile crossed her face as she turned the card over and began to read Freda's words. It was lovely to hear from her old friend. Although it was only days since Molly had left Erith, it felt like months since she'd begun training to be a Butlins redcoat. Her smile turned to a look of horror as she scanned Freda's words.

A quiet cough alerted Molly to Johnny, who was still standing close to where she sat. 'I'll see you later at the bingo game, Molly,' he said with a glimmer of humour on his handsome face.

'Bingo?'

'Yes. We are in need of assistance for tonight's game. Be in the ballroom at seven thirty sharp.' He walked away, but not before Molly saw him laughing to himself.

Molly leaned back in her seat and groaned.

'Whatever's wrong?' Bunty asked. 'You've turned a deep beetroot colour. Do you feel ill?'

'No, I'm fine, thanks, Bunty, but I'm in need of a quick lesson on how to play bingo before the boss man realizes I'm a complete novice and hauls me over the coals for not knowing my job.'

Bunty started to explain the intricacies of the game as Molly tucked Freda's postcard into her pocket. If only her old chum had not enquired about Molly's passion for Johnny Johnson the matinee idol. She squirmed in embarrassment as she tried to listen to Bunty's instructions.

The rest of the day went without a single hitch. Molly had volunteered to help with the children's donkey rides on the beach close to where the

129

stables were situated. The ponies and donkeys did indeed live a life of luxury in draught-free accommodation with plenty of food. Plum had sworn they had better accommodation than the staff, and Molly had to agree, as she'd noticed a draught whenever a breeze blew from the sea towards their own quarters. Perhaps they could patch up their chalet a little to make it cosier. Spud would be able to advise her on what to use. He seemed to know the camp inside out.

After directing a few latecomers to their chalets, she headed back to change into clothes more suitable for working with children and animals. She found Bunty sprawled on her bed with her arm across her face.

'Do you fancy coming to help with the kiddies' rides?' Molly asked.

Bunty rolled to one side and faced the wall. 'No. I have a headache coming on. I'll have a short rest and see you at dinner. I'll be fine by then,' she murmured.

'If you're sure... Can I get you anything? Perhaps some water or a pill from the medical centre?' Molly was worried about Bunty, as she'd been fine when she'd left her not an hour before.

'No,' Bunty muttered a little irritably. 'I just need to sleep.'

Molly drew the curtains against the late-afternoon sun, trying to be as quiet as possible. After she'd pulled on white shorts and slipped into ankle socks and plimsolls, she crept from the room, leaving her fellow redcoat to sleep.

Bunty stirred as she heard the door to the chalet

close; she hated to miss her duties and deceive her new friends. She enjoyed her job at Butlins, but at this moment Bunty just wanted to hide away from the world. It wasn't so much a headache that had made her take to her bed as an overwhelming weariness that made her feel as though she no longer cared what happened in her life. It had been so long since she'd seen her parents and slept in her own bed. It was unlikely she'd see her family for some time to come. If only she could rewrite the past so that she hadn't fallen head over heels in love with a handsome doctor. She knew her sister, Sadie, would be marrying soon, and by rights Bunty should have been there as chief bridesmaid to see her sibling walk down the aisle on their dad's arm. Her family understood the situation, but still it hurt not to play her part in such a special day. Regardless of the danger, she needed to see the man she loved and keep him safe.

It was great fun helping the children onto the docile donkeys and leading them by their reins along the beach. Most enjoyed themselves. Several refused to get off at the end of their turn, and one little toddler screamed in fear as Molly tried to lift her onto the smallest of the animals, who stood patiently waiting to set off. 'He won't hurt you, sweetie,' she soothed. The little girl went rigid with fear and screamed for her mother.

'She ain't seen anything like it before,' the mother apologized as Plum marched over to see what was holding up the rides.

Taking the young girl from her mother's arms,

Plum rocked her gently before producing a carrot from her pocket. 'Here, why don't you give this to Jenny? She likes carrots.' The child thought for a moment and then nodded her head in agreement as Plum stood her down on the sandy beach.

The little girl held out the carrot to the donkey, who took it gently as if it knew the child needed to be handled with care. The child giggled and held her palm out to Plum for another carrot.

'I think we should take her for a little walk before she has another carrot, don't you?' Plum whispered to the child as she lifted her back into her arms. 'Do you want to sit on her back for a little while? Then you can give her another carrot.'

The little girl was delighted and giggled with pleasure as Plum headed off alongside Jenny, chatting away to the child.

'My, she's a natural with kiddies, isn't she?' the child's mother said to Molly. 'Our Edith don't usually calm down like that. Once she gets the fancy, she can scream for hours.'

Molly watched as young Edith disappeared along the beach on Jenny's back. She had to agree that Plum had a way with children. Gone was the posh-sounding woman and in her place there was a softer Plum who knew exactly how to handle a fractious child. She shaded her eyes against the sun, which was slipping lower in the sky. As she did so, Molly noticed a flash of red and white further along the top of the beach. It was one of her fellow redcoats heading in a hurry towards the fairground. Squinting against the sunshine, Molly recognized the woman who was now running through the sand dunes. It was Bunty. Whatever was she up to, and how had her headache cleared so quickly? Molly thought to herself.

Molly had no idea how she got through dinner. The dining room was full to bursting with happy holidaymakers from Kent House, and as well as eating her own meal, she spent time talking to guests about the week ahead and answering questions they had about their accommodation and the facilities. For many people, it was the first holiday they'd had since the outbreak of war. Molly was aware that a member of the family was much missed in some cases and she reminded herself not to ask about a missing mother or father.

''Ello, miss,' a young lad called out as Molly walked between the impressive, regimented rows of tables, each with a clean cloth and flowers. The catering and waiting staff were working non-stop serving meals and clearing tables. 'You helped our Edith on the donkeys this afternoon.'

She looked at a label tied to the lad's jacket: every child was labelled with their name and chalet number. She'd lost count of how many parents she'd helped label their kids. 'Hello, Freddie. Are you enjoying yourself?'

Freddie nodded. 'I'm coming on your nature walk tomorrow. Will you help me find some crabs? I've never seen real ones and Mum said there are some in the sea.'

Molly smiled at the keenness of the lad. These children had missed so much by growing up under the shadow of war. At least they were safe now. She decided at that moment to do everything she could to help as many people as possible enjoy their time at Butlins. 'I think we'll be able to find a crab or two for you to look at.' She smiled down to the boy. 'You know where to meet tomorrow morning, don't you?'

The boy nodded enthusiastically. 'You bet. I can't wait!' he declared, before climbing back onto his chair and tucking into a bowl of jelly.

'Thank you, miss,' Freddie's mum called from the table, where she was spooning food into little Edith's mouth. 'I wasn't sure about bringing the kiddies somewhere like this, but their dad had told me so much about the place before the war that I knew I had to come and check it out.'

Molly could see the only other chair at the table was being used by an elderly lady, who nodded politely but kept silent.

'That's my mother-in-law,' Freddie's mum said. 'I'm Gladys Sangster. We come from Woolwich.'

'Why, that's not far from where I hail from,' Molly said. 'I'm an Erith girl.'

'Bless my soul. Did you hear that, Mother? This young lady's from Erith. That's only a few stops from us on the train.'

The older woman's face lit up for a moment. 'That's a nice place to live. By the Thames, isn't it? We went there once to visit family and had a trip on the river.'

'That's right,' Molly said. 'Was it on *Kentish Queen*, the paddle steamer?'

'Bless my soul, so it was. It's a small world and no mistake,' Mrs Sangster Senior declared, holding out her hand to Molly. 'I'm pleased to meet you, miss.'

'Please, call me Molly,' she said as she shook

134

the lady's hand. 'I hope you enjoy your week's holiday.'

'We're here for two weeks,' Freddie called out as he scraped the last of the jelly from his bowl.

'I had a bit of insurance paid out to me and thought we might as well treat ourselves,' the younger Mrs Sangster whispered to Molly.

Molly nodded. 'Well, enjoy your time here, and if ever you need anything, just find me and I'll help if I can.'

She walked away from the table marvelling at how some people coped with what life threw at them. Those children would remember their holiday at Butlins for the rest of their lives. If ever she met Billy Butlin, Molly would tell him what his holiday camps meant to people. Then again, he probably knew already, she thought, as she stopped to chat with another family.

As the sun set on her first day as a Butlins redcoat and children's auntie, Molly headed off to the main ballroom to carry out her bingo duties. She wished that when her mum and Kath had attended bingo sessions in the church hall, she'd gone along to keep them company. As much as Bunty had explained about numbered balls being pulled out of a machine and campers covering numbers on printed cards until they had a line, or a 'full house', Molly still found the game confusing. She had no idea how she was supposed to be involved and hoped fervently she was not on stage instructing the audience in something about which she had no idea.

Nervously entering the ballroom, Molly smiled brightly. She recalled her training and the most important instruction from Connie: however nervous or unhappy they felt, a Butlins redcoat always pinned a smile to their face and made every holidaymaker feel welcome. She did just that and nodded to the campers as she headed towards a group of colleagues who stood close to the main stage.

'Ah, Molly, come and join us.' A redcoat from the entertainment team she'd been introduced to as Terry beckoned her over. 'I want you to work the back part of the hall with Dave. He will show you what to do. We have four games, plus the special.' He saw a few questioning looks. 'The special is a straight full house with the prize of a week's family holiday at the end of the season. There will be a break before the final game, so encourage the campers to buy extra cards and join in. The rest of the games will be either a line or the four corners, followed by a full house.' Molly nodded her head; she understood Terry's instructions. Fingers crossed she'd get through the evening in one piece.

'A family holiday is a very generous prize,' Molly said as she followed Dave towards the back of the large ballroom. They'd stopped at the bar to buy a drink on their way. Terry said they'd need a drink to see them through the evening. This puzzled Molly, as she knew Billy Butlin did not like his staff to be intoxicated while on duty. She chose a glass of orange juice, while Terry had a pint glass of bitter shandy.

'It keeps the camps full during the final weeks of the season when the weather changes,' Dave explained. 'The punters love it and often book to come the following year. It worked before the war and we expect it to work again.' Dave was one of the older redcoats and had worked at the camp before war broke out.

They reached the back of the hall and placed their drinks on the edge of a nearby table, which was occupied by the two Mrs Sangsters.

'Hello,' Molly said. 'Are you enjoying yourselves?'

The older lady patted a vacant seat next to her. 'Sit yourself down, love. You're going to be run ragged before too long. Might as well have a little sit-down.'

Dave nodded for her to take the offered seat as he leaned against a nearby wall and drank deeply from his glass.

'How are the children, Mrs Sangster?'

'Please, you must call me Gladys.'

'And I'm Olive,' her mother-in-law added. 'It always confuses people, what with there being two Mrs Sangsters.'

'We lost my husband, Joe, last year–' Gladys started to explain.

'It was his chest,' Olive interrupted, rubbing her own ample bosom. 'He'd not been right since Dunkirk. Too long in the sea,' she added wisely.

'I'm sorry,' Molly said. 'I lost my own parents last year. It must be hard for the children.'

'I'm sorry for your loss, love,' Olive said, patting her knee. Molly felt a lump form in her throat. Would she ever be able to accept condolences without wanting to cry?

'Edith is too young to remember much, but young Freddie's been a bit of a handful since,'

Gladys said ruefully. 'That's why we thought a holiday would be nice. Joe had an insurance policy he took out when we first married. A penny policy, they called it. Blow me down if it wasn't a fair windfall when the man from the Prudential came round the day after the funeral.'

'So we decided there and then to have a nice holiday when the weather was brighter,' Olive said. 'I stuck the money in my post-office account. We used a bit to have a nice Christmas. After all, money's no good to you when you're dead. That's what my old man always said.'

'And that's why the old man left you penniless,' Gladys was quick to point out.

Olive ignored her daughter-in-law. 'We'd heard about Butlins from Joe and thought the kiddies would like it. So here we are.'

'I hope you and the children have a wonderful time,' Molly said, wondering what it would be like to be left without a husband when you had two young children to bring up.

'We get by. Family stick together through thick and thin,' Olive said proudly. 'As long as the kids are happy, then we're happy too. I reckon they're gonna have a great time here. Young Freddie could hardly settle in his bed he was that excited about going along to your nature trail tomorrow. Gawd help you if you don't find him a crab to look at. I hope he doesn't wake our Edith. We don't want them calling out our chalet number to say a youngster's crying before we get to finish playing bingo.'

Molly held up both hands with her fingers crossed. 'Let's hope so.' She grinned.

Dave tapped Molly on the shoulder. 'Time to start, love.'

Molly rose to her feet. Butterflies danced in her stomach. 'I'd better get ready for the bingo. It's my first time.'

Gladys laughed out loud. 'You're a bingo virgin? As long as you don't get your "Kelly's eye" mixed up with your "legs eleven", you'll be all right.'

Molly's butterflies grew into vultures. Whatever was Gladys talking about?

Dave whispered to Molly as lively music from the stage alerted everyone to the start of the first game. 'Keep your eye on our tables to make sure no one's having a problem marking off their numbers. If someone shouts, check that Terry can hear you from the stage, then make sure it's the right card and read off the numbers so he can check them. We collect the envelope with the money prize, or a bottle if it's a bottle game, and hand it to the winner. Got it?'

Molly nodded nervously. 'I think so. What tables are we watching?'

'From here down to the pillars near the end of the bar.' He pointed to an area with around fifty tables.

'Crikey, that's a lot of campers.' She grinned at Dave. 'I'll do my best.'

'That's my girl. You'll be fine.'

Terry introduced the first game. Campers had to cover a line on their card to win a voucher for one of the many shops on the campsite. A female red-coat started to turn the handle on a circular wire basket and small coloured balls within began to rattle as they rolled inside. The noise travelled

139

around the room as the microphone in Terry's hand picked up the sound. 'Eyes down and looking. The first game this evening is on the green card. Good luck, everyone. The first ball is ... "two little ducks"...'

Molly was confused. Why was everyone making quacking noises?

'...twenty-two,' Terry announced, placing the ball on a table in front of him before taking a second ball from the basket. '"Was she worth it?" Seven and six, seventy-six.'

Molly giggled as the men in the room shouted a loud 'No!' to Terry's question. She knew he was referring to the price of a marriage licence, seven shillings and sixpence. It was then the penny dropped. The numbers in the bingo game had funny sayings attached to them. Once she knew the numbers, she could join in with the shouts. What fun!

Terry continued to call out numbers. Molly could hear people in her area grumbling as they waited on one number for a full line. A shout of 'Here you are!' was heard from midway down the ballroom. A redcoat waved his arms and called out, 'We have a winner!' Some people cheered, while others groaned. The redcoat then called out the colour of the card, followed by the five numbers in a line. This time, just the numbers were called. No one used the funny names – this was too serious for funny games.

Once the numbers were checked and the prize handed over, Terry announced, 'Eyes down for a full house,' and the next round began.

Molly listened intently for each number: legs

eleven; Kelly's eye, number one; two fat ladies, eighty-eight; top of the shop, blind ninety.

You could have cut the atmosphere with a knife as Terry pulled number after number from the basket. Molly was aware of several people near to where she was standing muttering that they only needed one more number. All at once, a lady close to the front screamed, 'Bingo!' at the same time as a man in her own section shouted, 'House!'

She glanced at Dave and he nodded for her to attend to the man. Molly took a deep breath and waved her arms to attract Terry's attention.

'We have two claims for the full house. That'll be thirty bob for each winner. Redcoat Molly, you go first.' Molly felt all eyes on her as she cleared her throat and called out the colour of the card followed by the winning numbers. Dave collected an envelope with the prize money and handed it to Molly.

The man who had won his game gave Molly a big kiss as she presented his prize. 'Thank you, my love. I'll stand you a drink later,' he beamed as his wife snatched away the envelope and tucked it inside her handbag.

The evening passed quickly, and before she knew it, it was time for a short break before the final game. Molly went to the bar to buy a round for Dave and herself. Many of the campers offered to buy her a drink, but Molly wasn't sure if she should accept. It was something she would have to check with Connie at the next staff meeting.

'Are you enjoying the bingo?'

Molly froze; she would know that voice anywhere. To her left, she spotted Johnny Johnson

141

sitting at the bar as a camper moved away carrying a heavily laden tray of drinks. Please don't knock the tray, she thought to herself, as the man brushed her arm in passing. Johnny was wearing a well-cut tuxedo and sparkling white shirt. At his elbow was Gloria, a woman Molly recognized who worked in an office behind the reception desk. From the deep blue satin gown she was wearing, it was apparent the pair were not here to play bingo.

'It's been interesting, thank you,' she replied politely as she paid for her drinks. 'Do you play?'

Gloria smiled as she tucked her arm through Johnny's. 'Does it look as though we do?' she replied. Her smile did not quite reach her icy-blue eyes.

'I do play, but I prefer to be doing what you're doing,' Johnny said, which made his companion scowl.

Molly felt uncomfortable. 'I have to get back. It's the big game next,' she said as she concentrated hard on not spilling the contents of the two glasses, only too aware that Johnny was watching her as she threaded her way across the room.

She had just placed the drinks down when Terry called attention for the big game.

There was much cheering as campers were told the prize was a week's family holiday at Butlins. Then the room fell silent apart from the sound of the balls turning round in their basket and Terry's voice as he announced each number. This time, there wasn't a prize for a line, or the four corners of the card, as there had been in the previous games. The tension increased as each number was called. Molly felt the stirrings of excitement as she

142

watched the campers in her section of the ball-room. She really hoped one of them would win the valuable prize. Just as she was beginning to think that no one was going to call out, there was a scream near where she was standing.

Gladys Sangster leaped to her feet, waving the card above her head. 'I've won! I've only bloody won!'

9

Molly sipped the hot cocoa. It had been a good idea of Plum's to fill a thermos flask in the cafe and take it back to their chalet for their night-time drink. Plum was already snoring gently in her bed. As her duties were different to the redcoats', she was often in bed earlier than them, then up with the lark to tend to her charges.

It had been a wonderful evening, and when the Sangster family had won a week's holiday at the camp, Molly had been delighted to join them to celebrate. She had really taken to the two ladies. They'd been through so much, what with losing a son and husband, but their outlook on life and how to enjoy themselves had made her think she could learn from this in her own life. Then again, the Sangsters hadn't had two mysterious relatives arrive out of the blue and lay claim to their family's property. Molly had never been materialistic, but something just wasn't right about Harriet and Simon. She shuddered as she thought of the man's

143

advances, and snuggled under the bedcovers, warming her hands on her mug. It was close to summer, but the evenings were still chilly. The holiday camp was settling down for the night. For the first time that day, silence fell, broken only by the hoot of an owl and by occasional footsteps and whispered words as campers headed down the rows of chalets to their beds.

Placing her mug on the small table by her bed, Molly reminded herself to post the letters she'd managed to find time to write before heading off to the bingo game that evening. Her letter to Kath and George described the camp and the chalet she shared with Plum and Bunty, whereas the letter to Freda included more about Johnny Johnson and how she felt he was not quite the dashing matinee idol she'd formed a secret crush on in the days when she went to the Erith Odeon. As the envelopes had not been sealed, Molly opened her letter to Freda and added a postscript describing Johnny's appearance at the bingo along with his snooty companion. Johnny had approached the Sangsters' table after their win to offer his congratulations. Like Molly, he had accepted the invitation to sit with the family for a while. He'd not only charmed the two ladies but had also bought a round of drinks to celebrate their win. His companion, Gloria from the office, had walked off in a huff. Johnny hadn't seemed to notice and spent the time charming the two ladies and even promised to dance with Olive when she mentioned wistfully that she hadn't been old-time dancing since her husband had passed away, some years ago. Molly speculated that perhaps it didn't bother Johnny that Gloria had not joined the party because he was so used to having women on his arm or fluttery around him. She realized she would be a fool if she didn't admit to being just slightly attracted to the handsome man, but nevertheless assured herself, and Freda, in her letter to her, that it was more the allure of the world of the movies than of the man she had met in the flesh. The Johnny Johnson of her dreams was not the man she knew at Butlins. The film star Johnny would have swept her off her feet, as he had done more than once in her dreams, whereas the Butlins Johnny simply annoyed her, and his presence seemed to bring out her clumsiness.

Molly was just drifting off to sleep when she heard the door to their chalet slowly open and saw Bunty, outlined by the light of the moon, creep in, clutching her shoes. Looking at the luminous hands of her bedside clock, Molly noticed it was past one o'clock.

'What's going on?' Plum muttered from her bed.

Bunty switched on the light. 'I'm sorry I woke you,' she whispered.

'I wasn't asleep,' Molly said, squinting in the harsh light. 'Were you working late?' she asked, although she couldn't think what duties a Butlins redcoat could have at this time of night, before she noticed Bunty was not wearing her uniform and was clutching a small doll.

'I'm sorry – I lost track of the time.'

Molly could see Bunty had been crying, as her eyes were red and puffy. Apart from that, her face was as white as a ghost and she was shaking.

Quickly climbing out of bed, she helped Bunty to her own bed and made her sit down. Pulling a cover around herself, Molly sat beside her and put an arm round the girl's shoulders. 'Now, tell us what's happened.'

Plum poured the last of the cocoa into a mug and placed it in the girl's hands. 'Take a sip of this. There's plenty of sugar, and that's good for shock. Did something happen at the fairground?'

Molly frowned. 'How...?'

Plum nodded to Bunty's feet and then the doll. The girl still had sand between her toes, and the small doll was identical to ones they'd seen being given away as prizes on several of the have-a-go stalls. She then remembered having spotted Bunty heading along the beach in the direction of the fairground that afternoon. 'What happened to you, Bunty? You can confide in us. We won't tell a soul.'

Plum nodded her agreement and reached for her brown flannelette dressing gown, pulling it on over the striped men's pyjamas that she favoured. It was chilly in the wooden cabin without any form of heating.

Bunty sipped her drink and looked into space, deep in thought, before speaking. 'It's Gordon, my fiancé. He says they know where he is...'

Plum looked towards Molly and frowned, silently mouthing the word 'What?'

'Who are these people, Bunty?' Molly asked, full of concern for her new friend.

'Private investigators ... perhaps even the police. Gordon said he'd been sent word they know where we are. He wants us to leave, move on...' She looked at Molly and started to weep. 'I'm so fed up with having to run all the time,' she gulped. 'I thought we'd be safe here for a while. Well, at least for the summer.'

Molly felt helpless. Whatever was this all about? From the look on Plum's face, she was thinking the same. 'I think it's best if you get yourself into bed and try to sleep,' she advised the weeping girl. 'We can talk about this in the morning. That's if you want to confide in us.'

Bunty nodded before wiping her eyes and blowing her nose on the handkerchief Plum had passed her. 'Thank you. I'd like that. I don't have anyone else. Well, apart from Gordon.'

'Then that's a plan,' Plum said, pulling off her dressing gown and climbing back into bed.

'I'm on breakfast duty in the morning, but I have an hour before I help with your nature ramble,' Bunty said to Molly as she started to unbutton her cardigan.

'Then I suggest we meet up and have a little chat, and until then you pin a Butlins smile on your face and we'll see what can be done,' instructed Molly.

'You'd better meet me at the stables,' said Plum. 'I'll be halfway through mucking out by the time you two have eaten and spent your time smiling at people. Some of us have to start work at the crack of dawn. Now, turn the light out and let me get some shut-eye.'

Molly grinned at Bunty and patted her shoulder. From the sound of it, whatever was behind Bunty's problem, she wasn't sure a little chat would solve it. Then again, having a shoulder to

147

cry on when one felt low helped enormously. She knew that to be true.

The sun was shining brightly as Molly and Bunty headed for breakfast the next morning. Both were wearing white shorts and blouses with their red jackets on top and received admiring glances from a few of the younger male campers. Knowing she would be leading the nature trail after they'd met up with Plum for their chat, Molly had left her equipment in a staffroom close to reception. With her hair pinned up in a neat pleat, she looked as cool as a cucumber and prepared for whatever would be thrown at her during the morning's trek with a crowd of children. She'd organized a few surprises for the children during their walk and was looking forward to seeing the expression on their faces.

Breakfast passed quickly, with campers enjoying plates of eggs, sausages and tomatoes, mopped up with thick slices of bread and margarine prepared in the vast Butlins kitchen. Molly stopped to chat with parents who had children old enough to go on her nature walk. Announcements were made during the meal urging people to join in with physical fitness on the lawn near the swimming pool or to help make Kent House the winning house that week by entering the swimming gala, boxing match or even the knobbly-knees competition. Announcements were always greeted with cheers by the holidaymakers, who took all suggestions in good spirit.

Molly spotted Bunty across the dining room cheering and applauding the redcoat who was on the microphone. She looked as though she hadn't a care in the world. With a healthy glow on her face and not a spot of make-up, she appeared closer to eighteen than the twenty-eight years of age that Molly knew her to be. What the girl had blurted out last night worried Molly. Was Bunty really in trouble with the police?

Once breakfast was finished, Molly headed over to the stable block. It was a little early for campers to begin lessons and Plum was alone mucking out the last of the stables. She'd expected to see Bunty already there, but the girl had not yet arrived.

'Hello, Plum. I've brought you a bacon sandwich. I thought you might have missed your breakfast.'

Plum took the food, wrapped in greaseproof paper, and sat on a nearby bale of hay. 'Scrummy. Thanks a bunch. I never seem to find time to eat in the mornings. Take a seat and make yourself comfortable. Where's Bunty?'

Molly shrugged her shoulders. 'I've no idea. I thought she'd have been here by now.' She checked her wristwatch. 'I only have half an hour before the children's nature trail starts and Bunty is supposed to be helping. I don't want to be late, as Mr Johnson has decided to tag along and I'm always making mistakes when he's around. For once I want to show I can do a job properly.'

Plum finished chewing a mouthful of bacon and wiped her mouth with the back of her hand. 'Have you known him long?'

'Goodness, no. I met him in London during my interview, then saw him again outside a theatre while I was doing "The Lambeth Walk". Before that, I'd only ever seen him on the cinema screen.'

'What?' Plum hooted with laughter. 'And there's me thinking you were the quiet one.'

'What do you mean about me being the quiet one? What about Bunty?'

'Oh, come on – you must have thought there was something strange about her creeping of to the fairground so many times,' Plum said.

'I've only seen her going once, yesterday, but she did seem distant that time we visited the fair together.'

'It was twice yesterday,' Plum said knowingly. 'The first time, she was wearing her uniform, but last night, she was in civvies. Before that, I spotted her going a couple more times. I did ask her about it, but she ducked the question and never gave me an answer.'

'I'm sorry about that,' Bunty said as she joined the pair and sat down beside Molly. 'I didn't know where to begin and you both deserved the truth.'

Molly felt embarrassed at being caught discussing Bunty. 'I'm sorry. I didn't mean to talk behind your back. We are worried about you. Connie warned us about hanging around the funfair during the first staff training session.'

Bunty sighed. 'If it were only that simple.'

'You'd better tell us before my punters arrive for their morning ride and our heart-throb Johnny comes looking for his latest conquest,' Plum announced, screwing up the wrapper from her sandwich and stuffing it in the pocket of her dungarees. 'That's if you still want to confide in us?'

Molly glared at Plum. 'Don't take any notice of

Plum – she's only larking about. We're both worried about you, Bunty. Why not start at the beginning?'

'I'll try. The truth is... The truth is...' Bunty held her breath, almost afraid to speak. 'I've been in prison. So has my fiancé, Gordon.' She noticed the look of horror on Molly's face and saw Plum's eyes open wide in shock. 'I knew I shouldn't have said anything.' She got up to walk away.

'You can stop right there. You've started now, so sit down and tell us what happened. I'd rather like to know if I'm sharing a chalet with a murderer,' Plum said, not unkindly. 'Come on, kid – spit it out,' she added in a mock American-gangster voice.

Bunty sighed but did as she'd been instructed. 'I'm not sure where to start.'

'At the beginning is as good a place as any,' Plum said. 'Tell us how you met Gordon.'

Bunty nodded. 'I was a nurse in the same hospital where Gordon worked as a doctor. I was attracted to him from the first day we met. You could say we were flung together. That first day, there was an air raid and so many injured were brought to the hospital. We worked non-stop helping those who were hurt, holding hands with people who weren't going to make it through the night and consoling their relatives. Gordon patched patients up, and I was there to dress wounds and help where I could. Afterwards, when we'd done all we could, we found ourselves sitting together in a pub and chatting. It wasn't until much later that I found out he was married, and by then it was too late.' Her face had taken on a haunted look as she

151

gazed into the distance, her mind now on a time and place long gone.

'So you had an affair with a married man?' Plum said, her face taking on a hard look.

Molly was surprised by Plum's attitude. 'Let Bunty finish her story,' she said, giving the girl a nod to continue speaking.

'I didn't know about Aileen for a long time. Gordon and I were just colleagues. I wasn't even sure he felt anything for me. We were thrown together because of the Blitz...'

'Don't tell me you blame Adolf for this,' Plum scoffed.

'No, I only blame myself for falling in love. We worked night and day together and got along so well. We were friends before ... before anything happened.'

'And his wife? Where was she while you were working with Gordon?' Molly asked. 'Did she find out about you?'

Bunty nodded, causing Plum to sniff in disapproval. 'Yes, but it's not like you think. Aileen had gone to live in Scotland with her parents. She had taken Jamie, their son, with her. They thought it would be safer than living in London. She didn't like the bombing. Her nerves weren't very good, and with Gordon working such long hours at the hospital, she was alone with the child and afraid. This all happened long before I met Gordon,' she added hastily.

'She found out?' Molly urged her, aware that time was passing and they would need to head towards reception for the start of the nature ramble.

'Aileen was making a trip to London, as she had

an important meeting to see the family solicitor on behalf of her parents. Or so she told Gordon. They'd been apart for two years by then. Gordon had hoped to see Jamie, but he'd been left with his grandparents. She said it was for his safety.'

'That's understandable,' Plum said. 'No one wants a kiddie to be in danger.'

'Gordon decided to tell Aileen about us. He went to see her alone. It was a very dignified meeting. She asked to meet me.'

'You went to see your lover's wife?' Plum asked in astonishment.

'We weren't... It wasn't like that. We were close but nothing more at that time.'

'But you went to see her?' Molly asked.

'She sent a note to tell us when she would be at her hotel. You've got to understand about their marriage. Aileen had never been close to Gordon. He married her to save her reputation.'

Plum burst out laughing. 'I've heard it all now. He's made excuses to you so he could have an affair behind his wife's back.'

'No, please believe me. It wasn't like that at all. I just wish someone would believe me.'

Molly put her arm round Bunty as she started to sob and tried to soothe her. 'Plum, let's give Bunty time to explain, shall we? She didn't have to tell us about her past life. I like Bunty. I don't think she's a bad sort. Come on, Bunty. Tell us what happened next.'

Bunty wiped the tears from her eyes and continued. 'She instructed us to be at her hotel at three and go straight to her room. I was almost sick with nerves. To face a man's wife and tell her

153

we were in love and wanted to marry isn't something I'd done before.' She gave a sad laugh. 'I really didn't want to wreck someone's life. I was so frightened. I was even offered a glass of water by the bellboy, who saw how nervous I was as we travelled up in the lift. He said he'd call a maid to fetch me one.'

'That sounds like a posh hotel,' Molly said.

'It was one of the larger hotels in Mayfair, which made me even more nervous,' Bunty added.

'Forget the glass of water and the posh hotel. Tell me what you meant about Gordon saving Aileen's reputation,' Plum insisted.

'Gordon married her in 1938 because she was expecting another man's baby. He felt responsible. He'd introduced Aileen to the man. Gordon's family had known Aileen's family. They'd both grown up together,' she blurted out through shuddering breaths.

'This gets worse by the minute,' Plum muttered as she got to her feet. 'Look, I'd like to hear more but I have people over there waiting for a pony. You'll have to tell me the rest later.' She patted Bunty's shoulder. 'It's not that I don't believe you, but I didn't expect to hear something like this. Chin up – I'm sure it's not as bad as you think.'

'It was. It is. You see, when we arrived at Aileen's hotel suite, the door was slightly ajar and we found her collapsed on the floor.'

'Oh my goodness, the poor woman,' Molly gasped. 'Whatever did you do?'

'Gordon checked to see if there was a pulse. There was, but it was faint. She was trying to speak but was very agitated. We did our best to calm her, but she wanted to talk. We couldn't make out much. She was worried about Jamie and begged Gordon to take care of him. She also kept speaking of Richard. He's Jamie's father,' she added, seeing Molly's puzzled expression. 'Gordon promised to take care of the boy. He has always provided for him, but we could see she was fading fast.'

'Was she ill?' Molly asked.

Bunty shook her head violently. 'We thought she'd tried to take her own life. The empty bottle was in her hand. She kept waving it at us. We assumed she was trying to show us what she'd done, but then she pointed to an empty tumbler on a side table. We realized she was trying to reach it and that must have been why she was lying on the floor. Gordon picked it up and checked the dregs at the bottom of the glass. It seemed the pills had been crushed and mixed with whisky.'

'My goodness, how awful. She must have been desperate,' Molly declared.

'She wasn't desperate and she hadn't taken her own life. She managed to tell us that she had found out Richard had taken all her money. She had come to London to confront him, but they'd had several drinks before he'd drugged her and left. She managed to explain that to us. She'd also wanted to set Gordon free so we could marry. Her trip had been to put her life in order, but instead she died.'

Molly was puzzled. 'Did you not tell the police what she had said?'

'We tried. It was as Gordon was lifting Aileen onto the bed that a maid arrived with my glass of water. After that, it was a blur, as the maid's screams brought people to the room. The police arrived just as Aileen passed away.'

Molly didn't know what to think. There were so many questions she wanted to ask. 'Did they catch the person who did it, this Richard?'

Bunty sighed. 'They never looked for anyone else.'

'What do you mean, they never looked for anyone else?' Molly exclaimed. 'Surely if it was foul play, there would have been an investigation?'

Bunty looked sad. 'It was the height of the Blitz. There was enough evidence to show the culprits were in the room. I was charged along with Gordon and we went to prison.'

'Did the police find out the truth?'

Bunty shook her head and started to sob. 'No. I was let out a couple of months ago and met Gordon here.'

Molly was mystified. 'But if they didn't find the real murderer, why did Gordon get out of prison so soon?'

Bunty gulped and tried to speak between her sobs. 'Gordon escaped during an air raid. He's been on the run these past years and waiting for me.'

10

Molly was surprised that she managed to get through the next couple of hours with so many thoughts buzzing around inside her head. It wasn't until she was marching the crocodile of children along the beach with a bracing wind in her face that she was able to focus on what was happening around her. After Bunty's disclosure about Aileen's death in the hotel and how Gordon had escaped from prison, the girl had burst into hysterical sobs that had only subsided into quiet tears when Plum had rushed over and slapped her face to bring her to her senses.

They'd helped Bunty back to the chalet and tucked her up in bed. Molly then dashed to reception, where she'd reported to Connie that Bunty was unwell and most likely off duty for the day. She'd found another redcoat to cover her friend's duties on the nature trail and had managed to get her large brood of happy children under control just as Johnny Johnson arrived to observe proceedings. Fortunately, he was content to take the tail end of the long line of excited children as they marched off towards the beach.

'Come closer, children,' Molly called loudly as they reached the shoreline. The tide was out as far as it would go, so at least there was no chance of the more adventurous youngsters being knocked over by an incoming wave.

'Are we going to fish for the crabs now, miss?' young Freddie Sangster asked.

'We don't fish for crabs. They crawl out of the sea and bite our toes,' a girl with a large white bow in her hair informed Freddie. She stood a head taller than the boy and looked down on him as some children tittered and others shrieked, trying to stand on one leg in case the dangerous crustaceans crept up on them. 'Doesn't your daddy teach you anything?'

Molly felt nothing but sympathy for young Freddie, but needn't have worried. 'My dad's dead.' He squared up to the girl. 'But he did tell me about crabs, and you can go fishing for them,' he announced pointedly.

The girl opened her mouth to continue the conversation, but before she could utter a word, Johnny stepped forward. 'Whoa there! You are both right,' he said, kneeling down so his face was level with theirs.

The girl was not going to back down easily. 'Crabs can't swim like fish,' she said, staring back at Johnny indignantly.

Molly fought the urge to laugh and had to place her hand over her mouth to hide her grin. How ever is he going to get out of this? she thought.

Johnny looked at Molly and smiled. For just a moment she felt a connection with the man. Perhaps beneath that movie-star persona there was a perfectly normal man who didn't have women falling at his feet and glamorous starlets on his arm.

'You are right, Susan,' he said, looking at the label pinned to her cardigan. 'Crabs can't swim,

158

but they do live in the sea and we can catch them.'

Susan thought for a moment before answering. 'I've only seen them in rock pools, and there aren't any pools here, so we can't catch them.'

Freddie sidled closer to Johnny. 'Tell us how you fish for them, mister.'

'Well, Freddie, it takes a special kind of fisherman to catch a crab. We need a length of string, a rock and a piece of bacon,' Johnny explained.

'Nah!' Freddie laughed. 'You're pulling my leg.'

The children who had gathered round expecting a fight between Susan and Freddie joined in with his laughter.

'Who would like to come crabbing?' Johnny asked.

Excited children raised their hands and started to shout, 'Me, me!' and jump up and down.

'Perhaps we can ask Redcoat Molly to arrange a crabbing trip.' He looked at Molly and winked.

'I'm sure that can be arranged.' Molly nodded. 'If Redcoat Johnny will come along and show us what to do.'

Johnny agreed. 'Now, let's get cracking with this nature trail. Is it a competition, Redcoat Molly?' he asked as he brushed sand from his trousers.

Molly quickly called the children together and put them into their house groups with a redcoat in charge of each. 'You have an hour to find all the items on the list I've given to your group leader. When your time is up, I'm going to blow my whistle. Then there will be a quiz about what you've found. Points will be awarded for your house. Good luck, everyone. Three, two, one, go!' Molly blew her whistle and the children raced off with their redcoat leaders in hot pursuit. It was going to be a busy hour!

Johnny had been put in charge of Kent House, much to the glee of young Freddie, who had taken the entertainment adviser by the hand and was busy chatting about crabs as they headed off to find seaweed and shells.

Molly checked that each group of children was engrossed in their tasks and then sat down on the soft sand to check her notes. She didn't want to miss out even one part of the itinerary she'd planned for the children but was finding it hard to concentrate after learning about Bunty and her fiancé.

The wind had eased off and Molly enjoyed feeling the sun on her face. If she didn't have the responsibility of her job, she could easily have closed her eyes and dozed for a while. A shadow passed over the papers on her lap, making Molly squint up into the sun. She shaded her eyes to see more clearly. A tall man dressed casually in slacks and an open-necked blue shirt, his hair a little too long and stubble on his chin, stood over her. Molly jumped, more in surprise than fear. 'Can I help you?' she asked for want of something better to say.

'Good morning,' he replied in a polite, well-spoken voice. 'I was looking for Bunty Grainger. I thought she would be on duty here today.'

She frowned. 'Gordon?'

'May I?' the man asked, before sitting down next to Molly when she nodded her approval. 'You must be Molly. Bunty has spoken of you. Do you know where she is? It's important I speak to her as soon as possible.'

'She's unwell. I thought it better she stay in our chalet and rest today.'

Gordon looked alarmed. 'What's wrong? I should go to her. I may be able to help.'

Molly held on to the man's arm to stop him jumping to his feet and racing off towards the holiday camp. 'It's best you don't. She was sleeping when I left her. She became distraught after she told us what happened with Aileen.' She watched a look of concern spread over Gordon's face.

'Who else did she tell?' he asked.

'It's all right. Only Plum and myself know about … about what happened. Even then Bunty didn't tell us everything, as she became distressed. We only know you escaped prison during an air raid and you've been hiding ever since. She was upset about what you told her yesterday evening.'

'So you know?'

'Yes, Gordon. I know you both went to prison. I don't understand why you escaped, and I do question why you would do such a thing. However, that is your decision. I'm just concerned for Bunty. She seems to have ruined her life because of you.' Molly felt her anger rising. Bunty was a good sort. She didn't deserve to be dragged into Gordon's problems.

'I love Bunty. I'd never do anything to hurt her. Please don't get her in trouble with the police. If they found out she knew where I was hiding, she would no doubt be sent back to prison. I don't think she could cope if that were to happen.'

Molly knew this to be the truth. 'I want to help Bunty. If that means helping her to move away

161

from Skegness and forget you ever existed, then so be it,' she said, raising her voice to push home her point.

Gordon ran his fingers through his hair. 'What can I do to show you I care for Bunty? Please meet me this evening and I'll explain.'

'Molly will not be meeting you this evening,' Johnny said as he approached the couple. 'Aren't you one of the fairground workers? You've been told not to mix with the campers. We've had problems with your sort in the past.'

Molly cringed. How much had Johnny heard?

Gordon rose to his feet. 'I meant no harm,' he said to Johnny. 'Molly, please consider what I've said.' He turned and walked back along the beach, his hands in his pockets and his head bent as though he had the troubles of the world on his shoulders.

Molly felt a twinge of regret for the way she had spoken to Gordon. It couldn't be easy to be on the run all the time and not know whom to trust. How do you prove your innocence when the world thinks you've done something wrong? she thought as she watched Gordon head towards the funfair.

'How long have you known that chap?' Johnny asked, staring down at Molly.

Molly felt herself bristle. How dare he question her in this way? 'What I do and who I associate with is no concern of yours, Mr Johnson,' she answered indignantly. Getting to her feet, ignoring the hand he held out to help her, she checked the time on her wristwatch, not wishing to spoil the children's competition. Holding her chin high, she faced him, feeling her face start to glow with

162

anger. 'Have I ever questioned your choice of female companion?' she asked. 'Now, if you'll excuse me, I have children to look after.' Walking away from Johnny, she stumbled as she caught her foot in a length of dried seaweed. Righting herself, she headed to where the children were congregating, Johnny's laughter ringing in her ears.

The nature trail was a complete success. As the tired but happy group headed back to the holiday camp for lunch, Molly was asked repeatedly what she was organizing next.

'Perhaps Redcoat Molly can arrange our crabbing expedition. We will announce details on Radio Butlins and at mealtimes,' Johnny told the children.

There were cheers and shouts of happiness as the children thanked Molly and the other redcoats before heading to find their parents.

Molly planned to leave her equipment in the staffroom before collecting sandwiches for lunch to take back to the chalet for herself and Bunty. She wasn't on duty until later in the afternoon, when she would be helping out around the swimming pool, where the beauty pageant would be judged. She heard Johnny calling her name.

'Molly, I just wanted to say well done for this morning's entertainment. Apart from your little dalliance, it went very well. We must plan more adventures for the children,' Johnny said before disappearing into his office.

She wanted to stamp her foot on the floor in anger. The infuriating man made her so mad. How dare he question whom she spoke to when she'd spotted him with many different women on his arm? What worried her more was why she cared so much.

Bunty was sleeping soundly when Molly arrived at their chalet. She left the sandwich and cold drink by the girl's bed and took her own lunch outside along with her notepad. Molly wanted to write to Kath and George again to let them know how she was getting on in her new job. She also wanted to ask a favour of Kath. It would have been her mother's birthday in a few weeks, and as Molly would not be able to travel to Kent to lay flowers on her grave in person, she wanted Kath to do this for her. Molly's heart ached whenever she thought of her mum. Would she have approved of her working in a holiday camp? She tried to console herself with the thought that she was working with children and this was no different to when she helped out with the Brownies and Girl Guides. She smiled to herself when she decided that her mum would have loved to have known about the camp and the many exciting events her daughter was involved with. She would have laughed knowing that a matinee idol was one of the redcoats. Charlotte Missons had always enjoyed the cinema.

After tucking a ten-shilling note inside the letter to cover the cost of a bouquet, she wondered about arranging for Kath and George to visit the holiday camp. They would love it, she was sure.

She next dashed off a letter to Freda, in which she included more about Johnny. Brushing crumbs from her lap, she went inside the chalet to wash her hands and face, and prepare herself for the afternoon's entertainment. Changing out of her shorts, she pulled on a white skirt that was part of her uniform. The redcoats were much admired in their red-and-white uniforms, and staff were proud to represent Butlins in their official attire. Molly loved the feel of the pleated skirt as it swished round her legs.

After dropping off her letters at the post room, she headed to the swimming pool along with crowds of campers. Already she was beginning to remember names and was touched when the holidaymakers remembered hers. She bumped into the Sangster family as they were settling themselves into deckchairs for an afternoon of entertainment.

'Our Freddie really enjoyed himself this morning,' Olive Sangster said. 'He hasn't stopped telling us about those blooming crabs. Is it right your young man is taking the kids crabbing?'

Molly blushed. 'Yes, there will be a trip to the pier where they can fish for crabs. Mr Johnson is arranging it, but he isn't my young man,' she added quickly.

'Well, I wouldn't say no,' Olive declared loudly. 'You snap him up before someone else does, my love.'

Molly laughed at Olive's joke. Goodness, did any of the other campers think they were a couple? 'Are you going to enter the beauty pageant?' she asked Gladys.

'I've told her she should enter. She'd give the younger women a run for their money.'

Gladys blushed. 'I don't know about that. I'm a

165

married woman ... I mean a widow,' she faltered. 'Isn't it for the younger girls?'

Molly could see that Gladys was wavering. 'Other mums are entering, Gladys. Why not give it a go? It's just a bit of fun.'

'Go on, girl – get up there. Wave the flag for Woolwich. Our Edith and Freddie will be that proud,' Olive insisted, giving her daughter-in-law a playful push. 'I'll keep our deckchairs safe.'

Gladys grinned and reached for her bag. 'In that case, I'd best pull a brush through my hair and put a bit of lipstick on. I don't want to let the side down.'

'Good luck,' Molly said, before moving on to encourage more young women to join in. Secretly she hoped Gladys Sangster would win, as she was such a likeable woman and had been through a lot in her life. Then again, so had many other people she'd met at Butlins that week.

By the time announcements had been made over the busy tannoy system and the judges had settled behind their table, pens poised to take notes, there were quite a number of young women lined up round the side of the swimming pool hoping to win the coveted title of that week's 'Butlins Beauty Queen, Skegness'. The judges were announced: two older campers who had holidayed at Butlins before the war, the local mayor and also a young starlet whose parents lived nearby. She was appearing in a well-received film that was currently doing the rounds in cinemas. Molly had seen the movie with Freda not long before she left Erith to start her new job at Butlins. Going by the way the young woman hung on to Johnny's arm as he led her to the table, she either knew him very well or was unable to walk unaided, Molly thought to herself with a grin. He certainly attracted the women.

Campers cheered and whistled as the judges were announced and Johnny took to the stage, microphone in hand. After welcoming one and all to Butlins, he explained that today's winner would go through to the next stage of the competition, which would culminate in an all-expenses-paid final at London's Albert Hall early next year to find the Butlins Beauty Queen of 1946. Not only that, there were many prizes for runners-up, along with sashes for the lucky ladies.

It took some time for each contestant, number card in hand, to be introduced and parade in front of the judges, who wrote furiously and conferred with each other after each lady had walked by. Gladys looked pretty in her green bathing costume, her shining auburn hair bouncing on her shoulders as she walked confidently before the judges. Not as tall as many of the other contestants, some of whom seemed to be old hands at such competitions going by the way they posed for the judges, she stood self-assuredly in front of the table with a friendly smile. When asked where she came from, she announced, 'Woolwich in southeast London,' and quickly added, 'with my two children and mother-in-law.' At which point, there was more cheering from the large crowd watching. No doubt all Londoners.

There was a break while the judges conferred. Johnny explained to the holidaymakers that there were so many beautiful contestants that ten women would be called forward before the winner was announced. The entertainment team stood round a piano and sang a selection of songs to keep the audience amused.

Silence fell over the crowd of holidaymakers as Johnny approached the microphone once more with a card handed to him by the head judge, the mayor of Skegness.

'Ladies and gentlemen, the following ten contestants will step forward and compete to be crowned this week's "Butlins Beauty Queen".' He slowly announced each number, pausing for effect to encourage those watching to wonder if their mum, sister, daughter or girlfriend was one of the lucky ten finalists. 'The final contestant is ... number thirteen, Gladys Sangster from south-east London.'

Molly cheered loudly along with the crowd, who all seemed to support the pretty redhead. She could see Edith and Freddie were wild with excitement that their mum's name had been announced. Olive, too, was waving her sun hat in the air.

The unlucky contestants left the swimming-pool area with much sympathetic clapping from the happy crowd. The fortunate ten ladies again walked round the pool as the judges contemplated who would be in the final three and the entertainment team sang 'A Pretty Girl Is Like a Melody', which Molly recognized from one of her favourite films *The Great Ziegfeld*.

As the young women once more lined up in front of the judges, a hush fell over the crowd. Johnny again took a card from the head judge and smiled as he announced third place; a popular choice among those watching, a tall brunette girl from Scotland accepted a sash and an envelope that the campers were told contained a voucher to be used in one of the onsite Butlins shops.

Silence fell again as the anticipation grew among the crowd. They were not disappointed when Johnny announced that Gladys Sangster had won a prize of five pounds, a voucher for a Butlins shop and another for the hairdressing salon. Molly could see Gladys's family jumping for joy and Olive fishing for a handkerchief in her handbag. She felt quite emotional herself.

The competition culminated with a pretty blonde girl from Birmingham being crowned 'Butlins Beauty Queen' of the week. The three happy women again paraded round the pool to much applause and cheering.

Molly helped clear up and stopped to chat to some of the contestants before popping over to see the Sangster family and offer her congratulations to Gladys.

'I think we ought to have a quiet holiday after all this excitement,' Gladys said. She appeared embarrassed by the attention of fellow holiday-makers who had offered their congratulations. 'I'm all of a fluster what with the bingo win and now this. People like us aren't usually this lucky.'

'Enjoy your prizes, Gladys,' Molly said as she gave the woman a hug.

'I don't need prizes,' the modest woman replied. 'Olive can have her hair done, and the kids can use the shop voucher to buy themselves a toy each. The money will go into our savings pot. I'm

169

just happy to have taken part.'

'Don't forget to have your photograph taken along with the other finalists. It's going to be done on the lawn near reception. Do you want me to walk over with you?'

'Please, Molly, that would be lovely. I'm more than a little embarrassed by the attention,' Gladys said.

The two women headed towards reception chatting amiably about the area of the country they knew so well. Molly explained how her parents always took her to Woolwich Market as a child and she had fond memories of the special trip to buy fruit and nuts each Christmas Eve. 'That was long before the war,' she added wistfully.

'Why, my father-in-law probably served you – he had a fruit-and-veg stall in the open-air market. What a small world it is,' Gladys said. 'Olive always says we couldn't rob a bank as someone would probably know us,' she added with a laugh.

'The same could be said for those of us who live in Erith,' Molly agreed. 'Do you work on the market?'

'Goodness me, no. I work in Woolworths. It's too much like hard work for me out there in all weather.'

'My friend Freda works in the Erith branch,' Molly said.

'There, didn't I say it was a small world?' Gladys declared. 'Did you hear about the Bexleyheath branch being hit with an oil bomb and staff and customers being killed?'

Molly nodded. 'Freda told me about it, but

170

only after the war. Her boss and friend were injured. Many of the employees went to work at Erith while the store was being rebuilt.'

Gladys nodded. 'We had a few join us. Who'd have thought it could happen and remain such a secret?'

'We didn't want Hitler hearing about it and thinking he was winning the war, did we?' Molly said.

'Certainly not,' Gladys agreed, 'and it worked 'cos he didn't, did he?'

'Thank goodness or we'd not be here having a lovely time now,' Molly said as they arrived by the flower-bordered lawn. 'Here we are, and the photographer has just arrived by the look of things. Do you want me to wait?'

'Please. I've not had my photo taken since my wedding day. If only my Joe could see me now,' she said sadly.

'I'm sure he'd be more than proud, just like Mrs Sangster and your children,' Molly said.

Gladys gave her a grin. 'I think he would have been. If he'd been with us now, he'd have put his name down for the sports team as well as the boxing. If only things had been different,' she added reflectively.

'Hello, ladies,' the photographer said as Molly and Gladys approached. 'Now, would you stand just there next to this lovely lady and we will have this over and done with in a flash. Would you stand away a little?' he asked Molly, who dutifully stepped behind the man so she didn't appear in the photographs.

Butlins had a group of official photographers

who not only worked at organized events but also walked around the camp taking pictures of happy faces and holidaymakers enjoying themselves. Within hours the photos would be displayed in reception and also in a special shop where campers could buy copies to take home as mementos. This particular photographer had been on the beach at the children's nature trail earlier in the day and had taken photographs of each of the teams.

Molly noticed the sash worn by that week's winner had slipped slightly and the word 'Butlins' could not be seen. 'Excuse me,' she called to the man as he clicked away with his camera. 'One of the sashes needs adjusting.'

The photographer tutted. 'Then adjust it, please.'

Molly dashed forward and straightened the sash, making sure the word 'Butlins' could be seen on the other two finalists' sashes as well. 'That's better.' She returned to stand behind the man. However, as he continued to stay in one spot and click away with his camera, Molly became puzzled. Why was he not taking individual photographs of the three women? They would be bound to purchase more, and she knew that Butlins loved campers to take home anything with the word 'Butlins' inscribed on it, as then friends and families of the holidaymakers would show interest and hopefully book their own holiday at the camp. 'Do you think you could take some individual photographs as well?' she asked.

The photographer sighed. 'Everyone's an expert,' he said to no one in particular. 'OK, ladies, let's be having you.' He pointed to Gladys. 'Stand over there by the flagpole, darling, and give me a big smile.'

Gladys did as she was told, but again Molly was puzzled. 'Er, excuse me, but aren't you taking photographs straight into the sunshine?' Her father had been a keen photographer and had taught her the fundamentals of how to take a good photograph. Surely, as a professional, this man should know such basic rules.

The man, who had been clicking away with his camera, turned and glared at her. 'I knew that.' He looked towards the three women in their bathing suits and smirked. 'Redcoat Bunty should be doing my job.' He laughed.

Molly noticed Gladys open her mouth to say something and then think better of it as Molly grinned at her. It was strange, though, that the man would think she was Bunty.

Molly returned to her chalet. She wanted to check on Bunty. If the girl was still poorly, they would have to decide what to do. She was pleased to see Plum there and Bunty not only out of bed but dressed in her Butlins uniform.

'How are you feeling?' she asked.

'A hundred times better. Thank you for taking me in hand. I don't deserve such good friends. That's if you still want to be my friend now you know I've been in prison,' she added, looking pensively between Plum and Molly.

'Don't be an ass,' Plum said. 'If you said you didn't kill Aileen, then we believe you.'

Molly checked the time on the small alarm clock by her bed. 'I have a suggestion. Why don't we get ready for the evening and take ourselves over to the cocktail bar? I'm not on duty this evening, but I'm expected to be in the ballroom for the old-time dancing. We would have an hour to chat about events.'

'What a good idea! I'm on entertainment duty too in the dance hall,' Plum said. 'That's why I'm out of the jodhpurs and wearing a frock.' She gave a twirl and the two girls clapped. Plum looked so different with her hair pinned up and in a yellow dress with a tight bodice and flared skirt. 'You'd best check me over for any traces of straw. It gets everywhere.'

Bunty grinned at Plum. There wasn't a hair out of place, let alone the chance of finding straw. 'I'm on duty for dinner and in the ballroom afterwards. I'd love to taste a cocktail. I've never tried one before. It all sounds so glamorous,' she sighed.

'Then now's the time to try,' Plum said. 'I'll be your teacher.'

Molly rushed to get ready and join her new friends, though she did wonder what world Plum lived in to be an expert on cocktails and horses.

11

'You've converted me. I'll never drink anything but cocktails from now on,' Molly declared as she placed a straw in her second drink of the evening. 'What did you say this was called?'

'It's a Manhattan, and if you keep drinking

them at the rate you're going, we will have to carry you back to bed.' Plum laughed. 'Do you like your snowball, Bunty?'

'Mm, it's delicious. I must confess it doesn't feel as though I'm drinking alcohol. This is more like a bedtime drink.'

Plum hooted with laughter. 'I don't believe the pair of you. First you choose your drinks by their colour, and then one of you knocks them back as if it's lemonade and the other thinks it's the same as a cup of cocoa.' She sipped her own drink delicately before pulling an olive from the cocktail stick and placing it in her mouth.

'What's yours called?' Bunty asked. 'It looks rather posh.'

Plum picked up the long-stemmed glass and raised it to both girls. 'This, my loves, is a Martini. If it's good enough for Churchill, then it's good enough for me. Cheers!'

'Cheers!' they both echoed as they raised their own glasses in return.

'Now, can you please explain to me why Gordon scaled the walls of his high-security prison and legged it?' Plum asked in a ghastly cockney accent.

Despite the seriousness of the question, the girls laughed. 'It wasn't quite like that,' Bunty said. 'He was so miserable knowing that I was locked up for something I'd not done that he was desperate to have someone know the truth. When the opportunity arose during an air raid, he took it and escaped. He doesn't want to implicate me in his escape. He feels so guilty for me serving time as it is.'

Molly could see that Plum was trying hard to keep her temper in check as Bunty extolled the virtues of her fiancé.

Plum sighed. 'Are you sure that this Richard chappie killed Aileen, and Gordon hasn't been stringing you along?'

Bunty looked blankly at both girls for a moment. 'It was Richard. I am sure of it.'

Molly frowned. 'Honestly?'

Bunty nodded. 'Most definitely. Aileen whispered it to us before she passed away. She'd spoken to Gordon the last time he went to Scotland to visit Jamie and told him that Richard needed money as his investments had done badly. Richard had suggested that Aileen should divorce Gordon and marry him so that he could settle his debts.'

Molly and Plum fell silent as they absorbed this new information.

'But how can Gordon ever clear his name?' Molly asked.

'By going to Scotland and looking for Aileen's diary,' Bunty said. 'We thought that if we worked our way slowly north, then by the time we reached Dumfries, anyone looking for Gordon would have given up, thinking he was heading to where Jamie lives with his grandparents.'

'Did Aileen always live with her parents? Molly asked. To her it seemed strange that a grown woman with a child would still live at home.

Bunty sighed. 'I've not lied to you once, and yes, Aileen had continued to live in Dumfries with her parents. They had a vast estate there and she wanted Jamie to be safe. Her marriage to Gordon

176

was for convenience only so that Jamie had ... had a proper name. She only came to London for business and that wasn't often. That is why Gordon was confident he would find her diary.'

'Surely the police...' Plum started to speak.

'No. As far as they were concerned they had the murderers, and why waste time making more investigations when they were short-staffed and the Blitz was at its height?'

'It's beginning to make sense to me, Bunty. In the little time I've known you, I haven't for one moment thought of you as being able to kill someone.'

Bunty gave Molly a watery smile. 'Thank you.'

Plum drained her glass and picked up her purse to buy another round. 'So, what makes you think you've been followed here?'

'I sent a postcard to my mum to let her know I was fine and she wasn't to worry about me.'

Plum rolled her eyes in mock despair. 'Not a view from Butlins?'

Bunty nodded. 'I never gave it a thought until my sister wrote to say that a stranger had come asking after me. Mum got annoyed, as she said I'd served my time and people should mind their own business. She waved the postcard at him to show how I had a proper job and sent him packing. I feel awful that I've deceived them, as I promised I'd not see Gordon again. The shame would kill my mum. That's why I've not been home.'

'So this man knows that you're here and there's a possibility that Gordon is in the area as well,' Molly said. 'Did your sister give you any idea what he looked like?'

'She just said he would be in his fifties and was a short man with weaselly features...'

'And an ill-fitting coat?' Molly finished for her.

Bunty was astonished. 'How did you know that?'

'Because he's here and she's seen him,' Plum announced.

Molly nodded. She was thinking of the irritable photographer who'd called her by the name of 'Bunty' that very afternoon. She quickly explained to her two friends about the man and how he had called her by the wrong name.

'It doesn't make sense. Why would he think you were me?' Bunty asked.

'Because he's a member of staff and would have seen the staff rota and known where you were working,' Plum explained.

'And he thought you'd be on the beach this morning for the nature trail so he appeared there to take photographs. Fortunately, he mistook me for you,' Molly declared with a smile on her face, 'and that's why he called me Bunty when I took Gladys to have her photograph taken this afternoon.'

'I'd say that was a lucky break,' Plum said as she placed fresh drinks on the table. 'It means you can come and go for a while without Mr Snoop following you. It won't be so easy for Molly, though, as he will be hot on her heels expecting to find Gordon.'

Molly groaned. 'He may have found him...'

'What?' the other two girls asked.

'Gordon came looking for you on the beach. He sat and spoke to me for a while.'

Bunty turned pale and gulped her cocktail,

which made her cough. Plum thumped her on the back. 'Cough it up, girl,' she said.

'I'm not sure if Mr Snoop was there when I was talking to Gordon. Fortunately, Johnny Johnson was not amused with someone from the fairground talking to a redcoat. He sent him packing.'

'I should be annoyed at Mr Johnson for treating Gordon like that, but for once it may have done him a favour.' Bunty sighed with relief.

Plum clapped her hands together in delight 'I have an idea that might just help Bunty and Gordon, but it all depends on whether Mr Snoop is a copper or a private investigator. I don't fancy deceiving the police.'

Bunty frowned. 'It's awfully decent of you, Plum, but I don't want anyone getting into trouble to protect us.' Plum looked over her shoulder to make sure no one was within earshot. Fortunately, those who had been nearby were now heading for dinner, as the tannoy was booming out announcements for the first sitting. 'If we fooled Mr Snoop into believing Molly was you for a while,' she whispered to Bunty, 'it may give you a few days to get away from the area.'

Bunty's eyes lit up for a moment before she looked glum. 'Don't forget the police know Gordon escaped prison. Even though he isn't guilty, he needs to prove it. If I disappear, Mr Snoop might hear and then you could be hauled over the coals for protecting us. It was a lovely idea, though. Thank you.'

Molly had been thoughtful as Bunty spoke. 'I do believe we should check who Mr Snoop is before we do anything else. Who do you think could do that for us?'

Plum jumped to her feet and grinned. 'I reckon Spud is our man. He knows everything that goes on in the camp. I've known him for years. I'll scoot down to the gatehouse after dinner and sound him out. Now, let's finish our drinks and hurry to dinner or we'll be in trouble with Mr Johnson, and we don't want him sniffing about.'

Molly raised her glass to her two chums and sipped the last of the Manhattan through the straw. Again she found herself wondering about Plum. How could she have known Spud for so long when she'd only worked at Butlins the same length of time as she had?

Plum set off at a brisk pace down the long drive to the gatehouse, where she knew Spud would be working. She smiled to herself. It had been reassuring to know someone at the holiday camp when she'd started her job. She'd thought long and hard about returning to work, but knowing there was a friendly face at Butlins had encouraged her to accept the position of running the busy stables. She knew Spud had put in a good word for her with 'the governor' and would never be able to repay him for his generous help. Plum had been brought up to believe that blood was thicker than water, but that hadn't been the case since her William had died. In fact, if it hadn't been for Spud and his sister, Tilly, she'd have been alone without a penny these past few years. No, family meant nothing, despite being able to trace her line back to William the Conqueror.

'I do feel dizzy,' Molly exclaimed as she collapsed in the seat next to Plum.

'Those cocktails take a little getting used to,' Plum said as she lit a cigarette, waving smoke away from where Molly was fanning her hot face with her hand.

'No, it's all this dancing. I didn't imagine for one minute I'd have to join in so much. I haven't missed one since the band started playing.'

Plum passed her a drink and laughed as Molly sniffed the contents. 'Don't worry – it's only orange squash. I thought you'd need one, so I picked it up when I bought mine.'

'Aren't you dancing?' Molly asked.

'Thankfully no. The campers apparently associate me with my donkeys and give me a wide berth.'

Molly laughed. 'If you want, I can tell them you've had a bath since mucking out the stables.'

Plum raised her eyebrows. 'Best keep them in ignorance. I'm enjoying just sitting here ... and thinking.'

'I take it you spoke to Spud?'

'Yes. He's a good sort is Spud. I told him everything we know. It's all right – he won't tell a soul,' she added quickly, seeing the horrified look cross Molly's face.

'I know he won't tell. It was just a shock realizing that someone else knows about Bunty and Gordon,' Molly said thoughtfully. 'I agree Spud is definitely a good sort. He took care of me the day I arrived, when I was ready to turn tail and run home.'

'Why didn't you?' Plum asked, looking Molly in

the eye.

'I couldn't ... but that's a story for another time,' she added wryly. 'We need to help Bunty right now.'

'Spud said it would mean a bit of ducking and diving for a few days, but then things would be fine. Do you know what he meant? He also reckons our Mr Snoop gave us the answer when he called you Bunty.'

Molly laughed. 'I've heard the saying before, and yes, we can duck and dive around our Mr Snoop.' She noticed the puzzled expression on Plum's face. 'Imagine a boxer jumping and swerving in the ring to avoid an opponent's punches. We need to do the same with Mr Snoop.'

'I think we can do that, but what about the rest?'

'Mr Snoop thinks I'm Bunty, so let him carry on believing it for a few days. It will mean Bunty is safe from his prying eyes. As long as we're careful, we won't be doing anything wrong. I don't want Mr Snoop arresting us for breaking any law if he *is* a copper.'

'That was something else Spud told me. Our Mr Snoop isn't a police officer or a private eye. He's a journalist and goes by the name of Charlie Porter. He's from one of the seedier national newspapers, so we can have our fun with him and keep Bunty safe at the same time,' Plum said with a glint in her eye. 'Look out – here comes the boss man. I'll tell you what else Spud said when we are back at our chalet.'

Molly turned to see Johnny Johnson making a beeline for her across the dance floor. She sipped her drink and tried to remain calm. She only had to look at the man and her heart skipped a beat. She placed her glass back on the table before she spilt it down her dance frock.

He held out his hand. 'May I have the next dance?'

Molly nodded. As he led her to the middle of the floor, the band started to play. She recognized her favourite tune, 'Moonlight Serenade'. The lights dimmed and the dance floor became illuminated by the glitterball twinkling above their heads. A saxophonist played the romantic Glenn Miller tune as a female singer stepped forward and started to sing. The words were so romantic. Johnny held her close in his arms. He was wearing the tuxedo she'd so admired the evening before. She breathed in the scent of his lightly spiced cologne. They slowly covered the floor and she was putty in his hands as he guided her past other couples who were enjoying the romantic moment. Time seemed to stand still and she wished the song would never end. Johnny's lips were close to her hair; she could feel his breath, slow and controlled. It would be so easy to wrap her arms around his neck and guide his lips to hers. She tried to pull herself together, but the music and being in his arms swept her along on a wave of desire.

The dancers applauded as the song came to an end. Molly, still feeling the effects of being held by Johnny, turned to go back to her seat. 'Not yet.' He smiled. 'There's a special request next I know you'll enjoy it.'

The lights were undimmed as the compére

stepped up to the microphone. 'Ladies and gentle-men, we've received a request for that well-known dance "The Lambeth Walk". Please take your places on the dance floor. If you don't know the steps, just put one foot in front of the other and walk!'

The band started playing an intro as campers flooded the dance floor. Molly found herself grabbed and pulled along in the wave of dancers as they started to sing and step out. Looking around, she could see Johnny standing by the side of the room lighting a cigarette as he watched her dancing with the campers. Had he made the request for this dance? Molly wondered. As she looked at his smiling face, she thought perhaps he had and recalled that night in London when she'd seen him at the stage door with the glamorous actress who'd been splashed with muddy water.

'You make a lovely couple,' the lady who'd linked arms with Molly shouted, competing with the music and singing.

'I beg your pardon,' Molly said, trying to catch her words above the din.

'I said that you and Johnny make a lovely couple.'

'Oh no, it's nothing like that. He's just my boss,' Molly assured her.

The woman nudged her and winked. 'It didn't look like it to me. It's not every girl that can hook a film star. You hang on to him, lovey.'

Molly had no choice but to continue dancing and singing along with the campers, but she was horrified to think that anyone would assume that she was chasing after Johnny just because he'd appeared in films. No, she'd still find him infuriating if he were a butcher, a baker or a candlestick-maker.

'The Lambeth Walk' finished and led straight into Butlins own 'Goodnight, Campers', based on the well-known song 'Goodnight, Sweetheart'.

'Come on, miss – give us your arm. We can't have you standing there on your own for the last dance of the evening. Budge up there, Sal, and let the lovely redcoat join us,' a rather merry camper exclaimed as they linked arms and sang along together. Molly had found the song amusing when she first heard it, with its humorous references to holiday-camp life, but tonight it seemed a poignant end to the evening.

Heading back to where Plum was sitting, she was surprised to see her nodding in a pointed way. 'Bunty, there you are. It's time we got ourselves off to bed. We have a busy day tomorrow.'

Molly was puzzled but thought it better not to reply, so just finished her drink, which was still on the table, and collected her handbag. As the pair left the ballroom, they passed Mr Snoop with his camera. Had he been listening to Plum?

'Goodnight,' Plum said emphatically to the man. 'Come along, Bunty – I'm that exhausted I could fall into bed right now.'

The two girls giggled as they headed to the chalet, where they found Bunty tucked up in bed reading a book. It had been Bunty's turn to collect the thermos flask. She jumped out of bed to pour the hot cocoa into three mugs while the girls prepared for bed.

Plum told Bunty what Spud had said about Mr

185

Snoop. 'It seems that he's not long back working on the paper after being in the Observer Corps during the war. Spud reckons him to be a cocky so-and-so. Didn't stop bragging about his work when he popped into the gatehouse to ask Spud a favour.'

'A favour?' Bunty looked worried.

'Yes. He said that if Spud spotted anything unusual with the campers, or got a sniff of a story, he would see him all right for a few bob. I must say Spud's turns of phrase confuse me at times,' Plum said with a frown.

Molly laughed at Plum's puzzlement. She was very fond of her new friend, but sometimes it was so funny when Plum didn't understand common expressions. She wondered how someone like Plum got to be working at Butlins. 'I was going to ask how our Mr Snoop could mistake me for Bunty if he knew the story of Aileen's murder, but you've answered my question. It sounds as though he is following up old stories from his newspaper, and with Bunty not long released from prison, he must think he can find Gordon.' She wrinkled her nose. 'I really don't like this man.'

Bunty again looked worried. 'I'm not happy with you pretending to be me. If I leave with Gordon and he finds out after a few days, he may cause trouble for you. I wouldn't want that to happen to my worst enemy.'

Plum thought for a while as she sipped her cocoa. 'I don't think you should leave Butlins.'

'But...' both girls said together.

Plum placed her mug down on the bedside table. 'Spud suggested, and I agree with him, that

186

if we continue with fooling Mr Snoop for a few days, it would give you time to help Gordon plan to leave the area and hopefully get to Scotland. His best chance of leaving would be on a Saturday, when we have the changeover of campers. There will be hundreds of people catching coaches and trains, so Gordon can join them without being noticed. If we continue to pretend you are Bunty' – she nodded to Molly – 'until the following Saturday, then revert to your right name, he will have one hell of a time trying to track Gordon, as we'd have had two changes of campers by then.'

Molly watched Bunty as she considered Plum's suggestion. After being separated from Gordon for so many years, could she say goodbye to him once more? 'Whatever you decide, Bunty, I'll support you,' she said, reassuring her new friend. She knew what it was like to have a friend when times were hard.

'Count me in too,' Plum added.

'Thank you, both.' Bunty took a deep breath before continuing. 'I know this reporter chap can't arrest Gordon, but if his story is published in a newspaper, it could lead the police to find him before he has a chance to clear his name. We all understand that Gordon is in serious trouble for escaping from prison. I would probably go back to prison for helping him. I don't know if I could see you both get into that much trouble for me.'

Plum considered what Bunty had said. 'I appreciate we may be getting into hot water, but I'm prepared to risk it. What if we say we did it as a prank and never knew about Gordon? Would that make you feel better? I don't feel Spud would have suggested we swap names if he thought we would get our collar felt.' She looked at Molly and grinned. 'I do know some working-class terms. I may come from landed gentry, but I'm also a working girl. I have a daughter to provide for.'

'A daughter? That's lovely,' Molly said. 'Is she with your husband?' She was aware that since the war many men were either injured or not yet in gainful employment.

For a moment, Plum looked sad. 'No. William died during the Battle of Britain. He was a Spitfire pilot and was killed before Elizabeth was born.' She looked at Molly and Bunty's distressed faces. 'Please don't be sad for me. Time has moved on and I'm coping. I have much to live for, and that's why I want to help you, Bunty, so that you and Gordon have something to look forward to.'

Bunty hugged her friends. 'I'm truly blessed to know such lovely people. I hope we can meet Elizabeth one day.'

Plum nodded, her face lighting up as she spoke. 'Most certainly. You must come to tea. I have a cottage a few miles from here. A good friend cares for Lizzie. I get to see her on my days off, and even on a half-day. How about you, Molly? You must be the only one among us with a normal family life...'

Molly gave a sad sigh. 'Unfortunately, my life is as complicated as yours. That's the reason I'm here.'

12

'So you see I had no choice but to leave Erith, at least for a few months, until my parents' solicitor returns from abroad and can hopefully sort out the whole sorry mess,' Molly said, giving a deep sigh. It was the following morning and she'd just explained to her two friends about her flight from Erith and what had led to her securing a job at Butlins.

Bunty placed her cup and saucer on top of the wall beside her. The girls had fallen into a routine of meeting for morning coffee whenever they could escape from their duties and were taking advantage of the late-May sunshine. Around them, campers were relaxing in deck-chairs or chatting with new friends made since arriving at Butlins. Sounds of splashing water and excited children could be heard from the nearby swimming pool. Along with Molly, Bunty would be heading to the pool to help with the weekly knobbly-knees competition when they had finished their drinks. 'I can see that these cousins would be a problem for you. It does seem strange that you never knew they existed.'

'The whole thing stinks, if you ask me,' Plum said, throwing her cigarette to the ground and stubbing it out with the toe of her riding boot. 'You handled Simon the right way, though,' she snorted.

Bunty glanced with annoyance at Plum. 'Molly hasn't long lost her parents, Plum. She shouldn't have experienced all this added worry. I don't think I'd be able to cope with what she's been through.'

Molly smiled at her friend. 'How can you say that when you've been in prison? I think you are to be admired for getting through that in one piece,' she said in amazement.

'I had my family,' she said, shrugging her shoulders. 'My parents didn't believe I'd done anything wrong, and they were there supporting me throughout my time in prison. I've not told them I'm with Gordon,' she added quickly. 'I know he's innocent, but I don't want them knowing anything that could get them into trouble if people like Charlie Porter start sniffing around.'

'But he *is* sniffing around,' sighed Molly, 'and they unwittingly gave him details of where you are.'

'At least they're not involved in what I get up to.' She smiled, thinking of her parents back home. 'I worried so much while I was locked away. They were in the thick of the bombing. The East End had it bad. At least my younger sisters were sent away with their classmates, though that worried Mum even more. Her letters to me were full of her wondering if they were safe. I felt powerless to help.'

'I felt the same when I joined the Land Army. Mum and Dad were in Erith, which is by the Thames, and were sitting targets for the Luftwaffe, with the docks nearby and factories like Vickers doing such important war work in nearby Crayford. There were times I wanted to jump on the next train and head for home just to see they were safe.' She looked into space as she added softly, 'They survived the Blitz only to die together in a car crash just a month before the war was officially declared over.'

'I can't begin to understand how you must be feeling, and you an only child.' Bunty put her arm round her new friend. 'Was there no way you could stay in Erith and fight it out?'

Molly shook her head, causing curls to bounce on her shoulders. 'I'm grateful I have good friends back in Erith, but I'm worried George and Kath will be harassed by Simon if he gets wind of the way we lied about ownership of the shop, or the fact we don't believe his mother owns the house. They're getting older and it just wouldn't be fair of me to saddle them with my problems. As for Freda, she's been a brick, but I'd hate her to be around if Simon became violent, or what if he sought her out in Woolworths and caused trouble in front of her bosses?'

'I'm sure your friends know what they've let themselves in for,' Bunty said.

'The shop is in good hands, Kath is caring for my parents' grave, and Freda is keeping her ears open and eyes peeled should anything untoward happen. I shall just have to stop worrying,' Molly agreed.

'They seem a good sort. Hoorah for good friends is what I say,' Plum added with a faraway look in her eyes. Giving herself a little shake, she jumped down from the flower-bordered wall on which she'd been sitting, next to Bunty, and brushed biscuit crumbs from the front of her overalls. 'I'm back to the stables before the queue of kiddies waiting for rides take things into their own hands. There's always one bright youngster wanting to take over my job. Who knew donkey rides would be so popular?' She headed towards the stable block but turned back sharply. 'Be on your guard, girlies. Connie and Cecil Beaton at six o'clock,' she said before raising her hand and walking away.

'Who is Cecil Beaton?' Bunty asked Molly.

'A society photographer. I didn't get the six o'clock part, though.'

Bunty laughed. 'It's pilot-talk for–'

Both girls froze as Connie and Charlie Porter headed towards them.

'Cripes, we'll be lucky if we get out of this without being rumbled,' Bunty whispered.

'Quick – take a gulp of your coffee and start coughing ... and don't stop.'

Bunty did as she was told as Connie came within earshot.

'My goodness, has something gone down the wrong hole?' Connie asked with concern.

'She'll be fine,' Molly said, thumping Bunty's back.

'I wanted to let you know that Mr Porter here would like to take some photographs of the female redcoats by the pool. He suggested you, Bunty, and a couple of your colleagues.'

Bunty tried not to look alarmed. How could she reply without alerting the photographer to the fact that *she* was Bunty, rather than the redcoat he'd been watching the last couple of days? She took a mouthful of coffee and started another fit of coughing.

'I'll make sure we're there, Connie,' Molly replied, as she helped Bunty to her feet. 'Come along – let's get you a glass of water in the cafe,' she said, taking Bunty's arm and dragging her away.

'That was close,' Molly said as they turned the corner and collapsed against the wall. 'I just wonder how long we can keep Charlie Porter from finding out who is the real Bunty Grainger. The sooner Gordon is far away from the camp and not likely to be found by the wretched man, the better for all concerned. When do you think you'll be able to go to the fairground and update Gordon?'

'I agree I need to do it as soon as possible, but I'm on duty all this afternoon with you at the knobbly-knees competition, and then it's the children's talent show straight after dinner. By the time I get to the fairground, Gordon will be busy working and we'll be unlikely to grab more than a few words before he gets called away.'

'Then you must go this afternoon. Why don't you slip away once we have all the contestants lined up and the judges picked? You'd have two hours at least while we pick the man with the knobbliest knees. I suggest you change first so no one questions why a redcoat is heading to the funfair. You'll have plenty of time.'

'But what about the group photograph of the redcoats? Won't I be missed?'

'I doubt it. As long as I'm there and pretending to be Bunty, then Charlie Porter will be happy. Besides, it's better you avoid being included in any official photographs in case he sends a group picture to his newspaper and someone points you out as the real Bunty Grainger,' Molly said.

Bunty gave Molly a hug. 'You are a wonderful friend. I couldn't think of half the cunning ideas you have. Wherever do they come from?'

'Too many afternoons spent watching Johnny Johnson play secret agent Clive Danvers in B-movies at the cinema.' Molly laughed. 'I'm learning how to duck and dive, as Spud would say.'

Bunty's eyes opened wide with amazement 'Johnny is a film star? I know he is good-looking, but ... wow! No wonder you are sweet on him.'

'I'm not,' Molly said far too quickly. 'Now, let's go and find as many knobbly knees as we can. I spotted some likely candidates earlier.'

The afternoon was filled with fun and laughter as the redcoats encouraged male campers of all ages to join the line-up to find the knobbliest knees of the week. Even Molly was astonished to find they had forty men competing for the title.

The sky started to cloud over as the last of the contestants were encouraged to compete. The judges and contestants were told to head for the ballroom, where the entertainment continued. In the confusion, Bunty slipped away to change her clothes and visit Gordon.

Molly made sure that she kept Charlie Porter in her sight as much as possible. If he was watching her, then Bunty was safe to talk to Gordon without fear of being caught She found that when she stopped to speak to men in their late thirties, Charlie came closer and started taking photos of holidaymakers nearby. She had no doubt that she would appear somewhere in the background of each photograph. The man was certainly crafty. She also wondered if Charlie thought Gordon was one of the campers.

Holidaymakers and redcoats found the knobbly-knees competition most entertaining, all howling with laughter as the judges, made up of female campers, felt and prodded each set of knees. The men took it all in good sport, rolling up both trouser legs and parading around the ballroom, much to the amusement of their families, who cheered on their menfolk. After prizes had been awarded, and winners congratulated, campers started to wander outside, the rain having stopped and the sun shining once more.

Molly was becoming fed up with being shadowed by Charlie Porter so gathered a few colleagues who were standing nearby and called him over. 'Mr Porter, would you like to take your photographs now, please, before we have to move on to our other duties?'

Charlie Porter was quick to agree and began to take photographs of the redcoats, although he was unsure of his equipment and fumbled with the settings quite a lot. Molly decided to have a little fun with him and constantly moved to the back of the group. He became quite agitated, pulling her to the foreground and becoming flustered when she put her hand in front of her face or turned to chat to a fellow redcoat. Some of her colleagues began to sing 'Oh, Mr Porter, What Shall I Do?', much to his embarrassment, when he ran out of film. Under the circumstances, Molly didn't think it was uncharitable to join in. After all, the man would be utterly beastly if he did locate Bunty's Gordon.

'It's ever so exciting, isn't it?' Gladys Sangster said to Molly as she stretched out on her towel on the beach. 'Such a shame you won't get to meet Billy Butlin, though.'

Molly nodded. 'Yes, it is, although we've been asked to step in and help out, as the pool area will be crowded with campers wanting to catch a glimpse of the famous man himself and possibly speak to him. He's supposed to be judging the Butlins beauty pageant. I hope you are entering again. You look even lovelier now you have a tan. You are so lucky. I just turn as red as a lobster if I'm not careful.'

The two women had become close since the Sangster family started their holiday at Butlins. Knowing they lived not far from each other, they'd promised to meet up once Molly finished working at Skegness and would write to each other in the meantime.

'I don't think I should enter. After all, I won a prize last week and it would be greedy of me to try again, even though I'd love to see what Billy Butlin is like up close,' Gladys added wistfully.

'Then you should enter,' Molly declared as she checked her wristwatch. 'I think we ought to make a move. You need to make yourself beautiful, and I have to change into my uniform.'

'You've convinced me,' Gladys said as she got to her feet and shook sand from her towel. Looking around at the gently lapping waves and golden sand, she sighed. 'I'm going to miss all this when we head back to south-east London. The children are thriving in the sun, and being away from the bomb-damaged buildings and rationing has done me and Olive the power of good.'

'Then you should think about taking day trips to the Kent coast, or perhaps even go on the paddle steamer *Kentish Queen*. I heard from my friend Freda that it is running again and taking day-trippers from Erith down to the coast. Margate and Ramsgate took a fair bashing during the war, but now the beaches are safe, it will be a nice day out.'

'That sounds like a good idea. I'll look into it as soon as we get home. We so enjoyed our trip before the war. I'm pleased I met you, Molly. I feel as though I've discovered a sister.' She hugged her new friend and called to the children, who were building sandcastles nearby. Arm in arm, they headed back to the holiday camp.

'I don't believe it! I don't believe it!' Bunty kept squeaking with excitement. 'Billy Butlin has just kissed Gladys Sangster.'

'So he should. After all, she has been crowned this week's beauty queen. Look at her family cheering. Even her mother-in-law is jumping up and down,' Molly said, wiping a tear of happiness from her eye. 'I'm so pleased for Gladys. If only her husband was alive to see this.'

'Chances are she wouldn't have entered, or even been here if he were,' Bunty reminded her. 'Didn't she say that it was an insurance-policy payout that made the holiday possible?'

'It was,' Molly said as the two girls pushed through the excited crowd towards the winning bathing belles, who were to be escorted to the rose garden for their official photographs. 'I'm sure she'd rather have her husband with her than all the attention she's getting today. Now, watch out for Mr Snoop in case he catches us out.'

'We are safe today. I heard he is on duty taking photographs of Billy Butlin with the campers. Spud told Plum the odious man has even done a deal to sell some to the newspapers.'

'In that case, you keep well clear. We don't want to draw attention to you until Gordon has cleared his name. Why don't you go and help Plum with the donkey rides? It's part of our duties as Butlins aunties so won't look too suspicious.'

'Good thinking,' Bunty said as she gave Molly a hug and turned away into the crowd. 'Whatever would I do without you?' she called over her shoulder.

'You'd manage.' Molly laughed.

The redcoats had been totally unaware of Billy Butlins visit until an hour before he arrived in his chauffeured limousine. Johnny and Connie had called the staff together to inform them of his imminent arrival and to ask those who were off duty if they'd be prepared to work an extra shift. Not one redcoat complained, as most had never met the great man and were keen to see the show-man-turned-holiday-camp-owner in the flesh. So, it seemed, were the campers, and as word spread through the camp that he was visiting to judge that afternoon's beauty competition, there was an extra buzz in the air. Little did the holidaymakers know that besides shaking hands and being a sociable, smiling face, Mr Butlin would also be going behind the scenes and checking a hundred and one things to ensure his camp was being run just as he liked. Not one staff member could breathe easy until the great man had departed the camp and they were told that all was as it should be.

It was a memorable day for staff and campers, who would tell the story of how they met Billy Butlin to their children and grandchildren in the years to come.

'I'm sorry to see the Sangster family leave,' Molly said sadly as she waved goodbye to the last coach as it headed out of Butlins on the Saturday morning.

'It feels as though I've worked for Butlins for months,' Bunty said as they turned to head back to reception.

'Let's have a drink in the coffee bar before our staff meeting and the new intake of campers arrive and we start all over again,' Molly suggested.

The girls linked arms and strolled towards the coffee bar. They often enjoyed their breaks with fellow redcoats, catching up on news of the camp and also the outside world while popular records played in the background.

'Miss Missons, I have something for you.' Gloria, the receptionist whom Molly had seen on Johnny's arm a few times, strode towards her. 'I don't make a habit of delivering redcoats' post, but Mr Johnson told me you were out here.' She handed a white envelope to Molly. 'I told Mr Johnson it's most likely just a love letter from one of the many young men who follow you around the camp, but he insisted that I give it to you all the same,' she said with a thin smile that did not quite reach her eyes.

Molly took the letter and thanked Gloria. 'I have no idea who would write to me.'

'Probably one of those "many young men",' Bunty sniggered for the benefit of Gloria, who was walking away far too slowly, intent on listening to what the two friends were chatting about.

'Oh, it's from the Sangster family,' Molly said with a smile as she removed a pretty card from the envelope. 'They are thanking me for looking after them during their holiday and reminding me to write. Isn't that nice?'

'It's all right, Gloria. You can report back to your boss that Molly doesn't have a missive from a young man and all is in order,' Bunty said loudly, making sure the receptionist could hear. She did, as she stuck her nose in the air and headed back to her office at a fast pace. Bunty started to giggle, then froze. 'Oh, blast. Whatever have I done? Trust me and my big mouth!'

Molly frowned and looked to where Bunty was staring. It was Charlie Porter and he wasn't at all happy. 'Oops. I think it's time we put Mr Porter in the picture, don't you? Let's invite him for a coffee.'

'I think you've got some explaining to do,' Charlie Porter said as he placed his cup on the table and sat down next to the three girls.

Molly and Bunty had been pleased to see Plum already in the coffee bar when they arrived and they'd quickly informed her of Bunty letting the cat out of the bag and that Charlie now knew Molly was not Bunty. Plum, being slightly older and more worldly-wise, would be able to deal with whatever happened next.

'We have no idea what you mean,' Plum said, stubbing out her cigarette in a tin ashtray that advertised a well-known brand of beer.

'Come off it, girls. I reckon you've been leading me a merry dance this past week or so. You're not Bunty Grainger,' he said, nodding towards Molly.

'I never said I was,' Molly replied.

'So, come on, love,' he said, ignoring Molly and turning to Bunty. 'Where's the boyfriend? I know you're hiding him here somewhere.'

'He's not–' Bunty started to say before Plum placed her hand on Bunty's arm to stop her speaking.

All eyes turned to Plum, who slowly lit another cigarette before speaking. 'What's it to you who we are and if we have boyfriends?'

Charlie leaned back in his seat and nodded. He could see that Plum would be a problem if he didn't tread carefully. Posh birds always were. 'Sorry, Lady Plumley. I didn't know you was part of the crime. I s'pose your mates here know they are sleeping in a shed with an aristocrat?'

Plum felt her heart beat a little faster. The man was good at his job. She'd known her secret would come out before too long. She only had herself to blame for not telling the girls sooner about her past. After all, they'd been above board with her.

Molly squeezed Plum's hand under the table. Whoever Plum was, she deserved privacy, and regardless of her family, she was a good sort. She'd no doubt explain later if she wanted to. 'We know who Plum is, thank you, Mr Porter. We also know who you are. I wonder if Billy Butlin knows you are spying on his staff and pretending to be a camp photographer, when in fact you are a reporter for a tacky national newspaper.'

Charlie thought for a minute, then gave them a toothy grin, showing his nicotine-stained teeth. 'You've got me there. I s'pose you could call this a stalemate. You haven't got any little secrets, have you?' he asked, looking at Molly, whose cheeks suddenly turned pink. 'Ho, ho, perhaps I'll leave you until later.'

'Mr Porter, I'll tell you what you want to know. Just leave my friends alone, please,' Bunty begged. She was surprised at what the man had said about Plum and knew that Molly felt uncomfortable with anyone knowing about her problems at home. Not that it would be of interest to the kind of people who read the newspaper he wrote for. Then again, if he even got a sniff of the fact she was keen on Johnny Johnson – and Bunty was sure it was reciprocated in some small way by the screen idol – then he could create a very unpleasant headline.

Charlie nodded. 'I want an exclusive interview with your boyfriend, the murderer Gordon Taylor,' he said, glancing at Molly and Plum as if he were revealing a big secret.

'Give over, Charlie,' Plum said, blowing smoke into his face. 'We know about Gordon and we've met him, so you can stop being so dramatic.'

'So I was right. He did follow you here,' he said, looking around the busy coffee bar.

'No, I followed him here, but he's been gone for over a week. You've missed your story,' Bunty said, feeling a little braver with Plum and Molly by her side.

'I wouldn't say that. You've been helping to harbour a criminal – all three of you. He's a murderer on the run and you three are accomplices.' He smiled. 'That'll be a nice little earner for me and will put me in my editor's good books as well as stick my name on the front page.' He rubbed his hands together. 'Very nice, if I do say so myself.'

Plum looked at the faces of those sitting round the table – Molly and Bunty, both a little fearful, and Charlie Porter grinning like a cat who'd got the cream. 'You could do much better than naming us in your newspaper, you know.'

Charlie frowned. 'What do yer mean?'

'We may know where Gordon is and what he's up to. Do as we say and you could have a prize-winning article and not something that'll be wrapping the next day's chips. You've got to trust us, though.'

Charlie thought for a moment before looking Plum straight in the eye. 'For some reason, I trust you. I'll go along with what you say for now, but I want details of everything that's happened or I'll shop the lot of you to the police and write what I know.'

Plum stood up. 'It's a deal, but you'll have to forgive us. We have a meeting to attend. You can have your story tomorrow after lunch. Come along, ladies,' she said as she headed towards the door. 'We have work to do.'

'So what do we do now?' Bunty said as she sat in bed hugging her knees. It was the first chance the girls had had to chat since they'd met Charlie Porter in the coffee bar. 'I really don't want to tell him where Gordon is, assuming he's reached Dumfries. It's been over a week since he left the funfair. Goodness knows what's happened. I haven't been able to concentrate on a thing knowing we have to talk to that infuriating man tomorrow.'

'I noticed,' Molly said as she climbed into her own bed. 'You didn't even hear that camper shout, "Bingo," when he won the full house and he was standing not ten feet from you.'

'He did make me jump.' Bunty smiled. 'I did my best to pay attention after that.'

Plum leaped onto her bed and picked up a pen and notepaper from the nearby table. 'I've made some notes and think I know how to handle our Mr Porter. We give him the news that Gordon did not murder his wife and that he knows who did kill Aileen. We tell him how Gordon acted on impulse when he escaped during the air raid and that all he thought of was that the murderer needed to be behind bars so Bunty's name could be cleared and she would be able to nurse again, and of course he would be able to work as a doctor once more.'

'That would certainly tug at his heartstrings,' Molly said.

'But what if the police see the story and go after Gordon and the real murderer, Richard, is never caught? He will be sent back to prison and the three of us will no doubt be in trouble as well.'

'But we don't know where Gordon is, do we?' Plum said, giving them both a wink.

'But he is staying–' Bunty was cut short by

Plum and Molly placing their fingers in their ears and singing, 'La, la, la, la, la, la,' extremely loudly.

'Did you hear something?' Plum asked Molly.

'Not a sausage, Plum,' Molly answered with a cheeky grin.

'Do you remember that poster from the war "Careless talk costs lives"? Keep anything about Gordon to yourself. We don't want to know.'

'I can't even tell you what he says when he writes to me?' Bunty asked.

'Definitely not! In fact, he isn't going to write to you.'

'Whatever do you mean, Plum? We have no reason to think Richard has moved from the area as he would want to see his son – even if Aileen's family believe Gordon is the true father.'

'That's where you're wrong. The only letters arriving here will be for me from my aunt Gertrude, and this is what she'll be saying.' Plum handed a page of neatly written words to Bunty. Molly leaned over her shoulder to see what Plum had noted down.

'Let me get this right. When Richard has been located, Gordon is to write to you pretending to be your aunt Gertrude saying she's "located the right shade of embroidery silks to complete her tapestry of the family coat of arms",' Bunty said.

'Yes, and if things go pear-shaped, Aunt Gertrude will write that "The old brown cow has died."'

'It seems very straightforward,' Molly said. 'You seem to have a statement for every eventuality. How will Gordon know to use these phrases?'

Plum passed her notepad to Bunty. 'You are

going to write to him this instant and enclose the list of Aunt Gertie's comments. I'll post the letter first thing when I exercise the ponies. There's a letterbox down the lane. It's best not left in reception for collection. You never know who's watching. I assume you have an address to contact him?'

'Yes, it's–'

Again the two girls put their fingers in their ears and started to sing.

Bunty giggled. 'I get the message.' She started to write her letter to her fiancé but looked up. 'By the way, what's all this about you being called Lady Plumley?'

Plum grinned. 'That story, my sweetie, is for another time.' She lay down, turning her back on Molly and Bunty. 'Night-night, girlies. Turn the light out when you've finished. Don't be too late. We have our rehearsal tomorrow for the Redcoat Variety Show.' As she closed her eyes, she heard her two friends groan.

Molly had known since her interview in London that she may have to perform as a Butlins redcoat. She could belt out a song if need be, and had been a regular in the church choir, but to stand up and sing in front of over a thousand campers was another thing completely. Standing in the wings of the theatre waiting for her turn to perform, she felt more than a little sick and hadn't been able to eat her dinner, even though it was her favourite, fish and chips. In her hand were the words to a well-known song, which she was expected to sing alone in the centre of the stage with a spotlight picking her out in the darkness. She was word-perfect and had sailed through rehearsals that afternoon, despite having no knowledge of the running order of the acts. The wardrobe department had supplied her with a beautiful grey satin gown with fitted bodice and flowing skirt. With her hair brushed away from her face and pearl earrings clipped to her ears, she felt glamorous and a little giddy. Perhaps she could get through this if she just focused on the words. Pulling black satin evening gloves up her arms and patting her hair, she laid the sheet of music aside and concentrated on her performance.

On stage, Plum was using her husky voice to great effect as she leaned on a piano singing Cole Porter's 'Night and Day'. The late-night show contained popular American songs. She knew that Plum would take a bow and leave the stage, then return for a short performance before it was Molly's turn. She clapped along enthusiastically with the audience as Plum took her bow before heading to where Molly was standing. Unlike Molly's full-skirted dress, Plum's midnight-blue gown fitted tightly, emphasizing her slim form with a train of glittering voile trailing behind her. Reaching Molly, she grinned before turning to go back on stage.

'Ouch – that hurt!'

'Whatever's wrong, Plum? Have you hurt yourself?' Molly asked as Plum leaned over and rubbed her ankle.

'It's these blooming shoes. I don't wear heels much these days and I caught my ankle as I turned,' Plum replied. 'I really can't walk. Look, you are going to have to go on in my place.'

Molly's face went pale. 'But I can't. I don't know what to do. Will I have to sing?'

'No, just stand by the piano while the man sings and try to look interested,' Plum instructed as she hobbled to a nearby chair and plonked herself down. 'Hurry – the curtain will be going up soon.'

Molly had no choice but to help out her friend. She walked to the piano and stood on the mark the pianist pointed out to her as he started to play. In front of the red velvet curtain she heard the compère announce the next song. Slowly, as the curtain rose, the first lines of 'The Way You Look Tonight' were sung. Molly knew the song well from a Fred Astaire film she'd seen. It was very romantic, and if she'd not been so nervous, she would have found the whole experience wonderful.

As the curtain rose higher and higher, Molly tried to pose as she felt a woman being serenaded by her beloved would have posed. It was then she realized who was singing. It was Johnny. His face was a picture as he turned towards the piano and saw Molly standing there. Being a professional, he continued singing without missing a beat and moved towards her. Taking Molly into his arms, he moved her gracefully round the stage before continuing to sing.

If Molly could have drawn breath, she would have noticed his fresh cologne; instead, she felt his strong shoulders under the white tuxedo jacket and his arms holding her close. *Please don't step on his toes,* she screamed inside her head. She'd heard Johnny sing in several of his movies so was not surprised by his tenor voice and how meaningful he made each word sound.

All too soon the song came to an end and she curtsied as he took a bow. 'Ladies and gentlemen, Miss Molly Missons,' he announced, before kissing her hand and leaving the stage without a backward glance.

The piano struck a note, indicating she should start her song. Molly controlled her feelings as she watched Johnny depart the stage. *'Someday he'll come along, the man I love...'*

She felt every word was true as she poured her heart out on stage. To rapturous applause, her fellow entertainers returned to the stage for a final song and the curtain went down for the last time.

'You did very well, Molly,' Johnny said as he approached her.

'Th-thank you...' was all she could stammer before running to the dressing room and closing the door. What was happening to her? It was only a song...

13

'It's wonderful to hear your voice, my love. Do you have enough coins, or should I try to telephone you back?'

Molly smiled. She knew that Kath was fearful of using the telephone in the shop and would jump if it rang when she was nearby. She treated it like a piece of furniture, having crocheted a small mat for it to sit upon and polished the black phone until it shone. It was treated with reverence, as it could bring news, good or bad. 'I have plenty of pennies, Kath. I've been saving them specially to speak to you all. Now, tell me what's been happening at home.' Molly made herself as comfortable as she could in the red telephone box she'd found down a narrow, winding lane not far from the Butlins holiday camp and prepared to listen to the latest news from Erith.

Kath chatted away happily about the goings-on in the town and what the neighbours had been up to since Molly moved away. Molly listened quietly, wishing she was once more sitting at Kath's kitchen table enjoying the company of the older woman. She closed her eyes and imagined being back home.

'I've been up to see to the grave. The cemetery is awash with colour. There are so many beautiful flowers blooming at the moment. The roses from you look a treat. I hope you don't mind, love, but I wrote a little card to say happy birthday to your mum. It sounds daft to say it, but I'm sure Charlotte's looking down and smiling on us all, as I'm sure Norman is as well.'

'I hope so, Kath. Thank you again for looking after the grave. As soon as I'm home I'll pay a visit and let them both know how I'm doing.'

There was a silence as both women thought of Charlotte Missons.

'Hark at me going all quiet on you when you rang to speak to our George. I'll give him a shout. He was standing here just now. I'll just put the phone down for a minute...'

Molly could hear Kath calling George and then a quick exchange of words as she scolded him for walking away from the phone. She smiled to herself. Nothing seemed to change back home. Thank goodness her dad had installed a telephone at the ironmonger's. She only needed to walk to a telephone box to be able to ring her friends in Erith. Not that she wanted to disturb them or make it look as though she missed them, and her home town, as much as she did. Plum and Bunty were good company, and she was growing to love the loud brashness that was Butlins, but all the same, there was no place like home.

'Hello, my love. How's it going with you? Breaking the hearts of all those campers, are you?'

Molly felt a lump form in her throat as she heard George's gruff voice. She laughed at his words, although she could have cried. She couldn't wait for the day she saw the elderly couple again. 'Things are going well and I've yet to break one heart. It's only you I love. Now, how are you, and what's been happening while I've been learning the art of bingo numbers and rules about fancy-dress competitions?'

George started to talk about stock lists and sales figures until Molly's head was in a spin. Inserting a few more coins, Molly listened to the mechanism churn away for a few seconds before giving her more time to talk to her friend. 'George, I didn't telephone you to ask about the shop. I know it's thriving in your hands. As long as you can take a wage each week and aren't going without, I'm happy.'

'Then stay happy. We are busy most days, and the new lad is coming along a treat. So much so that me and Kath are going to be coming to Butlins at the end of July for a week just to see what your holiday camp is all about. Kath is that excited she took her bathing suit out of mothballs and is at her Singer sewing machine most nights making dresses and the like.'

Molly squealed with delight. 'That's next month! I'm so happy you are taking a holiday and I'll get to see you for a whole week.' She fell silent for a moment. 'What about the shop?' she asked, then felt guilty for asking the question.

'That's what I said to Kath when she told me we were off on our holidays. Then she pointed out that Ted Parker's son, Dave, was demobbed last month and had more time on his hands than he knew what to do with and would be perfect to run the shop. So it's all arranged. I was thinking we might even consider taking on Dave after our holiday. Perhaps part-time to begin with until we know when you'll be returning home,' he added as an afterthought.

'Don't give a thought to me, George. I'd rather Dave Parker had a job to go to each day. It's only right after he served his country and was injured into the bargain. I can always find work. You know I wasn't meant to see out my days at Missons. Mum and Dad both wanted me to consider my future and not cling to the shop. I might even get a job at Woolworths and work with Freda.'

George gave a roar of laughter that vibrated down the phone line. 'I'd eat my hat if you ended up working at Woolies. I couldn't see you obeying orders and jumping to attention every time one of those bells rang.'

'It's not much different at Butlins, George. Just you wait until you get here and Radio Butlins is blaring out news dawn to dusk. Now, tell me, is Mr Denton back in his office yet?' She crossed her fingers, silently praying that George would say yes.

'I stuck my head over there the other day. There was only the young chap in there. He reckoned the last he heard, it could be another month before the old boy's back in town. Looking at the office, I don't think he'll have a business to come home to. I said to Kath I couldn't see why someone who was a solicitor would leave that young chap in sole charge of the office. He doesn't know one end of a pencil from the other. It's a queer business.'

'He's family, George. Mr Denton probably trusts him.'

'You've hit the nail on the head there, love. My Kath nigh on said the same as you. I just wish the old bloke would pull his finger out and get home to his business. But then I'm just selfish. He no doubt has reasons for being away for so long.'

'I do hope he has some news once he returns to Erith. Even if it's not what I want to hear, we can get on with our lives. I can't bear the thought of Harriet and Simon living in Avenue Road, though.'

'What will be will be, Molly. Now, I have Freda here jumping up and down to talk to you. I'll say bye-bye for now and see you next month. Take care of yourself, love...'

Molly could hear the catch in George's voice. She missed him so much.

'Hello, Molly. Have you still got time to talk? Do you have enough money for the call? I have lots to tell you.'

'Hello, Freda. It's my day off, so I've all the time in the world to chat.' She looked at the pile of pennies by the telephone, which was fast diminishing. 'I have enough coins to talk for a while yet.' Molly did wonder what Freda had to tell her, as she'd only received her weekly letter the day before and that was packed full of news about their friends and Freda's work. She pushed a couple more pennies into the slot and the mechanism clunked as it swallowed her money. 'Talk away. I've fed the telephone. What's happened since your last letter?'

Freda took a big breath. 'You know I wrote about one of my Woolies colleagues getting engaged? Well, I was invited to her party at the Prince of Wales and guess who I bumped into.'

Molly didn't need to guess. 'Cousin Simon.'

'Yes.'

'You were careful, Freda? Was he drunk?' Molly asked, worried for her friend.

'When isn't he the worse for wear? I spotted him by the public bar, but as we were in the hall at the back of the pub, I thought he'd not see me. Unfortunately, he was outside when I left. He asked about you.'

'Oh my gosh. Whatever did you say?' Molly didn't want her violent cousin hurting her best friend. She shuddered as she thought of his clammy hands on her body. 'He didn't try to touch you, did he?'

'No. I was with my landlady, Ruby, and her

214

grand-daughter, Sarah. They'd been to the party as well. All Woolworths girls together.' She laughed. 'We'd decided to get a bag of chips before heading home and he was there, watching me. I think it took a while for him to work out where he'd met me.'

Molly shuddered. 'Then what happened?'

'He asked if you were at the party. I replied that you weren't likely to be, as not only did you not work at Woolies but were still away from home. Fortunately, I'd told Ruby and Sarah about the situation. You don't mind, do you? I think Ruby would have floored him with her handbag if he'd been nasty.'

'No, I don't mind Ruby and your friends knowing about my problem with Harriet and Simon. They were good to me when Mum and Dad had their accident.' Molly had also heard how Ruby helped catch a criminal when he broke into her home during the war. The old lady was a good person to have on her side in a battle, she thought with a smile. 'Did Simon say anything else?'

Freda fell silent, but Molly could hear her take a deep breath. 'Yes, he did. He came up close to me and said he knew something was going on as he'd seen Kath walking through town the other day and she didn't look ill, and that if Kath was home, you would be too.'

'Oh my goodness,' Molly gasped. She knew how intimidating her cousin could be when up close. She could almost smell the whisky and stale cigarettes on his breath. It wasn't fair that her friend should be dragged into her problems.

'Don't worry, Molly – Ruby pushed him away

and told him not to be daft and that of course Kath would be home for her own husband's birthday, whereas you were invited to stay a little longer in Cornwall and who could afford to turn that down? Then she gave him one of her looks and asked him how Kath should appear when she had "women's problems". His face was a picture.'

'Bless her,' Molly said. 'I'd love to have seen his face when he heard that.'

'It was worth seeing,' Freda said. 'However, he made a parting shot as he staggered up the road. He said that if I was to get in touch, I was to tell you that you'd never win. Isn't that creepy?'

Molly felt her stomach churn. She'd had a good breakfast at the camp of scrambled eggs, tomatoes and toast, so it wasn't hunger but fear. Pulling herself together, she replied, 'Let's just assume from his words that whatever he and Harriet are up to, it isn't entirely honest. When Mr Denton gets back to Erith, then I'm sure that all will be settled satisfactorily,' she assured Freda.

'I have some other news,' Freda added.

'I hope it's better news than what you've just told me.' Molly laughed.

'It is. I'm going on holiday. I'm so excited.'

Molly felt instantly saddened. She was happy for her hard-working friend, but they'd always planned to go away together. Although Butlins was a holiday camp, it was still her job and she'd have loved to spend a week with her chum. 'I'm pleased for you,' she said, trying to keep her voice upbeat. 'Are you going with the girls from Woolies?'

'No, you ninny. I'm coming to see you at

Butlins along with Kath and George.'

Both girls shrieked with excitement. It was the best news Molly had heard in a long time. They chatted for a while, until the pips announced that Molly's coins were about to run out.

'Don't feed the phone with any more money,' Freda said. 'Perhaps we could speak next week, and I'll write as usual. Take care, Molly, and don't be too sad today. We are all thinking of you.'

Molly scooped the remaining pennies into her purse and pushed button 'B' to check there weren't coins to be returned to her before stepping from the telephone box. It was stifling in the confined space, and try as she might to lean against the door to let in a little air, it had proved fruitless. The June day was going to be warm. It was only just past ten o'clock and already she could feel the sun on her face from the open fields on one side of the lane. Molly kept in the shade as much as possible as she headed back towards the holiday camp.

With a day free to do as she pleased, Molly's mind wandered back to a year ago, when she had helped celebrate her mum's birthday – breakfast served in bed by a dutiful daughter, and then Charlotte and Molly had caught the train for the short journey to the nearby market town of Dartford, where they'd wandered from shop to shop before stopping for a leisurely lunch. Norman Missons had told them to be ready at four in the afternoon as he had tickets to take them both to London to see a show. Molly could still see her mum's face when she realized they had tickets for

Irene at His Majesty's Theatre. Charlotte had so enjoyed the film version of the musical and had seen it three times at the cinema a few years earlier. Charlotte had hugged Norman for joy as they'd stood in front of the theatre and he'd handed his wife tickets for the stalls. For days after Charlotte could be heard singing the song 'Alice Blue Gown' as she'd gone about her housework and thought she couldn't be heard.

If only she'd known it would be the last birthday her mum would celebrate, things would have been so different. She scolded herself for her selfish thoughts. Who knew what the future held? They'd celebrated victory in Europe only months before and everyone was preparing to face life anew after six years of war.

As Molly neared the holiday camp, she heard the excited shouts of campers around the swimming pool and the sound of Radio Butlins reminding people to attend that day's sports activities. It wasn't a day to be around people. She didn't feel she'd make good company and wished to be alone thinking of her parents on her mum's birthday. Next year would be different. Although no doubt she would always grieve for her parents, who had been taken too soon, she would at least have come to terms with what had happened and her wounds would not be so raw.

Heading to the chalet she shared with Bunty and Plum, Molly decided to change out of her slacks and into a pretty cotton sundress and take a walk along the shoreline. Kicking off her white pumps, Molly heard one thud against the suitcase stored under her bed. It reminded her that her mum's small attaché case was stored inside the larger case. Today would be the perfect time to sift through the photographs and reminisce of happier times. Placing the small leather case onto her bed, she flicked back two small brass catches and tipped the contents onto the candlewick bedcover. She smiled at the few blurred pictures of her as a child and another of her parents on their wedding day, similar to the one in a frame that had stood on the hall stand before being damaged when Simon attacked her. Flicking through yellowing cuttings, she saw several news items from the *Erith Observer* from years gone by when her dad had won a darts tournament and done well in a cricket match for a local team. Charlotte had also kept past advertisements for Missons Ironmonger's January sales, and even a birth announcement she and Norman had placed in the popular local paper when Molly was born. It was then that Molly came across a bundle of papers. Impatiently picking at the knot in the faded red ribbon, she hoped that perhaps there was a copy of her dad's latest will. It would solve all her problems, or at least tell her if Harriet was in fact the true owner of the house in Avenue Road and possibly the family business. If that were the case, her life would change forever.

Molly was just about to start reading the papers when the door to the chalet burst open and Plum rushed in. 'Where's Bunty? I've received a missive from Aunt Gertie.'

Molly frowned. She'd been so deep in thought as she looked through her mum's possessions she'd forgotten for a moment their plan for Gordon to keep in touch with Bunty, It had been some weeks since Gordon had left in a hurry after the girls realized journalist Charlie Porter was snooping about after a news story.

'My goodness, it actually worked,' Molly said. 'Let me take a look.' She took the proffered page from Plum, sniffing the note before reading. 'He's really playing the part, but the perfume's a little on the whiffy side. I take it this means he has located the real murderer and is in hot pursuit?'

'Well, it means he has arrived in his home town and has an idea where Richard is living. I'm not so sure he is in hot pursuit, as you put it. Have you been watching Clive Danvers movies again?'

Molly felt embarrassed; she'd commented earlier that Plum's plan was like something from one of her favourite B-movies. 'I believe Bunty is supervising the children's playground this morning.' She checked her wristwatch. 'Yes, she should still be there. I reckon she will be over the moon to know that Gordon's been in touch.'

Charlie Porter had been placated with the information Bunty had given him about her life since leaving prison and her insistence that Gordon was innocent. However, he was sworn to secrecy, otherwise he would be given no more information. The man had a nose for a good news story and knew better than to cross the three girls at this time. Molly did wonder how long he'd be prepared to wait for his scoop, though.

Plum turned to leave the chalet but noticed the papers and photographs on Molly's bed. 'Feeling homesick?' she asked, nodding to the photos on top of the pile.

'A little. It would have been Mum's birthday

today. I was just taking a look at some things of hers that Freda put in my case. I've not seen these before.'

'Me and my big mouth,' Plum said, rushing over to give Molly a hug. 'Look, don't stay cooped up in here. It's a lovely day. Get yourself out in the fresh air and let the sun warm your bones. You can still think about your family. It'll do you good. I can get someone to cover me so I can join you, if you like. I'm only on duty this morning. I was going home this afternoon but can put it on hold if you would like some company.'

'Thank you, Plum, but I don't want you to miss seeing Lizzie. I appreciate your offer, but I'll be fine. It means a lot to me that you and Bunty are my friends. Bunty and I have so many problems. I'm sorry you got stuck in this chalet with us,' Molly said as Plum stopped hugging her.

'Lovey, open any door in this holiday camp and you'll find people with problems. No one has a perfect life.' A shadow had crossed her face. 'Now, are you taking yourself off out of here, or do I have to drag you by the hair?'

'I thought I'd get changed and take a walk along the beach as it's so nice,' Molly replied, looking at Plum's face. Was Plum hinting she had problems herself, or was Molly imagining things?

Plum opened the door to the chalet, her face once again wearing its usual smile. 'You do that. I'll see you later this evening.' She gave Molly a big wink and left.

Molly changed her clothes and started to pack her mum's things back into the attaché case. She stopped for a moment and pulled out the papers

221

that had been held together by the red ribbon, then placed them carefully in her handbag. She would sit on the beach and read through the documents. Out in the sunshine, life would feel more positive than here in the little wooden chalet.

Molly walked at a slow pace for almost an hour, stopping to dip her toes into the waves as they lapped at the sandy beach. She found a spot where she was alone apart from a few seagulls swooping overhead. It was the perfect place to rest and read the papers she'd placed in her handbag. Settling herself on the soft sand, she opened her bag and took a deep breath. Praying that what she held in her hand could solve her problems, she started to read. The first documents were birth certificates – her own, followed by her mum and dad's. Eager to move on to something that might be more important, she reached for a large, flat, sun-bleached stone to weigh down the documents. Some words on her mum's certificate caught her eye and she picked up the faded paper to read them. Charlotte's father, Harold Kenyon, and his wife, Molly, were, or had been, farmers at the time of Charlotte's birth and lived in a place called Spilsby. Molly felt a tingle of excitement spread through her body. It wasn't the sunny day that did it but the thought she had a link to a family she'd never known existed. Whatever had happened for her parents to leave their home town and head to Erith?

Molly stared at the piece of paper. Why did Spilsby ring a bell? Of course – she'd seen the name of the village on the large map pinned to a wall in reception. The map showed places of interest for campers to visit if they wished to venture out of the camp. Molly and Bunty had planned to borrow bicycles and tour nearby villages when their days off coincided.

She wondered where her dad had come from. As her parents had never mentioned life outside of Erith and had always been secure in the close-knit community, Molly had never thought to ask. Why had she not questioned her parents?

Peering at the small, neat writing on her dad's birth certificate, she was astonished to see that her dad had been born in the same area as her mum. No wonder Charlotte Missons had shown an interest in visiting Butlins at Skegness before the war. Molly knew she had been disappointed when the camp had been taken over by the navy for the duration, but had always thought it was because she'd longed for the novelty of visiting the well-known holiday camp rather than because she wanted to go back to a place close to her birth.

Excited now at what other information she would discover in the small bundle of papers, she unfolded the next document. It was the deeds to the house in Avenue Road. Surely these should have been kept with Mr Denton, the family solicitor? If only she knew more about such legal matters. The next document was a life-insurance policy. Framed by ornate scrollwork, the fancy wording boiled down to the fact that Molly was the beneficiary of a sum of money if anything should happen to her parents. She would need to contact the London and Provincial Insurance Company to inform them of her parents' passing.

Although she felt some assurance for her future, Molly would have given every penny she owned to have her parents alive.

There was one more item. An envelope. Molly was disappointed. She wasn't sure what a will would look like but thought it probable that the document was more substantial than the envelope she held in her hand at that moment. She opened the envelope with some trepidation and gasped at what she read.

14

'Mama, look at my painting,' Lizzie called, running up to Plum who was wobbling on one foot pulling off the tight-fitting bicycle clips from around her ankles, shaking each leg in turn to free her cream-coloured slacks.

Kneeling down on a faded woollen rug, she held out her arms to her young daughter. 'Come and give Mama a big hug. Why, I swear you've grown six inches since I last saw you. It must be a year at least,' Plum said as she squeezed her daughter tight in her arms, breathing in the aroma of soap and her daughter's unique perfume.

'Oh, Mama, it was two days and ... three hours.' She giggled, looking at an ancient grandmother clock standing next to the fireplace.

Plum felt guilty that she had to leave her daughter with her old nanny, Tilly, while she worked at Butlins. If only Billy Butlin would allow his staff to live outside the holiday camp. Perhaps in time she could live at home again. After all, it was only a half-hour brisk bike ride with a good wind behind her. 'Now, let me take a look at you,' she said, holding the young girl at arm's length.

'Mama, I need to show you my painting. It's really special,' the child pleaded, trying to wriggle away as Plum stared hard into her face. She could still see a spark of her late husband. Yes, William was there in the glint of their daughter's eye and the toss of her head. Plum sighed with relief. What if the day came when Lizzie grew up and she could no longer see a living reminder of her late husband in her only child?

Tilly placed a tray on the table in the small living room and poured tea into two cups. 'Lizzie's been that excited about showing you her work. I've lost count of how many times she's been to the gate to see if you were on your way down the lane. Now, drink your tea before it gets cold. There's a letter for you to read, when you have time to draw breath. It's from you-know-who. I can tell by the postmark.' She nodded to where a letter had been placed behind a carved wooden candlestick on the mantel over the fireplace.

'Why don't you fetch this wonderful painting, Lizzie?' Plum said as she reached for the letter, a worried look on her face, ripping open the envelope as quickly as possible so the words inside could be read before Lizzie returned.

Tilly sat at the table and sipped her tea, waiting for Plum to speak. She'd cared for the woman since she was a child and now she continued her duties caring for Plum and her daughter so Plum could earn a wage at the holiday camp. Tilly may only have been Plum's nanny when she worked at the big house, but she thought of her as a daughter and Lizzie as her own grandchild. She still could not understand why Plum's family had closed their door to her when she arrived on their doorstep with a child in her arms and no husband. How could anyone do that to their own child? she thought. Why, there'd been a war on, and from all accounts Plum and William were to marry. Only his duties in the RAF had stopped him turning up at the church that day. Then he'd been shot down and there was no wedding and the baby arrived. There were many women like Plum who for one reason, or another did not have a man by their side. Thank goodness the girl came to her for help. She'd never turn her away.

'What does the old battleaxe say this time? It's been a while since she's written. I'd hoped after her last words that we were rid of her,' Tilly huffed, her cup rattling in its saucer as she placed it back on the table.

'William's mother says she wishes to meet me. Do you think she is trying to take Lizzie from me again?' Plum said with a fearful look in her eyes.

'I wouldn't trust the woman. In fact, I have a strange feeling in my water about this,' Tilly said with a shudder.

'She's alone in the world and may have regretted her actions. William was her only child, after all...'

Tilly stood up, her cheeks slightly pink. 'We don't need that woman interfering in our lives. Throw the letter in the bin. Better still, burn it. We are happy as we are.'

Plum slipped the letter into her pocket; she had a feeling it could change her future, but would it be in a good way? Lizzie should know her grandparent. Then again, Plum's own parents had let her down badly when she'd most needed their help. They cared more about what the county folk thought of a woman having a child out of wedlock than they did about their own daughter. Plum knew she would never forgive them. They were as dead to her as William had been since the day he disappeared in his plane. But was it right to ignore William's mother now she was possibly prepared to acknowledge her grandchild? She'd have to think about this very carefully.

Lizzie rushed into the room waving a large sheet of white paper. 'Look, Mama – I painted a picture of Daddy.'

Plum took the picture from her daughter and gazed at the painting of William, which had been carefully copied from the one photograph Plum owned of Lizzie's father. The six-year-old child had carefully copied her daddy standing by his Spitfire, possibly the one he was flying when he disappeared into the Channel. 'Why, this is very good. Tell me, who are the other people?'

Lizzie leaned against her mother and pointed first to her father. 'I painted his hair the exact colour of my own, as you told me we were the same. This is his plane, and here you are with your donkeys. These people are my grannies and grandpops. They are all in heaven,' she added sadly.

Plum stroked her daughter's hair from her face. It was indeed just like William's: light brown in colour with a touch of copper when caught in the sunlight. 'What makes you say that, my poppet?'

'Davie, in my class at school, has never seen his grandparents and he said they are in heaven. I've never met mine either, so they must be there too.' She looked at her mother with enquiring eyes. 'Are they?'

Plum looked over her daughter's head to where Tilly stood, a frown on her face. Soon she would have to explain to Lizzie about family. It could not be put off for much longer. But what could she say? 'Why don't I pin this on the wall next to your daddy's drawing? Then we will go for a walk and you can tell me what you've been doing since I last came home and I'll tell you all about my work at Butlins.'

The young girl's face broke into a beam, her question forgotten for now in her excitement to spend time with her mama. 'I'll find my sandals,' she said, dashing from the room.

'The apple didn't fall far from the tree with that child,' Tilly said as she looked at Lizzie's artwork, now pinned on the wall next to a sketch William had done of Plum. 'The child is showing talent. Even I can see that. If William's mother needs any more proof, it is here to see.'

Plum nodded. William had caught her likeness in his sketch. She remembered walking with him on the South Downs on one of his rare days off duty. They'd laughed and chatted, making plans for a life together once the war was over. Later, while lying in the sun watching a dog-fight overhead, William had become quiet. 'We will have a future, won't we?' he'd asked.

Plum had leaned over and kissed him; she'd

been wondering the same thing. 'My family will accept you even though you are a poor artist.' She'd laughed. 'They will love you as much as I do.'

William had continued to gaze up at the sky as an enemy plane burst into flames and spiralled down from the clouds.

'Here, why don't you draw my portrait?' she said, trying to distract him. 'You've been promising to do it for some time.' She picked up his sketchbook from where he'd left it on the grass and threw it to him.

William snapped out of his reverie and opened the page. 'This will be the first that we can frame and hang on the wall of our family home.'

Plum looked at the simple sketch now. Until she'd pinned her daughter's painting alongside, it had hung alone.

Molly pushed open the door of the little chapel and stepped into the semi-dark interior, away from the strong sunlight outside. She stood still while her eyes became accustomed to the light before heading to the altar to light a candle for her parents. The contents of the envelope had taken her breath away and she'd headed back to the holiday camp wishing no more than to go to her chalet and think about her discoveries. It was as she approached the chapel that Molly had decided to enter and contemplate her future. There was a calm in the small chapel that she'd not find anywhere in the holiday camp.

Molly pulled the two pages from the envelope and by the light of the candle again read the words. The first was a letter from Charlotte Missons to her parents notifying them of the birth of their first granddaughter, Molly. She spoke with pride of the opening of the ironmonger's shop and plans to buy their own home in Avenue Road, where they were currently renting. The letter signed off with hope that past differences would be forgotten and they could all move forward together as one big, happy family. Molly had smiled as she'd read Charlotte's words, but then wondered why the letter had been in her mum's possession.

The second letter soon answered her question. The few lines from her grandmother were straight to the point:

The shame you brought on this family when you ran away with Norman Missons can never be mended. You are no longer a child of mine. We do not wish to be associated with any member of the Missons family.

Molly winced as she read the words written by her grandmother, a woman she had never met. A further line simply said that Charlotte's letter was enclosed as she had no need to keep it.

Sitting down on a nearby seat, she buried her head in her hands and sobbed. Why, she could have had a family to turn to after her parents' accident if only she'd known about her grandparents. For some reason, her parents had been ostracized, and because of that, she was alone in the world, and on a day that should have been filled with happiness because it was her mum's birthday. It was then she heard a creak as the door to the chapel opened and the sound of footsteps announced someone else was present in this sacred place.

'Why, if it isn't Molly Missons. Are you praying for divine intervention so you don't have to help in tomorrow's children's fancy-dress competition? Life can't always be a walk on the beach or drinking cocktails with your friends.'

Molly's back stiffened. Why, oh, why did Johnny Johnson have to come into the chapel at this moment? She pulled open her handbag to look for a handkerchief but couldn't see beyond her tears. She did her best to wipe them away with the back of her hand, hoping he wouldn't get too close. No such luck.

Johnny appeared in front of her, a wide smile on his face, ready to make another joke until he saw her expression. 'Whatever has happened? Has someone hurt you?' He sat beside Molly and reached in his pocket for a handkerchief before passing it to her. 'Here, use this. It's clean.'

Molly mumbled her thanks and quickly dabbed at her eyes. 'I'm sorry you caught me like this. I didn't expect anyone to come in. There isn't a service today.'

'I saw you walk into the chapel just now. I wouldn't have intruded if I'd known you were upset... What I mean is, I would haven't acted such a fool just then. Please forgive me.'

'Think nothing of it. You weren't to know I was upset and had come in here to hide away.'

Johnny reached for her hand. Molly turned to face him and was surprised by the concern she saw etched on his face. 'It must be something pretty awful that upset you so much. Now, why don't you tell Uncle Johnny all about it? That's if you want to?' he added quickly.

Molly took a deep breath and blurted out, 'It's my mum's birthday and I miss her. She died last summer, along with my dad … and … I feel so lonely.' She started to sob again, holding Johnny's freshly laundered handkerchief to her face.

Johnny slid his arms around her and held her close, making soothing noises and gently rocking her until the worst had passed. 'Now, tell me everything and I promise I'll try to help. You know what they say – a problem shared is a problem halved.'

Molly looked into Johnny's eyes. She could see true concern and at that moment trusted him enough to share her story. Words flowed with ease as she started to talk while Johnny listened.

'Molly, I'd like to help you,' Johnny said as he handed back the birth certificates and letters.

'There's no need, Mr Johnson. You aren't responsible for your employees' problems outside of Butlins,' Molly replied, embarrassed by how she had so easily told Johnny everything that had happened since her parents had died.

Johnny took Molly's hand. 'I feel we are more than employer and employee, Molly. Besides, I'm sure Billy Butlin would be pleased to know all his staff were problem-free and able to put a hundred per cent effort into their duties.'

'I've never let my problems affect my work,' she said quickly, feeling embarrassed that he would think she was shirking her duties while wallowing in her misery.

'I know you wouldn't. There's never a moment when I don't see you smiling. You are a true redcoat. Whatever problems you have in your life, the campers are not aware of them,' he said, squeezing her hand tightly. 'Believe me when I say I truly want to help you and I know a way.'

Molly felt embarrassed and pulled away her hand. 'I'm sorry but I don't see how you can sort out my problems. You hardly know me.'

Johnny shrugged. 'I've felt there was a connection between us. You seem to see me as a person rather than as a matinee idol. So many people want to be friendly because of the characters I played on screen. You ... well, you just treat me like a normal person.'

Molly laughed. 'You mean I give you a hard time. I wouldn't say that was treating you like a normal person. We are here to give the holiday-makers a good time. I hope that's what we do.'

'I enjoy our weekly nature trips with the children, and I'm impressed with your organizational skills. You've never once introduced me as a film star or tried to flatter my ego.' He looked past her, deep in his own thoughts.

Molly noticed small frown lines on his forehead and forced herself not to reach out and run her fingers across them. Since arriving at Butlins, she'd seen another side to the actor she'd fallen in love with from the stalls of the Erith Odeon. She often scolded herself for even thinking that the character he played would be anything like the real man. However, in the few weeks she'd worked with Johnny, she'd witnessed a strong, decent man, very much like the secret agent on the silver screen. Perhaps the character wasn't so far removed from the man in front of her now. What must he think when she'd been almost rude to him at times? 'I have a confession to make. You may not be amused.'

Johnny glanced back at her serious face. 'You're going to leave Butlins?'

'Goodness, no. Why would I do that? No, it's more serious and you may not want to help me when you know.' She tried not to laugh, but a small smile crept across her face, which did not go unnoticed by Johnny.

'Don't tell me you are really on the run for undertaking some dastardly deed?'

'Oh, much, much worse. Back home in Erith, I have a photograph of you on my bedroom wall. Furthermore, I've watched all the Clive Danvers films at least twice.' She looked him in the eye before bursting into laughter. 'I'm a lost cause and not different to all the other admiring females.'

Johnny joined in with her laughter. 'Most definitely not a lost cause,' he said, running a finger across her cheek, brushing away a few stray hairs.

Time stood still. For a few seconds they looked at each other, until the door to the chapel creaked open, releasing them both from the magical moment. An elderly couple entered, apologizing for interrupting the redcoats. Johnny helped Molly to her feet and assured them they had not interrupted anything important. The look he gave Molly as they left the little chapel and stepped out into the mid-morning sun showed he thought otherwise.

'I accept,' Molly said after a few moments of awkward silence.

'Accept what?' Johnny looked confused.

'Your offer to help me... That's if there is still an offer. Although I'm not sure how you can...'

Johnny grinned, looking down at Molly's eager face. 'Right. I'll meet you in the coffee bar in half an hour. Get yourself organized and make sure you have all that paperwork with you, as we'll need it.'

Molly nodded and set off for her chalet. There was just time to wash her face and do her make-up before meeting Johnny. He was a decent sort. She felt more relaxed than she had since opening the envelope on the beach, and thanked God Johnny had walked into the chapel and discovered her in distress.

'Finish your coffee and we can be on our way. My car is parked by the gatehouse,' Johnny instructed Molly. He'd changed out of his Butlins uniform into grey slacks and a white open-necked shirt. They looked like any other holidaymaker sitting in the popular cafe.

Johnny placed his hand on Molly's back as he guided her through the campers; some stopped them to ask questions about the events being held that day in the camp. They both answered politely, although Molly was eager to know where Johnny was taking her.

They'd just reached the door when they heard someone call out Johnny's name and Gloria caught up with them. 'Johnny, I need to speak with you about the London trip. You will excuse us, Molly,' she added, bestowing her with a brittle stare.

'It will have to wait, Gloria,' Johnny replied to the Butlins receptionist as he continued to walk away. 'Molly and I have an appointment' – he checked his watch – 'and we will be late if we don't hurry.'

'As you wish, Johnny,' Gloria answered with a sideways glance at Molly. 'I'll see you this evening.'

Johnny did not answer as the couple headed towards the gatehouse and his car.

'Will you tell me where we're heading?' Molly asked as Johnny drove out of the camp and headed down the leafy lane past the telephone box where she'd made her call only a few hours before. It seemed a lifetime ago.

'Be patient,' he said, not taking his eyes from the road. 'We will be there in less than an hour.'

Molly leaned back in the comfortable leather seat and slowly closed her eyes. The warmth of the sun on her face through the windscreen made her feel sleepy. It was good to just relax and do nothing after the surprises she'd uncovered today. Hopefully, whatever Johnny had planned would not be too much of a shock.

'Wake up, sleepyhead – we're here,' Johnny said as he opened the car door and gently shook her shoulder.

'Oh my goodness, I must have fallen asleep. I'm so embarrassed ... I do apologize. Whatever must you think of me? I hope I didn't snore.'

'I thought you looked beautiful while you slept, although I'm too much of a gentleman to say if you snored or not.'

Molly felt her cheeks glow just imagining Johnny watching her as she dozed. She tried to ignore the look he gave her and ran her fingers through her hair. 'I feel a mess.'

'You look lovely. Now, come with me. I may have some interesting information for you.'

Molly looked around her. Johnny had parked the car close to a large, imposing church. 'Where are we?'

'This is Spilsby, and we are about to meet the vicar of St James's Church,' he explained, leading her towards the building.

'Spilsby? But that's—'

'Yes, it's mentioned on the certificates you found in your envelope,' Johnny said as a tall man bounded from the side of the church dressed in long black robes. 'I know this area, and also a man who may be able to help. Here he is.'

The vicar took Johnny's hand and pumped it up and down enthusiastically. 'Johnny, old chap, it's a pleasure to see you again. Seems an age since you were at the airfield. Where have you been hiding yourself?'

'Bertie, it's good to see you. Thank you for seeing us at such short notice. I'd like you to meet Molly Missons. I mentioned her in my telephone call.'

Molly shook the vicar's hand, rather bemused as she had no idea why they were visiting this man. He seemed to know Johnny well, as they chatted about people they knew in common, many of whom had RAF titles.

Bertie stopped talking to Johnny and apologized

to Molly. 'Excuse us, my dear. We don't meet so often now the war is over and we've taken different paths in life.'

Molly frowned. 'You were an actor?' she asked.

Bertie roared with laughter. 'If only I had such talents. A short shift as the back legs of a donkey is as far as my talent runs. No, I was referring to the days when we both flew up into the wide blue yonder,' he quipped.

'Molly doesn't know of my time in the RAF,' Johnny said with an apologetic look.

'I thought you spent the war making films?' she said.

Bertie, laughing once more, nudged Johnny in the ribs. 'If only they knew the truth, old chap. Our Johnny here is a hero. Flew Spits, when he wasn't seconded to help keep up the morale of the British public as a dashing hero.'

Molly looked at Johnny, who was showing some discomfort. 'I never knew you were a hero in real life as well,' she murmured. 'You are full of surprises.'

'Enough about me. Bertie, did you manage to lay your hands on what I spoke about?'

'Indeed I did. It may not be what you expected, but I hope it will help.' He handed over a scrap of paper to Johnny. 'Now, would the pair of you care for a spot of lunch?'

'That's good of you, Bertie, but I'd like to check this out first. I'll stand you dinner soon, I promise,' Johnny said.

With much shaking of hands and slapping of backs, Bertie bade them both goodbye. Johnny led Molly back to his car and started the engine.

Molly stayed silent. She had an idea that whatever lay at the end of their journey would answer some questions about her unknown family. After a short drive, Johnny pulled up by a small cemetery and held the door open for Molly, who climbed out of the car and felt her legs wobble as she attempted to stand. 'I didn't expect to come to a cemetery,' she said quietly.

'Be brave,' he said, taking her hand.

'"Molly Charlotte Kenyon, devoted wife, mother and grandmother,"' Molly read from a carved headstone. 'This is my nan's grave.'

'Would you like me to leave you alone with your thoughts?' Johnny asked.

'No... Please stay. I don't quite know how I feel. I know nothing of the person buried here.' Apart from the letter she wrote to my mum, she thought. 'My parents never spoke of their families. This is all alien to me. It could be anyone lying here. I don't understand how she could be a devoted mother and grandmother when she never acknowledged my existence.' She looked at Johnny with tears in her eyes. 'Does that sound awfully bad of me?'

'No, not at all. No one could ever say that,' Johnny said, enveloping Molly in his arms and stroking her head as she shed silent tears. 'It's been a shock for you to go from discovering you have family to me bringing you here all within a few hours. Can you forgive me?'

Molly looked up to his concerned face, her lips still trembling. 'I can forgive you anything.'

He lowered his mouth to hers and kissed her

gently at first until they were both consumed by the intensity of their passion. Johnny pulled away. 'I'm sorry. I should know better than to take advantage while you are distressed.'

'Then I should also ask for forgiveness as I wanted the kiss to continue,' she replied, surprised again that she was able to speak to Johnny with such ease. She wondered if his leading ladies felt this way after just one kiss.

'I think it's time we had something to eat,' Johnny said, trying hard to change the subject. 'We passed a teashop a way back. Can I tempt you?'

'Yes, please,' Molly whispered as they both gazed into each other's eyes, not wishing for the moment to stop. Something significant had passed between them. Molly was astonished by the feelings she experienced when she was in Johnny's arms.

As they walked from the cemetery, Molly looked back to her nan's grave and wondered what life would have been like if she'd known this woman.

15

Bunty jumped when Charlie sidled up to her as she sat by the children's paddling pool, and almost dropped the glass of squash she was holding. Deep in thought, wondering what Gordon was doing and if he was any closer to proving that Richard had murdered Aileen, she had not seen the photographer approach. Bunty worried constantly that

Gordon could be in peril while she was at Butlins enjoying herself, albeit also working hard.

'Is there any news from the escaped prisoner?' he asked as he lit the cigarette that dangled from his thin lips.

Bunty looked around her in case anyone had heard what he'd muttered none too quietly. Fortunately, it was noisy in the children's play area and no one had noticed. Bunty felt so uncomfortable when the journalist, still posing as a camp photographer, appeared. Perhaps she was uneasy because he knew so much about her. Whatever the reason, she hoped that Gordon would soon be in touch with developments. There'd been several postcards to Plum from her 'aunt Gertie' with the cryptic comments that were part of Plum's plan for Gordon to let Bunty know what was happening. She longed for the day when Gertie announced, 'The eagle has landed,' as then she would know that Richard was in the hands of the police and she would soon once more be in the arms of the man she loved.

'I've not heard a word from Gordon, if that's what you mean,' Bunty said, her chin held high in defiance. 'I promised I'd tell you when I'd received news. I'm not a person to go back on my word.'

Charlie spat a stray piece of tobacco from his mouth and sneered. 'It's not likely I'd take the word of a woman not long out of prison. Now, if it was that posh mate of yours, or her pretty friend, it'd be a different kettle of fish.' His gaze took in the area around them, where mothers watched their children at play. 'No sign of them today. When one of you appears, there's usually another close behind. Like buses you are.' He laughed at his feeble joke. 'On your own today, I see.'

Bunty shuddered, wishing fervently that Molly and Plum were by her side. They could be relied on to put Charlie in his place. For once, both girls' leave had fallen on the same day. Plum had gone home to see her daughter, and Molly had left a note to let Bunty know she wouldn't be able to meet her for their afternoon break as she'd been taken out by Johnny Johnson and would tell her all about it later. It had been this delightful piece of information that Bunty had been pondering when Charlie had crept up and caught her by surprise.

She raised her chin and stared him in the face, something she'd been taught by her friends, who'd told her to be brave and unashamed of what had happened. 'The girls are around and about. We are not joined at the hip. I'm not a liar, Mr Porter. I went to prison for telling the truth. When I hear something, you will be the first person I inform. That was our deal, was it not?'

Charlie eyed her thoughtfully for a couple of seconds before nodding. 'Just make sure it is. My editor won't wait forever for the story. He may just run it with what I've told him so far.' A grin covered his face. 'That alone would make for interesting reading. It might even give Butlins some publicity. At least then I'd be shot of the place. It's far too happy here for my liking.'

A silence fell between them as Bunty contemplated his words. The last thing she wanted was for

Butlins to be implicated in his tacky newspaper's lies. She was sure as eggs were eggs that most of what he wrote would be fabricated. Bunty loved her job and had hoped that once Gordon received a pardon, they would continue to work for the holiday-camp company. Nearby, a child screamed out in pain as he fell to his knees.

'I suggest you go and look after your charge and wipe away his tears, but think on. I want news ... and soon.'

Bunty hurried to soothe the sobbing youngster. 'Please, Gordon, send me news soon,' she whispered to herself.

'Would you like more tea, my loves?'

Johnny raised an eyebrow at Molly. 'I know I'd enjoy another cup. How about you?'

'Yes, please. That's if you're in no hurry to close,' Molly added, noticing that it was close to four o'clock. They were the only remaining customers in the quaint little teashop.

'It's no trouble at all, my lovelies. Now, would you like another slice of my seed cake? It's freshly made.'

'That would be delightful, thank you,' Johnny said, giving the woman one of his heart-melting smiles, which often had female campers almost swooning in delight.

'I couldn't eat another morsel,' Molly said, rubbing her stomach. 'Why, I'm fit to burst. I can't remember the last time I ate so much, and that's something, considering the food Butlins lays on for us.'

'Oh, you're staying at that Butlins. On your

243

holidays, are you?' the waitress asked with interest. 'Never been there myself.'

'No, we both work there. This is a rare day off for the pair of us,' Johnny said as he passed an empty teapot to her. 'I was based at the airfield for part of the war,' he added quickly when the woman gave him a quizzical look.

'I thought your face was familiar.' She nodded thoughtfully. 'I suppose you must have come in here occasionally. Yes, that must be it. I'll go and fetch your tea.'

Molly giggled as the waitress disappeared through a door marked, 'Staff only'. 'I suppose you get a lot of that kind of thing. It must be a problem?'

A smile crossed Johnny's face. 'It can be at times ... when I want to be alone, that is. At other times, I'm more than happy to play the man from the movies and answer questions. It's all part of the job.' He took Molly's hand and lightly kissed her fingertips. 'I'd rather be incognito right now and simply be a guy out with his girl.'

Molly felt a tremor of excitement course through her body. 'Are you playing another role, Johnny?'

'My acting days are over, Molly.'

She was lost for words. How many times had she wished to be in this situation? Sitting alone with the dashing actor as he spoke words of love was a dream come true. But now she knew the real man, rather than the matinee idol. The moment was lost, as the waitress bustled back into the room with a tray laid with fresh tea and clean cups. Molly snatched back her hand, not wanting the pleasant lady to assume they were a courting couple and ask embarrassing questions. She was unaware it was obvious to anyone close by that her cheeks were flushed pink, her eyes shone brightly and that she was a woman in love with the handsome man who gazed at her in adoration.

'I wonder if I could ask you something,' Molly said as the waitress placed their order on the table.

'Ask away, my lovely. I'm always being asked directions.' She hugged the empty tray to her ample bosom, waiting for Molly to speak

'We've been to visit my nan's grave and I wondered ... what with you being a local ... if you knew of my family.'

The woman frowned. 'Lost touch, did you, my love?'

'You could say that...' Molly didn't want to tell the waitress she had never known her family.

'Molly doesn't come from around here. She lives down south,' Johnny added helpfully, giving the waitress another of his smiles. 'You know what it's like what with the war and everything.'

If the women didn't know 'what it was like', she never said, but took the seat that Johnny offered. 'I'll help if I can,' she said.

'I know very little apart from their names and that they farmed around these parts when my mother was born. I believe they must have still lived locally, as my nan was buried nearby.' She looked at the woman with hope in her eyes.

'It would help if you gave me their names,' the waitress suggested.

'Oh, silly me.' Molly laughed. 'The surname is

245

Kenyon, Harold and Molly Kenyon. Do you know the name?' she asked hopefully.

The woman thought for a moment. 'I went to school with a Sally Kenyon, but that's a good few years ago now, so she'd most likely have married and be known by her husband's name. Hang on a minute and I'll ask my mum. She's out the back washing up. She knows everything worth knowing around here.' The waitress hurried through the staff door and returned only a minute or two later with a small, wizened woman, her hair tucked into a turban and her body swathed in an oversized cross-over apron.

Molly jumped as the women came into the tea-room. She chewed her lip nervously, not wanting to look at Johnny or imagine what news she would hear.

'Sit yourself down, Mother, and tell the young lady all you know about the Kenyon family.'

Johnny, who had stood when the women appeared, helped the woman into a seat. 'If you can recall Miss Missons's family, we would be most grateful.'

'Missons? I thought your name was Kenyon.' The elderly woman looked at her daughter, then Molly. 'I do know that name, though...' she said thoughtfully.

'I'm Molly Missons. My mum was a Kenyon before she married my dad. He came from this area too,' she added expectantly.

The woman nodded her head. 'My girl here was right. She did go to school with Sally Kenyon. She had a sister ... Charlotte. Yes, that's right – Charlotte Kenyon. She was a fair bit older, though. A surprise baby, by all accounts, was Sally. That Charlotte, well, she left the area many years ago. I can't quite remember why...' She tapped her head, trying to think. 'I'm not as quick up here as I used to be, but it'll come given time.'

'Charlotte was my mum,' Molly prompted. 'But what about Sally? Is she still living in these parts?'

'Oh yes. She married Dan Dempster and lives in one of the Turners' farm cottages over a mile or so away. She has a bonny pair of twin girls.' The elderly woman squinted at Molly. 'There's a likeness between you... Yes, there's definitely a likeness. But then the apple never did fall far from the tree with the Kenyon women.'

'A successful day, don't you think?' Johnny said as he helped Molly from the car.

'Beyond my wildest expectations,' Molly said, pulling her cardigan around her shoulders and picking up her handbag from the seat of the car. 'I had no idea when I woke this morning that by the evening I'd have information about a family I never realized existed.'

'It's a shame your aunt Sally wasn't home. It would have been the perfect end to a perfect day if you could have met her.' Johnny took her hand and tucked it through his arm as they headed up the driveway towards the Butlins buildings, waving to Spud as they passed the gatehouse.

'Yes, it's been a perfect day,' she said, looking up at the handsome man. 'In so many ways. I don't know how to begin to thank you. If it hadn't been for your help, I'd have still been a miserable mess and most likely have taken to my bed to brood over my problems.'

Johnny turned and pulled Molly to the side of the road, so they were hidden from view of the camp by a large rhododendron bush, before taking her into his arms. 'Oh, you darling girl, it should be me thanking you.'

He held her close, his lips seeking hers. She melted against Johnny's body, reaching up to his broad shoulders as he held her as close as was humanly possible. She'd dreamed of this moment for so many years. However, this was not a girl's crush on a matinee idol but a woman falling in love with a man. A man she thought would never love her back in a million years.

Johnny pulled away from Molly, running a finger across her cheek while controlling his laboured breathing, then placing a gentle kiss on her forehead. 'I need to catch up with some work, but I'll see you later in the ballroom. Yes?' he almost pleaded.

Molly stood on tiptoe and kissed him back, longing to hold Johnny tight and never allow him to leave her arms. 'I'll look forward to that.' She smiled.

They walked hand in hand towards the large reception building before parting company. Molly had just started to follow the footpath to the staff chalets when she heard her name being called. It was Gloria.

'Molly, Molly...' The woman strode towards Molly waving her hand dramatically so that passers-by stopped to look. 'Oh good, you heard me. I wondered if you'd seen Johnny.' The look she gave Molly showed that Gloria was aware that Molly had just parted company with their boss. Had she spotted the couple kissing? Molly wondered.

'I believe he is going to his office to do some work,' Molly replied, trying hard to appear as if she hadn't just been kissing the man they were now discussing. Not that it was any business of Gloria's.

'Oh right. I'll catch him there. I just need to go over some of our travel and accommodation arrangements.'

Molly's face fell. 'Accommodation?'

'Yes, Johnny is taking me to London for a couple of days. We are really looking forward to our trip,' the woman replied, and she smiled at Molly with her thin lips pressed tightly together. 'Mr Butlin has given his approval for our trip.'

Molly was puzzled. Did the kiss she shared with Johnny count for nothing if he was going away with Gloria? She'd seen the woman clinging to Johnny's arm a few times since she started work at the holiday camp. Perhaps they were a couple. If Billy Butlin knew about them, then it must be true.

'I hope you have a lovely time,' Molly said, trying hard not to show how affected she was by the many thoughts whirling through her mind. 'If you'll excuse me, I have to change before dinner.'

'There is one other thing before you go. It seems one of the redcoats who should have been on bingo duty this evening has gone down with a summer cold. You are required to stand in for her.'

Molly nodded glumly and walked away. Her perfect day was no longer perfect.

A sneer crossed Gloria's face as she watched Molly walk away. She could see by the slump of the girl's shoulders that her words had hit home – just as she'd hoped they would. That'll show Molly Missons, she thought to herself. It was fortunate she'd spotted her with Johnny as she was heading down to the gatehouse with a message, and she thanked her lucky stars that Spud Jenkins hadn't answered his telephone and she'd had to go in person. Gloria had hidden as soon as she'd seen the tender moment between the pair. Gloria intended Johnny to be hers, and after their trip to London, she was confident Johnny would no longer be interested in the young red-coat.

Molly slumped down onto her bed, too drained even to cry.

'Whatever is the problem? You look as though you have the troubles of the world on your shoulders,' Bunty said, concerned for her friend. She had her own news to share of her encounter with the horrid camp photographer but knew that could wait now she'd seen how down Molly appeared to be. Bunty had been aware that today was Charlotte Missons's birthday and Molly would be sad, but felt there must be something more for her to be this miserable.

Molly threw off her cardigan and lay back on the pillows, staring at the ceiling of the chalet. 'So much has happened since breakfast. I don't know where to begin.'

Bunty sat on the edge of her friend's bed. 'Why

not tell me the highlights? You can fill in the rest later.'

Molly chewed her lip and thought for a moment. 'George, Kath and Freda are coming here for a holiday at the end of next month...'

'That's excellent news. I'm longing to meet them. I feel as though I know them already – you've told us so much about them. Surely that's not why you're so sad.'

'There's more. I found out I have family and know where my mum's younger sister lives.'

'Why, that's marvellous. How did you find out? And I still want to know why you are unhappy.'

Molly sat up and hugged her knees to her chest. 'Johnny took me out for afternoon tea and he kissed me. That was wonderful,' she sighed.

'Oh my gosh,' Bunty exclaimed. 'How can you be so down when your dream came true and Johnny Johnson kissed you?'

Molly frowned. 'How...? What...?'

Bunty brushed Molly's questions aside. 'It's been written all over your face for ages. You're in love with the man, regardless of what happens whenever you meet. Plum and I just knew it would happen before too long. So?'

'So what?' Molly was surprised her attraction to Johnny was so obvious.

'So why are you so unhappy? Come on – spit it out.'

'I found out he is going to London on a trip with Gloria.'

'Oh my, that does put a different perspective on things. Perhaps in the circles he moves in, it's the done thing to have a few women friends?'

Molly thought of the times she'd seen Johnny with a starlet on his arm coming out of the theatre and on the Pathé News at some grand event or other. He was never short of a glamorous female as an escort. Perhaps she'd been fooling herself to think he was as interested in her as she was in him. She was just a silly young thing he could spend a couple of hours with and kiss without any strings attached. She sighed. She had hoped for so much more. It was time to forget about her longing for the matinee idol and get on with her life. She was at Butlins, she enjoyed her job, and she intended to have fun with other men – with no strings attached.

Johnny leaned back in his chair and stretched his arms above his head. His paperwork had taken longer than he'd thought, as Gloria had placed more on his desk. He just had time to wash and change before finding Molly in the ballroom. They were both off duty, but the life of a red-coat was such that they hardly ever left the confines of the large holiday camp. Today had been a good day. He'd make sure he took his allotted time off so he could treat Molly to more trips into the surrounding countryside to look for her family. He thought for a moment of their kiss and smiled to himself.

'You look pleased with yourself,' Gloria said from the doorway.

'You could say that, Gloria. Everything is up to date, and now I'm off to the ballroom for a relaxing evening. There's not anything else, is there?'

'No, apart from a few changes to the staff rota.

I called in that Molly Missons to cover tonight's bingo game, as we are a redcoat down.' She looked at Johnny to see how her news affected him.

'I thought it was her day off,' Johnny replied.

'It was, but as you often say, Johnny, our work at Butlins comes first. She said she wasn't doing anything important this evening and was happy to oblige. It hasn't stopped her enjoying her day off, as I spotted her in the bar earlier with a crowd of male redcoats having a good time.' She watched again to see if her lies had hit home and was pleased to see Johnny was not amused.

'If there's nothing more, Gloria, I'll have an early night, thank you. I'll see you at nine o'clock tomorrow. It's a long drive to London in the car and I want to make an early start.'

'I won't let you down,' Gloria said, simpering at Johnny. 'I'm looking forward to our time together.'

Johnny frowned as the woman left the room. Switching off the desk lamp, he went to the window of his office and stared out over the footpath leading to the ballroom and theatre. He could see couples arm in arm, enjoying the cool evening air. He envied their happiness and carefree lives.

Plum took the glass of lemon squash from Molly and sighed with delight after taking a sip. Since the weather had become warmer, they'd changed their nightly cup of cocoa to something cooler. 'It was lovely to spend the day with Lizzie. I really didn't want to leave her today.'

'It must be a wrench,' Bunty said. 'I'm not sure I could do it.'

'At the moment, I have no choice. Someone has to put food on the table, and I think myself fortunate that not only is Lizzie safely taken care of but I have a job that is flexible enough for me to spend time at home. Though, it would be good to sleep in my own bed each night and be able to travel into Butlins each morning, rather than make haphazard trips home when the duty rota allows,' she said wistfully.

'Why don't you ask if you can change your shifts?' Molly suggested.

Plum shook her head. 'I don't want them to think I can't cope. After all, I'm doing a man's job. Spud told me the chap who ran the stables before the war worked all hours. I don't want them to think I can't at least equal what he did. It would just be nice to be able to tuck my daughter up in bed occasionally and read her a bedtime story, then be there in the morning when she has breakfast,' she added longingly. 'Now, that's enough about me. What have you two been up to today?'

Bunty and Molly looked at each other.

'Come on, you two. Spill the beans. I can see something has happened by the looks on your faces. Have you drowned a camper in the pool or something?' She laughed.

'If only it were that simple, Plum. You go first, Bunty. I feel my news will take much longer,' Molly said.

Bunty explained about the newspaper reporter, currently masquerading as a camp photographer, hounding her for news of Gordon. 'I fear he will give the game away if he doesn't hear something of interest soon.'

'Surely this is blackmail,' Molly said. 'Why not go to Connie, the staff officer, and ask for help?'

'If I do, I may might well lose my job. I've been honest with Butlins and they know I spent a while in prison, but they know nothing of Gordon, and he was working on their fairground ... and he did run away from prison. I feel as though my life is on a knife-edge at the moment. I'm not sure what to do,' Bunty said sadly. 'I just wanted a fresh start when I joined Butlins, but it hasn't turned out to be the case at all.'

Plum thought for a moment. 'I don't think it's the right time to tell the bosses about your dilemma. We just need to keep that oik Charlie champing at the bit for a few more weeks. With luck, Gordon will catch up with Richard or find proof that he did not have a hand in Aileen's murder. Perhaps Aunt Gertie should be a little more frequent with her letter-writing?'

'But how...?' Bunty looked confused.

Plum pulled open the drawer of her bedside table and lifted out her writing set. 'I'll get writing first thing tomorrow and arrange to have the letters posted back to me at the camp. Flap a couple in front of Charlie and we'll have him eating out of our hands within days.'

'But the postmark will be wrong... How...?' Bunty was perplexed.

'Just leave things to me. With a little help from Spud, we can get around most problems.' She smiled.

Bunty hugged Plum then Molly. 'I don't know how to thank you both. I've never had friends like you who trust me enough to help me get out of trouble. You seem to be able to solve any problem, Plum.'

Plum hugged Bunty back, then reached for her cigarettes and lit one with shaking hands. 'I just wish I was as good at sorting out my own problems,' she said as she inhaled deeply, then exhaled, waving the smoke away from her friends. 'I have family problems that if not handled properly, could have my daughter ostracize me in years to come.'

'We will help if we can. That's if you want to share with us?' Molly said.

'A problem shared and all that,' Bunty added quickly.

'If you are sure?'

Both girls nodded. Plum was a mate, and if she needed their help, they'd do their best to support her.

'You may be shocked by what I tell you. The thing is, I was never married to Lizzie's dad, William. Do you think I'm an awful person?'

'Oh, not for one minute. A few of the women who were in the same prison as me were unmarried mums. Whatever they'd done to be locked up, they seemed decent sorts when it came to their children. So many times they would be in tears because they worried for their kids and missed them. You don't shock me, Plum.'

'Me neither,' Molly was quick to say. 'Women who had children outside of marriage used to be frowned on in my community, but the war changed many things. You have my support, Plum. Is this why you never speak of your parents?'

Plum nodded. 'They turned me away at the door. I wasn't even allowed to cross the threshold when they knew William was missing and I was expecting his child. Oh, they offered me money, but I was to move away and not shame the family name. I threw the money back at them and walked away. I wrote when Lizzie was born, but the letter was never answered.'

Molly was shocked. She knew that if she had gone home to her parents with a baby, they would have been disappointed in her, but they would have supported her and the child. 'Where did you go? What about William's family?'

'William's mother is a widow. She wouldn't accept I was carrying William's child, as there was no marriage licence. I could have been any woman out to gain money from a widow woman who had not long lost her only child. Fortunately, Lizzie is the image of William, and although I visited and did my best to encourage her to share Lizzie's life, the woman really didn't wish to know.'

'It's so awful. Where did you live?' Bunty asked.

'My own nanny took me in. That's how I came to work here, as her brother is Spud who works in the gatehouse.'

'You had a nanny?' Bunty gasped.

'Oh yes. I come from the full landed gentry. I wouldn't give you tuppence for the lot of them. In fact, I took William's name, Appleby. Plum is the nickname he gave me when we first met. In my old life, I was Lady Elizabeth Plumley, born with a silver spoon in my mouth.'

'I feel as though we should be curtsying to you,' Bunty said.

Plum threw a pillow at her. 'Don't be so daft.'

'So what is your family problem?' Molly asked. 'You have a good home and a nice job as well as a lovely daughter. Has something changed?'

Plum lit another cigarette and offered the packet to the two girls, who both refused. 'You could say that. I tried to keep in touch with William's mother by sending photographs of Lizzie and little notes on how she was progressing. After all, she was the only thing she had left that was linked to William. She ignored me until three years ago, when a letter from her solicitor arrived. She wanted to take Lizzie from me and bring her up herself. She wanted to pay me off, would you believe? It was a mess for a while. I had to use most of my savings to employ my own solicitor to send her packing.'

Molly and Bunty didn't speak. They couldn't believe their friend had experienced such terrible events in her life.

'I felt sorry for the woman but dared not visit with Lizzie or even write as I feared she would take my daughter from me. Perhaps she'd finally realized that William would never return. It's the not knowing that eats at you the most. Many nights I've spent awake wondering what happened to my beautiful man. But I knew that someone had to be strong, and if that was to be me, then so be it. I decided to stop all communication with her, and things went quiet until a few months ago, when letters and even a telegram arrived asking me to get in touch.'

'Did you?' Molly asked gently.

Plum shook her head. 'No. I didn't dare. I'd secured the job here and if she had found out that I was leaving Lizzie alone with someone while I worked at a holiday camp, it might have meant she could take my daughter from me. Would she have understood that caring for donkeys and ponies and doing shifts in a ballroom was the right job for a mother? Then today this arrived.' She pulled a crumpled letter from the pocket of her slacks and handed it to the girls to read.

'Crikey, she's coming to visit you?' Molly said. 'What will you do?'

'I really don't know. One part of me thinks she will snatch my child, but another part of me keeps thinking about you, Molly.'

'Me?' Molly was surprised.

'Yes. I've seen how much you miss your own parents and how the strangers who appeared at your home have caused such problems for you. You've told us how you never knew about your grandparents. If I denied my Lizzie contact with William's mother, she would never know her own family...'

'But I *have* found out about my grandparents,' Molly said, reaching for her handbag to show Plum the paperwork that had been such a surprise earlier in the day. 'I've even seen where my mum's sister lives, and I have maternal cousins. Johnny Johnson drove me there today. I have family, Plum. I have proper family.'

'That's splendid,' Plum said, hugging Molly until she couldn't breathe, before letting her go. 'That's bloody splendid.'

'And Johnny kissed her,' Bunty added with a beam.

'Bloody hell, what a day!' was all Plum could say.

16

'How are things?' Plum asked, as she collapsed into the seat next to Molly in the coffee bar. 'We've hardly had time to breathe, let alone speak these past few days. I've taken on two more stable hands and been promised six more donkeys, so hopefully there won't be so many queues for rides.'

'It has been mad. Connie told us things would get busier. I love my job, but my head is bursting with so much going on. I'm supposed to be on duty now, as it's the children's swimming races, but Bunty is covering for me for half an hour. Then I'll do the same for her.'

'At least it doesn't give us time to think about our problems, does it? Have you spoken to Johnny since his return?'

Molly shook her head. 'No. I've seen Gloria a few times when I've been in reception. She's like a cat who's stolen all the cream.'

'Or the redcoat who nabbed her man,' Plum butted in. 'I'm sorry but I just can't take to the woman. I don't know why, but that's how it is.'

'I try to be friendly with her, but she has such a superior air. Now she has her claws into Johnny, she seems so much worse,' Molly said with an unhappy look on her face.

Plum took a noisy slurp from her coffee cup. 'Sorry, I'm such a pig – being in a hurry all the time makes for bad manners.' She noted Molly's sad face. 'Does it hurt? I mean about Johnny, not me slurping my coffee.'

'It did, but I'm being sensible about things. Johnny and I come from different worlds. To me, a kiss means something special. No doubt in the world he moves in, it isn't so important. I won't be taken for a fool again and won't be giving my kisses away so easily in future.'

'Molly, there's no need not to enjoy yourself just keep it to having fun and enjoying a kiss or two. It doesn't make you a girl of easy virtue. Just don't wear your heart on your sleeve.'

'Was it that obvious? I didn't think people were aware I liked Johnny so much.'

'Those who were interested would have seen. Your friends and people like Gloria. Perhaps that's why she's been such a bitch.'

Molly raised her eyebrows. 'That's a bit strong coming from you, Plum. Thank goodness Gloria isn't a holidaymaker or we'd be forced to be pleasant. I'll just try and avoid her from now on.'

'You do that. I'll be having words with her if I find her being beastly. Now, I'll have to love you and leave you, as I have staff to keep an eye on and kiddies to fight off. I must say my job makes me very popular with the children.' Plum hugged Molly, brushing away a few stray pieces of hay that had attached themselves to her friend's red jacket. 'I'll see if I can catch you tonight for a chat if you aren't fast asleep.'

'I'll be late, as I'm working in the Butlins Theatre this evening. It should be a great show.'

'In that case, I may just try and make it, if I don't fall asleep in my smelly overalls again.' Plum had been ribbed by Bunty and Molly after they'd found her snoring soundly and the chalet smelling of the stables. The chalet door had to be left open to let in some fresh air before they could sleep. Plum's overalls were now put outside overnight to air.

Molly was just finishing her drink when a shadow fell across the table. Looking up, she saw Johnny with a frown on his face. 'Have you been avoiding me?' he asked. 'I've left several notes for you in reception.'

Molly felt a thrill of excitement run through her to see Johnny standing just inches from where she sat. She tried to keep calm. How dare he stand there expecting her to have responded to messages she'd not even seen, especially after he'd been off gallivanting to London with the Butlins receptionist? Molly decided to keep calm and not let Johnny know how shaken she felt. 'I have no idea what you are talking about. I've not received one message from you. Are you sure they weren't sent to another female redcoat?' She felt awful for being so brusque. It wasn't in her nature as a rule.

Johnny pulled out a vacant chair and sat beside her. 'You don't mind, do you?' he asked, ever the gentleman.

'Not at all. I'm about to go back on duty,' she replied, trying hard not to look in his direction for fear of crumbling under his gaze. She picked up her handbag and tried to leave, but Johnny grabbed her hand and she had no choice but to sit down. 'I'm not sure what it is you want, Johnny,' she said quietly.

'Molly, I want to know what has changed between us. You're treating me like a stranger. I thought we meant something to each other.'

Molly could feel her heart melting. Johnny sounded so sincere. Perhaps there had been a mistake. She decided it would be fair to give him another chance. She was far too fond of him to cut him off completely and then see him around the holiday camp each day. She knew it would break her heart. With nowhere to go, she had no choice but to stay friends with Johnny, at least until the end of the season.

'Hello, you two. You look very cosy. Has Johnny been telling you about our trip to London, Molly? I'll never forget it as long as I live.' She fluttered her eyelashes at Johnny, who was frowning once more.

Molly raised her eyes and looked at Gloria standing in front of their table. 'Johnny hasn't told me a thing, Gloria. Please sit down and join us.' She nodded to a vacant chair.

'I'll get the coffee,' he said, rising quickly to his feet and heading towards the busy counter.

'So, tell me about your trip. I'm eager to know all about it,' Molly said, forcing a smile onto her face. If Gloria and Johnny were now a couple, she should try to make friends with the woman and hide her own heartbreak, all thought of avoiding her flying out of the window.

Gloria tucked her hair behind her ears and smiled. 'It was lovely to be able to spend time away from the holiday camp and get to know Johnny a little better. He made me feel very special. I hope we can repeat the trip again when he isn't busy.'

'Lucky you,' was all Molly could think to say before trying to change the subject. 'I'm looking forward to the show in the Butlins Theatre this evening. We have stars from the radio show *ITMA*. Will you be there?' Like all redcoats, Gloria was often working evenings, helping out with the campers' entertainment.

'I'm hoping to be there to watch the show, but it depends on how busy Johnny will be. He still has to catch up with work after whisking me away to London,' she said with authority while watching Molly closely.

Molly felt like a goldfish in a bowl with Gloria the cat watching from outside. Why was she showing off like this? Of course Molly felt jealous. She knew Johnny had a place in her heart, but if he was promised to someone else, she would not fight for him. It would be hard, but she'd hold her head high and try not to look disappointed. In time, it wouldn't hurt so much.

'Excuse me, Auntie Molly,' a little girl said as she tapped Molly's arm for attention. 'I wondered if you would help me with my fancy dress. Mummy isn't feeling well, and I'm not allowed to use her sewing kit.'

Molly recognized the little girl. Her mother was in a wheelchair. Often it was her father who took her to join in the games and events while his wife slept in their chalet. 'Of course I can help you, Cynthia. In fact, I can spare a few minutes right now.' She took the young girl's hand and got to her feet. 'Give my apologies to Johnny, please, Gloria. I'll not have time for that coffee.'

'Before you go, I have something for you,' Gloria said, putting her hand into the pocket of her jacket and pulling out a few scraps of paper. 'I meant to pass them on to you the other day, but you know how it is.'

Molly glanced quickly at one of the papers and spotted Johnny's name scrawled on the bottom. Were these the notes Johnny had mentioned? Why did Gloria have them? 'Oh, I know what these are about already, but thank you for passing them on,' she said, shoving them into her pocket before walking away with the little girl.

Cynthia skipped along beside Molly. 'I don't like that lady. She told my mummy off this morning.'

'I'm sure she didn't mean to do that, Cynthia. Perhaps you heard wrong?'

'I did hear right, and I saw Mummy crying afterwards,' Cynthia said with a stubborn look on her face.

Molly was unhappy to hear that the child's parent had been upset. 'Perhaps I can have a little chat with your mummy while I help with your costume,' she suggested.

Cynthia smiled. 'I'd like that. Mummy likes you. She says you have a warm smile. Does it hurt having a warm smile? Does it burn your face?'

Molly laughed with the little girl as they headed towards the chalets. This was what she loved about her job. If she could only avoid Gloria and not feel so unsure of Johnny's feelings towards her, then her life at Butlins would be almost perfect.

Molly stepped into the chalet and noticed that Cynthia's mother was sitting up in bed with a bundle of coloured paper and material in front of her. The woman's face was pale, and she seemed to be having trouble with the task in front of her. 'Hello, Mrs Smithson. Would you like me to help you with Cynthia's costume?'

The woman's expression was welcoming as well as worried. 'I hope our Cynthia hasn't been bothering you? She's that excited about entering the children's fancy-dress competition. I'm afraid my fingers aren't as good as they used to be.'

'I'd love to help you, Mrs Smithson,' Molly said as she sat in the chair offered to her by Mr Smithson. 'Can I let you into a little secret? I miss making costumes. I used to help my mum with the Brownies and we were always making costumes for one event or another.'

Cynthia's mother visibly sighed and Mr Smithson grinned. A short, slight man with greying hair, he seemed to carry the troubles of the world on his shoulders. Molly thought it was likely he'd had a lot to put up with now that Mrs Smithson was confined to a wheelchair.

Cynthia climbed onto Molly's lap and cuddled her. 'I knew you would be able to help us. If your mummy is here at Butlins, can she come and help too?'

Molly gave the child a hug. 'No. My mummy isn't able to come to Butlins, but I'm sure she'd have loved to have helped you. You will just have to put up with me instead.'

Molly caught the sympathetic look that Mrs Smithson gave her and returned it with a smile.

It was only later she realized she'd been able to talk about her mother without shedding tears. 'Now, what exactly is it you would like to be in the competition?'

'I want to be a bingo queen,' Cynthia said, sliding from Molly's lap and jumping up and down with excitement.

'A bingo queen? That's a costume I've never seen before. What made you think of that?' she asked the child with some alarm. The competition was later that afternoon and she had no idea how to proceed.

Mr Smithson sat on the edge of the bed to explain. 'Our Cynth has been fascinated by the bingo. It's something we both enjoy attending if Joan is feeling up to it.'

'I love playing bingo,' Joan Smithson added. 'It's something I can do in my wheelchair. Ernie and I go often when we are at home. We play each week in our village hall.'

'We were sitting with another couple,' Ernie Smithson continued, 'and the husband told us his wife was so addicted she must be the queen of bingo. This fascinated our Cynth and she's spoken about nothing else since.'

As Molly listened, a few ideas popped into her head. 'I do believe we could make you the best bingo queen ever. We don't have much time, and I first must pop over and speak to a colleague for a few minutes,' Molly said, thinking of Bunty, who was waiting to be relieved from her duties for her tea break. 'Mr Smithson, would you mind collecting a few ping-pong balls from the gift shop and perhaps a small notebook?'

267

'Please, call me Ernie. Yes, I can do that by all means. Anything else to help our little princess?'

'Queen, Daddy, I'm going to be a queen, not a princess,' Cynthia interrupted.

'I'd like to help as well,' Joan said, 'although I'm not up to making a dress.'

'I don't think we have time for that.' Molly laughed. 'Do you have a sewing kit?'

Joan Smithson showed Molly her tin of sewing equipment, which contained safety pins, something Molly knew would come in handy. Feeling assured they had the basics, Molly set off at a fast pace to see Bunty and collect items that no bingo queen should be without.

'There! What do you think about that, Cynthia?'

The young girl twisted and turned in front of her parents, showing off her bingo-queen outfit. Molly had found some used bingo cards, which had been pinned onto Cynthia's sundress, while Joan Smithson had written bingo calls on slips of paper, which were now pinned round the hem. Cynthia was tickled pink to have 'legs eleven', 'Kelly's eye', 'top of the shop', 'two little ducks' and other well-known sayings on her dress. Ernie had been kept busy making a cardboard crown and had attached ping-pong balls to the top with numbers written on them.

'You've done a wonderful job, Molly. I wouldn't know where to start to thank you,' Joan said.

'It's all part of the job,' Molly replied cheerfully as she cleared away the mess they'd made on the single bed, which had been used as a makeshift table while the costume was created.

'Beyond the call of duty, I'd say,' Ernie replied. 'You've made one little girl very happy. We must repay you in some way.'

'No, no, there's no need at all. I've enjoyed myself. It brought back some happy memories.'

'Of your mother?' Joan asked.

Molly nodded but didn't wish to say any more in front of young Cynthia.

Sensing the situation, Ernie took charge. 'Come on, young lady. Let's go and show your outfit off to our neighbours, shall we?' he said, taking the excited Cynthia by the hand and leading her out of the chalet.

Joan patted the bed close to where she was sitting in her wheelchair. 'Sit yourself down, Molly. I sense you've lost your mother.'

Molly nodded as she sat down. 'Yes, last summer. I lost both my parents in a car crash. Would you believe that today is the first time I've not cried when mentioning Mum?'

'I saw the grief on your face when you mentioned her. She must have been a very special person to bring such a caring daughter into the world. I've been through the wars myself,' she said, tapping her legs. 'I may never walk again, and yes, it was a car accident.'

Molly took Joan's hand. 'I'm so pleased you survived. I'd never wish Cynthia to go through what I have this past year. It's been very hard at times.'

'You've survived, Molly. You are a good person, and I have a feeling good things will happen to you. Do you have any other family?'

Molly chatted to Joan about the discovery of

family she never knew about, although she kept quiet about Harriet and Simon, as they didn't feel like family to her.

A tap on the door from Ernie to tell them it was almost time for the fancy-dress competition gave them both a start. 'My goodness. I must go and help prepare the ballroom for the competition or they'll be giving me my cards.' She laughed. 'But there was something I wanted to ask you. Cynthia mentioned that Gloria, one of the receptionists, had upset you. I wonder if you would tell me what she did. I do have my reasons for asking,' Molly added quickly, in case Joan thought she was just being nosy.

'Of course you can ask. I feel a little silly now for being upset. I spotted the young lady with her colleagues in the reception area today and said that we had attended the big parade in London last week to celebrate the end of the war. It had been wonderful to watch. Ernie took part because of his war work. He's still not allowed to talk about it,' she added quickly. 'Anyway, I saw this particular young woman wearing her redcoat out-fit at the parade and recognized it, as we would be at Butlins the following week. I only said how it had been lovely to see a redcoat marching in the parade and she became rather unpleasant. Ernie quickly wheeled me away.'

'What did she say to you, Joan?'

'Only that I must have been mistaken. She said she'd been in London with her boyfriend. I think she said his name was Johnny. Yes, it was Johnny. For some reason, her colleagues began to laugh at her and that was what infuriated her. Did I say something wrong, Molly?'

Molly gave Joan a quick hug. 'No, you did nothing wrong at all. In fact, you have cleared up something that has been worrying me. Now, I must dash, but I'll be there to cheer young Cynthia on. I'll see you all later.'

Molly left the Smithsons' chalet and headed along a flower-bordered path towards the ballroom feeling as though she was walking on air. Gloria must have been telling lies when she intimated she and Johnny were a couple. It sounded more like work that took Gloria to the capital city if she'd taken part in the parade to celebrate the end of the war. Why shouldn't redcoats have taken part? Spud, the gatekeeper, had told her that Billy Butlin did sterling work during the war years when the holiday camp was closed. No doubt there were other redcoats representing the company as well. Molly had heard about the big parade through the streets of London. Perhaps if she had been living in Erith, she would have taken the train up to Charing Cross and waved and cheered with the thousands of other spectators. She wondered if Johnny had taken part. Molly gave herself a stern talking-to. Why shouldn't he go to London, and why shouldn't he give Gloria a lift in his car? She was making mountains out of molehills, and it wasn't helped by Gloria's attraction to Johnny. After all, she'd never seen him reciprocate. He had always appeared to be a gentleman. She would ignore Gloria's cheap jibes in future.

'Molly!' As if by magic, she heard Johnny calling out to her as he rushed down the busy path, stopping to say hello to campers who called out to him.

She waited until he caught her up. 'Did you want something, Johnny?' she asked pleasantly.

'Yes, look'– he ran his hand through his hair distractedly– 'I wanted to talk to you this morning, before that even, but my notes seem to have gone astray. I could have sworn I placed them in your cubbyhole in reception.'

'Not to worry. You can tell me in person now you're here.' Molly was aware of the pieces of paper in her pocket, but no good would come of telling Johnny that Gloria had taken them and only just passed them on. The troublesome woman was best ignored. 'Was it important? Would you like me to take on some more duties?'

'No. I mean yes... It's important, but nothing to do with work. I have a few hours free tomorrow and plan to go over to Spilsby to visit the airfield. I wondered if you would like a lift to visit your newly discovered aunt. We could meet for a meal later. That's if you want to?'

Molly felt a thrill of excitement course through her. It wouldn't hurt to go out with Johnny for the afternoon. It wasn't as if they would be together, as he had business to deal with, and she could visit her mum's younger sister. 'I'm owed a few hours' leave, but there is a small problem.'

'I'm sure it's nothing that can't be overcome,' Johnny said as he took her arm and guided her away from a family who were cycling towards them.

'It's just that I wrote to my aunt and I've not yet received a reply. Perhaps she doesn't want to see me.'

Johnny considered her words for a few seconds before answering. 'How about I wait to see if you are invited into the house before I leave? If she slams the door in your face, I can drop you in the town and you can visit the shops. I'll cut short my meetings and get back to you earlier than planned. Perhaps we could meet in the teashop.'

'Oh, please no. I wouldn't wish you to miss your meetings on my account. If my aunt doesn't wish to speak to me, I can make my own way back to Butlins. I'm sure a bus runs back to Skegness.'

Johnny could see that Molly was not going to change her mind and agreed to what she suggested. 'All right, but I don't see how anyone could slam the door in such a pretty face.'

Molly laughed. 'Then you don't know me very well, do you?'

'I'm willing to learn,' he said quietly.

Molly felt her cheeks start to burn. Plum was right: she did wear her heart on her sleeve. Perhaps she should act more like Gloria and toss her hair and lay claim to the man. She giggled as the thought crossed her mind.

'Is something funny?' Johnny asked with a frown.

'No. Sorry – it was something a friend said to me earlier. It's not important,' she added as she noticed his frown. 'I'm on duty at the fancy dress. Are you going my way?'

'I most certainly am,' he said, taking her arm. 'I'm the compère for the event.'

'Can I ask you something?' Molly said as they reached the busy entrance to the ballroom, where

273

the fancy-dress parade was taking place.

'Ask away.'

'It's just that I helped a family with their daughter's fancy-dress outfit. Was it the right thing to do? I hope I haven't given her an unfair advantage.'

It was Johnny's turn to laugh. 'I've no doubt that many redcoats have been helping the children. I was called in to advise on a rather nifty Spitfire costume.'

'You mean the child is going to enter dressed as a plane?' Molly said in astonishment.

Johnny opened the door and they headed towards their colleagues. 'You'd be surprised how inventive the families can be. The children's fancy dress is one of the most hotly contested competitions of the week. How have you missed it for so long?'

'It's usually been my afternoon off, but I'll make sure not to miss it in future.' She laughed as Johnny took the microphone and got the proceedings under way.

'That was so much fun,' Molly said as she joined Plum and Bunty at the bar of the Pig and Whistle Inn. She had to keep refusing drinks from the holidaymakers as she made her way across the pub or she'd have been drunk within the hour.

'I spotted you with the heart-throb earlier,' Plum said as she handed Molly her drink and then sipped her half-pint of brown ale. 'Are things back on?'

Molly nodded. 'He's taking me to visit my aunt tomorrow. That is, he's dropping me off at her house.'

'What about Gloria? You don't want to be tread-ing on her toes,' Bunty said, checking her watch. 'We'd better hurry – the show is starting soon at the Butlins Theatre and we are supposed to be there mingling with the campers and helping people to their seats.'

Molly finished her shandy and placed her glass on the bar. 'I do believe she's been making up the story about her and Johnny being a couple. How-ever, to be on the safe side, I don't intend to be-come romantically involved. Hurry up, you two, or we'll not get a seat, let alone help the campers.'

As Bunty and Plum followed Molly through the busy throng, they raised their eyebrows at each other. They did not believe for one moment that Molly wasn't already in love with Johnny Johnson.

'I'm sorry the weather isn't so good,' Johnny said as he helped Molly into his car.

'It's not your fault it's raining, Johnny. At least the campers are happy with the indoor competi-tions,' Molly said, removing her headscarf and checking her face in the small powder compact she took from her handbag. She watched as he took a cloth from the glove compartment and wiped the car windscreen. Dark hair, dampened by the light rain, flopped over his forehead as he worked at his task. He looked up and grinned at her, brushing his hair back into place with one hand. Even with tousled hair and more than a little wet, he looked as handsome as he had when Molly had watched him on the cinema screen at the Odeon back home in Erith.

'Right, I think we're ready to go,' he said, climbing back into the vehicle and starting the engine. 'Did you hear from your aunt?'

'No. I had hoped a letter would come today. I checked again just before I headed over to meet you. I do hope she will see me.'

'I'm sure she will. Perhaps it's been a shock and she needed time to think,' he said, driving carefully out of the camp, careful to avoid a group of cyclists, all of whom were wrapped up in wet-weather clothing and pedalling frantically against the rain, which was beginning to fall more heavily. He steered his car towards a road sign-posted to Spilsby.

'I suppose it has. I never imagined after Mum and Dad died and I became an orphan that I'd discover a family, even if some of them are not very pleasant,' she added as an afterthought, thinking of Harriet and Simon.

'Which family are these?' Johnny asked. 'I was under the impression you hadn't met any yet.'

'Two of Dad's cousins arrived earlier this year. I had no idea they existed, let alone that Dad had left the house to them. That's why I came to Butlins – to keep out of Simon's way until the will was sorted out. It became unbearable to live under the same roof, even though I'd lived in that house all my life.'

Johnny was thoughtful for a while as he negotiated the narrow country lanes. 'Would you like to tell me about it? I'm a good listener.'

'I've nothing to hide from my friends. Plum and Bunty know all about my problem, as do George, Kath and Freda, who are coming to the camp for a holiday. They are almost like family. I don't know what I'd have done without them after the accident.'

Johnny reached across and squeezed Molly's hand. 'I like to think we are friends, more than friends, so please start at the beginning and tell me everything.'

The journey passed quickly as Molly told Johnny of her life in Erith and all that had happened before she arrived at the holiday camp.

'That's why I was so nervous at the interview in London. I didn't intentionally mean to spill tea over you or step on your foot. I'm sorry,' she said, trying not to smile at the memory.

Johnny burst out laughing. 'Or drown that poor woman I shared a taxi with.'

'She wasn't your ... your–'

'No, she wasn't my ... my ... so get that idea out of your sweet head. Being who I am means that sometimes I have to escort people and be seen in public at certain events. It doesn't mean I like doing it. It's part of the job, and that's why I want to change my life.'

Molly felt her heart thump in her chest. 'You do?'

'Yes, but you will always be a part of my life, if you wish to be.'

'What about Gloria?' The words burst out before Molly could stop them.

'Gloria? There's nothing going on between Gloria and me. I gave her a lift to London recently. Why? Has she been upsetting you?'

'She may have said something, but I'm not upset,' Molly said shyly. Suddenly Gloria and her awful words were a million miles away. She was here with Johnny and that's all that mattered.

'Forget Gloria. Listen, I'd like to help with your family problem, but now isn't the time,' he said as he parked his car across the road from Molly's aunt's house. 'The sun has come out, and over there are family members you've never met. I'll wait here until I see you are invited into the house. I'll come back at five to collect you and we can dine somewhere quiet and catch up on each other's lives.'

Molly leaned over and kissed Johnny's cheek. 'I'd like that very much.'

17

Molly turned back to see Johnny still sitting in his car watching her. He raised a hand and waved encouragement as she knocked on the door of the small cottage. It seemed an age before she heard footsteps approach and the door open. She was faced with a younger version of her mum. The shock caused Molly to lose the power of speech as she stared back at what was surely her aunt Sally. The woman, wiping her hands on a tea towel, in turn looked shocked at seeing Molly on her doorstep.

'Well, bless my soul. You've got the look of the Kenyons, that's no mistake. You must be Molly.'

Molly could only nod in agreement.

'Come along inside. It looks as though we're about to have another shower of rain. I had a feeling you'd be on my doorstep before too long.'

Molly was just able to wave to Johnny as her aunt ushered her inside.

'Sit yourself down, Molly, and I'll put the kettle on. You're probably wondering why I never replied to your letter. We've been all of a tizzy here, what with my two having the measles. Joe's working all hours on the farm now the land girls have left, and I've just not had time to get into the village and post my reply to your letter.' She walked over to a dresser that filled one wall of the kitchen and reached up for an envelope. 'Here you are. Read that while I make us a brew.'

Molly realized she'd not spoken a word since knocking on her aunt's door. 'Gosh,' was all she could think to say, as her aunt burst out laughing and Molly joined in. 'I thought you didn't want to know me. I just had this mad idea to knock on your door and find out once and for all,' she said to her aunt.

'Why ever would you think that, my love? I've waited years to hear from Charlotte and Norman, and to have their daughter turn up out of the blue is wonderful,' she said as she poured boiling water into a brown earthenware teapot. 'Receiving your letter and knowing you are working not far away was the answer to my dreams,' she added, pulling a knitted tea cosy over the pot and settling herself across the table from her niece.

'You have a very nice home,' Molly said as she admired the crockery on the dresser and the pretty gingham curtains hanging at the leaded windows.

'We make do. The cottage comes with the job.

Perhaps in time my Joe will have his own farm, but for now we are content.' She poured tea into two pretty cups and passed one to Molly. 'By rights this tea set and the china on the dresser should be Charlotte's, but it was passed to me after Mother died.' A wistful look appeared on her face. 'If only we'd had Charlotte here at the time, but no one knew where she was,' she added, looking sad. 'I was only seven when she ran away with Norman. I was the surprise baby that Mother never expected. I remember how she would take me to Brownie meetings, where she helped out. In fact, my most vivid memories are of her teaching me the Brownie Promise and the Brownie games. Your dad, Norman, would take me for a drive in his car when he was courting Charlotte. It was such fun for a little girl stuck on a farm with no young friends nearby.'

'I have the same memories. Mum was Brown Owl and also ran the Girl Guides where we live. So many people have the same memories that you have,' Molly said. It felt strange to meet someone who had known her mum so many years ago.

'Whatever happened for them to disappear out of my life I'll never know. Mother and Father never mentioned Charlotte again. Even at Mother's funeral, when my sister's name was mentioned, Father just turned his back and refused to speak about her. His face looked like thunder when someone mentioned Norman. If only they'd kept in touch...' she said again.

'But they tried...' Molly said. 'At least, Mum did.' She reached for her handbag, in which she had the papers that had led to her finding her aunt. 'I found them recently, after...' Molly faltered. How did you explain to someone that a sister they'd not seen for many years, and had hoped to see again one day, had died at too young an age?

'Has something happened, Molly?' Sally asked gently.

'Mum and Dad died in a car accident almost a year ago,' she said, knowing of no easier way to break the sad news.

'Oh my,' Sally said, placing the teapot back on the table with a thud, causing the pretty cups to rattle and tea to slop into the saucers. 'That wasn't what I expected to hear, and that's no mistake. There was me thinking I would be seeing my sister again before too long, after I heard from you.' She pulled a handkerchief from the cuff of her cardigan and dabbed her eyes, tears threatening to start.

'I'm sorry. I didn't want to upset you,' Molly said, distressed at upsetting her new-found aunt. 'If there had been any other way of telling you...'

Sally left her seat and went to Molly, then hugged her tightly. Both women wept. Molly felt as though it was her mum hugging her. She could smell baked cakes and the faint aroma of lavender water and soap. For a moment, she felt she was with her mum once more. She prayed her mum was happy that her daughter had found her young sister.

When the tears subsided and they'd wiped their eyes, Sally checked the tea. 'It's stone cold. I think we need something stronger, don't you?' She went to the dresser and took a bottle of sherry from one of the cupboards. 'This'll do nicely.' Pouring a generous amount into each of two small glasses, she handed one to Molly. 'To Charlotte and Norman, God bless them.'

Molly raised her glass. 'Mum and Dad,' she whispered, praying she wouldn't start to cry again. She must be brave and think of the future now she'd found her family. She hoped her mum would have approved.

A clatter from the staircase announced the arrival of Sally's two daughters. 'Come into the kitchen, girls. I have a surprise for you.'

Two little girls entered the room and shyly stood by their mother when they spotted Molly. 'This is your cousin Molly. Doesn't she look like your nana Kenyon?' Sally said. 'Molly, these are my twins, Avril and Annie. Say hello to your cousin, twinnies.'

The two girls stepped forward. Avril shook hands politely, and Annie curtsied before they both burst into giggles.

'Oh my, I feel like Princess Elizabeth. No one has ever curtsied to me before. Can I tell you a secret?' Molly smiled at the two girls.

'Yes, please,' Annie said as they both crept nearer.

Molly leaned close to their heads and whispered, 'I've never had a cousin before. Now I have two.'

Both girls' eyes grew wide as they thought about what Molly had told them.

'We look like each other,' Avril said. 'But your hair is darker than ours.'

'Daddy calls us his blonde bombshells. Mummy's is mousey.'

Sally laughed loudly. 'Out of the mouths of babes.'

'I wouldn't say you are mousey,' Molly said, looking at her aunt. 'It's just like my mum's. Light brown.'

'Is your mummy here?' one of the girls asked. Molly was having trouble working out which child was Avril and which was Annie.

'She's gone to heaven. Perhaps Molly has a photograph she could show you sometime?'

'I have one here,' Molly said, delving into her bag, 'It's one of when Mum married Dad.'

Sally and her daughters huddled close as they looked at the photograph.

'Were you a bridesmaid?' Annie asked.

Sally and Molly grinned at each other. 'Molly wasn't even born then, my love. They are rather interested in bridesmaids and weddings, as Dan's brother is getting married in August and both girls are to be bridesmaids. They talk of nothing else.'

'Our dresses will be older kneel, and we are going to be carrying flowers,' Annie announced.

Avril sighed. 'It's "eau de Nil". That's green,' she added knowingly to Molly. 'Will you come to the wedding and watch us be bridesmaids?'

Molly was flustered. 'I'm not sure. It's usual to be invited to weddings, and the bride and groom don't even know me.' She looked to Sally for help.

Sally shrugged her shoulders. 'It's not a posh affair. We will be having the wedding breakfast here. If the rain holds off, we will use the barn and garden so we can spread out. You will be very welcome to join us, I'm sure. After all, you are family.' Sally's eyes were drawn to the photograph she was now holding. 'Your dad was very handsome.'

'He can come to the wedding too,' the twins said excitedly.

'He's in heaven,' Sally explained gently.

'With Nana Kenyon?' Avril asked.

'I would think so, my love.' She ran her finger over the image of her sister and brother-in-law. 'If only they'd not been so stubborn and got in touch...'

As much as Molly liked her aunt, she didn't want anyone to think badly of her parents. 'It wasn't quite like that,' she murmured.

Sally sensed Molly needed to explain and called her daughters' attention. 'Girls, why not find your cardigans and wellies and we can show Molly the farm? Wash your faces first.'

As the girls scampered upstairs, Sally placed the photograph on the table. 'Can you tell me anything?'

Molly sighed. Where should she begin? 'I grew up an only child in Erith, Kent. It's not far from London,' she added.

'They went south, then? I've often wondered,' Sally said thoughtfully.

'I never knew I had family. Dad had an ironmonger's shop in the town and we lived nearby. After the car accident, I had to leave Erith for a while and come up this way to work at Butlins. It's only recently I found these documents and realized I had family in the area. A friend helped me find Nan's grave and by chance the owner of a teashop recalled the family name. She said she went to school with you.' She passed the documents to Sally, who looked carefully at them.

'But what makes you think there was more to Charlotte and Norman being unable to return?'

'I found these letters as well,' Molly said, handing them over.

Sally read the letter her sister had sent first and smiled. 'It must have been such a happy time for her. I wish we could have shared it.'

'So do I,' Molly agreed. 'Our lives would have been so different. They may even have still been alive.'

Sally then read her mother's reply. 'That'll have been Dad making Mum write those words. Oh, he's a miserable bugger,' Sally declared, before clamping her hand over her mouth. 'I'm sorry for my language, Molly, but your grandfather can be a most disagreeable man at times, and once he has a grudge against someone, he never changes his mind. He's a curmudgeonly old so-and-so. I only visit out of duty so the children know who their grandfather is.'

Molly, who had always wanted to know about her grandparents, was horrified. Whatever could have made the old man that way?

'What does "cum–", "cumudg–" What does that word mean, Mummy?'

'It means little girls shouldn't listen to adults who are having a private conversation. Now, get those wellington boots on and we can get going. I have a pair that I think will fit you, Molly. Come on – I want to know all about Butlins, as well as about that rather handsome man who dropped you off at my door.'

Molly followed her new-found family out of the kitchen and into the boot room to change her shoes. She felt that life would never be quiet again and she looked forward to getting to know her aunt Sally and the adorable twins.

'What is Butlins like, Auntie Molly?'

'Molly is our cousin, Annie, not our auntie,' Avril said with a childish superior air.

'I know she is, but she's too grown-up to be a cousin. Besides, if she was a cousin, she'd play with us.'

Molly, who was walking between her two small cousins, laughed at the chatter. 'I'm most definitely your cousin, and I'd love to play with you another time. Today, I want to get to know my auntie Sally and learn about my family. Do you mind?'

Both girls hugged Molly and skipped off happily towards the barn, where their father was working. 'You have the perfect life,' she sighed, leaning against the wooden railings of a fence and gazing out to where cows were grazing. The rain had stopped and the sun was shining. She could smell the warm grass and feel the heat of the day returning.

'I love it here, and I love my life. I can't imagine living anywhere else,' Sally said. 'I'll ask Annie's question, as I'm curious to know. What is it like working at Butlins? I can't conceive of being with hundreds of people every day. Do you ever get time to yourself?'

'I wasn't sure what to expect. A good friend suggested I apply for a job when I needed to get away from Erith, but I really took to the life and have made new friends. I never know what I'm doing from one day to the next. Yesterday, I helped make a bingo-queen fancy-dress outfit for a little girl, and in the evening, we had a show with comedians from a radio show. Other days, I'm organizing nature trips for the children or assembling contestants for glamorous-grannies and knobbly-knees competitions. One day is never like another. I'm busy all the time and it takes my mind off being away from home.'

'That does sound fun. I'm not sure I could make fancy-dress outfits, though.'

'We don't do it all the time. It's just when a camper has a problem I like to step in and help. Cynthia, the little girl whose costume I made yesterday, was in a fix as her mother is in a wheel-chair. How could I not help? She came third. Her parents were so proud. I like to think it's my mum's days with the Brownies that gave me those skills.' Molly smiled at the memory. 'Mind you, a colleague helped a little lad with his Spitfire outfit and disaster struck when the wings fell off during the judging.' Molly chuckled at the memory of Johnny's embarrassment.

Sally laughed. 'Never a dull moment by the sound of it.' Her face took on a serious look. 'You say you had to leave Erith. Would you tell me why? I thought it was where you grew up and lived with Charlotte and Norman?'

'It's a long and complicated story, but I don't mind telling you. After all, you are my family.'

Sally thought for a moment. 'Let me check the girls are behaving themselves and not bothering

Dan. Then we can go back to the cottage for a cup of tea and you can tell me everything. That's what family are for.'

Molly watched as Sally walked over to her daughters to have a word. Sally reminded her so much of her mum. She was so grateful for being accepted into the family fold. A family that, for some reason, she had been denied for many years.

'I've never heard of Harriet and Simon Missons,' Sally said after Molly had told all that had happened since her parents' deaths. 'I just wish my mother had spoken more about the past. I know she always feared your grandfather's temper, but it always struck me as strange that she didn't share what went on with your parents. It must have been something awful for them to move away as they did.'

'I'm sure they didn't do anything wrong. I have no way of proving it, but in my heart I know they were good people. I just wish I knew. Then for Harriet and Simon to appear...' She gave a shudder.

Sally was quite indignant. 'No, I'd never believe that my sister and Norman had done wrong. I may have been a child and not much older than Avril and Annie are now, but I know they were good people. I'd fight any man who said otherwise.'

Looking at her aunt's angry face, Molly knew that her own gut feeling was correct. Whatever the reason for them to flee south, they had not done wrong. 'Do you know anything of my dad's family?'

'I'm sorry – I don't, but I'll certainly make some enquiries. Now, would you like another cup of tea and a teacake?'

Molly rubbed her stomach. 'Thank you, but I couldn't drink another cup.'

Sally laughed. 'I do like a cup of tea when I'm chatting. We seemed to have chatted for an age. It's been lovely, though. You will stay for dinner, won't you?'

Molly looked at the clock on the kitchen wall. 'Oh my goodness, it's gone five. Johnny will be waiting for me.'

'Is that the handsome young man I saw when I opened the door to you?'

'Yes, he's a friend. He was the one who helped me to find you. He said he'd pick me up at five o'clock.'

'Then we had better invite him in if he is waiting.' Sally headed to the front door with Molly close behind. 'It looks as though he has just arrived,' she said as they heard him turn off the engine. Sally waved and headed towards the car, where she chatted to Johnny through the open window before he climbed out and followed her towards the cottage. 'It's all settled. Johnny is staying to dinner.'

Molly raised her eyebrows and grinned at Johnny. 'It seems my aunt is a force to be reckoned with,' she said as he greeted her with a kiss on the cheek. Molly spotted Sally watching with interest and prayed she wasn't a matchmaker as well.

'It's only stew and dumplings, and one of my apple pies, but we have plenty, and now we have a new member of the family, it's only right she joins us for a meal.'

Johnny rubbed his hands together. 'As long as I'm not intruding, I'd be delighted to join you. Butlins may feed us well, but you can't beat a home-cooked meal.'

Sally showed Johnny to the front room and ushered Molly in after him before heading to the kitchen, insisting she didn't need help to prepare vegetables when Molly offered.

'You don't mind eating with my family, do you?' Molly asked.

'Not at all. That's if you don't mind?' Johnny replied as he stretched out in an overstuffed arm-chair. 'I'll take you for a meal another time if you like?'

'I would like that very much. Thank you, Johnny.'

'There's no need to thank me. I enjoy taking you out and having you to myself,' he said. He looked tired and his eyelids were starting to droop.

'No, I mean thank you for helping me to find my family. I'd never have done it on my own.'

'You deserve to have a nice family.' He smiled as his eyes closed.

Molly sat on a footstool close by. 'Have you had a busy day?'

'It was tiring. I attended a memorial service for comrades at the airbase who died during the war. Families were invited to the service, so it was rather emotional.'

'I'd have helped if you'd told me. I feel awful having had a lovely day while you had such a sad one.'

Johnny reached across and took her hand. 'There will be other times. I want you to know your family. You can tell me all about it on the drive home.'

The moment was lost as the twins burst into the room. They froze as soon as they spotted Johnny.

'Johnny, these are my mischievous young cousins, Avril and Annie,' Molly said as the girls stared at him.

'I'm pleased to meet you both. Who is who? I can't tell you apart.'

'I'm Annie. Avril has a freckle on her cheek,' Annie said as she approached Johnny and leaned on the arm of his chair. 'Are you Molly's boy-friend?'

Johnny laughed out loud. Molly wished a hole would open up and swallow her.

Avril joined her twin and smiled at Johnny. 'We are going to be bridesmaids.'

'Whoa there. A moment ago, I was a boyfriend and now there's a wedding!'

Molly felt herself blush. 'No, Johnny, the girls don't mean us. I mean...'

Johnny gazed at Molly and gave a gentle smile that reached his eyes. 'What's it to be, Molly Missons, boyfriend or husband-to-be? I'm open to offers.'

Molly couldn't breathe. Surely he was joking with her. What should she say? Her beating heart was urging her to say, 'Yes, please.'

'Would you like to play tiddlywinks with us, Johnny?' Avril asked.

The moment was broken. 'I'll help Sally while you play with the girls,' Molly said as she escaped to the kitchen before Johnny could say another word.

Everyone enjoyed the meal. Sally was a good cook and served fluffy dumplings on top of tender mutton, and vegetables she'd grown herself in the kitchen garden. Even the cooking apples in the pie were from their small orchard. Molly remained quiet as she ate and listened to Johnny chat to the family. Dan, Sally's husband, was soon telling them about the farm and his work. Johnny seemed interested, and when Dan announced he had a problem with the tractor and would need to go out to work on it before they lost the light, Johnny was quick to volunteer his help.

'Johnny, you're not dressed to work on a greasy old tractor,' Sally protested.

'You have overalls, don't you?' he asked Dan.

The farmer nodded. 'And work boots. You'll not want those ruined.' He nodded to the polished black shoes Johnny was wearing.

'Then let's get cracking,' he said, rolling up his sleeves and following Dan from the kitchen.

It was late when they left Sally and Dan's. The repair to the tractor had taken longer than expected. Molly was amused to see Johnny's face covered in streaks of grease when he finally followed Dan into the cottage. She'd only ever seen him in smart clothes and the Butlins uniform. Sally had insisted on providing hot drinks and sandwiches after Johnny had cleaned himself up, before they bid the couple goodbye.

'I like your family,' Johnny said, as he headed the car up the dark lane and on towards Skegness. 'You seem to get on well with them.'

'I feel very fortunate to be accepted into the fold. It must have been hard for Sally to not see her sister and wonder what happened to her all these years.'

'It must have been the same for your mother and father,' Johnny suggested.

Molly thought for a moment. 'Yes, it must have been, but they never spoke of family matters. Whatever happened was kept locked away for over twenty years. Sally mentioned that my grandfather was inclined to be strict and rather miserable at times. Once Mum left, she was never mentioned in the house again. I hope to meet him and at least ask what happened.'

'It makes one wonder what can have driven a man to turn his daughter away like that. I hope I never do such a thing,' he said, staring ahead into the night.

Molly could see a serious frown on Johnny's face. 'I don't think you would, Johnny,' she said. 'From what I've seen, you are a fair man.'

'Even when a nervous woman tips drinks over me and treads on my feet?'

Molly smiled to herself in the darkened car. 'Are you never going to let me forget that?'

'Never,' Johnny chuckled.

'Molly, Molly!' a voice shrieked from somewhere in the throng of campers alighting from a packed coach. It was Saturday, changeover day at Butlins,

Skegness, and Molly had lost count of the number of hugs and kisses she'd received from campers leaving for their homes. Shouts of 'Keep in touch' and 'See you next year' could be heard from the parting holidaymakers. It was a special day for Molly: she was expecting George and Kath to arrive, along with her best friend, Freda, and was on tenterhooks waiting for them to appear.

'If I'm not mistaken, that shout is from your friend Freda. Unless there's someone else trying to catch your attention.' Bunty grinned as she pointed towards the coach, where an excited Freda was hanging on to the door and waving frantically from the steps. 'Why not go and help your friends settle in? There are plenty of us here to do the meeting and greeting. Tell Freda I'm looking forward to meeting her later.'

'Thank you, Bunty. You're a real chum.' Molly pushed through the crowd and hugged Freda as she jumped from the bottom step of the coach and made way for George and Kath to alight.

'Molly, love, you look a picture in your uniform,' Kath said as she gave Molly a kiss. 'Your hair looks even lovelier with it a little longer. Here, George, leave those suitcases and come and see our Molly.'

George gripped Molly so tightly in a bear hug that she could hardly breathe. Holding her at arm's length, he studied her face carefully. 'I was hoping you'd be pale and wasting away so I could pick you up and take you back home to Erith, but that's not the case. You are blooming, Molly. I can see that working here has done you the world of good. I hope this doesn't mean we'll never see you back with us?'

'Wherever I am in the world, Erith will always be in my heart, George. Besides, where else would I go when the season ends if not home to you? That's if you'll have me? I can't hide away from horrid Simon forever,' she said, picking up the smaller of their suitcases. 'Now, let's collect the keys to your chalets and settle you in, shall we?'

'This is so exciting. I can't believe we're going to be together for the whole week,' Freda said, linking arms with her friend. 'I'm going to stick by your side for the next seven days. I might even be tempted to become a redcoat.'

'You mustn't feel you have to stay with me, Freda. I do have my work, and you may want to try other activities.'

'We are bound to see lots of you. How big can this place be?' Kath said.

Molly laughed. 'You'd be surprised, Kath. Just wait and see. Now, here we are. Leave your cases while we get you registered.'

18

'Oh my, I haven't laughed so much in a long time,' Kath said, wiping her eyes on a sparkling white handkerchief. 'I never expected to see a redcoat thrown into the swimming pool.'

Molly had headed back to her job of greeting new campers in the reception area after seeing that George and Kath were settled in their chalet. She found them later, sitting in deckchairs by the pool, watching the fun and games as campers entered races and fooled about. 'I've seen redcoats thrown into the pool on many occasions now, but it never ceases to make me laugh,' she said.

'Have you been thrown into the pool?' Freda asked. She was stretched out on the grass, wearing the cutest shorts and matching top. Molly made a mental note to ask about the dress pattern Freda had used to make the outfit. Something similar would be ideal for her afternoons off when she headed to the beach to relax.

'My goodness, no. I'm working mainly with children during the day and they don't do such things. Many things have been thrown over me, but I've not yet ended up in the pool. Now, I have a half-hour break. Would you like to accompany me to the coffee bar and have an ice-cream sundae?'

Freda jumped to her feet. 'That would be good. I was beginning to feel quite sleepy in this sun. Are you coming, Kath, George?'

The older woman looked at her husband, who had placed his newspaper over his face and was leaning back in his deckchair. 'I'd prefer to stay here for a while and rest. The train and coach journey took it out of us a bit. Perhaps you could bring back a tray of tea? I see other campers have them.'

'Yes, we can do that. Perhaps a sticky bun as well to see you through to dinnertime?'

'That sounds grand,' a muffled voice was heard to say from beneath the newspaper.

The girls giggled as they headed off for their ice cream. 'This week is going to be such fun,' Freda said. 'I just hope George doesn't overdo things. He needs a rest after what he's been through.'

Molly stopped dead in her tracks. 'What do you mean, Freda? What's happened?'

Freda sighed. 'Me and my big mouth. We didn't want to worry you...'

Molly grabbed Freda's elbow and steered her towards a rose garden, where they could talk away from other campers. 'Now I am worried. What the hell's been happening?'

Freda sat on a bench and twiddled her fingers, trying hard not to make eye contact with Molly. 'Simon roughed him up and George bumped his head.'

Molly was furious. 'Tell me everything, Freda, and don't leave out a single thing or I swear I'll be back home in Erith before you've even finished your holiday and I'll never leave town again.'

'I don't really know where to begin...'

'Try the beginning.' Molly was not only angry with her friends for keeping her in the dark over what had happened but with herself for enjoying her time away from Erith without a thought that her second cousin had been causing as much trouble for George as he had for herself.

Freda absentmindedly picked at the petals of a yellow rose as she thought of what to say to Molly. 'It was three weeks ago. George had been playing darts for the Prince of Wales team. It was a home game against the Railway Hotel from Slade Green. He went alone as usual. After all, it's only a short walk, and no one was to know that he'd bump into Simon like that.'

Molly frowned. 'Like what?'

'George was a little late and in a hurry. You know how he likes to be punctual.'

'Yes, we can usually set our watch by him. Go on,' Molly urged. She dreaded hearing what Freda would say next but wanted to know all the same.

'There was a crowd standing out on the pavement. It was a warm evening and he remembers saying hello to people he knew and making apologies as he pushed through the crowd. It is always busy in the Prince on darts nights. Someone jolted his shoulder and he stumbled as he reached out to steady himself. The person pushed him away and he fell. As he went down, he noticed it had been Simon Missons who had shoved him. Simon knelt beside him, and rather than help him to his feet, he grabbed George's hair and banged his head hard onto the pavement George doesn't remember much after that, apart from Simon whispering in his ear.'

Molly felt herself shudder. 'What did he say? Was George badly hurt?'

'He said he is going to get the house and the shop and nothing will stop him. George spent the night in hospital. He had two stitches in the back of his head where he hit the kerb. We made sure he didn't go into the shop for the rest of the week and took things easy. When he did, Kath went with him. She said that nothing would happen to George or the shop while she was there. She even sat by the telephone most of each day ready to call the police if Simon or his mother should appear.'

Molly sat down next to Freda and put her head

in her hands. 'I wish this would stop. Why is Simon doing this? None of you deserves to be in danger because of me. Surely a house and shop aren't worth all this trouble. George has already told Simon the ironmonger's belongs to him and not me just so he didn't bother us. I thought that would be enough to keep him away.'

'I stayed with Kath the night George was in the cottage hospital. We thought long and hard about what happened and also made some decisions. The first was that we would not let you know what happened, as chances were you'd rush back and Simon would like that. With George out of action, you'd be more vulnerable than you were before, and we don't want Simon putting you in a compromising situation again. It could turn out worse than before.'

Molly shuddered as she thought how Simon had forced himself upon her. If it had not been for quick thinking, goodness knows what would have happened. 'I know you did the right thing, but I can't help thinking this is all my fault.'

'Don't be silly,' Freda said. 'You're our friend, almost family really, and family stick together.'

Molly gave a weak smile. 'I don't know what I'd have done without you this past year.'

'We made another decision,' Freda added. 'We intend to be firmer with Mr Denton's nephew and insist he contact his uncle and help us resolve this business with your dad's will. No one has seen the will Harriet says she has, so how do we even know she is telling the truth?'

Molly felt confused. 'Why would someone know to turn up out of the blue if they didn't have a claim on Dad's property? It's so confusing. I shall have to ask my grandad when I meet him at the family wedding.'

Freda looked surprised. 'What's all this about an aunt and a grandad and a family wedding? When did this happen?'

Molly laughed. 'You're not the only one who can keep secrets. I wanted to wait until I could tell you all face to face. I've found Mum's younger sister. She lives not far from here. She is married and I have twin cousins. Oh, Freda, they are delightful. You will love them when you meet them. My life seems to have changed so much since I came to Butlins.'

Freda felt shell-shocked. 'Blimey, what a surprise. Now it's my turn to say I want to know all about it. First, I should collect that tea for Kath and George. I'll be back in two shakes. You'd better do your job. That lady's been hovering over there for a few minutes. She looks as though she needs help. We can have our ice-cream sundaes another time. We have all week.'

Molly walked over to where an elderly lady was standing looking lost. With a few helpful words, Molly explained about dinnertime and where the lady should go. She sat back down on a bench between fragrant rose bushes and thought about what Freda had told her. Perhaps she should sell the ironmonger's; then Simon and his mother could not get their grubby hands on it. George and Kath were close to retiring and she would see they were well provided for. That's if she could get a good price for the business. She had no idea about such things. She was deep in thought when she heard footsteps approaching. It must be Freda.

'Is there something wrong, Molly?'

Molly turned quickly at the sound of Johnny's voice. 'I'm sorry. I know I should be working,' she said quickly.

'No, please stay where you are. I passed by a little while ago and thought you looked distressed. I didn't want to interrupt as you were talking to one of the campers.'

'That's my friend Freda. I believe I mentioned to you that she was visiting, along with George and Kath, who have taken care of me since my parents died. She gave me some disturbing news, but I'm fine and can return to my job.' She started to head back towards the path that led to the main Butlins building. From the large clock on the wall, she could see that time was passing quickly. She should be in reception recruiting children for the activities she was involved in, as well as helping late arrivals collect their chalet keys.

Johnny took Molly's hand and led her back to the bench she'd just vacated. 'You work hard for Butlins, Molly – a few minutes here or there won't matter. What's more important is that you are upset and I intend to get to the bottom of it before we leave this rose garden.'

'Oh, Johnny, even you can't help me with this problem. You've been a good friend to me in recent weeks, but I can't burden you with every-thing that is less than perfect in my life.'

'Molly, my intentions are to be burdened with every problem you have in your life, however large or small. I'm here for you, Molly, and will

301

be as long as you need me.'

'But, Johnny–' She didn't have chance to utter another word as Johnny took her in his arms and kissed her gently. She gave herself up to his kiss as he held her close, oblivious to the world around them.

'I treated us to an ice-cream cone as we missed out on a sundae. I hope you don't mind... Oh my gosh!'

Molly jumped away from Johnny and spun round to face her friend. 'Freda, I believe you've met Mr Johnny Johnson before.'

Freda's eyes grew wide before she came to her senses and held out her hand to shake his, not realizing she still had hold of the ice cream.

Johnny took the cone and passed it to Molly before shaking Freda's hand. 'It's a pleasure to meet you, Freda. I've heard a lot about you. Please, take a seat before your ice cream melts.'

Freda didn't speak a word as she sat down next to Molly and licked the dripping ice cream. Her puzzled expression changed to a giggle as she looked at her best friend. 'I should have guessed this would happen. I must say he looks more normal in real life than he does in the magazines you had stashed in your bedside table back home.'

Johnny roared with laughter. 'I need more people like you in my life, Freda. It's a refreshing change not to have starlets and fans throwing themselves at my feet.'

'Will the pair of you stop it?' Molly grinned. 'You are embarrassing me. I thought you were here to help me, not show off to my friend!'

Johnny looked serious. 'I am. I want the pair of

you to explain what's going on. Don't leave anything out. I may not be a secret agent in real life, but I'll make a damn good show of solving any problems you have.'

If Johnny knew everything that is going on in my life and that of my friends, he might regret what he just said, Molly thought to herself.

Molly had no idea how she worked through the next few hours. Thank goodness she knew her job and could point campers towards the correct chalet blocks and advise about the medical centre and children's activities. Satisfied she'd done a good job, she bid goodbye to the last camper in the reception area and decided to speak to George. Freda had begged her not to mention the altercation with Simon, but Molly felt that George might just mention it if she were alone with him. Heading back through the camp past the swimming pool to the grassed area where her friends had been sitting earlier in the afternoon, she spotted George. He was not alone. Sitting next to him was Johnny, his long legs stretched out as he sat in the striped deckchair deep in conversation with her dad's oldest friend. As she approached, both men stood up.

'There you are, my love. I hope you've not been working too hard? It doesn't seem right when we are all enjoying ourselves,' George said, giving her a peck on the cheek. 'Kath and Freda have gone back to change for dinner. I've been having a chat with your young man here.'

'George, Mr Johnson is a work colleague,' she said, feeling embarrassed in front of the two men.

'That's not what Johnny has told us, or what Freda said when she came back earlier. Why, Kath and Freda have nigh on planned a wedding.' He laughed at his own joke.

Molly could have curled up and died. 'I'm sorry, Johnny. I apologize for my friends. They do get carried away sometimes.'

'I'm happy to go along with wedding plans.' He smiled gently, noticing Molly's embarrassment. 'To whom should I address my request for your hand in marriage?'

Molly frowned. She had no idea if Johnny was joking or not.

'I would have said that was my duty now, but Freda says you've unearthed family since being here at Butlins,' George said.

'I was saving the surprise for when you arrived here. So much has happened recently.'

George patted her arm. 'I'm pleased for you, Molly. You are entitled to your secrets. Have you met your grandparents?'

'Not yet. I've only met my aunt and her family. My grandmother has passed away, and I'm told my grandfather is a bit of a recluse. But talking of secrets, don't you have something to tell me, George?'

George rubbed the back of his head where he'd been injured. 'I was biding my time for the right moment, but your friend here had other ideas.'

'Molly, George has been telling me what happened and more about your problems with your dad's cousins. I've offered my assistance.'

'But there's no need... When Mr Denton arrives back in Erith, it will all be resolved.'

'I've accepted Johnny's help, Molly. He has a friend in the legal trade who I can speak with. It doesn't hurt to have another pair of ears listen to the problem. How much longer will it be before Simon goes further than knocking an old man over and making threats that no one else heard? Besides, when you are back home, I'd never forgive myself if he tried to ... you know...'

Johnny looked from George to Molly and could see there was more they'd not explained. 'Is there something I've not been told?'

Molly didn't wish to tell Johnny what had happened. It didn't feel right to speak of how Simon had attacked her. She looked pleadingly at George.

'Simon tried to force himself on our Molly a couple of times,' the older man said.

Johnny looked angry. 'Did he hurt you?'

'No. I'm sure it was the drink that made him do it.' She looked away, unable to make eye contact while she spoke of such personal things.

'He tore your dress, Molly,' George said gently, 'and if I'd not dropped that suitcase on his head the second time, God only knows how it would have ended. We need help, Molly. I know I'd sleep much better knowing those dear to me were safe.'

Molly thought for a moment. 'Thank you, Johnny. I appreciate your help. If you believe your friend can advise us, then I'd be most grateful.'

'Once you're home, I'll have my friend contact you, George. Molly, if you want time off to go back to Erith, then I can arrange it,' Johnny said. 'Now, if we aren't quick, George is going to miss the first sitting for dinner.'

305

George looked his watch. 'Kath is going to have my guts for garters. She wants me suited and booted just to eat my dinner.' He shook hands with Johnny. 'You've picked a good one in our Molly. I know you'll take care of her.'

Johnny walked with Molly back to the staff office to check their duties for the evening. 'I'm on baby-crying duty after dinner.'

'Will you come to the Pig and Whistle afterwards? It's Connie's birthday and the staff who are available are going to throw a surprise party.'

'That's a lovely idea. I doubt I'll be finished until around ten, but I'll see you then.'

Johnny kissed her cheek. 'We never get to spend much time alone. Our courtship seems to be carried out in front of hundreds of people all the time.'

'Is this what this is? A courtship, I mean. It seems such a formal word,' Molly said.

'Haven't we just discussed the wedding with George?' Johnny smiled.

Molly thumped his arm. 'I never know when to take you seriously,' she sighed.

Johnny looked from left to right before sweeping her into his arms. 'Is this serious enough?' he asked before seeking her lips.

Molly closed her eyes and gave herself up to his kiss. For a few brief seconds, she knew what it was like to be in heaven.

As they drew apart, he took her face in his hands and looked into her eyes. 'Where you are concerned, Molly, I am always serious. Please believe that.'

Molly watched as he strode away to his office.

For the first time in almost a year, she felt content with her life and looked forward to the future.

Molly enjoyed her shifts listening out for crying babies. It was a well-executed routine whereby parents notified the nursery that they were leaving their children alone in their chalet while they enjoyed the evening entertainment that Butlins provided. Butlins staff then cycled between the rows of chalets listening out for distraught youngsters. If they heard one, they returned to base and checked a log showing where on the camp the parent could be found. An announcement was then made or displayed in the entertainment area showing a *baby was crying in chalet 150* and the parent would soon arrive to soothe their child. With so many chalets on the site, Molly would cycle miles in a few hours and was usually ready for her bed by the end of her shift. This evening, she couldn't keep her mind off meeting Johnny and had cycled past the reception area before she realized her own name was being called. Turning back, she saw Spud waving to her.

'Molly, do you know where Bunty Grainger is? There's a telephone call for her. I've just checked the staff duty list and she's not working this evening.'

Molly leaned her bike against the wall and thought for a moment. 'She will most likely be in the Pig and Whistle at this time of night. Some of the redcoats are celebrating Connie's birthday. Do you know who is on the telephone? It must be urgent to ring the camp at this time of night.'

'It's a man. He didn't give me a name. He just

307

said it was urgent family business.'

'Oh dear. I do hope her parents are all right. She was telling me today that her mother had written that her father was poorly with his chest again.'

'Look, would you speak to him? You're a friend of the girl and they may let you take a message. I must get back to the gatehouse. Anyone can get in the camp without me there to question them.'

'Yes, I'll do that. It's almost time to go off duty and I can find her and pass on the message.'

Spud nodded his thanks. 'Tell her she can use my telephone if she likes, as reception's about to be locked up for the night. I'll even throw in a cup of cocoa. The kettle's on,' he said as he marched off down the drive.

Molly picked up the telephone in the darkened reception area. A security man was already standing by the door, keys in hand, waiting to lock up. 'Hello. This is Molly Missons, Bunty's friend. We can't locate her at the moment. Can I take a message?'

'Molly, this is Gordon, Bunty's fiancé.'

Molly gasped and looked to see if the security man had noticed. Thankfully, he'd propped himself against the open door at the front of reception and was engrossed in reading the sports page of his newspaper. 'Gordon, you aren't supposed to telephone. Why don't you send a postcard to Plum as we planned?' The system Plum had devised in which Gordon sent postcards to Plum pretending to be her aunt Gertie had been a resounding success.

'Look, Molly, it's urgent. I must speak to Bunty at once. Her life is in danger.'

'Gordon, whatever do you mean? Bunty is here at Butlins. How can she be in danger?' Molly whispered, trying hard not to alert the security man to what she was saying.

'I can't talk for long, as I'm using the hospital telephone and I'm not supposed to be out of bed.'

Molly felt her heart thump in her chest. 'Gordon, what's happened, and why are you in hospital?'

'I found Richard. He bragged that he'd fed the drugs to Aileen that caused her death. He thought we were alone and he'd been drinking. What he didn't realize was that he'd been overheard by Aileen's father.'

'That's good news, isn't it? But why are you in hospital, and why is Bunty in danger?'

'I'd gone to see Aileen's parents to tell them my side of the story. Stupid, I know, but I'd always got on well with her father and he was prepared to listen to what I had to say. It seems his impression of Richard has changed in the years since I was imprisoned. He agreed to invite Richard to his home to confront him. It was while he was out of the room that Richard bragged to me he'd drugged Aileen and was pleased I'd been accused of her murder.'

'But how were you injured? I'm assuming you were as you are in hospital…'

'A minor injury. It's Aileen's father who was really injured. He was shot in the chest and it's not looking so good.'

Molly was horrified. Her hands were clammy as she held the telephone receiver, and she felt light-headed. 'Shot? How?'

'Aileen's father was enraged with what he overheard and there was a struggle. The old man had a handgun in his desk and went to retrieve it. Richard grabbed the weapon and pointed it at me. There was a tussle and it went off, hitting Aileen's father in the shoulder.'

'How awful. But why is Bunty in danger?'

'It was as I went to help the old man that he told me he believed me and would speak to the police to help clear my name. In the meantime, I was to return to Butlins and marry the woman I loved, as life was too short not to be together.'

'But what about Richard? Where was he?'

'I thought he'd run away, but it seems he was still in the room. The next thing I knew, the gun had gone off twice. I took a bullet in my arm, and the second hit the old man, this time in the chest. It was then that Richard ran off. He still has the gun...'

Molly was finding it hard to focus on what Gordon was telling her. 'How long ago was this, Gordon?' She prayed it was only a couple of hours ago, as Richard would not have been able to travel to Skegness from Scotland in that time and Bunty would be safe once they'd informed the police.

'It was this morning. It's been hell just trying to get the police to understand that Richard must assume we are dead and believes Bunty is the only person alive who knows the truth about him. All they would focus on was that Aileen's father had been shot and an escaped prisoner was in the room. I was under guard in hospital for a while until he came round from his operation and managed to speak a few words. Thank God he did.'

Molly glanced at a clock on the wall and tried to count in her head. 'Then it could be eleven or twelve hours ago. Could he be in Skegness yet?'

'My motorbike is missing, so yes, he could be at Butlins already. Please, Molly, you must find Bunty and protect her.'

19

A cough from the security guard reminded Molly that the office was due to be locked for the night. She scribbled down the name of the hospital and a telephone number, and promised Gordon to do all she could to make sure Bunty was protected.

Leaving the office, Molly climbed onto her bicycle, unsure of what she should do. From the ballroom, she could hear strains of music. Within the hour, the band would be playing 'Goodnight Campers' and holidaymakers would be filling the paths and heading to their chalets for the night. She decided to cycle over to the Pig and Whistle to talk to Bunty, Her first consideration must be for her friend's safety. She left the bike and headed into the crowded pub, nodding to holidaymakers who called out to her. It was hard to pin a smile to her face when she was so worried about her friend. She spotted Plum with some colleagues by the far end of the bar and headed in that direction, hoping that Bunty was with them.

'Drink?' Plum called as Molly reached the edge of the group of redcoats.

'Not at the moment, thank you. I'm supposed to be on duty for another half-hour. I'm looking for Bunty. Have you seen her?'

Plum glanced around her. 'She was here a short while ago. 1 spotted her wishing Connie a happy birthday. You look worried. Is there a problem?'

'It's a little noisy in here. Can you come outside and I'll explain? I can't really shout.'

'Let me just give Connie her drink and I'll be with you. I must say you certainly seem worried,' Plum said, giving her chum a quizzical look.

Molly pushed back through the crowd, stopping to ask a few redcoats if they'd seen her friend. By the time Plum joined her, she was beside herself with worry.

'Now, tell me what's troubling you. I've never seen you look so serious.'

Molly explained about Gordon's telephone call. 'We need to find Bunty at once, but I don't know where to start. I had hoped she would be with you in the pub celebrating Connie's birthday.'

'I asked Connie if she'd seen Bunty. Apart from when Bunty wished her a happy birthday, she's not seen her. Connie reckons it was about half an hour ago.'

The two friends sat in silence for a few seconds, wondering what to do next, until their thoughts were interrupted by an announcement over the tannoy saying a child was crying.

'That's it!' Plum said, jumping to her feet from the bench she was sitting on. 'You go to the ballroom and ask for them to broadcast that Redcoat

Bunty is required in the staffroom. I'll ask for the same in the Pig and Whistle, and the theatre. See you by the staffroom in five minutes.'

Molly climbed back onto her bicycle and cycled as quickly as she could to the ballroom. En route, she asked staff she passed if they'd seen Bunty. Each time she drew a blank. Reaching the ballroom, she found a redcoat to relay the message over the loudspeaker system.

Heading back to meet Plum, she had but one thought: what if Richard had already arrived at the holiday camp and found Bunty? She couldn't begin to imagine his state of mind after this morning's events in Scotland.

'Whoa, hold up there. Where are you going at such a speed?'

Molly gripped the brakes of her bike as she saw Johnny step out in front of her. It was only his quick thinking that stopped her flying over the handlebars. As it was, she stumbled from the bike and fell into his arms as it crashed to the ground. 'Oh, Johnny, we need your help. It's Bunty...' she managed to say in between taking great gulps of breath.

'Has there been an accident?' he asked, holding on to Molly so she didn't fall.

'No, but I fear for her life. I have to get back to the staffroom to meet Plum. I'll explain on the way.' She went to pick up her bike, which had landed in a flowerbed.

'Leave it. I'll get someone to collect it later,' he said, placing an arm round Molly's waist and guiding her along the footpath to where Plum was waiting with some colleagues, including

313

Charlie Porter.

'What are you doing here?' she asked in an unhappy voice.

'It's all right, Molly. I asked him to join us. I thought perhaps it was time he knew what was happening, if you-now-who has arrived.' She glanced towards Johnny.

'I've told Johnny. You've no need to speak in code,' she assured her friend. 'What should we do next?'

'Perhaps we should call the police,' Plum suggested.

Johnny thought for a moment. 'It would take too long, and it would be very hard to convince them of what has happened. By the time they contacted the police in Scotland, it would be too late... That's if this Richard is here and has Bunty,' he added.

'Oh, please don't say that,' Plum said, turning more than a little pale.

'If we think the worst, we will be able to cope,' Molly said, patting Plum's arm to console her.

'We need to make a search of the camp,' Johnny said, calling staff members closer so they could hear. 'I don't want to alert or alarm the campers, but we need to be thorough. For those of you who have just arrived, we have reason to believe our colleague Bunty may have been abducted by a man. She was last seen in the Pig and Whistle just over an hour ago in her Butlins uniform. The man may be armed. If you spot Bunty, report back to me. I will be in my office calling in extra security staff before joining the search. Whatever you do, be careful, and remember, we don't want

314

to alarm the campers, and we don't need heroes.'

Johnny then divided the group and gave instructions where they should search.

'Plum and I want to search together, and I think we should start in our chalet,' Molly told Johnny.

He nodded. 'As long as a male colleague goes with you,' he said, looking around as staff headed off to look for Bunty. Only Charlie Porter remained. 'Charlie, will you accompany Molly and Plum, please?'

The two girls looked at each other but accepted they needed an extra pair of hands. 'At least we can watch what he's up to,' Plum whispered, and Molly agreed.

They set off down the long pathway lined by chalets until they reached the end of the row of staff accommodation. The door to their chalet was swinging on its hinges from a light breeze blowing in from the sea.

Charlie put his finger to his lips and crept forward, reappearing several seconds later. 'It's empty, but the door lock's been broken. You'd better both check if anything is missing.' He lit a cigarette and settled into a deckchair outside the chalet. Pulling a notebook and pencil stub from his pocket, he began to write.

'I can't see that anything of mine is missing. How about you?' Molly said as she straightened an upturned bedside table close to Bunty's bed.

'There is something missing. I feel it in my bones,' Plum answered as she moved to the centre of the chalet and closed her eyes.

'Whatever are you doing?'

315

'Trying to remember what the chalet is like.'

Molly watched as Plum screwed her eyes tight, waited for thirty seconds, then opened them and looked around the room. 'Over there by Bunty's bed. There were a couple of photographs on the bedside table.'

Molly knelt down and checked under the bed. She pulled out a small photograph of Gordon in a wooden frame. 'This is the only one I can find.'

'The other one wasn't in a frame,' Plum said.

Both girls checked thoroughly, pulling back bedcovers and even looking between the pages of Bunty's library book.

'He must have it. Richard must have broken into the chalet to find Bunty and taken the photograph,' Plum said, sitting down heavily on her bed and sighing.

'So he doesn't remember what Bunty looked like? I suppose it's been years since he last saw her, when they all worked at the hospital. I doubt he'd have taken much notice of a nurse with so many working in a large London hospital.'

'But he's made a mistake. He took the photograph of you from when Charlie thought you were Bunty. He has your picture with "Redcoat Bunty" printed at the bottom. It's you he's looking for, Molly.'

Molly felt the blood drain from her face as she sat down beside Plum. 'But it doesn't explain where Bunty is, does it? Charlie, you'd better come in and hear this,' she called out.

Charlie listened as the girls told him what was missing. 'I'm going to shoot over and update Johnny and get maintenance to fix your door,' he said. 'Don't do anything stupid while I'm gone, you hear me? In fact, you stay here and don't move an inch.'

The girls nodded and watched him leave the chalet.

'Do you think Bunty came back to the chalet and disturbed him?' Plum asked. 'She could be lying hurt somewhere.'

'I think we should go and look for her. I can leave a note for Charlie,' Molly said, reaching for her writing set. 'It's best we take something to protect ourselves in case we do come across the detestable man.'

Plum rummaged under her bed and pulled out a riding crop. 'This'll give him a nasty sting if he crosses me,' she said, slapping her hand with the object.

'I have a putting stick that I've been meaning to take back to the sports store. That will give him more than a sting if I wallop the man.' She finished scribbling the note for Charlie, slipped a torch into her pocket and grabbed her weapon. 'Come on – let's go.'

The girls crept out into the dark night, moving slowly in case anyone was listening. The chalet ranks were dimly lit by a couple of lamps further down the path.

Plum prodded Molly in the back. 'Let's head up between the chalets towards the boating lake. It's always quiet there this time of night, apart from a few courting couples.'

Molly nodded and took a few more steps before turning left between two chalets that were in darkness. 'Oh my goodness,' she exclaimed as she

317

stopped suddenly. Plum ploughed into the back of her, and both jumped as an indignant voice yelped in pain. Molly flashed her torch downwards and found Freda looking up at her. 'Whatever are you doing down there, Freda?'

Freda stood up and brushed her skirt. 'I was coming over to find you. George and Kath are having an early night so I wondered if you fancied a drink if you were off duty. I was peering at the chalet numbers when I tripped over this.' She bent down and picked up a lady's white plimsoll.

Plum took the shoe and examined it. 'Look ... inside ... I thought as much. It's Bunty's name.'

'Is Bunty one of the girls you share with?' Freda asked. 'And why are you carrying those?' She pointed to the putting stick and whip.

'This is Plum, my other chalet mate. Bunty has gone missing and we think she's been abducted.'

The two girls smiled a hello to each other in the torchlight.

'And the man has a gun, and he thinks Molly is Bunty...' Plum's words rushed away with her.

'Blimey! It's all go at Butlins, isn't it? I have a hundred questions, but perhaps you can explain as we search. What does she look like?'

Molly described Bunty as the friends set off. 'You will like Bunty. She's good fun but has been through a lot.'

'Haven't we all!' Plum hooted aloud, before slapping her hand across her mouth with an 'oops'.

'We thought we'd look around the boating lake first,' Molly explained.

'That's a good idea. Then perhaps down by the beach,' Freda suggested. 'I took a walk this afternoon and it's not far to take someone.'

'The tide's coming in. It's almost high tide,' Plum exclaimed. 'Richard could drag her there and leave her, and ... and she could have drowned...'

'Perhaps we should go to the beach first,' Freda suggested.

The girls headed off at a brisk pace towards the beach, with Molly explaining to Freda as much as she could about Bunty and Gordon's problem and how Richard was likely to be at the camp hunting for their friend.

'What I don't understand is why, if Richard thinks you are Bunty, why then she has disappeared?'

Plum explained to Freda about Charlie Porter the journalist and how they wanted to deceive him to protect Bunty and Gordon.

Freda sighed. 'Honestly, Molly, I think it was safer back home in Erith when you only had Simon to contend with.' She stopped and looked around her. 'The beach looks so romantic in the moonlight.'

The girls could just make out the shoreline. It was almost high tide, with clouds hiding the moon. A gentle breeze chilled the air and Molly shivered. Where was Bunty? 'Look – what's that?' She pointed to something on the beach up ahead caught in the beam of her torch.

Plum hurried forward and picked up another shoe. 'It's Bunty's, and look – her redcoat jacket is over there.'

Freda retrieved the jacket. 'It's ripped, but it's dry.' The girls huddled round the jacket and checked it by the light from the torch. 'One of the sleeves is hanging off, and there's a big tear up the back. It looks as though this Richard has been quite rough with her.'

'I would think there's been a struggle around here. Bunty must have escaped or...' Plum took the torch from Molly and shone it ahead. The moon chose that moment to appear from behind a cloud. The girls could see the shape of a person slumped at the edge of the sea.

Plum was there first and threw herself onto the wet sand, grabbing Bunty under the arms and dragging her away from the incoming waves. 'She's breathing, but it's very shallow. Come on, love, wake up. You're safe now.'

Freda and Molly joined Plum and helped move Bunty to dry sand.

Freda checked the unconscious girl. 'I can't see any broken bones or bleeding, although there appears to be some bruising round her neck and here on her arm. We need to keep her warm until help arrives.'

The two redcoats removed their jackets and Freda her cardigan. Molly propped her friend onto her lap and wrapped her in the dry clothing. 'You're safe now, Bunty. You're safe,' she said, hugging her close.

Bunty's eyelids flickered and opened. 'Gordon... He killed Gordon,' she murmured, before her eyes closed again from the exertion.

'Gordon is fine, Bunty. I spoke to him on the telephone. He rang to warn you. If it hadn't been for Gordon, you would be dead,' Molly reassured her.

'We need to get medical help for Bunty,' Freda said. 'It's best I go, as you two know her and she will need friendly faces around her when she comes to.'

Molly nodded. She was worried that Bunty was becoming delirious. 'Go to the staffroom. It's in the reception building. Johnny will be there. Tell him what you know and say we think that Richard may still be in the grounds of the camp. Please, Freda, hurry.'

Freda headed towards the bright lights of the camp's main building. Plum and Molly watched until she disappeared.

'It won't be long now, Bunty. We'll soon have you tucked up warm and snug in bed,' Plum assured her.

Bunty opened her eyes slowly. 'Molly?'

'Yes, my love. I'm right here. Try not to fret,' she said, wanting to soothe her friend, who was becoming more agitated and attempting to sit up.

'Richard is looking for you... I tried to tell him I was Bunty, but he ... he thinks you are me. I tried to stop him, but...'

'It's that bloody photograph,' Plum said. 'Why did Richard drag you away? We found your plimsolls, by the way.'

Bunty licked her lips and frowned as she tried to think. 'I found him in our chalet. He was holding the photograph by my bed. He demanded to know where you were.' She stopped to think for a minute. 'He has a gun ... I thought he was going to kill you. I chased after him as he went to look for you. I said I knew who he was and what he'd done... That's when he hit me and forced me away

321

from the camp to here. I shouldn't have said I knew who he was ... I think he was going to kill me, but something disturbed him.'

'You were lucky he didn't shoot you,' Molly said.

'I was too close for him to get an aim. I clung on to him... He put his hands round my throat... I must have blacked out... Each time I came to, I felt water around me and tried to get away, but I felt dizzy.'

'And he didn't recognize you from when he worked with Gordon?' Plum said.

'I was just one of many nurses on duty. Some doctors are blind to what we look like when out of uniform. Please be careful,' she added, looking wildly around while hanging tight to Molly's arms.

'He can't be far away,' Molly whispered, aware that they were extremely exposed on the beach. She prayed help would not be long in coming.

'Nurse Grainger?'

Bunty gasped and clung even more tightly to Molly. 'That's him... That's him...'

Molly gazed up as a wild-eyed man limped towards them. A gun, held at arm's length, was pointing at her.

He indicated for Molly to move away from her friends. Molly could see nothing but the gun, and heard only the blood pounding in her ears. 'I think there's been some kind of mistake,' she said. 'I'm Molly Missons. I'm not who you think I am. The girl you want is back at the holiday camp.'

Molly tried to think. If she could only play for time, then perhaps help would arrive, but what else could she say? She stumbled slightly as an incoming wave caught her by surprise. As she did so, she heard a grunt and Richard crumpled to the ground. He'd been knocked out cold.

'That'll teach you to try and hurt my friends, you blighter,' Plum announced, retrieving the putting stick she'd thrown at the gunman. 'Now, stay down there, and no funny business or I'll bash your brains in.'

'I don't think he can hear you, Plum – you knocked him out.' Molly crept forward and grabbed the gun that had flown from Richard's hand when he was poleaxed by Plum. 'Wherever did you learn that?' she asked.

'You're not the only one who goes to the cinema. I just happen to prefer Westerns,' Plum replied as she placed one foot on Richard's back so he couldn't move if he came round. 'And just like in the best movies, here comes the cavalry,' she added, nodding to where a group of redcoats and security staff were running down the beach towards them.

'We've got him, boss,' Plum said, tapping a now groaning Richard with her riding crop.

Molly bent over her friend as Johnny appeared. She'd never been so pleased to see someone in her life. 'Look, Bunty, it's all over. Help has arrived,' she said, trying to rouse the girl as a stretcher was unfurled beside her.

Johnny called out to the security team, who dragged the groaning Richard towards the camp.

Molly sipped the hot, sweet cocoa. Senior redcoats had stepped in to make sure their colleagues were taken care of. She'd been moved into Freda's

323

chalet while the door on her own was being repaired. Molly was secretly grateful not to be alone, even though Richard had been caught, and was pleased that there were no objections to her staying with a camper.

'This is just like old times when I stayed over at your house,' Freda said as she tucked an extra blanket around Molly.

Molly couldn't stop trembling. Each time she closed her eyes, she could see Richard and the gun. 'Thank goodness things turned out all right. I dread to think what could have happened. You must have run like the wind, Freda.'

'I didn't have to go far. I bumped into Johnny and some of the security men by the boating lake. They'd found Bunty's handbag and knew she must be in the area. What I don't understand is why Richard dragged her away if he thought she was you.'

'All I got from Bunty was that Richard feared she would call for help and he wanted to get her away from the camp. Thank goodness we arrived when we did or she could have drowned.' Molly shuddered.

'Or been shot by that despicable man. I'm so glad it's all over for Gordon and Bunty. Just fancy being imprisoned when you've not done anything wrong. I can't begin to know how I'd feel if it was me,' Freda said.

'Bunty's family stood by her while she was in prison. It's good to have friends as well. Thank you for always being here for me. I don't know what I'd have done this past year without you.' Molly started to sob, loudly and uncontrollably.

'I'm sorry for blubbing like an idiot.'

Freda took the cup from Molly and hugged her close. 'There, there. This has all been a big shock, on top of everything else that's happened. Anyone would blub after what has occurred this evening, so go ahead and cry as much as you like. It will help you sleep,' she promised.

Molly's tears had not long subsided and she was starting to fall asleep when there was a quiet knock on the door of the chalet. She jolted awake and looked fearfully at Freda.

'Don't be afraid, Molly. Richard is being held at the gatehouse until the police get here. No one is going to let him try to hurt you or Bunty ever again.'

For all her words of support, Freda crept towards the door more than a little afraid of who was on the other side. It crossed her mind to have something in her hand to protect them both, but then she scolded herself for being so silly.

Opening the door, she found Johnny standing there holding a single red rose. She stepped outside and pulled the door shut, placing a finger on her lips. 'She's finally falling asleep, so I'll not invite you in.' She smiled. 'Is that for Molly?'

By the light of a nearby streetlamp, Freda could see that Johnny's face looked grey and drawn. 'I wanted to leave this, and a note for Molly. It wouldn't be proper for me to come into the chalet. The note explains what's happened. I hope it means she can put her mind at rest and sleep.'

Freda took the rose and inhaled the heady fragrance. 'It's beautiful. Molly will love it. Roses are her favourite flowers. It's so thoughtful of you.'

She smiled. 'Don't worry, Johnny – she will be fine after a good night's sleep.'

'I don't want to see Molly back at work for the remainder of the week. I've rearranged the staff rota so that she can rest. Bunty has been taken to the local hospital. Connie is with her, and Spud has driven Plum home. She should be with her daughter after what happened today. She's under orders not to return to work until Saturday.'

The door creaked open behind them. 'I want to work. Please let me. I'll go crazy if I have time to think about what could have happened,' Molly whispered.

Johnny took Molly's hands and kissed her lips gently. 'I'm only thinking of what is best for you,' he said.

Freda slipped quietly back into the chalet and closed the door. There were times when a best friend was surplus to requirements.

20

'Are you absolutely sure about this, Freda? You're supposed to be on holiday.'

Freda sighed. 'We've been over this umpteen times, Molly. You know how much I've longed to be a redcoat. To have my offer to help you this week accepted is like a dream come true. I get to be a redcoat and a Woolies girl at the same time. What could be nicer?'

'All the same, you've paid for a holiday and

you're spending your time working.'

'Ah! I'm not. Take a look at this.' Freda passed a sheet of paper over the breakfast table to Molly. 'I've been given a complimentary holiday for the last week of the season, so you don't need to worry about me being overworked. Now I have to go and collect my uniform before I join you for the children's nature walk. This is going to be just like the times we helped your mum run the Brownie pack.'

Molly smiled at her friend. Freda's excitement was infectious. 'That's wonderful. What about George and Kath? It feels like we've abandoned them.'

'I had a word with George this morning. You know me – I'm always up with the lark. Kath had sent him to join in with the keep-fit class. As you can imagine, he was overjoyed to see me so he could escape exercising and stop for a chat. I told him what had happened but left out the part with the gun. There was no need to worry him unduly. He sends his love and said they will both see you at bingo this evening. He reckons I'll make a good redcoat.'

'Hmm, I'd better look to my laurels, then, or I'll be out of a job before long, Redcoat Freda.' Molly grinned. 'Now, you'd better get ready for the nature trail. After a morning spent with inquisitive children, you may well want to hang-up your red coat for good.'

'Whatever were you thinking of, my girl? If that madman had killed you, where would we be then? I couldn't be more surprised when Spud

327

turned up with you last night and told me what you did. I've not slept a wink all night worrying about what might have happened.'

Plum hung her head in shame. In the light of a new day, the thrill of catching Richard and knowing a murderer would soon be locked up for a long time didn't feel quite as exciting as it had the evening before. Tilly was right: she hadn't thought about the consequences of rushing off to look for Bunty and then tackling an armed man. 'I'm sorry, Tilly. I've been an absolute fool. I could have left Lizzie an orphan. Can you ever forgive me for being such an impetuous idiot?'

The older woman looked at Plum. The girl was as near to a daughter as she'd ever had. Her sleeplessness had been caused not only by the thought that young Lizzie could have been left without both her parents but also that she could have lost someone she considered to be her own kin. 'No doubt I'd have done the same given the circumstances,' Tilly said. 'Although my aim may not have been as good as yours,' she added.

Plum looked at Tilly warily. Had she forgiven her for being so foolhardy? Tilly's smile proved she had and they both burst out laughing.

'Now, not a word to Lizzie about this. We don't want her getting ideas in her head. Only the other day I had to explain how young ladies do not dive into a playground fight between boys and join in. I don't know where she gets it from,' she said primly, eyeing Plum, who tried not to smile. 'Now, pour yourself a cup of tea and I'll get your breakfast from the oven. Young Lizzie wanted to stay home from school to be with you, but I told her you'd still be here when she got home. A week off work, eh? That must have been quite a shock for you all.'

'Yes, afterwards, when the dust had settled, I admit I felt quite wobbly. We all did. Butlins have been very good to us. We were told that if the man had gone back to the main part of the holiday camp, it could have been much worse than it was.'

'What can be worse than a man framing someone else for murder, I don't know.' Tilly tutted as she headed for the kitchen. 'By the way, another of those letters arrived the other day. It's on the mantelpiece. Things can't go on as they are. It's time you made a decision and wrote to the woman.'

Plum sighed. She knew Tilly was right. What if something had happened to her last night? Her daughter would have been left without a single blood relative who knew her, and she may have been sent to live with William's mother. It was time that Lizzie got to know her grandparents, whether they accepted her or not. She would start by writing to William's mother. With a heavy heart, she reached for the letter and tore open the envelope. The few words scribbled in haste on the page caused her to shriek aloud.

'My, my, whatever is it?' Tilly asked, coming into the room holding a hot plate with a tea towel. 'Mind that – it's hot.'

'It's William. His mother's written that there has been news,' Plum said, her hands shaking so much she had to place the letter on the table before she dropped it.

'What news could there be? The lad died in action.' Tilly picked up the letter and scanned the few lines. What she read caused her to sit down quickly. 'Bless my soul, a prisoner of war. Who'd have thought it?'

'I need to go to William's mother. She must know more. This letter was written a week ago.' She rose to her feet quickly, causing the table to shake. 'I need to pack a case. Can you tell Lizzie I've had to go back to Butlins but I'll be home soon? I hate to lie to her, but it's too early to tell her the truth.'

'I'll start packing your case while you eat your food. You can't travel on an empty stomach.'

Plum picked up her knife and fork. 'Oh, Tilly, my William's alive,' she said, her eyes brimming with tears of happiness.

Bunty grasped Molly's hand and held on to it tightly. 'I can't believe I'm leaving Butlins. I'm going to miss everyone so much, but especially you and Plum. Thank you for coming to the station to wave me off.'

Bunty had spent three days in hospital recovering from her ordeal. It was there she'd learned that Aileen's father had survived the gunshot wound that had threatened his life. He'd been able to speak to Gordon and the two men had settled their differences now that it was clear Gordon hadn't killed Aileen. Bunty was eager to travel to Scotland and be reunited with her fiancé. Already proceedings were under way to absolve Gordon of his wrongful conviction.

'Will you stay in Scotland or move south?'

Molly asked. It seemed so far away.

'We have decisions to make. I want to help Aileen's father get well, and of course there is Jamie, Aileen and Richard's son, to consider. He has always been brought up by his grandparents, but I like to think we could help in some way.'

Molly hugged her friend. 'You're a good person, Bunty. As soon as you are settled, send me your address so we can keep in touch. You will, won't you?'

'Of course I will, you silly thing. I just wish Plum had been here so I could say goodbye.' She looked at her watch. 'The train will be here in ten minutes. Are you sure you want to wait with me?'

'Now it's you who's talking daft. I'm not only going to stay but I'll be watching the train until it's a dot on the horizon. Oh my goodness, I feel quite tearful, and you don't want me blubbing,' Molly said.

'It won't be for long. We can arrange to meet up once the season is over. I realize we've only known each other a few months, but it feels as though it's been much longer. We are true friends.' Bunty gave a weak grin. 'Now it's me who might start to blub.' She looked over her shoulder at the sound of a commotion coming from the entrance to the platform. 'My goodness, whatever is happening over there?'

Molly had already turned towards the double doors that led to the busy street outside. Past the baskets of racing pigeons waiting to be transported across country, sacks of mail and women laden with shopping, she could see Johnny hurrying along the platform, followed by a breathless Charlie Porter. 'It's Johnny and Charlie,' was all she could think to say.

'Thank goodness. I thought we'd missed you,' Johnny said. 'Quick, Charlie – give Bunty your news. The signals are changing. The train will be pulling into the station at any minute.'

'What is it? Has something happened to Gordon?' Bunty asked nervously.

'Not at all. It's my story. Look, it's on the front page – "Butlins Girls Catch Murderer."'

'Oh my!' Bunty murmured as she read Charlie's words.

'It's all there,' Charlie said proudly, pointing over Bunty's shoulder. 'This is the bit that says how Gordon escaped prison during an air raid as he knew who had killed his wife. And here' – he pointed further down the page – 'is where you all get a mention as the Butlins redcoats who caught the real murderer on the beach.'

Molly felt slightly sick. 'You've named us all?'

'Yes,' Charlie said proudly. 'I covered everything. I've done such a good job my editor's given me a permanent position, so if you know of any other crimes, I'm your man.' He handed Bunty a crumpled card from his pocket. 'You can always get me at the paper.'

'Does this mean you're handing in your notice, Mr Porter?' Johnny asked, trying hard to look stern.

Charlie's face dropped. 'I was thinking of nipping off right now, if that's OK with you, boss?'

'I believe we can just about manage without you, Charlie,' Johnny said, his lips twitching as he tried not to smile. Charlie's photographic skills had not improved in the time he'd worked at the camp.

'Here's your train, Bunty,' Molly said, trying hard not to look upset by what she'd seen in Charlie's article.

'Oh, these are for you,' Johnny said, handing Bunty an envelope and a posy of roses from the Butlins rose bed. 'I thought a small bunch would be easier to carry.'

'Thank you. They're lovely. I'll press one and keep it in my Bible to remember you by. But what is in this envelope? You gave me my pay and cards last night at my leaving party, along with my lovely leaving gift.' She looked down at the smart new suitcase by her feet.

'It's a letter from the governor. He wants you and Gordon to consider coming back to work for us next season. We can always make room for a doctor in the medical centre, and a nurse if you are interested. Unless you'd rather remain a redcoat? It'll give you time to sort yourselves out. There's also a little something in there to tide yourselves over for a while.'

'Gosh, I don't know what to say. I never expected any of this. I was just going to slip away quietly.'

'No one does anything quietly at Butlins,' Johnny said, kissing her cheek. 'I suggest you get yourself on the train and find your seat. I'll put your suitcase in the guard's van.'

Bunty shook hands with Charlie, who insisted she keep the newspaper, and hugged Molly so tightly she could hardly breathe. 'I'll send a postcard as soon as I reach Dumfries. I promise.'

As the train chugged out of the station, Molly stood watching. She felt as desolate as she had the day she'd left her life in Erith back in May. In a few days, she'd be waving goodbye to George, Kath and Freda when their holiday came to an end. She felt so lonely.

Johnny took her arm and tucked it into his as they left the platform, stopping only to see the last puff of white smoke from the train as it disappeared into a tunnel. 'She'll be back. There's no-need for such a sad face.'

'I know she will. It's not the end of our friendship,' Molly said. 'I suppose I'm not used to so many changes in my life. I feel as though I've done nothing but say goodbye to people I love over the past year.'

'There are still people here who love you, Molly.'

She looked up to his face and knew he was sincere. But could she step into his glamorous world of theatres, movies and starlets, and be truly happy?

'There's something else, isn't there?' he asked as he guided her to where his car was parked.

Molly was startled. Did he realize she had concerns about being involved in his life? 'I don't know what you mean,' she said, looking away from his gaze.

'That newspaper article... Something worried you. I was watching your face as you read it'

'Oh, that. Yes, something is worrying me. It's Simon, my second cousin,' she added as Johnny looked puzzled. 'He reads that newspaper. I remember seeing it lying about when we all lived in my parents' house.'

'I suppose many people read that particular paper. It's one of the most popular, I believe.'

'Don't you see? If he reads this edition, he's hardly going to miss the Butlins story splashed across the front page, and my name's mentioned twice. Johnny, he will know where I am.' Molly looked anxiously at Johnny as he started the car and pulled out of the parking space. 'Perhaps it's time for me to leave as well.'

Johnny slammed his foot down on the brake and the car came to a sudden halt. 'Now look here, you are not going anywhere. I've waited years to find a woman I could love who wasn't chasing me for my contacts to help her on the stairway to stardom. I love you, Molly, and I'll be damned if I'm going to let you walk out of my life now. I will never let anyone hurt you. You've got to believe me. If Simon comes anywhere near the camp, I'll have him locked up before you can say, "Read the headlines." I've instructed my legal friend to look into your problem with your cousins, so in time this will all be over. Can you hang on here with me until then? What do you think?'

Molly laid her hand over Johnny's, who was gripping the steering wheel so tightly his knuckles had turned white. 'What I think is that I love you too, Johnny,' she said in a whisper.

'You look bright-eyed and bushy-tailed,' Molly said as Plum burst into their chalet. 'Those days off certainly did you good.'

'You could say that. I have the most marvellous news, and if I don't share it with both of you, I shall burst.' She looked around the room and noticed there were only two beds made up. 'Where's Bunty? Has something happened?'

'She's gone to Scotland to be with Gordon. I asked Spud if he could let you know, but he said something about you not being at home. It was a shame you missed saying goodbye. We gave Bunty a lovely send-off. But I'll tell you about that later. What are you bursting to say?'

Plum leaped onto her bed and jumped up and down. 'I'm so happy. You'll never in a million years guess what's happened!'

Molly had never seen her friend so excited. 'For heaven's sake, tell me before you break all the springs in that bed.'

'It's William. He's alive!'

'Whatever do you mean?' Molly sat down, looking puzzled. 'Darling, your William was lost during the war. Are you feeling poorly?' She felt concerned for Plum, who was grinning like the village idiot.

Plum sat down and said rather breathlessly, 'I received another letter from William's mother. It was there waiting for me when I arrived home. I believe I told you how I'd burned much of her correspondence as I feared she wanted to take Lizzie away from me.'

'Yes, I know how worried you were,' Molly prompted.

'After our little escapade on the beach, I decided Lizzie ought to get to know her grandmother. If anything had happened to me, she would have been alone in the world. Yes, I know that Tilly and Spud would have cared for her, but they are elderly and they are not blood relatives,' she added as Molly was about to speak. 'The letter that I could have thrown onto the fire was a note to say that William had been found and he was alive.'

'My goodness,' Molly said. 'What...? How...? Have you seen him?'

Plum grinned. 'I was on the next train south and arrived at his mother's home in Surrey that same evening. She couldn't have been more charming. I accompanied her to the authorities to find out more. Although we were engaged to be married at the time of his disappearance, and I then gave birth to William's child, it was still his mother who was listed as next of kin. We held each other's hands throughout the myriad interviews and paperwork.'

'Unbelievable. I'm so happy for you, Plum,' Molly said, rushing to hug her fellow redcoat.

'It's all very sketchy – wretched red tape and all that – but from what I can make out, he crash-landed and was badly injured, and ended up being held by the Germans for a while. However, he was handed over to the Red Cross and brought back to England due to his injuries.'

'Why were you not notified? It's been so long.'

'All that we can make out is that William was not carrying identification when he was handed over to the Germans. As he'd lost his memory, try as they might, the authorities could not locate family or even ascertain his name.'

'My goodness, all these years. But how did they find out who he was?'

'That is the amazing part of the story. The convalescent home encouraged him to learn to paint. You know he was an artist before the war?'

Molly nodded.

'Well, he kept painting the same scene. A woman lying in a field watching a dogfight overhead.'

'Isn't that the one sketch you have of William's?'

'Yes, it sounds very much like it. The staff at the convalescent home built on that memory, which gradually grew until one day he remembered the name of the woman in the picture – Plum. A fellow patient who knew a little about the art world and had got to know William recognized his style and started to investigate. It took months and months, but finally, with William remembering more, and with the RAF finally able to help, my lovely man was identified.'

'It's such wonderful news, Plum. I'm thrilled for you. Have you seen William yet?'

'Yesterday. It was extremely emotional. He recognized me as soon as I walked into the room. It is going to take a long time for William to be the man he once was, but the consultant in charge of his case is confident that he will regain much of his memory, and with their help and his family, we will make it happen. We've decided not to let Lizzie visit just yet but to leave it a month or two so he is stronger and recalls more of his past. One excitable little girl may be too much to handle at this stage, although I have told her she has a daddy. She's been busy painting pictures for me to take to him, and also her grandmother.'

'Another artist in the family, do you think?'

'It looks that way,' Plum said proudly. 'It would have been good to have another horsewoman in the family, though, as I'd hoped Lizzie would help me here at Butlins during the school holidays when she is a little older. However, I must first think about today, and if I don't get a move on, there will be a queue a mile long of children waiting for rides.'

Molly smiled as she listened to her friend's plans. It was good to know that she would continue to work at the holiday camp. She wondered if she too would be here when the next season started in 1947.

'You both look so pretty,' Molly exclaimed as she spotted her two young cousins, Avril and Annie, standing outside the church. The sun shone brightly. It was a wonderful day for a wedding.

'Mummy's been looking for you,' Avril said. 'She's inside the church helping Daddy with his tie. He doesn't like wearing one.'

'He's the best man.' Annie giggled. 'Doesn't that sound funny?'

'He's a very important man today, as he has to make sure the groom is here on time so he can marry the bride,' Molly explained. In the short time she'd known her aunt Sally and her family, she had grown to adore her two little cousins.

'Is Uncle Johnny coming to the wedding to see me in my bridesmaid's dress?' Avril asked, giving a little twirl in her eau de Nil dress.

'He is going to join us this evening. It's a busy day at Butlins, with lots of new campers arriving. He sends his love and asked me to say that he expects to have a dance with both of you.'

The two girls dissolved into yet more giggles until Sally appeared and scolded them for messing about. 'Try to stay tidy until the bride arrives, please, girls. Avril, stop pulling petals off your posy, and, Annie, use your handkerchief. Molly, I'm so pleased you could make it. I know Saturday is a busy day for you at the camp. Now, let's go and find our seats, shall we? There's someone I wish to avoid for as long as possible.' She ushered Molly inside the cool interior of the small church. 'I must say, I do like your outfit.'

'Thank you. It's just a summer frock I made before I came up to Butlins. Plum lent me a hat and bag. To be honest, I feel rather strange to be out of my Butlins uniform.'

The two women found an empty pew and knelt to say a short, silent prayer. Molly's was for her mum and dad. She knew her mum would have enjoyed being here today to see her nieces, whom she'd never met or even known existed, looking so cute in their long dresses and white floral headbands.

The organ that had been playing quietly in the background as guests arrived struck up a loud note and the wedding procession started to walk down the aisle. Sally craned her neck to see her two girls following behind the bride, each holding a corner of her long lace veil. Both behaved impeccably. She breathed a sigh of relief, until she spotted a man sitting at the back of the church. She moved closer to Molly and whispered, 'That's your grandfather at the back of the church. I'm surprised the old so-and-so turned up. He's not known for being sociable.'

Molly turned to watch the bride pass by and glanced quickly in the direction that Sally had indicated. She could see a fairly short, grey-haired man standing almost to attention as he stared straight ahead. For a moment, Molly felt he was glancing her way. He looked surprised. She turned to face the altar as the service began. So that was her grandfather Kenyon. She felt no connection to the man whatsoever.

'Here, let me help you,' Molly said, relieving Sally of a tray of dirty crockery. 'Why don't you go and enjoy yourself? I'm quite happy to help with the washing-up.'

'I'd rather stay out here in the kitchen, if you don't mind. Weddings can be so tiring. But you can help me if you like?'

Molly removed her cardigan and picked up a tea towel. 'Why don't you like weddings?'

Sally shrugged her shoulders. 'I'm not keen on crowds and am not much of a drinker. Besides, out there I might run into my father, and at the moment I'm none too happy with him for keeping secrets and bearing grudges that should have been sorted out years ago. Even my mother went to her grave not standing up to the old bugger. It makes my blood boil when I think about it.'

'Perhaps it's best to let things lie now. It's been too long, and it won't bring my mum and dad back,' Molly considered as she added another clean plate to the growing pile on the kitchen table.

'He shouldn't be allowed to get away with it. I'd like to know what it was that made my sister and her husband-to-be run away so suddenly.' She threw her dishcloth into the bowl of hot water and dried her hands on a tea towel. 'Come on, let's go

341

ask him now while I've got the nerve. He won't dare argue with me if there's a crowd about.'

Molly hurriedly dried her hands and followed her aunt through the throng of wedding-reception guests, who had spilled out into the garden and the field beyond, where children were running around excitedly. Avril and Annie were among them, no longer the demure little bridesmaids, with their hair flowing freely and their dresses tucked into the legs of their knickers so they could play. She spotted her grandfather sitting alone at the far end of the vegetable garden, a pint glass in his hand.

Sally reached Harold Kenyon first. 'Father, I'd like you to explain to me what made my sister, Charlotte, and Norman leave the area in such a rush.'

Harold looked up at his younger child and studied her flushed face. 'There's no need to dig up old troubles.' He eyed Molly, who had joined her aunt. 'So my elder daughter has sent her child to do her dirty work after all these years? I must say you have the look of your mother, rather than that man she chose to marry.'

Molly was stung by his words. 'No one has sent me to do their bidding. I'm here as a guest, just as you are. I, too, would like to know what it was that sent my parents away.'

He drank deeply from the glass of beer and wiped his mouth with the back of his hand. 'Your father never told you?'

'As far as I knew, I had no family. It has only been in recent months that I found out of your existence,' Molly said, resenting his attitude. She always thought a grandfather would be pleased to see his offspring. This bitter man seemed not to care about anybody. 'I came across my parents' birth certificates and two letters that were sent just after my birth. Apart from that, I have no information about my family.'

Harold Kenyon threw his beer glass to the ground, where it shattered into dozens of pieces. 'Let's get this clear, shall we? You are no kin of mine. Anything that comes from the loins of that thief Norman Missons has no place in my family. You can go back to where you come from and tell your mother and father just that. You can also ask them not to send a young slip of a girl to do their dirty work. It'll be a cold day in hell when a Missons steps over my threshold.'

Molly gasped. How could he be so hurtful?

'Father, there's no need to speak to Molly like that.'

'Molly, eh? He even had the cheek to name you after my wife. Be off with you back to your parents.'

Molly felt tears stinging her eyes, but she wouldn't let this man see that he had upset her. She was proud of her parents and knew that whatever had happened before she was born, and however her parents were involved, they would never have done anything wrong. She raised her chin defiantly and stared the old man in the face. 'I refuse to listen to your insinuations about my parents. They lived blameless lives and were held in high regard by everyone in our town. It's a shame you didn't witness their joint funeral and make note of the many people who turned out to pay their respects. You will not speak this way about my mum and dad unless you can prove they did wrong.'

She waited for the old man to speak, but he simply stared at her. 'Dead, you say?' he said eventually.

Molly stared back and nodded her head. 'Yes, a year ago this month.' She felt Sally reach for her hand and squeeze it tightly.

'Father, your bitter ways have lost you your family. Now you'll never see Charlotte again. You cannot take this to your grave. Please tell us what happened or I'll never let you see your granddaughters again. You think you are stubborn? Think on, as I can be just as stubborn as you.'

The old man looked away and cursed. 'I help no one who has Missons blood in their veins.'

Sally put her arm round her niece and guided her away. 'Come along, Molly. We have no time for this man.'

Molly glanced back at her grandfather. He sat hunched up, in a world of his own. He was her own flesh and blood. Things could have been so different.

21

Molly sipped the brandy her aunt Sally had picked up from the makeshift bar in the barn. It burned the back of her throat as she swallowed the amber liquid but brought her to her senses.

344

She'd felt close to screaming. How could anyone think her kind, sensitive dad was a thief? 'Do you think what Grandfather said is true?'

Sally thought for a moment. They'd wandered away from the wedding party and were leaning on a wooden fence close to a small paddock where a donkey grazed. 'If you want the honest truth, Molly, I don't know.'

'What? You believe Dad did something criminal?'

'No, love, that's not what I mean. I was a child when Norman and Charlotte left the area. I can only remember the pair of them with warm affection. They were good to me, taking me out and filling my life with fun, but as to whether your dad committed a crime, I don't know. My gut feeling is that this is some kind of misunderstanding. The old goat back there is so volatile that no one could talk sense into him. Perhaps that is why your mum and dad went away, rather than because of any wrongdoing.'

Molly thought for a moment. 'I do believe you are right. I'd really like to get to the bottom of this and find out what happened, if only for some peace of mind. Perhaps if Mum and Dad hadn't died so young, they would have told me what happened. I was young when the war started, and life was so hectic that the past just wasn't discussed. I like to think that in time my parents would have told me about before they arrived in Erith and built such a wonderful life.'

'It's important that you hold on to that thought, Molly. They had a good life, from what you've told me, and they are remembered with fondness. In my book, that counts for something. All the same, you're right it's time we got to the bottom of this, even if it's so we can confront that miserable bugger and tell him he's been wrong all these years. Now that would be worth doing,' Sally said with a grin.

'But how can we? I have no idea how to look into the past, or where to look.'

Sally smiled. 'That's where I can help. I shall make it my business to find Norman's family and then we can ask them what they know of this sorry affair. They can't have vanished off the face of the earth, can they?'

Molly thought her aunt was becoming over-enthusiastic, although she loved her for wanting to help. 'They could have passed away by now. Plus I'm concerned that they too consider Dad to be some kind of thief. Why else would there have been no communication with his family all this time?' Molly's thoughts went to Harriet and Simon. Harriet had married her dad's cousin. Would she have been told about the family having fallen out all those years ago? Perhaps she should speak to her. She quickly shrugged off that idea. It would be better for her parents' past life to remain a mystery than to involve Harriet and her son. She wasn't even sure if she would believe what they told her.

'Then we have to find out once and for all. There is one thing that bothers me, Molly. What if we do find out your dad did something wrong? How would you feel?'

Molly thought for a moment. 'It would make no difference to me. My dad was a good man in

346

my eyes and that will never diminish, whatever we uncover. Thank you, Aunt Sally. Please find out what you can.'

'One final thing, Molly. Please stop calling me "aunt". I'm only ten years older than you. "Sally" will do for me. Now, let's head back to the house. I see that Johnny has arrived and is at the mercy of my daughters. They will have him making daisy chains and playing princesses before too long. He seems to be putty in their hands. He's a good one, Molly, like my Dan. You're a lucky girl.'

'Yes, Sally, I'm beginning to believe I am indeed extremely lucky.'

Molly hadn't expected to enjoy the wedding. The black cloud that was her grandfather quickly dissipated and she enjoyed meeting Sally and Dan's friends and family. Johnny was soon busy talking food production with the men, and Molly was not surprised to learn he intended to discuss buying local produce with the governor when they next met. The biggest surprise of the day was when Johnny handed the twins an envelope just before they left the reception.

'We're going to Butlins,' Avril and Annie chanted together, before flinging themselves on Johnny, almost pulling him to the ground in their glee.

Sally took the envelope and looked at the contents. 'Why, Johnny, I don't know what to say. This is far too generous. A whole week at Butlins in a family-sized chalet. My goodness.'

'It's the last week of the season. Many campers will be returning after having won a free holiday

347

in one of our competitions. It will be a special week to end the first Butlins season since the war. Next year, there will be more chalets and even more entertainment for visitors,' he explained.

'It would be lovely to show you the camp. Please say you can come,' Molly urged.

'I know I'd like to see where you both work. I've always had a hankering to visit Butlins. Knowing it's not far away from here, the camp has always held a fascination for me. I'd love to accept, and I know the girls wouldn't forgive me if I said no. Dan will have to find someone to cover his work for the week. I'll put my foot down if his boss objects or we will come on our own,' she said, looking at her husband as he read the contents of the envelope.

Johnny laughed. 'I don't want to cause dissent between husband and wife. If you can't get time off from the farm, Dan, I can change the booking to next season.'

'Oh no!' Sally said. 'We will be there and can't thank you enough. Life for farm workers doesn't give much time for holidays. We are going to enjoy ourselves.'

The twins became more excited and Molly, who had been dreading the end of the season at Butlins, was overjoyed that her last week at the camp would be spent not only with Sally and her family but Freda as well, who was returning to Butlins after forgoing her previous holiday in order to work at the camp.

'What will you do once the camp closes, Molly? Will you go home to Erith?' Sally asked as she walked her niece to Johnny's car. 'I know things aren't right for you at the moment in your home town, but there are people who love you and will make sure you are safe.'

'Yes, I'm going back to Erith and will stay with George and Kath to begin with. I'll help out in the shop for a while, but there are enough staff who can do the job better than I can, and I'm not sure the profits can carry another person on the payroll at present. When I thought Mum and Dad's house would be passed to me, I was considering taking in paying guests, but that isn't going to happen now.'

'Before you head south, I'd like to invite you to stay with us for a week. I can't offer the same entertainment as Butlins, but the girls would love to spend time with their new cousin. They've never had one before.'

'I've never had a cousin before either, and now I have two, as well as an aunt and uncle,' Molly said as she kissed Sally goodbye. 'I'm a lucky, lucky girl.'

Molly leaned back in the car seat and sighed. 'Despite the disastrous meeting with my grandfather, it has been a lovely day. It was so good of you to give such a generous gift to Sally and Dan. Thank you, Johnny.'

'Don't thank me – thank Butlins. I can use my discretion when awarding prizes, and if there are chalets empty in the last week, why not fill them? It's good publicity for the company. Holiday-makers tell their friends and next season some of those will book. Besides that, I like your relatives.'

'Whatever you say, I think it was pretty good of

you to treat them,' she said, giving him a big smile.

'It was worth it just for that smile.'

Molly slapped his arm. 'Don't be daft.' She thought for a moment. 'What about your family? You've never mentioned them. Here I am always crying on your shoulder about my family problems and accepting your help, but you never mention your own family. Do you mind me asking?'

'Not at all. It's rather boring really. I'm an only child, just like you, although my parents are alive. My father runs a successful talent agency in London and owns a hotel in Margate, Kent.'

'So we both have roots in Kent. That's nice. There's no better county to live in,' Molly said enthusiastically.

'I agree. I've lived there, man and boy. I hope to settle in the county one day.'

'Do you mind if I ask why you are working for Butlins and not your father's business?'

'Of course not. In fact, I used to work as a junior talent agent in the agency but had itchy feet to try something else. I fell into acting through the agency and enjoyed it. Then the war came along and made me think long and hard about my future.'

'You joined the RAF?'

'Better to jump than be pushed in the wrong direction. I enjoyed myself as a pilot – if you can say you enjoyed war. As a minor celebrity, I was able to make the occasional film. Patriotic movies in which good triumphs over evil. They were made to keep up morale and show the world England would not be walked over by the enemy.'

'Your films kept up my morale, thank you very much, as well as that of many other women.' Molly grinned and was surprised to see Johnny's cheeks turn pink. 'Are you blushing, Mr Johnson?'

'That's the side of show business I don't enjoy. I'm happy to put my minor fame to good use for others, but I'm not a natural movie star. I've turned down offers to go to Hollywood.'

'Instead you came to Butlins?'

'I was offered the job of working on the entertainment team as an adviser for the season. The job interested me because I'd be working as part of a team creating memorable holidays for families, and it would give me the summer to think about my future,' he answered, turning the car right into Butlins at the end of their journey. 'As it is, my decision has been made for me.'

'You're returning next season?' Molly asked hopefully.

'No. I had intended to return for at least one more year, but circumstances have dictated otherwise. I travelled down to London a couple of months ago to see my father. He's been insistent I return to the family business. He's not getting any younger, and my mother wants to travel and enjoy their retirement before he gets too old. He begrudgingly gave me another year but was taken ill soon after and it has rather forced my hand.'

Molly took his arm as he helped her from the car. 'I'm sorry your father is unwell. Is it serious?'

'Yes and no. He will recover but is under strict instructions from his doctor, and my mother, to retire and take things easy.'

Molly was disappointed that Johnny would not

be working at the Skegness camp next season but knew that under the circumstances his father's health came first. 'How do you feel about the changes?'

'Not as bad as I thought I would. The old man has given me carte blanche with the business, so at least he won't be interfering. A bonus has been that the governor has invited me to remain part of the overall entertainment team. I'll be involved with finding entertainers for the camps, and that will be done through my London office.'

'So you'll not be visiting the camp?'

'Possibly, but my work will be more office-based. Does that disappoint you?'

Molly sighed. 'Yes. So much of my life has changed in the past year that I was hoping for some stability. Now Bunty has gone, Plum has William back, Freda is in Erith, and I don't know what to do with my life. Should I come back to Butlins in the spring or stay in Erith, if that is possible? If truth be known, I feel a little tired and more than a little scared of the future.' She turned to face Johnny as he locked the car doors. 'I was looking forward to being here next year and seeing you every day.'

Johnny pulled Molly into his arms and held her close. 'My dear girl, do you honestly think I'd walk away and forget you? I thought I'd made my intentions clear. I love you, Molly. I want us to spend the rest of our lives together.'

'You're moving too fast, Johnny,' Molly said. 'I feel as though everything is being rushed. Can we not spend time getting to know each other? I enjoy being with you, and I do love you, but so much of my life is still a mess. I don't want to bring that into a relationship.'

Johnny kissed the tip of her nose. 'I can make everything right for you. I'll spend my life caring for you and protecting you...'

Molly pulled away. 'No, Johnny. I need to be able to fight my own battles sometimes. Don't think I'm not grateful for all you've done, but I must be prepared to stand on my own two feet. Do you hate me for saying that?'

Johnny thought for a few seconds and then smiled gently. 'You're right. I was running away with the notion of us being together. I won't push you. I promise. I had another suggestion, but it may be the wrong time to mention what it is.'

Molly thought she loved Johnny more then than she had ever done. She could have lost him forever for saying what she had, but instead he was prepared to wait. 'Johnny, I adore you,' she replied, reaching up to kiss him. Johnny's response took her breath away as he held her as close as was humanly possible and returned her kiss until she could hardly breathe.

He groaned. 'We'd better say goodnight before you drive me completely crazy.' He took her hand and they walked towards the main building, where campers could be heard singing 'Goodnight Campers'.

'By the way, Johnny, what was your suggestion?' she asked shyly.

'I was going to ask you to come and work with me in my London office over the winter while you decided whether to return to Butlins in 1947 or perhaps marry me...' He grinned.

Molly stopped dead in her tracks. 'I shouldn't have asked. Now you've given me something else to think about.'

He looked sideways at her and laughed. 'You mean marrying me is a problem?'

'I'll ignore that,' she said, joining in with his laughter. 'It was the suggestion of a job that I was referring to. Can I think about it?'

'Take as long as you want. The job is yours until you say you don't want it.'

'You haven't told me what the job entails. I can't type, and I'm useless at taking telephone messages.'

Johnny led her to a nearby bench, where they sat side by side. 'I need someone to devise holiday activities for children. You'd be ideal for the job, Molly. I've seen you work with the children here and you are a natural. Furthermore, you're good with the parents, and you care about the holiday-makers.'

'But I don't have any qualifications or training, Johnny. You need someone who trained as a teacher or perhaps a nurse.'

'No, I need someone who cares about the job. I need you, Molly.'

'I'm seriously interested, Johnny, but shouldn't this work be done in the holiday camp rather than your office?'

Johnny shook his head. 'This is for the family hotel in Margate. I want to offer families with young children the same kind of entertainment that is available at Butlins. Why shouldn't children have aunties and uncles whose sole job is to entertain them so they have enjoyable holidays?'

Molly nodded. 'I think it's a wonderful idea. I'd say yes straight away, but there are things I need to do back home before I commit to another job. Would that be possible?'

'It's more than I thought you would agree to. What if we say you start at the beginning of December? If you feel you wish to start work earlier, then you just have to say.'

Molly agreed. She'd been wondering about finding work once Butlins closed for the winter. A job as a shop assistant in Erith would have been the obvious choice, but until the ongoing problem with Harriet and Simon was resolved, she felt it was better she didn't work in the town she called home.

'It doesn't seem five minutes since we were waving goodbye to you,' Gladys Sangster said as she sat down next to Molly in the busy ballroom, 'and now here we are, on the last night of our second holiday at Butlins. We will definitely be back next year. I suppose you'll be moving on as well soon?'

'Yes. At the end of next week, I leave the employ of Butlins, but I've been invited to return as a redcoat next year.'

'You sound unsure,' Gladys said as she nodded to a man who had asked for the next dance.

'I have a few options and will consider them carefully.'

'We'll miss you if you aren't here next year, but either way you will visit us, won't you?' she said as the man took her hand for the Gay Gordons.

Molly nodded with a smile as the young woman

was whisked away. She knew she'd be seeing plenty of her new friend in the months and years to come.

Molly had been delighted to see the Sangster family back at the holiday camp, after they'd won a free week's holiday during that memorable bingo game during the first week the holiday camp reopened. It was the change to Gladys that had astonished Molly. The shy widow had disappeared and in her place was a confident, self-assured, pretty woman who was facing life full on and enjoying the experience. Molly had watched Gladys as she'd entered sports events, the adult fancy-dress competition and the Butlins beauty pageant. The first time she'd entered, she'd come second, and the next time, she'd won, much to the excitement of her family and redcoats, who remembered the family with affection.

'We've got you to thank for the change in our Gladys,' Olive Sangster said as she moved over to sit next to Molly.

'Me?' Molly was confused.

'Yes. You encouraged her to enter the beauty competition back in May. It played a big part in her regaining her confidence. Understandably, she'd not been the same after my boy passed away. Now we have our old Gladys back.'

'You don't mind that she will be courting again?'

Olive shrugged her shoulders. 'I won't say I don't wish my boy wasn't still alive, but life has to go on and she's a good girl. She deserves to be happy.'

Life goes on, Molly thought to herself. If the Sangster women could move on from losing a loved one, she should be brave and do the same thing. It didn't mean she loved her parents less, but if it meant letting go of the family home, then so be it. An idea began to grow in her mind from that evening on.

Sally, Joe and the twins enjoyed their holiday at Butlins so much Molly was amazed at the energy of her two little cousins, who didn't stop from dawn to dusk. As the cousins of a redcoat, they assumed the role of junior redcoats and had their own followers. During Molly's popular nature trail, Avril and Annie instructed the younger children and showed they were true leaders.

'I'm thinking of teaching them both to ride; then I can have a couple of days off while they take over.' Plum laughed as she watched the twins organizing their house team during the junior sports day. 'I wouldn't be able to cope if my Lizzie was as lively as those two. Thank goodness she takes after her father and prefers to draw and paint.'

'How is Lizzie getting on with her father?' Molly asked.

'They are still getting to know each other. Lizzie's been to visit him in the convalescent home three times, and although it's early days, they seem to be bonding.' She smiled to herself as she thought of William patiently showing his daughter how to draw a horse. Lizzie had been so keen to show her father how her work had improved that she'd spent a day at Butlins drawing the ponies and donkeys in the stables. 'I never thought in a million years that I'd see my William alive. I wake each morning and have to pinch myself to believe it is true that he is back with us. It will be a while before he's strong enough to be home with us, but each day brings us a step closer.'

'I'm so pleased for you. Butlins seems to have worked miracles for you and Bunty. Just look at how your lives have changed. There's Bunty reunited with Gordon, and him a free man again, and you have the miracle of William's return. Who'd have thought it?' Molly said.

'How about you? You've discovered you have an aunt, and you've also fallen in love. You have your future laid out before you and it includes Johnny. There could be three brides in our chalet...'

Molly shook her head until her glossy curls bounced. 'Most definitely not. Johnny has mentioned marriage, but I can't think about such things until I'm confident that all my family problems have been ironed out. Johnny has been a darling helping me and being a shoulder to cry on, but I don't want to enter a marriage with a sack load of trouble following on behind.'

Plum sighed. 'Molly, no one's life is ever completely free of problems. Johnny loves you for who you are. Don't push him away and expect him to wait around forever. There are far too many women who would gladly take your place. In some cases, even a wedding ring would not prevent them making a play for your man. Grab your happiness now and stop worrying about your family troubles.'

Molly looked away. It was all right for Plum to tell her to grab her happiness now, but what if she found out something truly awful had caused her parents to run away to Erith all those years ago? For her grandfather to act as he had done since, it must have been something terrible. Mud sticks and she would not wish Johnny's business and future to suffer because of his wife's reputation. No, she needed to find out what had occurred, and until then Johnny would have to wait.

'It's such a relief to hear birdsong instead of Radio Butlins every hour of the day.' Molly sighed as she sipped her tea. She was sitting in the small garden of Sally's cottage enjoying the warm September sun on her face. Already the leaves were starting to take on a golden hue; summer would soon become a memory. A very happy memory.

'I enjoyed our holiday at Butlins, but I'd not be able to work there as you did. My life is busy but in a different way.'

Her aunt's life was indeed busy. It was only a day since Molly had arrived, having been picked up by Dan in the farm truck, and already she had seen what the life of a mother and wife of a farm worker entailed. Dan's day on the farm was long, and so was Sally's. Early to rise, she would have bread baking in the oven, chickens cleaned out and fed, and if they were lucky, there would be eggs to collect during the day, although Molly was told this was mainly Avril and Annie's job. The girls would be back to school soon, so Sally's working day then revolved round walking to the village school to drop off the twins and returning to collect them.

The girls were thrilled to have their cousin staying with them, and since their visit to Butlins, they had greeted her at every opportunity by chanting, 'Hi-de-hi!'

The two women heard the gate open at the front of the cottage. 'That sounds like the afternoon post,' Sally said, getting to her feet. 'Time to get myself back in the kitchen.'

Molly went to follow.

'No, I insist you sit there and finish your tea. You are our guest, not a skivvy,' she said, disappearing round the side of the house.

Molly refused to take advantage of her new-found family members and had offered to pay for her keep, but it had been refused. So she did as much as she could to help around the house without annoying her aunt. Noticing bed sheets blowing on the washing line, Molly went to check if they were dry enough to take down, ready for ironing. She was just reaching for the pegs when Sally called her name.

'Molly, come and look at what's arrived,' she called.

'Is it good news or bad?' Molly asked as she spotted a letter in Sally's hand.

'Good, I hope. As you know, I've been making enquiries to find out where your dad's parents moved to. I was hitting my head against a wall at every turn. Then I thought I'd write to Florrie Hepsom.'

Molly was puzzled. 'Should I know her?'

'I doubt it. She was a teacher at the village school for many years and may have known your dad. I heard she now lived in a home for retired ladies near Boston and was clutching at straws when I wrote to her. I should have known that she'd have followed the lives of many of her pupils over the years. She was sad to hear about Norman and Charlotte, but did know where your paternal grandparents moved to all those years ago.'

'Is it far away?' Molly asked, hoping they hadn't moved overseas like Harriet's husband, Bert, had done.

Sally grinned. 'Would you believe that Leonard and Joan live in Skegness?'

Molly gave a large sigh of relief. 'I suppose they might have moved to a larger town to disappear if something awful had happened in their own small community?'

'Miss Hepsom writes that they moved to make it easier for Leonard's job in insurance. As luck would have it, she kept their address as she was one of his customers. Look.'

Molly took the letter and read the neat copperplate lettering. She made a note to visit the lady to thank her for her help and tell her about her parents. 'What should I do next?'

'You, young lady, are getting up bright and early tomorrow and taking the first bus to Skegness to visit your grandparents.'

'But what if they are like Grandfather Kenyon?'

Sally laughed. 'They broke the mould after my miserable father was born. Will it hurt to meet them? What harm could it do? If they don't want to know you, then jump back onto that bus and come straight home to us. We love you.'

Molly hugged her aunt. 'I'll do just that.'

22

Molly held her breath as she knocked on the door of the small mid-terrace house. Crossing her fingers behind her back, she prayed that whoever opened the door was not as nasty as her grandfather Kenyon.

A white-haired woman opened the door and stared at Molly, an inquisitive expression on her face. Molly could see her dad in the shape of the woman's nose and the twinkle in her eye. 'Can I help you?'

Molly had never felt so nervous before. 'Yes, I hope so. This sounds absurd, but I believe you may be my grandmother. My name is Molly Missons.'

'Oh my!' the woman murmured, ushering Molly inside. 'Len, Len, you'll never guess who I found on our doorstep...'

Molly was shown to a comfy armchair after shaking hands with a wiry man, who was sitting in another chair. 'I'm Molly Missons,' she repeated to him.

He frowned for a moment. 'I know all of the Missons around this way. There aren't many of us. I can't recall a Molly. Are you local?'

'My parents were. I come from Kent,' she replied, hoping that soon the penny would drop.

The man scratched his head thoughtfully. 'No, can't say I know any Missons in Kent.'

'Oh, for heaven's sake, Len. The girl says she is our granddaughter. That can only mean one thing.'

The man's eyes lit up. 'You're not our Norman's girl, are you?'

Molly nodded. 'Yes, I am. I have some papers to prove it if you'd like to see them?'

The couple brushed away her offer. 'No need for that. Why would anyone want to pretend to be our Norman's daughter? If you say you are, then we more than believe you,' Joan Missons said, pulling a chair from the dining table and sitting close to her husband.

'So who is your mum? Would we know her?' Len asked.

'My mum is Charlotte ... Charlotte Kenyon?'

Len and Joan Missons looked at each other in disbelief. 'I don't understand,' Joan said. 'I thought Charlotte was married to Bert ... Albert Missons.'

Bert? Could they mean Harriet's husband? she wondered. 'No, my parents were Norman Missons and Charlotte Kenyon. Here, I have a photograph of them on their wedding day,' she said, delving into her handbag for the same photograph she had shown Sally and handing it to her grandmother. Her aunt had suggested she take it with her to show the couple.

'You have the look of your mother,' Joan said as she ran her finger over the image of her son.

'I noticed you said they "were" your parents, rather than "are"... Does that mean they've passed on?'

Molly nodded. 'I hate to be the bearer of bad

363

news, but my parents died in an accident in August 1945. I had no idea I had relatives until I came across some papers recently. I have my birth certificate, and there are people who can vouch for me if you have any doubt I'm your granddaughter. I don't want anything from you. I just wanted to say hello.'

Len looked up from the photograph. His eyes were damp. 'I lived in hope that he would turn up one day. Some things were said long ago that were wrong...'

Joan patted his shoulder. 'Some things should have been mended and not left, but it's water under the bridge now. It's too late to see our son this side of the Pearly Gates, so let's make our amends with this young lass sitting here. She must think we are a right lot. I'm going to put the kettle on and we can chat. We have a lot of catching up to do.'

Molly sat with her grandparents and told them everything she knew of her parents' early life, the business and their home. They in turn asked questions and she answered as honestly as she could.

'One thing I'd really like to know is why my parents left this area and never told me they had family. What happened that made Grandfather Kenyon so bitter? He won't say anything apart from that my dad was a thief. I don't believe that for one minute. Even my aunt Sally has no idea: it all happened when she was a child.'

Len Missons jumped to his feet. 'Why, the old b–'

'Watch your mouth, man. Whatever happened, I'll have no bad language in this house. It all boiled down to money, love. Men and money. Harold Kenyon has been a miserable so-and-so all his life. God only knows why. Molly – your gran, that is – married him, but your mum was what's called an "early baby", so we can but guess.'

Molly listened intently. She found it fascinating to hear about her parents, but she was no closer to finding out what had happened. 'So why did Dad leave the area?'

Len Missons answered. 'Harold Kenyon owned Holcroft Farm at the time. Quite a big concern, it was. Our Norman was courting your mum, and his cousin Bert was seeing a barmaid from the Old Bull in the village. She must have been a good sight older than him, but he wasn't that choosy. They'd go out together quite often, as Bert had a car.'

'He was always a bit on the flash side was Bert,' Joan added.

'The first we knew was when the police turned up here one evening looking for our Norman. It seems the money for the farm labourers' wages had vanished from Harold's office at Holcroft, along with some other money. Harold wasn't one for banks. He didn't trust them. He also had cash in his desk from the sale of pastureland,' Len added, 'and probably more besides. It was all missing and he reckoned Norman had taken it, as he had been at the farm collecting Charlotte not an hour before.'

'Were there any witnesses?' Molly asked.

'They interviewed Bert and he confirmed he'd seen Norman walking up to the farm office as he drove by,' Joan said. 'I didn't believe him for one moment, but the police and Harold Kenyon did. But it got worse for our lad.'

'How ever could it get worse?' Molly asked.

'We only heard this later. Bert Missons went to see Kenyon and told him that Charlotte was expecting Norman's child. As our Norman would no doubt go to prison for being a thief, all kinds of shame would be placed on the whole family.'

Molly gasped. 'But she wasn't...?'

'No,' Joan continued. 'But we didn't know that back then. Bert offered to marry Charlotte, as his name wasn't tarnished like Norman's was, as long as Kenyon paid him well for saving the family name. Harold Kenyon coughed up straight away. The first your mum knew was when Harold Kenyon told her she had to marry Bert as Norman would be charged for the theft and would go to prison. Kenyon was a man to be feared back then and your mum was too afraid to cross him.

'Norman and Charlotte ran away that night. They left a note for us to say that whatever anyone said, Norman was innocent, but so as not to bring shame on both families, they planned to make a fresh start elsewhere.'

'Mum did write to her parents when I was born, but the letter was returned,' Molly said. 'I wonder why they didn't write to you.'

Len and Joan looked at each other. 'Love, we sold up and moved away. Your parents would have had no idea where we were. We kept very quiet about where we were going,' Joan explained.

'But why? You'd done nothing wrong,' Molly exclaimed.

Len leaned forward in his chair. 'We tried to

put things right after Bert scooted of with that barmaid. It was clear to us that he had pinched the money and fooled Kenyon into giving him more, but no one would listen. He had always been a bad lot. Kenyon was hell-bent on ruining our name, regardless of whether it was Norman or Bert who had taken the money.'

'I don't understand. Did the police not try to find Dad or Bert?' Molly asked.

'Kenyon dropped the charges,' Len said.

Molly was aghast. 'He doesn't strike me as the kind of man who would do such a thing. He is still bitter more than twenty-five years later. He didn't want to accept me as his granddaughter.'

Joan sighed. 'Molly, we sold up our home and gave Kenyon every penny he'd lost. We moved here and put the past behind us.'

Molly was horrified. To think that Bert Missons had caused such problems for her family and then Harold Kenyon refused to let bygones be bygones. 'Did you ever hear from Bert again?'

'No, not since the day he ran off with that barmaid, Harriet. He can go to hell as far as I'm concerned,' Joan said with passion.

'I know where she is,' Molly said, before explaining her side of the story.

'So that's about it,' Molly said, hanging the last of her clothes in the wardrobe. 'Harriet and Simon must have read about Mum and Dad's death and decided to profit from it. It wouldn't have taken much to read an obituary and know that a local businessman and his wife perished in an accident, leaving a daughter.'

Kath, who was sitting on Molly's bed listening as she unpacked, was outraged. 'We should go to the police at once,' she said.

'I want to speak to George first. It's only fair he should know all the facts. Most of what I've found out is hearsay. I'm not sure the police will act. Perhaps once Mr Denton returns, he can advise us. In the meantime, I have a little announcement of my own. I really wanted to tell you and George together.' She looked at the bedside clock. 'He seems to be late home from the shop.'

'He's doing some work on the building. We didn't want to bother you, but there was a water leak after the storm last week. It came in through the roof over the office. He's clearing everything out so a builder can come in and sort out the damage. It's a right mess, I can tell you.'

'I ought to go and help him.'

'We thought it might upset you to see your dad's office in a state,' Kath said with concern.

Molly sat beside her on the bed and hugged the woman. 'It may have done once, but I think I've grown up a little this summer. I realize that my parents are in my heart and I have my memories. I've found relatives I never knew I had, which is a dream come true, but above anything else, I have you, George and Freda, who are as much family as those I share blood with. Bricks and mortar mean nothing. Harriet and Simon aren't nice people – it could take an age for us to prove they are not entitled to claim my home, so I intend to move on. Then they can't hurt me.'

Kath kissed Molly's cheek. 'I can see the sense

in what you say. Time alone will show how things will pan out. So, what is this announcement you mentioned? Is it something to do with that nice young man Johnny?'

'Johnny and I are just friends for now. I have too much going on in my life to worry about marriage. You needn't raise your eyebrows at me like that, Kath. You'll be the first to hear when there's a wedding in the offing.'

'Then what is this news?' Kath asked, not believing a word Molly had just said.

'I was going to wait to tell George, but here you go. Freda mentioned that a house opposite where she lodges in Alexandra Road is up for sale. With the insurance-policy payout, as well as my savings, I worked out I could more than afford it. I wrote to the owner last week and offered to buy the house.'

'Well, that is a surprise,' Kath said. 'They are nice sturdy little houses. You've made a good buy there. I'll be sorry to not have you living here, but you'll only be a couple of streets away, so we can see each other often.'

'Most definitely,' Molly agreed. 'I'll need your help to turn my house into a home.'

'It's a shame you can't take some of your parents' furniture from the Avenue Road house. I can't see as how it belongs to Harriet. Surely she only inherited the house, not the furniture as well. But, I can see that you don't wish to antagonize your unpleasant relatives.'

'I thought the same, but I have time to think about it, as I won't be moving in until next month. How about I put the kettle on and we have a cuppa before I go and find George?'

'That's a good idea, and two letters have arrived for you.'

The women went through to the kitchen, and Kath fetched the envelopes while Molly filled the kettle and placed it on the stove. She settled down to read her correspondence as Kath laid out the cups and saucers. 'This is from Bunty. They hope to move in with her parents, in the East End, by Christmas while they go through the legal process after having been wrongfully imprisoned.'

'I hope it works out for them,' Kath said. 'Do you know if they will be compensated? I hope so after all they've been through.'

Molly checked both sides of the letter. 'Bunty doesn't say, but I would think something should be done. I hope so. They are such a nice couple. Bunty does say they will be getting married in the new year and I'm to be a bridesmaid. That's such lovely news.'

'You will make a beautiful bridesmaid. You would also make a beautiful bride, but I'll settle for bridesmaid for now.'

Molly laughed. 'Kath, you are just like my mum.'

'I'll take that as a compliment.' Kath smiled at her fondly. 'I'll pour that tea while you read your other letter.'

The second letter contained an invitation from Johnny for Molly and Freda to attend the screening of the film *A Matter of Life and Death* in Leicester Square in London. 'It seems to be very posh,' Molly commented. 'My gosh, the king and queen will be there.'

'I've read about that,' Kath said, flicking through

370

copies of the *Evening News* that were stacked in a corner ready for fire-making. 'Here it is. David Niven will be there, as well as many other stars. It seems very important. You and Freda will have a wonderful time.'

Molly sighed with delight. 'Freda will be over the moon. We shall have to decide what to wear. It sounds as though evening frocks will be required. These are very good seats. My goodness!'

After finishing her tea and a slice of Kath's treacle tart, Molly headed off to Missons Ironmonger's to see what George was up to. She found him stacking old floorboards outside the shop.

'Hello, my love. How long have you been back?'

'Only a couple of hours, George. What's been going on here?'

George pointed out the damage from the storm. 'Hitler started this during the war when that landmine went off over the back and shook the building. We had a heavy downpour last week and the water came in and finished off the job. I've emptied out the room and started to rip up the floor so the builders can come in during half-day closing to plaster the walls and lay new floor-boards.'

'I'll give you a hand. Kath said dinner will be ready at six thirty, so we'd best not be late. It's liver and bacon, and the liver will be as tough as old boots if we keep it waiting too long.'

'Let's get cracking, then, or Kath will be after us.'

George continued pulling up the wooden floor, while Molly carried the wood outside to add it to the growing pile.

'Well, I'll be...' George said, reaching down to where he'd just pulled up a loose board. 'There's something down here.'

Molly grabbed a torch from a counter display and shone it where George was reaching down. 'What is it, George?' she asked, peering over his shoulder.

George pulled out a box wrapped in oilcloth. He sat on the floor and unwrapped the parcel. 'It looks like a cashbox of some kind and a ledger. I wonder who it belongs to.'

Molly took the ledger. 'It's Dad's handwriting.' She flicked through the pages of numbers. 'The last entry is three days before the car accident. Is there anything in the cashbox, George?'

'It's locked, but hang on a minute.' He heaved himself to his feet and found the large bunch of keys that were used for the shop. George tried a couple of smaller keys until the lock clicked and the box opened. He tipped the contents of the box onto the shop counter. Out fell a small bank-account book, a bundle of ten-shilling notes, some loose change and an envelope.

'How much is there?' Molly asked.

George quickly counted the money. 'Thirty-seven pounds, twelve shillings and sixpence.'

She pointed to the last entry in the ledger. 'That's the amount Dad entered.' Molly took the bank deposit book and opened it 'The money paid in corresponds with the ledger. This must have been a second account where Dad deposited extra money. We've been running the shop on the current account and all the while there's been spare cash to pay the bills.'

'Norman must have placed this under the floorboard for safe keeping until he went to the bank. I wondered why this one was so loose. We'd always planned to get a safe fitted but never got around to doing it.'

'There's over three hundred pounds in this account,' Molly said in astonishment. 'What's in the envelope?'

George opened the brown envelope and pulled out a folded cream sheet of paper. Smoothing it out flat, they both peered at the last will and testament of Norman Missons.

They looked at each other and burst out laughing.

'All this time we've been worrying about Mr Denton being away and the paperwork was under our feet,' George said. 'Has he left the house to you, Molly?'

Molly looked up at George with tears in her eyes. 'Everything has been left to Mum. Dad never for one moment expected to die alongside Mum.'

George looked closer at the document. 'It is dated two weeks before they both died and was prepared by Mr Denton. If Harriet Missons does have a will, which I don't believe she has, it must have been prepared long before this one so will be void.'

'What do we do, George? Should we march up there and kick them out?'

George thought for a moment. 'I think we should tread carefully. We could do with a good solicitor to advise us before we speak to the police. With Mr Denton away, it is going to be hard to prove anything, as he knows your dad's business better than anyone else. I'm going to have a word with Mr Johnson's legal friend. Help was offered and we'd be fools not to take it up.'

Molly nodded. As much as she didn't want Johnny's help so she could stand on her own two feet, she knew it wouldn't hurt to consult Johnny's friend. 'Would you speak to him, George? I'll write down everything my grandparents told me about Bert Missons.'

'Leave it with me, love. Now, let's go and have that liver-and-bacon dinner before Kath gives it to the dog.'

Molly arranged a bunch of pink chrysanthemums in a short vase at the head of Norman and Charlotte Missons's grave. She'd given the headstone a wipe and pulled a few stray weeds from the grass surrounding the grave. So much had happened since the last time she had visited her parents' final resting place.

'Oh, Mum, you'd have loved Butlins. If only things had been different and we could have holidayed there together. Dad, I know you'd have liked Johnny. Even though our paths are destined not to run side by side through life, you can rest in peace knowing he is a true gentleman.'

Standing up, she brushed a few strands of grass from her coat and smiled down at her parents' grave. 'I miss you both so much it hurts, but you'd be proud of me and how I've coped. At least, I hope you would.' She blew a small kiss and walked away.

'It helps to talk to them,' an elderly man said as

he stood up from a nearby bench and raised his hat. 'I couldn't help overhearing. You must be Norman Missons's daughter? I'm Fred Butler. This here is my wife, Dot. I often pop up for a chat and tell her what I've been up to.' He pointed towards a carefully tended grave covered in flowers. 'Dot always appreciated a few flowers on the sideboard, so now I'm not digging for victory anymore, I can grow some blooms just for her.'

'They are wonderful,' Molly said, not quite knowing what to say. 'Did you know my dad?'

'I certainly did. He put me right a few times on what I needed to fix up my house. I miss his knowledge and his cheerful chat. He was a popular chap in Pier Road was your dad.'

'The shop is still open, so if you are ever in need of help, Mr Butler, please don't be afraid to ask. My knowledge is not up to scratch, but George is always available to give advice if it's needed.'

'I'll keep that in mind, young lady. You're a credit to your parents the way you've kept going after what happened.'

Molly, smiled and thanked the man. It was as she walked away she realized she no longer cried when people mentioned her parents. Norman and Charlotte Missons took a piece of her heart with them when they died, but at last she felt strong enough to cope without becoming a snivelling wreck. She raised her chin high as she stepped onto the bus and smiled at the conductor. She would take whatever life threw at her knowing her parents looked down with pride.

23

'This is magical,' Freda said in awe as the two
girls approached the Empire Theatre in Leicester
Square. 'Do you think we will see the king and
queen? I've been practising my curtsy in the staff
canteen at work.'

Molly smiled at her friend's excitement. She
couldn't quite believe they were attending such a
special event. She'd written to Johnny to thank
him for the tickets and had also rung his office, but
he'd not been available to take her call. She knew
he was busy in his new job but all the same felt a
little rejected, despite it being her who had refused
to talk seriously about marriage. She looked
around for Johnny but couldn't see him among the
crowd.

'I can't believe how beautiful the women look
in their gowns. Do you think we fit in properly?'

'Freda, you look wonderful. The red silk suits
you down to the ground.'

'I hope so – it's a long dress.' She laughed.
'Maisie did a good job altering your mum's
dresses to fit us, didn't she?'

Molly agreed. It had been her idea to utilize the
dresses that she'd rescued from Avenue Road.
Freda's friend Maisie was a whizz with a sewing
machine and had remodelled the dresses by
copying the latest styles from her fashion magazines. Molly had been particularly fond of her

mum's green velvet gown and was so pleased she could now wear it in a newer style. Wearing her mum's fur coat round her shoulders, and Freda a fur stole, she felt as though Charlotte Missons was with them on this special occasion.

'Look – there's Johnny,' Freda said, pointing to where a group of people were standing close to a roped-off area near the entrance to the cinema. 'I think they're waiting for the king and queen to arrive.'

The girls headed through the waiting crowd until they were on the fringe of Johnny's group. Molly raised her hand to catch his attention. He was looking particularly handsome in a black dinner suit and sparkling white shirt. Molly heard people calling out his name among the watching crowd of cinema fans. Johnny waved a few times to the fans and gave a smile before turning back to the people in his group. Molly edged forward, wanting to be with Johnny.

'Ouch! Watch out!' a female voice exclaimed as Molly was pushed into her.

Molly cringed: she recognized that voice. It was Gloria, the receptionist from Butlins.

'Oh, it's you. Johnny mentioned he'd invited a few staff members. I did tell him you'd all be out of your depth at a function like this.' Gloria looked Molly up and down and sniffed. 'Wherever did you find the rags?'

Freda leaned forward and hissed, 'These are from a fashion house. Would you like to see the labels and stroke the fur?'

Molly grinned at Freda. She could see Gloria looking at the gowns and she held her head high.

Her mum had always bought quality clothing, believing it was an investment, so she was proud to be wearing her outfit, as was Freda.

Johnny spotted the two friends as they chatted excitedly, and pushed through the crowd to kiss Molly tenderly on the lips and whisper, 'I'm so glad you could make it.' He kissed Freda on the cheek. 'You look a million dollars, Freda.'

She whispered something in his ear and he burst out laughing.

'Whatever did you say?' Molly asked as Johnny turned to shake hands with a man who had just arrived.

'I told him I bought it from Woolies.' She grinned.

The girls were still laughing when Johnny introduced them to his companion, David Niven.

Molly couldn't remember what she said to the famous actor but told Kath later that he had the most wonderful smile and was a true gentleman.

Freda tried hard not to curtsy and instead asked for his autograph, which her colleagues at Woolworths later said must have been a forgery, until they spotted both girls on Pathé News when they next went to the local Odeon in Erith.

They were led into the cinema before the Royal Family arrived. Johnny gave an arm to Molly and Freda, and escorted them both to their seats, next to his own. As the lights went down, he reached for Molly's hand and held it gently throughout the film.

As they left the cinema, Freda was overcome with excitement when she spotted Queen Elizabeth in her car. 'This is the perfect ending to the perfect day,' she whispered to Molly.

They stood outside as the crowds started to drift away. They would need to hail a cab to get back to Charing Cross Station before the last train of the night left for Erith.

'Molly, where are you going? I have a car collecting us. It should be here soon,' Johnny said as he walked over to where the two girls stood.

'Don't worry about us, Johnny. We can get back to the station by cab.'

Johnny looked puzzled. 'What about the reception at the Savoy Hotel?'

It was Molly's turn to look puzzled. 'I don't know what you're talking about. We need to catch our train.'

'The invitation included the hotel reception and an overnight stay. Didn't you read the letter that was with the invitation?'

Molly pulled the envelope from her handbag and held it out to Johnny. 'There wasn't a letter. I rang your office to say thank you for the invitation and no one mentioned a reception or accommodation.'

Johnny ran his hand over his hair in exasperation. 'I just don't understand.' He turned and called Gloria over. 'Do you know anything about the letter being left out of Molly's envelope?'

Gloria took Johnny's arm and pouted provocatively. 'I may have made a mistake. You work me so hard, Johnny, night and day,' she added, smiling towards Molly. 'You know what he's like. Come along, Johnny – I'm just dying for a cocktail.'

Fortunately for Molly, a taxicab passed at that

moment and she raised her hand to stop it. 'Thank you for a delightful evening, Johnny. I'll never forget this,' she said pointedly, and climbed into the vehicle, followed by a puzzled Freda.

As the vehicle sped away, Molly didn't see Johnny standing alone in the middle of the road, as her eyes were full of tears.

'This is very nice,' Kath remarked as she inspected the bay window in the front room of the terraced house across the road from where Freda lived in Erith. 'The last owners have left it very clean. We can have you moved in within days. You can take the bedroom furniture from your room at our house to get you started, along with some bedding. What about pots and pans?'

'Freda bought me some as a moving-in gift, and Mrs Caselton over the road has an armchair for me.'

'It's such a shame that there's so much furniture at your parents' house that belongs to you. I've a mind to walk up there and get some. Harriet Missons can't really say no, can she?'

'It's Simon who I'm more worried about. He's so unpredictable.'

Kath thought for a moment. 'Let's take a walk up to Avenue Road and see what happens. We can stop off at the shop and leave a note for George to pick us up in the van when he gets back from the supplier's. We'll be able to pack a fair bit in the vehicle and go back for some more another day.'

'I don't know, Kath. George said to keep away...' Molly said with a worried frown.

Kath wasn't having any of it. 'It won't hurt to

knock on the door. We can always walk away if your relatives are unpleasant.'

'All right, but promise to be careful,' she sighed.

It had been a week since she'd attended the film in London. Part of her had hoped that Johnny would get in touch, but she hadn't heard a word from him. Molly couldn't understand why Gloria was working for him. Had he promised a job to every female who'd worked at Butlins? But Gloria of all people... Didn't Johnny understand how troublesome she could be? Molly had hardly slept since that night; she just tossed and turned in her bed, trying to make sense of Johnny and asking herself if she cared. She'd still not come to any conclusions as they walked up to her parents' house that afternoon to look at the furniture. They'd dropped a note in at the shop to let George know to pick them up with the van at closing time.

They were surprised to see a for-sale board in the garden of the house in Avenue Road. Something would have to be done quickly, before Harriet and Simon sold Molly's inheritance when they had no right to the property.

Molly still had a key to the house and let them both in. She called out to Harriet and Simon, but there was no answer. 'Let's get the curtains and bedding from upstairs. We can bring it all down to the front door ready for loading.' She didn't want to be in the house a moment longer than she had to be.

'What about the dressing table and chest of drawers from your bedroom? We could pull them out to the landing for George to move downstairs?' Kath suggested.

'That's a good idea. I'd also like the little side tables from the front room and Mum's bureau. Plus the oil lamp that's in the bay window if that's possible.'

They were carrying the bureau between them when the front door opened and Harriet walked in, followed by Simon. 'Whatever do you think you are doing, taking my property from my house?' Harriet demanded.

'I think you'll find that the contents of the house belong to me,' Molly said bravely. She didn't wish to inform them that the newly discovered will left everything to her. That was best left for now until solicitors, and hopefully police, had investigated. She just wanted the furniture for her new home.

'You are wrong, Molly. Your father's will left everything to my husband, and as he has passed away, it now belongs to me.'

Kath rounded on Harriet. 'I'd like to see this will, please,' she said as pleasantly as she could.

'It is of no concern of yours, Mrs Jones. I own this house and you are both trespassing.'

Kath wasn't budging. 'I don't believe you. I want to see the will. You see, we know otherwise.'

Molly could see that Kath's words had annoyed Harriet. 'I'm afraid you are wrong, Mrs Jones. I have a vast knowledge of the legal world and the will in my possession is legal and binding. My husband was left all property by his cousin Norman, and now it is mine.'

'And I'm calling you a liar,' Kath spat back. 'We know more about you and your husband than you think. You're nothing but a jumped-up bar-maid from Skegness. You are both thieves.'

382

Molly gasped. Kath had let the cat out of the bag. Harriet and Simon would know that they had been found out.

Harriet looked at the brass clock on the mantelpiece. 'They will be here soon, Simon. Deal with these two before they cause any more trouble.'

He grabbed Molly and Kath by the arms and marched them through to the kitchen. Molly kicked and shouted, but he was too strong for them. Kicking open the cellar door, he pushed them both down the steep steps. Kath gave out a cry as she stumbled and fell to the bottom. Molly grabbed a banister rail and regained her balance. By the time she'd done this, she heard the bolts slide across the door. Simon had trapped them in the cellar. A groan from the bottom of the steps signalled that Kath had been hurt.

'Kath, are you all right?' she called down into the darkness. Feeling her way, she reached the bottom of the stairs and stepped carefully, knowing Kath would be close to where she stood. Her foot made contact with Kath and she bent down. 'Let me help you to your feet, Kath. I know this cellar well. There's an old seat to the right of us.' She moved Kath slowly until she reached the seat. By now her eyes were becoming accustomed to the dark. A small chink of light gave her an idea. 'Let me sit you down and check you over.'

'It's just my ankle. I twisted it as I fell,' Kath said as she felt her way onto the chair. 'It'll be all right when I've rested it. I feel such a fool for blurting what we knew to Harriet.'

'Don't be silly. I almost did the same,' she reassured Kath. 'There are some candles and matches here somewhere. I'm going to find them and then take a look at that ankle.' Molly felt along the wall until she reached a shelf. Running her fingers over the thin strip of wood, she found what she was looking for and struck a match, lighting the stub of candle before the match went out. 'That's better.'

'Yes, that is better. I'm not one for the dark,' Kath murmured.

Molly looked at her friend's face. She'd scratched it as she'd fallen and was looking pale. Molly bent down and checked her ankle. It was already swollen. Kath winced as Molly ran her hands over it. 'Don't worry, Kath – I'll have you out of here soon.'

Thanking her dad for being so organized, she went to a small sink in the corner of the cellar and ran the tap for a while until it was running as cold as possible. She found some clean rags, which her dad used to clean his car, and ran one under the cold tap.

Kath sighed as Molly wrapped the cold rag round her ankle and raised it up on a box.

'That will feel better in no time. I'm just going to see if I can hear anything.'

'Be careful, Molly,' Kath whispered.

Molly crept up the stairs and listened but couldn't hear a thing through the door. She went back down to Kath. Already there was more colour in her cheeks. 'There's a small, narrow window at ground level, but I don't think it's been opened in years, I'll give it a try,' she said.

However much she pushed, the window wouldn't budge. Taking off her shoe, Molly tapped at the glass, then listened. The noise hadn't alerted anyone. She hit the glass harder and it cracked. Pushing the pane with her hand, the shards fell away from the frame and shattered on the path outside. She held her breath but was lucky as it hadn't been heard by Harriet or Simon. She worked at the remaining pieces of glass that were left until the frame was free of jagged edges, then went back to Kath. 'I can just see the path that leads to the road from the window. I plan not to make a noise until George arrives. Then we must scream and shout until he hears us.'

'It's going to be ages yet. The shop doesn't close until half past five,' Kath said. 'What about making something we can wave through the window to alert a passer-by?'

'I'm not sure we should try that, as it could anger Simon and we don't want that. We'd best wait for George. However, something to wave at him would be a good idea.'

Molly had started to search for items she could turn into a flag when she heard voices outside. She blew out the candle and crept to the window to listen. Two men seemed to be discussing the house. They must be buyers. No doubt Simon wouldn't show them the cellar, where his captives were. Molly prayed for George to arrive and rescue them. She checked her watch. It would be another hour at least. Leaning against the wall, she closed her eyes. A slight breeze from the broken window chilled her face. She hoped the men would leave before George arrived.

Molly was startled awake as she heard the men make their goodbyes. Thank goodness, she thought. She crept back to Kath. 'The men have left. I'll finish making my flag and listen for George. If only the window was just six inches larger, I'd be able to wriggle out and get help.'

'Don't do anything to alert them upstairs,' Kath whispered. 'Stay safe until we are rescued.'

Molly continued knotting the rags together. She found a bean cane and tied the rags to the end. Satisfied she could attract attention, she went back to Kath and checked her ankle. The swelling didn't seem to be so bad. She ran the rag under the cold tap and reapplied it to Kath's foot.

It seemed an age before they heard footsteps. Molly listened at the window but didn't recognize George's voice. But ... was that Johnny? Yes, it was definitely Johnny, and she could hear at least two other voices. She grabbed her flag and poked one end through the window. 'Help, Johnny, help. We're in the cellar,' she called. 'It's Molly and Kath. Help!'

Feet approached the window. She could see knees and then Johnny's face as he peered through the small gap. 'Molly, thank goodness. We have the police here. I'll get you out of there in no time.'

Molly went back to Kath and hugged her. 'Help has arrived. I don't know how but Johnny has the police with him.'

Kath and Molly huddled together as they listened to raised and angry voices through the floor above. Within minutes the cellar door flew open and Johnny, followed by George, appeared in the small cellar and the women were helped upstairs into the front room.

'Is it safe?' Kath asked, fearfully looking around

for signs of Harriet or Simon.

'The police took them away. They won't set foot in this house again, or Erith, come to that,' George said as he settled his wife on the sofa.

'I don't understand how the police became involved and why you are here, Johnny,' Molly said as he handed her a glass of water.

'I've been working with George to get to the bottom of this business with Harriet and Simon Missons. I had a private investigator check them out and it seems they've spent a lifetime defrauding people out of their inheritances. They made a mistake when they discovered your parents had died and thought you'd be an easy target. We handed over the information to the police yesterday.'

'Did they live in South Africa?'

'No, the only boat they travelled on was the Woolwich ferry. They were living in Silvertown.'

'So many lies,' Molly sighed sadly.

Johnny took her arm and they walked out into the garden. 'It's all over. You're safe now, Molly. You have your home and your life back.'

'There's still something missing,' she said, gazing up at him, 'something I can't live without.'

'What would that be?' he asked as he pulled her into his arms.

'You. I know I need you in my life, Johnny. Today proved to me that you don't give a damn about the starlets and the fans or you wouldn't have come to rescue me. Being in danger, all I could think was I may never see you again. Is that job offer still open?'

He kissed her tenderly. 'I would think so.'

'How about the marriage proposal?'

'Most definitely.'

'There are a couple of things...'

He groaned into her hair as she pulled away slightly. 'What now?'

'I've purchased a house in Erith.'

'Give it to Freda.' He nuzzled her ear.

'I want to sign the shop over to George,' she murmured.

'Good idea.'

'Johnny?'

'Yes?'

'Kiss me.'

Acknowledgements

It is often said that writing is a solitary occupation. I couldn't disagree more. In the months since *The Woolworths Girls* was published and news of *The Butlins Girls* became known I've been inundated with readers informing me of their holiday camp memories. I've viewed photographs and heard of many happy memories from years gone by. A special thanks to my friends in the dog-showing world; I've known many of you for a good numbers of years now and appreciate your support of something that is 'non-doggy'!

I have to thank my students at The Write Place for their support and friendship. Many are now published in various forms and make me very proud to be part of their writing journeys.

I can't praise my literary agent, Caroline Sheldon, highly enough. Caroline is always there to answer my questions and calm me when I have a 'wobble' with my writing. I'm proud to be part of the agency's impressive stable of authors and still pinch myself to check I'm not dreaming.

Pan Macmillan are absolute stars. To have faith in my writing and produce such fab books with my name on the cover is a dream come true. I'm never left to wonder what is happening and have been included in every step of the publishing process.

The PR team is just great – I'm gobsmacked by the amount of work that goes into promoting an author.

My editor at Pan Mac, Victoria Hughes-Williams, is a delight to work with and her feedback on my writing is both inspiring and encouraging. Thank you so much.

I'm a great fan of The Romantic Novelists' Society – such a supportive community of writers. The legendary parties, fabulous conference and online contacts, which we all know is work, makes this writer feel as though she in never alone at her keyboard.

Finally my husband, Michael. You have always supported my writing and are the sounding board for my plots and ideas. I may not always listen, and yes we argue, but your input is appreciated xx

Author's Note:
My Holiday Camp Memories

It is said that Sir Billy Butlin came up with the idea for his first all-inclusive holiday camp after witnessing holidaymakers being booted out of their rooms after breakfast and not being allowed to return until late afternoon for their evening meal. Whatever the weather, the poor holiday-makers would have to find shelter from the sun and rain, and also entertain themselves.

This was a similar predicament for my parents when we had our two-week holiday each July in Ramsgate, and later the Isle of Wight, during what was then the shut-down period for industry in the UK. Having travelled by train or coach to the guesthouse we did not have the benefit of a car to jump in if the weather turned gloomy. Mum always planned ahead and saved money from her part-time job, not only for our holiday but also for rainy-day treats: an afternoon at the cinema to see *Those Magnificent Men in Their Flying Machines,* or a trip to the zoo where we would dash around between showers.

Once Mum discovered a brochure for a holiday camp, we spent many happy years touring the country enjoying all the camps had to offer. I'd like to say that it was Butlins where we enjoyed our vacations, but it wasn't. We visited Warners, which was similar to Butlins since Sir Billy Butlin and Captain Harry Warner had worked together in the early years, and had very similar ideas about family holidays. Meals were plentiful, the wooden chalets clean and there was day-long entertainment come rain or shine.

We were 'joiners', and as everything was free we signed up for putting, tennis and darts, as well as more energetic events. Points were won for our house and the overall winner of each event was presented with a voucher and a medal. I had decided one summer to enter 'women's cribbage', but had no idea how to play. An hour later I was sitting opposite a steely-eyed woman and I beat her! I didn't progress much further that year, but do recall winning a medal for ladies' putting with a hole in one, and also ladies' darts.

Come the evening we joined in with the talent competitions. Dad was a decent singer and could belt out an Elvis or Tom Jones number, while my sister and I would dance or perform a skit. Mum's skill was in the fancy-dress competitions. In those days no one bought outfits, so everything was made from crepe paper that was purchased in the camp's gift shop. Fancy hats based on a popular tune found Mum melting chocolate into a lump on my favourite sun hat and winning a prize for her 'On Mother Kelly's Doorstep' creation. However, to this day I can recall the horror of the 'Topsy Turvy' competition – for a fourteen-year-old to see her mother line up on the stage dressed as a bishop, complete with moustache, was too much to bear. I could see friends we made that holiday sniggering. I wanted to run away and hide, but Dad decided we had to clap as loud as we could. It must have worked as she won.

We stopped visiting holiday camps after Mum died in 1971. Even when quite ill she insisted we all went to Great Yarmouth, and I have bitter-sweet memories of her last holiday – and yes, she did manage to sew costumes and that time I had to wear them!

This Large Print Book for the partially sighted, who cannot read normal print, is published under the auspices of

THE ULVERSCROFT FOUNDATION